DATE DUE

OCT 03 06			APR 06
GAYLORD			PRINTED IN U.S.A.

NOTHING BUT TROUBLE

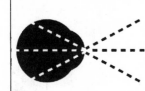

This Large Print Book carries the
Seal of Approval of N.A.V.H.

NOTHING BUT TROUBLE

TROUBLE

A Kevin Kerney Novel

Michael McGarrity

Thorndike Press • Waterville, Maine

This book is a work of fiction. Names, characters, places, and incidents either are the product of the author's imagination or are used fictitiously, and any resemblance to actual persons, living or dead, business establishments, events, or locales is entirely coincidental.

Published in 2006 by arrangement with Dutton, a member of Penguin Group (USA) Inc.

Thorndike Press® Large Print Mystery.

The tree indicium is a trademark of Thorndike Press.

The text of this Large Print edition is unabridged.
Other aspects of the book may vary from the original edition.

Set in 16 pt. Plantin by Ramona Watson.

Printed in the United States on permanent paper.

Library of Congress Cataloging-in-Publication Data

McGarrity, Michael.
    Nothing but trouble : a Kevin Kerney novel / by Michael McGarrity.
       p. cm. — (Thorndike Press large print mystery)
    ISBN 0-7862-8403-X (lg. print : hc : alk. paper)
    1. Kerney, Kevin (Fictitious character) — Fiction.
2. Police — New Mexico — Santa Fe — Fiction.   3. Santa Fe (N.M.) — Fiction.   4. Police chiefs — Fiction.
5. Large type books. I. Title. II. Thorndike Press large print mystery series.
PS3563.C36359N68 2006b
  813'.54—dc22   2005033812

For Sean and Meghan McGarrity

As the Founder/CEO of NAVH, the only national health agency solely devoted to those who, although not totally blind, have an eye disease which could lead to serious visual impairment, I am pleased to recognize Thorndike Press★ as one of the leading publishers in the large print field.

Founded in 1954 in San Francisco to prepare large print textbooks for partially seeing children, NAVH became the pioneer and standard setting agency in the preparation of large type.

Today, those publishers who meet our standards carry the prestigious "Seal of Approval" indicating high quality large print. We are delighted that Thorndike Press is one of the publishers whose titles meet these standards. We are also pleased to recognize the significant contribution Thorndike Press is making in this important and growing field.

Lorraine H. Marchi, L.H.D.
Founder/CEO
NAVH

★ Thorndike Press encompasses the following imprints: Thorndike, Wheeler, Walker and Large Print Press.

Acknowledgments

Thanks go to Cari Dyer and Joel Dyer of Hachita, New Mexico; Cheryl Wright and Norman Wright of Playas, New Mexico; and Deputy Sheriff David Arrendondo Sr. of the Hidalgo County Sheriff's Department. They all provided valuable information about the Bootheel of New Mexico that did much to contribute to my research.

A special thanks goes to an extraordinary top cop, Chief Beverly Lennon of the Santa Fe Police Department, who gave me virtually unrestricted access to the inner workings of the department.

Chapter One

For as long as Kevin Kerney had known him, Johnny Jordan had been nothing but trouble. But it had taken a long time for Kerney to realize the downside of being Johnny's friend.

Memories of Johnny flooded through Kerney's mind on a snowy April afternoon after he returned to police headquarters to find a telephone message on his desk from his old boyhood chum. Johnny was in Santa Fe, staying at a deluxe downtown hotel, and wanted to get together for drinks and dinner that evening.

Kerney stared out his office window at the fluffy wind-driven snow that melted as soon as it hit the glass. He'd last seen Johnny well over thirty years ago at the memorial services for his parents, who'd been killed in a traffic accident the day Kerney had returned from his tour of duty in Vietnam. Johnny had shown up at the church late, accompanied by a good-looking woman twice his age, with his left arm in a cast — broken in a fall he'd taken at a recent pro rodeo event.

He remembered Johnny waiting for him outside the church, standing next to a new truck with the initials JJ painted on the doors above a rider on a bucking bronc. Dressed in alligator cowboy boots, black pressed jeans, a starched long-sleeve white Western-cut shirt, and a gold-and-silver championship rodeo buckle, he'd flashed Kerney a smile, led him away from the truck where his lady friend waited, and offered his condolences.

"It's a damn shame," Johnny said with a shake of his head. "Are you going to be okay?"

"Eventually, I suppose," Kerney replied.

"But not yet," Johnny said.

"Not yet."

They caught up with each other. Johnny had been rodeoing since graduating from high school and had become a top-ten saddle bronc rider, while Kerney had finished his college degree and gone off to Vietnam as an infantry second lieutenant. Johnny's parents, Joe and Bessie, who owned a big spread on the Jornada, a high desert valley straddled by mountains in south-central New Mexico where Kerney had been raised, had sold out and bought another ranch in the Bootheel of south-western New Mexico. Joe had left his job as the president of a local bank in Truth or Consequences to take over a savings and loan in Deming.

Still in shock over the loss of his parents, Kerney didn't have much to say, but he promised to stay in touch with Johnny once things settled down. Johnny gave him a phone number where he could be reached and left with the nameless woman.

It had been typical of Johnny not to introduce his lady friend. He had a catch-and-release attitude toward woman.

Kerney never followed up. His friendship with Johnny had ended years before. At the age of sixteen Kerney had hired out as a summer hand on the Jordan ranch. On his first day at work he'd been sent with Johnny to repair a cattle trap in preparation for the fall roundup. The job consisted of replacing broken fence posts and stringing new wire.

By noon they'd almost finished the chore, when they ran out of steel replacement posts. Johnny took the truck to get more from a ranch supply store in Truth or Consequences, while Kerney stayed behind to string and splice wire. Four hours later Kerney was still waiting for Johnny's return when the ranch manager, Shorty Powell, had showed up.

"Is this as far as you've got?" Shorty asked, surveying the unfinished trap.

"We ran out of posts," Kerney replied. "Johnny went to get more." He didn't say anything about Johnny leaving him stranded in the hot desert sun for four hours with no water, no shade, on foot, and ten miles from the ranch headquarters. He didn't tell Shorty that while he'd waited for Johnny he'd rebuilt and rehung the gate to the trap by himself, using the old wooden fence posts.

"This job should have been finished today," Shorty said as he grabbed the mike to the CB radio in his truck and called for Johnny. "Where are you?" he asked when Johnny replied.

"Just leaving the store with the posts."

"I want you and Kevin out at the trap first thing in the morning to finish up. I'll bring Kevin back to the ranch."

At the ranch Johnny had not yet arrived. Shorty killed the engine and gave Kerney a long, appraising look. "That wasn't a full day's job I sent you boys out to do. What took so long?"

"We had a lot of wire to splice and the ground was pretty hard," Kerney replied,

12

so parched he could barely speak. "Pounding those posts in took a while."

Shorty grunted. "It's your first day on the job, so I'll give you some slack. But if you're going to work for me this summer, I expect you to put your back into it."

"Yes, sir," Kerney said.

The next morning, as they finished up at the trap, Johnny told Kerney how he'd stopped by his girlfriend's house in town on the way to the store and had gotten "distracted." He never once apologized for leaving Kerney in the lurch, nor did he thank him for covering up his absence with Shorty.

"Don't worry about Shorty," Johnny said as he pounded in the last post. "I'll make sure he keeps you on through the summer."

Kerney spliced a top wire with fencing pliers, clipped it to the post, and stretched it tight. "Don't do me any favors, Johnny."

"What's bugging you?"

"Nothing," Kerney replied, staring at Johnny, who stood grinning at him, showing his perfect white teeth. Unlike Johnny, who lacked for nothing, Kerney needed the job and the money it would bring. "Just don't expect me to lie for you again."

"You're taking this way too seriously."

Kerney wrapped the remaining wire around the post, took off his gloves, and handed Johnny the pliers. "You can finish up."

Johnny laughed. "When did the hired hand start giving orders?"

"When I found out my partner is a slacker."

Over the course of the summer Kerney distanced himself from Johnny and won Shorty's respect as a hand, which meant more to him than Johnny's friendship.

That year Johnny's wild streak took over. In his free time he organized beer busts on his father's boat at Elephant Butte Lake, made trips to sleazy Juárez nightclubs in Mexico, and got in fistfights over girls. When he wasn't working or partying, he was glued to the back of a horse, practicing his calf-roping and rodeoing skills.

As he considered Johnny's invitation, Kerney wondered if his old boyhood pal had changed at all over the years. Did he still have the big grin, the easy laugh, his charming, cocksure ways? As a rodeo fan he'd kept up with Johnny's career for a time. Johnny had been good enough to re-peatedly reach the national finals and had won two saddle bronc championships, but never the all-around title. Then he'd faded from view.

Kerney decided it was worth his time to have dinner with Johnny, just to find out what had prompted his phone call. He dialed the hotel and asked to be put through to Johnny's room. The operator asked for his name, and when he responded, she told him Johnny would meet him in the bar of an expensive downtown restaurant at seven o'clock.

Kerney confirmed he'd be there and disconnected, thinking maybe Johnny hadn't changed much at all: he still expected things to go his way and for people to do his bidding. Any nostalgia he had about his past friendship was erased by a sense of wariness.

He checked the time. If he left for home now, he could change out of his uniform into civvies and get back in town to meet up with Johnny at the restaurant.

At the Santa Fe Airport, Johnny Jordan sat with the woman he'd brought with him to Santa Fe, eager to put her on a flight home and be done with her. Brenda was a petite, hard-bodied workout maven who conducted trim-and-tone exercise classes at a Denver gym and spa that catered to professional women. He'd met her at a party three weeks ago, and by the end of the night he had taken her to bed.

Over the past three weeks Johnny had found her to be the perfect combination of what he liked in a woman: haughty, hot looking, and sluttish in bed. Two days ago he'd invited Brenda to accompany him on a short business trip, thinking it would be fun to have someone to play with who liked it wet and wild and didn't demand too much of his time. By the end of the drive down from Denver, Johnny realized he'd made a huge mistake.

From the moment she got in the car Brenda had talked endlessly, about her parents, her siblings, her job, her ex-husband, her hiking vacation to the Canadian Rockies, and anything else that just popped into her pretty head. In Santa Fe, Brenda's prattle turned to making hints about expensive items that caught her eye in the jewelry stores and boutiques on the Plaza and complaints about how she didn't like being left alone while Johnny took care of his business dealings.

Earlier in the day, realizing there was no way he could face driving Brenda back to Denver, Johnny had sent her off window shopping on the pretext that he had to make some confidential phone calls to clients. When she got back to the hotel room, he greeted her with a worried look and a tale that his father had just suffered a stroke at his ranch on the Bootheel. In fact, despite his eighty-three years, there was nothing wrong with his father, other than a recent hip replacement.

"I'm so sorry." Brenda stepped close and hugged Johnny. "Will he be all right?"

Johnny shook his head gravely. "I don't know, but I have to get down there right away."

"Of course, family comes first." Brenda drew her head back, looked up at Johnny, and bit her lip. "But you're not going to leave me stranded here, are you?"

Johnny smiled. "I wouldn't do that to you. You're booked on a flight to Denver this afternoon. I'll take you to the airport."

Brenda's expression lightened. "Thank you."

"Sorry about the change in plans," Johnny said.

Brenda shook her curly locks. "It's not your fault. What is the Bootheel, anyway?"

"It's a strip of land in the southwest corner of the state that butts into Mexico. It's shaped like the heel of a boot."

"And your father owns it?" Brenda asked with great interest.

Johnny laughed. "Not all of it by a long shot, but a pretty fair chunk."

"What time is my flight?"

"Five-thirty."

Brenda pressed hard against him and her hand found his crotch. "That's hours from now. Is there anything I can do to ease your worries?"

Johnny responded by slipping his hand down the front of her blouse, and Brenda spent the next half hour consoling him with her mouth and body.

At the airport Brenda's flight had been delayed because of the snowstorm, so Johnny forced himself to sit with her outside the boarding area, even though she protested that she would be fine on her own. He'd learned a long time ago to leave women feeling happy and cared about, especially if you had no intention of ever seeing them again. It caused much less trouble that way.

Because the Santa Fe Airport served only turboprop commercial carriers and private airplanes, the terminal was small. In the public area, a space with high-beamed ceilings, tile floors, and hand-carved Southwestern chairs, about twenty passengers, along with a few spouses and friends, waited for the last flight out to Denver.

From where Johnny sat with Brenda, he could see the tarmac. The inbound flight from Denver had just taxied to the ramp area. Soon he'd be shed of her, and the thought made him want to smile, but he stifled the impulse. When the gate agent announced that boarding would begin in a few minutes, Johnny stood, bent over, and gave Brenda a kiss.

"Thanks for being so understanding," he said.

"You've been so quiet," Brenda said, kissing him back.

Johnny gave her a solemn look. "You know, just thinking about my father." In truth, he'd used the fabricated family catastrophe to tune Brenda out. Actually, his only worry was whether or not over dinner he'd be able to talk Kevin Kerney into participating in a deal he'd just sewn up. Kerney had been an obstinate, straitlaced kid back in the old days on the Jornada, who'd occasionally dressed him down for his fun-loving ways. But what Johnny had in mind shouldn't get Kerney's ire up. It was a straight business deal with some good money built into it.

Brenda stood, kissed him again, patted his arm, and nodded understandingly.

"I'll call when I can," he said.

She buzzed his cheek with her lips and pranced toward the boarding area, looking pert and yummy in her tight jeans. She threw him a smile over her shoulder, and Johnny smiled back, thinking it was a real pity that she liked to talk as much as she liked to party.

Popular with the well-heeled set, the restaurant Johnny had picked wasn't one of Kerney's favorite places. Although the food was good, the dining rooms were small and dark, the tables crowded together, and most nights the din of nearby diners made private conversation difficult. In the summer, when customers could dine on the tree-covered patio, it was much more tolerable.

He waited for Johnny at the small bar in an alcove near the entrance. As the lone customer at the bar Kerney spent his time sipping an herbal iced tea and watching the bartender mix drink orders placed by the servers. He looked at his wristwatch, noting that Johnny was ten minutes overdue. But Johnny had always been one to stage flashy, late entrances. Thirty-some years ago, Johnny's show-off antics had been amusing, but Kerney wasn't about to cool his heels much longer. He'd give it five more minutes before blowing the whole thing off and heading home.

The thought had no more than crossed his mind when Kerney felt a hand come to rest on his shoulder. He turned to find Johnny smiling at him. His face was a bit fuller, but his wiry, small-boned frame was lean, and his restless brown eyes still danced with mischief. No more than five foot seven, he wore his light brown hair cut short. Lizard-skin cowboy boots added an inch to his height, and the belt cinched around his waist was secured by a championship rodeo buckle.

"Looks like you're hitting the hard stuff," Johnny said as he glanced at Kerney's iced tea and took a seat. "It's been a long time, Kerney."

"That it has," Kerney replied, not expecting an apology from Johnny for his lateness. "You look well."

"So do you." Johnny glanced up and down the length of the almost empty bar. "Where are all the good-looking Santa Fe women? Do you have your cops lock them up at night?"

"No, but we do try to keep them safe.

Are you still chasing skirts, Johnny?"

"Not me, I'm a happily married man. But I sure do like to look." He gestured to the bartender and ordered a whiskey. "Not drinking tonight or on the wagon?"

"Not in the mood," Kerney replied.

Johnny raised an eyebrow. "That's no fun. I hear you got hitched some time back."

"I did," Kerney replied. "Who told you?"

"Dale Jennings," Johnny replied. "Says you've got yourself a beautiful wife and a fine young son."

Dale was Kerney's best friend from his boyhood days on the Jornada. Together with Johnny they rodeoed in high school. In their senior year Johnny had taken the state all-around title, while Kerney and Dale won the team calf-roping buckle. Dale still lived on the family ranch with his wife, Barbara, and their two daughters.

"I do," Kerney replied. "Sara and Patrick. How about you? Any children?"

Johnny shook his head as the bartender handed him his whiskey. "Not a one."

"When did you talk to Dale?"

"I'll fill you in later." He knocked back the drink and waved the empty glass at the bartender.

"You're not driving, are you?" Kerney

asked, as the bartender approached with the whiskey bottle.

"Hell, yes, I am," Johnny said as he slid his fresh drink closer. "Stop sounding like a cop. I never figured you for one back in the old days."

"It's an honorable profession," Kerney said. "Tell me what you've been doing since you stopped rodeoing."

Johnny swirled the ice in the glass, deliberately took a small sip, and smiled. "There, is that better? I don't want to get in trouble with the police chief."

He put the glass on the bar. "Hell, I didn't want to stop saddle bronc riding. I was in my prime on the circuit. But after I got kicked in the head for the sixth time, the doctors said if I had one more head trauma it could kill or paralyze me. I had to quit."

"I'm sorry to hear it," Kerney said.

Johnny shrugged and downed his whiskey. "Back then, twenty-five, thirty years ago, nobody wore protective gear. Nowadays, all the boys wear vests and some are wearing helmets. If that had happened in my day, we would have laughed them out of the arena. Those boys with the helmets look like they should be riding motorcycles, not bulls and bucking horses.

But times change, and it's a damn hard sport on a man's body, that's for sure."

The hostess came to escort them to their table, and they were seated next to a group of eight women loudly discussing a planned fund-raising event for a local charity. Over their noisy chatter Kerney again asked Johnny what he'd been doing over the past years.

"Sports management, for one," Johnny said, taking a menu from the server, "and media relations. Most of my clients are pro rodeo cowboys, but I've got a few up-and-coming country singers in my stable, and some minor league baseball players who have the talent to make it to the big show. But I'm branching out. That's why I wanted to see you."

A server appeared with menus and recited the specials. Johnny ordered a salad, steak, and another whiskey. Kerney went with the asparagus soup and lamb. "Are you in town on business?" he asked. "Or just to see me?"

Johnny leaned back and grinned devilishly. "Both, but it's all business. I met with the director of the state film office yesterday and the governor today. You're the last person on my list."

"So are you going to tell me what busi-

24

ness you have with me or is it a secret?" Kerney asked.

"You're gonna love it, Kerney. I've just brokered a deal to film a movie in New Mexico. It will be produced by a Hollywood film company, costar two of my clients, and be shot entirely in the state. The governor and the state film office are putting a chunk of money into it."

"Sounds like quite an undertaking."

Johnny spread his hands wide to match the grin on his face. "It's big, and it's gonna be a hell of a lot of fun. I want to bring you in on it."

"Doing what?" Kerney asked, as the server brought Johnny his whiskey.

"First let me tell you the fun part," Johnny said. "The movie is a modern-day Western about a rancher who's facing bankruptcy due to drought and the loss of grazing leases on federal land. He decides to fight back by mounting a fifty-mile cattle drive to dramatize his plight. But when he tries to drive his cattle across closed federal land, the government bars his access. The story takes off from there."

"I've always liked a good Western," Kerney said. "Let me know when it hits the theaters."

Johnny laughed as the server placed his

salad on the table. "Hear me out. The fun part is that we're filming some of it on my father's ranch in the Bootheel, and we plan to hire as many New Mexico cowboys, wranglers, stuntmen, stockmen, extras, and qualified film technicians as possible. That's part of our deal with the state. I want Dale Jennings to be a wrangler and you to be a technical advisor on the film."

"So that's why you talked to Dale," Kerney said. "What did he say?"

"He's gonna do it."

Kerney tried the asparagus soup. It was good. "You can hire whoever you want?" he asked.

Johnny, who hated tomatoes, picked them out of the salad and put them on the edge of the plate. "For the key, non-technical New Mexico personnel I can. I'm an executive producer for the project. The story line was my idea. I'm even getting a screenwriting credit for it."

"I'm impressed. When does all this take place?"

"In September, after the rainy season, when it's not so damn hot."

"I've got a full-time job, Johnny."

"We're talking about three weeks on location, maximum. That's all you have to commit to. Use your vacation time. You'll get top dollar, housing, meals, transportation, and expenses. Plus, you can bring the wife and son along gratis. In fact, we'll hire them as extras. That's what I promised to do with Dale's wife and daughters."

Johnny finished his greens and slugged back his whiskey. "We have a ninety-day shooting schedule. Three weeks in the Bootheel to do the major cowboy and rodeoing stuff, then some other location filming around the state in Silver City and Las Cruces. We'll do the set work here in Santa Fe at the sound studios on the college campus. We're hiring film students as apprentices."

Kerney put his spoon down and wiped his mouth with a napkin. "Sounds like a major undertaking."

"It's big," Johnny replied. "My sister, Julia, is in on it. You know, you broke her heart when you came back from Vietnam and didn't marry her."

Kerney laughed. "Get serious, Johnny. Julia didn't want anything to do with me." A year younger than Johnny, Julia had been one of the prettiest, most popular girls in high school. A great horsewoman in her own right, she'd won the state high-school barrel-racing competition the year after Kerney, Johnny, and Dale graduated.

Johnny grinned and raised his hand to the sky. "I'm telling you the truth. She totally had the hots for you."

"What has Julia been up to?"

"Pretty much taking care of Joe and Bessie, now that they're older. What do you think about my proposition?"

"I'd need to know a lot more about it before I decide," Kerney answered. "What kind of technical assistance would you have me do?"

The main course arrived, and Johnny asked for a glass of expensive red wine before cutting into his steak. "Cop stuff," he said. "You'd make sure anything to do with law enforcement is accurate. The story pits a rancher against agents of the Bureau of Land Management. When he decides to move his cattle illegally across public land, federal agents and the local sheriff try to stop him. The chase turns into a stampede when the cops try to turn back the rancher and his neighbors who are driving the herd across BLM land."

Kerney's lamb came served on a bed of polenta. It looked perfect. "It doesn't sound like there would be much for me to do," he said.

Johnny chuckled. "Now you're thinking straight. It would be a working vacation,

Hollywood style. Besides that, when was the last time you went on a real cattle drive? I'm not talking about moving stock from pasture to pasture, or gathering cows for shipment. But a real cattle drive, pushing three hundred and fifty head across a mountain range."

"Can't say I've ever done that," Kerney said.

"Doesn't that sound like fun?" Johnny asked.

"Yeah, it does."

"You think about it," Johnny said, fork poised at his mouth. "Talk to Dale. Talk to your wife. This is a once-in-a-lifetime opportunity for us to do something we used to dream about back when we were kids."

"You were always good at organizing grand escapades," Kerney said.

Johnny nodded, his face flushed from the whiskey and wine. "And this one is a real moneymaker for everyone involved. Not that you need it. To hear tell, you've got a sweet little horse-ranch operation outside of town."

"Raising and training cutting horses," Kerney said, wondering who had been so forthcoming about his personal life with Johnny. He doubted it had been Dale Jennings.

29

"Are you in?" Johnny asked, his words slightly slurred.

"I'm not sure if I can spare the time."

"You're the police chief," Johnny rebutted. "Top cop, and all that. Can't the department do without you?"

"I'll think about the offer."

After dinner Johnny fumbled with his wallet for a credit card to use to pay the check. When he signed the charge slip his hand was shaky.

Kerney thanked him for dinner and held out his palm. "Give me your car keys, Johnny. I'm driving you to the hotel. The concierge can arrange to retrieve your vehicle."

Johnny flashed an annoyed looked. "Get real, Kerney. The hotel is only four blocks from here and I'm not drunk."

"I think you are. Your keys, Johnny."

"You're joking, right?" Johnny said, laughing.

Kerney shook his head and made a gimme motion with his outstretched hand.

Johnny shrugged, fished a hand into his pocket, and dropped the keys into Kerney's open palm, along with his business card. "I'm going to need an answer on the technical-advisor job in a week," he said.

"You'll have it by then," Kerney said.

At the hotel Kerney accompanied Johnny into the lobby. The concierge was off duty, so Kerney gave Johnny's car keys and a twenty-dollar bill to a valet parking attendant and asked him to bring the vehicle at the restaurant back to the hotel.

Johnny described his car and the attendant hurried off. "Let me buy you a nightcap in the bar," he said.

Kerney steered Johnny to the elevators and shook his head. "Not tonight, but thanks again for the meal. It was good to catch up with you."

Johnny hid his disappointment. He hated being alone in hotel rooms. Maybe he should have tolerated Brenda's chitchat and kept her around instead of sending her back to Denver. He pushed the elevator call button and said, "You're no fun at all, Kerney."

"Don't take it personally," Kerney replied. "I've got a busy day tomorrow. Next time, if you come to town on a weekend, I'll lift a glass or two with you."

"It's a deal," Johnny said. "When I get back to Denver, I'll send you a copy of the shooting script for the movie by overnight express, so you can see exactly what I've been talking about. You're gonna love it."

The elevator doors slid open and the two men shook hands and said good-night. Kerney left the hotel thinking it might be wise to check out Johnny and his offer before making up his mind about the proposal. On appearances Johnny seemed to be successful and living large. He drove an expensive car, stayed in the best hotel in town, and had treated Kerney to dinner at a pricey restaurant.

But Kerney wondered about Johnny's drinking. He'd studied Johnny's face carefully for any telltale signs of alcoholism — pasty gray skin, bloodshot eyes, the broken spider veins that showed on the cheek and nose — and had seen none. But that didn't prove anything.

He shrugged off his unanswered question about Johnny. Best to wait and see if he followed up and sent him the script. If he did, Kerney would talk to Sara about the idea of spending their vacation playing cowboy on a movie.

Actually, to Kerney, in spite of his reservations about Johnny, the idea sounded like a total hoot.

By morning the April snowstorm had passed, the sun had burned away the last traces of snow, and trees were greening up, about to bud. After a presentation to a civic organization at a breakfast meeting in downtown Santa Fe, Kerney hurried back to headquarters for a regularly scheduled monthly meeting with his senior commanders and supervisors from all shifts. Always on the lookout for new ways to combat and reduce crime, Kerney had recently instituted a computer-based system that identified patterns of criminal activity based on the types of offenses committed, the dates and times of each occurrence, and the specific locations of the crimes. Basic information from all incident reports and traffic citations was fed into the system, analyzed, and broken down into ten geographic areas within the city. The program allowed Kerney and his commanders to shift resources, set goals, coordinate case planning among the various divisions, and track progress.

The department had field-tested the system over the previous holiday season and had reduced auto burglaries at shopping malls by fifty percent. Now that it was fully operational, each commander was responsible for establishing targeted monthly goals to reduce crime on their shifts based on the current trends.

Over twenty senior officers were

crowded into the first-floor training room, filling the chairs at the large conference table and sitting against the walls. Kerney's deputy chief, Larry Otero, ran the meeting as commanders discussed the data, reviewed current activities, set new case plans, and decided upon special operations to be initiated during the coming month.

At the end of the table a slide projector connected to the computer displayed the maps of the city on a screen that highlighted high crime activity. In the downtown area, early evening, strong-arm robberies and purse snatchings were up, and in a public housing neighborhood near St. Michael's Drive, criminal damage to property and residential burglaries had risen by ten percent on the weekends. On the southern end of the city motor vehicle crashes were down on all shifts. But a perp had surfaced who was baiting patrol officers into high-speed chases and had yet to be caught.

The meeting wound down with a report on the completion of the latest citizen police academy program, and a decision was made to run a DWI blitz on a weekend two weeks hence. The last bit of business was an announcement of the arrival of twenty new patrol vehicles, which would be outfitted and put in service within several weeks.

Kerney thanked everyone for their good work and went to his upstairs office, where he reviewed the shift commanders' reports from the last twenty-four hours. A DWI arrest had been made on Cerrillos Road by a third-watch patrol officer, and a male subject named John Jordan had been taken into custody.

Kerney powered up his desktop computer, logged on, and read the officer's incident-and-arrest report. Three hours after Kerney had left him at the hotel, Johnny had been busted on Cerrillos Road two blocks from the city's only adult entertainment club. He'd been stopped for making an illegal U-turn and had failed a field sobriety test. At the jail he'd registered a 0.20 on the alcohol breath test, more than twice the legal limit.

Kerney called the jail and learned that Johnny had been released on bail. His phone rang just as he was about to dial the hotel.

"Hey, Kerney," Johnny said cheerfully when Kerney answered. "You should have had that nightcap with me at the bar, then I wouldn't have gotten into trouble with one of your cops."

35

"I just read about your 'little trouble,' Johnny," Kerney said.

"Didn't the cop call you at home? I asked him to."

"He had no reason to do that."

"Even if he had, I figured you wouldn't give a rat's ass," Johnny said sourly.

There was static on the receiver. "Where are you calling from?" Kerney asked.

"I'm on the road, heading home. Can you help me get out of this pickle for old time's sake?"

"Sorry, Johnny. Get a lawyer to handle it."

"Is it that cut-and-dried?"

"In my department it is."

"I thought as much. Even though I'm pissed, I'll still get that shooting script off to you. It will be on your desk tomorrow morning."

"I'll give it a look, Johnny."

"Good deal. My reception is breaking up. I'll talk to you soon."

Johnny disconnected and Kerney spent time running a quick background check on Johnny. In Colorado, Johnny had been cited twice for speeding but had no DWI arrests on his record. The National Crime Information Center showed no outstanding wants or warrants, and there was nothing on him in the New Mexico law enforcement computer system.

Although it appeared to be Johnny's first DWI bust, it wasn't something Kerney could take lightly. Because Johnny could be untrustworthy and downright conniving, he decided to pay a visit to the New Mexico Film Office to learn more about the movie project. He wanted to know if it was the real deal or one of Johnny's pie-in-the-sky fantasies.

Housed in offices on St. Francis Drive, the film office had undergone a resurgence with the election of a new governor who made trips to Hollywood to court production companies to film pictures in New Mexico. Under the governor's watch new state laws had been passed offering tax incentives and loan subsidies to moviemakers.

Kerney introduced himself to the receptionist, a young woman with light brown hair and plucked eyebrows, and asked if someone could tell him about a movie to be filmed in the Bootheel later in the year.

Somewhat taken aback by Kerney's uniform, the young woman cautiously asked why he was interested. Kerney told her he'd been approached to serve as a technical advisor on the project, and the receptionist passed him on to the director, a middle-aged woman named Vikki Morrison.

Trim and energetic, Morrison had short blond fluffy hair and high cheekbones. Her office walls were filled with framed, autographed photos of movie stars and posters of films shot in the state. A director's chair at the side of her desk carried the name of one of Santa Fe's best-known resident film celebrities. A bookshelf held a display of various shooting scripts signed by cast members, along with a carefully arranged display of copies of a book, *100 Years of Filmmaking in New Mexico*.

Kerney explained his personal relationship with Johnny Jordan and asked about the movie project in the Bootheel. Morrison told him that Johnny had been a driving force behind getting the film shot in the state. He'd brokered a deal to use the nearly abandoned mining town of Playas as the production headquarters. In addition to serving as a movie set, the town would house the cast and crew during filming in the area.

Kerney knew about the town through a recent article in a law-enforcement bulletin. Built in the 1970s, Playas had once been a company town of over a thousand people. But when the nearby copper-smelting operations were shut down, it became a virtual modern-day ghost town containing over 250 homes, 25 apartments, a bank building, post office, fire station, churches, community center, air strip, and other amenities. Recently, the town had been bought with Homeland Security funds and was in the process of being transformed into a national antiterrorism training center.

Morrison explained that Johnny had been active in securing part of the financing for the movie through a low-interest state loan. He'd just finished negotiating the final details of a contract that guaranteed the state a percentage of the profits from the film.

Kerney asked Morrison to tell him about the role of a technical advisor.

"Well," Morrison said, "it all depends on the project, the cast, and the crew. In some cases it can be a demanding, frustrating role, or it can be an enjoyable, low-key experience."

"I'm not looking to take on something that winds up being a heavy burden."

Morrison smiled. "I can certainly understand that. You should have an opportunity to meet with the producers and key personnel before filming actually begins. If what you learn isn't to your liking, you can always opt out of the project."

"That sounds reasonable," Kerney said. He thanked Morrison for her time and left with a copy of *100 Years of Filmmaking in New Mexico*, which she insisted he should have.

Johnny Jordan lived and worked in a late-nineteenth-century brick building in downtown Denver that had originally been a warehouse. The developer who renovated it had added a two-story penthouse with a wall of glass that looked out at the Rocky Mountains. It featured a large balcony, a media room, four bedrooms, two home offices, and a huge living room adjacent to the kitchen and dining area. This was where Johnny and his wife, Madeline, a partner in a law firm that specialized in corporate mergers and hostile takeovers, lived. Madeline retained sole ownership, having bought the property prior to their marriage.

Johnny loved living there, loved waking up to the city views and the distant mountains, and especially loved that it hadn't cost him a penny.

He didn't expect Madeline to be home, and she wasn't. Johnny always timed his trips out of town with other women to coincide with his wife's travel schedule. It reduced the odds of discovery. This week she was in Toronto, heading up a team of lawyers negotiating the merger of two multinational lumber companies.

Johnny cared about Madeline, maybe even loved her every once in a while when she wasn't obsessing about her career. But like every other woman he'd been seriously drawn to and married over the years — Madeline was wife number four — she now bored him.

With all his wives he'd been faithful until the boredom set in. Then he went fishing for fresh talent. At the end of his second marriage he'd tried to figure out why he became so easily disconnected from women he thought he loved. After pondering it he'd decided most women were like well-presented but uninteresting meals: nice to look at but no fun to feast on time and time again.

When his third wife left him, Johnny had struggled briefly with the question of why he kept getting married. The only thing he could figure out was that he was too damned impulsive. With Madeline he'd thought he had chosen more wisely. In her early forties when he'd met her, she was stunning to look at, had a great sense of humor, and was extraordinary in bed. He liked the fact that she was mature, sophisticated, and successful. He dated her for a year, seeing no other women during that time, before popping the question.

After the marriage she'd held him at the banquet table far longer than any of his other wives. But that had all gone south a year ago.

In his office Johnny stuffed a copy of the screenplay in an envelope for Kerney, filled out the airbill form, and phoned to have it picked up. Then he called his lawyer and left a message about his DWI arrest in Santa Fe. Finished with the small stuff, he dialed the private office number of Bill Esty, vice president in charge of programming at a cable sports network in New York.

"Is it wrapped up?" Esty asked.

"The film office is drafting the final contract. We can move ahead."

"Johnny, we still have some issues to clear off the table."

"What issues?" Johnny demanded. "I've got a movie deal in the bag that will feature two ex–national pro rodeo stars, two up-and-coming Hispanic cowboys from the circuit, and a screenplay with a humdinger of a gut-busting rodeo in it."

"We know all that," Esty said slowly,

"but it's been suggested that rodeo may already be nearing its saturation point. Bull riding is on cable almost every night and the numbers aren't moving."

"Rodeo is more than bull riding," Johnny said, "and right now everyone is presenting it in the same old way. Like we've been saying, this is a chance to do for rodeo what the X Games did for skateboarders and snowboarders. We can take this sport to the next level on your network."

"If I didn't think there was a chance of that, we'd have stopped talking a while ago. But I don't have a completely open field here."

"This movie is going to generate a wave of interest in rodeoing and cowboys. Do you really want to be standing on the sidelines when I produce the first rodeo Super Bowl? I've got the talent already tied up, sponsors interested, and an agreement in the works with two pro rodeo associations."

"Now that I know you have the full funding," Esty said, "I'll talk to the Spanish-language television people in Florida and Mexico City about taking the next step and formally bidding on a share of the rights."

"Why have they been dragging their heels?"

"It's human nature in the television business," Espy replied. "No one wants to go out on a limb with a project that doesn't already have the market's seal of approval. But they loved the footage of your Hispanic cowboys, Lovato and Maestas. Now that the production financing is nailed down, I don't think it will take too long to bring them on board."

Johnny had put every dime he had into developing the movie. He'd get a producer's fee for the film and an agent's fee for the cowboys who had appearances in the movie, but he was out advances against the rodeo stars he'd signed up for the new circuit. Unless he could get corporate sponsorships and seal the deal with Esty, his super rodeo circuit would be dead in the water and he'd be bankrupt.

"When do you expect a response?" he asked.

"No telling," Esty replied. "But I'd like to see us finalize contract negotiations by this summer. If it all falls into place, we can start preproduction right away, and you'll have a contract."

Johnny heard footsteps in the hallway. "Okay, I'll talk to you soon." He hung up to find Madeline staring at him from the doorway with a frosty look on her face. Five three with dancer's legs and pert little breasts, she was built just the way Johnny liked them. Her jaw was set and she didn't look at all happy to see him.

"You're back early," he said with a grin. "I didn't expect you home until to-morrow."

"I got home last night, just in time to find a woman named Brenda slipping a note to you in our mailbox."

"Who?" Johnny asked.

"Brenda," Madeline repeated, handing Johnny the opened letter.

"Did you talk to her?"

"No, she left before I could approach her. But I read her little note. She wants you to call her when you get home because she was worried about you in Santa Fe. Did you really tell her that your father had a stroke?"

"I don't know what this is all about," Johnny said, scanning the note, knowing that he'd been busted.

Madeline scoffed. "From what Brenda wrote, she appears to be smitten with you, Johnny. Those earrings you gave her made quite an impression."

"I can explain everything," Johnny said.

Madeline stepped to his desk and dropped a business card on the table in front of him. "No, you can't. The movers will be here in the morning to pack up all your personal possessions and get you out of my house. Here's their card. After you check into a hotel for the night, I suggest you start apartment hunting."

"Can't we talk this out?"

"We just have," Madeline said, her hand outstretched. "Give me your house key."

Johnny smiled sadly, looked crestfallen, spread his arms wide in a gesture of supplication. "Look, sweetie pie, I'm sorry. I screwed up. It won't happen again."

"You're damn right it won't. Pack an overnight bag, leave my house, and don't speak to me again."

He dropped the key in Madeline's hand and watched as she turned on her heel and left. He checked his wallet for cash, pulled out his last bank statements of his personal accounts, and studied his balances. He could rent a place and get by for a month or two before he would be forced to use his credit cards to cover his business and living expenses.

The thought struck him that maybe Brenda would put him up. She had an extra bedroom he could use as an office.

That way he could cut his overhead in half and save a chunk of money. He worked on a story to tell her as he dialed the phone.

"Hey, sweetie pie," he said when she picked up, "I got your note."

The following morning the script Johnny had promised arrived, and Kerney spent his lunch break at his desk reading it. The story was a good one, with some interesting plot twists. The climax to the film occurred during a working cowboy rodeo held at the end of the cattle drive, which turned into a free-for-all after the cops showed up to arrest the rancher and his friends for trespassing on government property. Although set in present time, it had the feel of a classic Hollywood Western.

He put the screenplay away. Tonight, Sara, his career-army wife, would be flying in with their son, Patrick, for a long weekend break from her current Pentagon assignment, which was scheduled to end in the fall. For the past two months they'd been debating how to spend the thirty days of leave Sara would take before her next posting. Mostly she'd talked about just wanting to settle in at their Santa Fe ranch to nest and relax. Would she consider giving up a large portion of her vacation time so that Kerney could work on a movie?

Last night he'd called Dale Jennings to get his take on Johnny's offer. Dale told him that Barbara and the girls were excited about it, the money was too good to pass up, and it would be fun to see firsthand how movies got made.

Dale's enthusiasm had made Kerney think more positively about signing on. But in the end it would be Sara's decision to make.

A worried-looking patrol commander who knocked on his open office door made Kerney postpone any further thoughts about the movie. He smiled, wrapped up his half-eaten sandwich, dropped it in the waste basket, and invited the officer to enter.

Usually a good traveler, Patrick was restless on the flight to Albuquerque. Sara tried, without success, to distract him with a picture book and the toys she'd brought along, a set of small plastic barnyard animals that ordinarily kept him occupied for hours. Today the book and toys held no attraction. He squirmed in his seat, kicked his feet, twirled his favorite toy animal in his hand, and repeatedly asked when he would see his daddy.

Patrick's question made Sara's heart sink. Her son had reached the age where he needed a full-time father in his life, and her long-distance marriage to Kerney made that impossible.

At the terminal Patrick spotted Kerney waiting near the escalators behind the passenger screening area and ran full tilt to him, his face breaking into a big smile. Kerney scooped him up and hugged Sara with his free arm. On the drive to Santa Fe, Patrick's fidgetiness vanished. He sat calmly in his toddler car seat and soon fell asleep.

They talked quietly about their work-weeks. By design Sara avoided two issues that were troubling her: Patrick's need for a full-time father and her next duty assignment. She'd just been told that she would be posted as a deputy military attaché to the U.S. embassy in Turkey. The assignment came with the promise of a fast-track promotion. If she turned it down, her climb up the ladder would stall and she'd never get to wear the eagles of a full bird colonel.

"Did you know that the first movie made in New Mexico was filmed in 1898?" Kerney asked.

"You always have such interesting bits of trivia to share," Sara replied, grateful that Kerney was making small talk. "Tell me more."

"It was made by the Edison Company and ran less than a minute," Kerney said. "In 1912 D. W. Griffith filmed *A Pueblo Legend* with Mary Pickford at the Isleta Pueblo south of Albuquerque, and later Tom Mix, the early cowboy movie star, made twenty-five movies up in Las Vegas."

"Where did you learn all this?" Sara asked.

"In a book I'm reading on New Mexico filmmaking."

"Why the sudden interest in movies?"

Kerney slowed to let a semitruck pass. "I've been asked to serve as a technical advisor on a movie to be shot here starting in September."

"Is it a shoot-'em-up or a cop caper?" Sara asked.

"A bit of both."

"How did this happen to land in your lap?"

"By way of an old boyhood acquaintance," Kerney replied.

He gave Sara the lowdown on Johnny Jordan and the movie. He told her that Dale Jennings had signed on to be a wrangler and planned to bring Barbara and the girls with him. The more he talked about the idea the more animated he became, particularly when he described the cattle drive and the rodeo that would be filmed in the Bootheel. He was grinning from ear to ear when he finished.

"You sound like you want to do it."

"Not without you and Patrick," Kerney said as he signaled his turn off the highway onto the ranch road.

"Let's talk about it some more."

Soon the ranch house came into view. Tucked into a saddleback ridge, it looked out on the Galisteo Basin, with the Ortiz and Sandia Mountains in the distance. Sara sighed as the car climbed the long hill. It was paradise, and the thought of spending a month at the ranch before heading off to Turkey was more than appealing to her. But the movie idea did sound like it could be a fun adventure, and Kerney was clearly drawn to it.

"There's one more thing," Kerney said as he pulled to a stop outside the house.

Sara gazed at the pasture and the horse barn across the field from the house. Four geldings were in the paddock, their heads up, ears forward, alerted by the sound of the car. To the west the sun was low, behind a thin bank of clouds, spreading a pink glow over the Jemez Mountains.

"What's that?" she asked as she got out of the car and slipped on her jacket to cut the chill of the April wind.

"The mayor told me privately that he doesn't plan to run for reelection next March. That means I'll probably be out of a job in less than a year."

Sara held back a smile as she unstrapped Patrick from the toddler seat and woke him up. Was it possible that both of her major concerns could be resolved within a matter of months? Would he be willing to resign his position before the municipal election and go with her on her next duty assignment? They could arrange for a caretaker to look after the ranch in their absence.

Kerney was a rich man by way of an unexpected inheritance several years back from an old family friend. He served as police chief not for the money, but because it had been the job he'd always wanted. Now that it would be ending, they could finally start living as a family, see a bit of the world together. Nothing would make Sara happier.

Kerney popped open the trunk and took out the luggage. "Did you hear what I said?"

Sara nodded, took Patrick out of his seat, put him on the ground, and bundled him into his warm coat. "Are you ready to retire?"

"It's about that time," Kerney said, looking stoical.

Patrick scooted away in the direction of the geldings in the paddock. "Can I go riding now?" he called. "With Daddy?"

Sara caught up to him and took him by the hand. "In the morning, young man."

"Can I give the horses some biscuits?" Patrick pleaded, trying to tug Sara along.

"Yes, you can." She turned back toward Kerney as Patrick led her away. "Watching how a film gets made and getting to play cowboy might be fun."

Kerney smiled. "That's what I think."

"You come see the horses, too, Daddy," Patrick called over his shoulder.

Kerney dropped the luggage and joined his family. Together, the threesome walked hand-in-hand toward the horses at the fence awaiting their arrival, heads bobbing in anticipation.

Chapter Two

June brought hot, dry days, high winds, a rash of snatch-and-grab thefts from local art galleries, and, at the end of the month, Johnny Jordan's return to Santa Fe. Kerney agreed to meet him for morning coffee at a downtown café, and not surprisingly Johnny was late again. He came into the crowded restaurant and spotted Kerney in one of the small booths along the back wall next to the kitchen. Smile flashing, he approached holding the local newspaper and pointed to the front-page headline:

RASH OF ART THEFTS STYMIES POLICE

"Seems you've got a crime wave on your hands," he said.

"Apparently," Kerney replied as he gestured to the waitress, who approached, filled Johnny's coffee cup, and offered Kerney a refill of his hot tea, which he refused. Johnny dumped cream and sugar into his cup and stirred it vigorously.

"So are you stymied?" Johnny asked.

"We're investigating all creditable leads."

Johnny laughed, put the newspaper aside, and laid a manila envelope on the table. "That means you've got nothing. Here's your technical-advisor contract for the movie."

Kerney didn't touch it. Two days ago, Johnny had called from Denver to say he was coming to town to hand-deliver the contract and talk to him about some unspecified business.

Interested in what that business might be, Kerney had contacted the municipal court. Johnny was scheduled to appear before a judge on his DWI bust later in the morning. He wondered if Johnny would ask him once again to get him off the hook.

"You don't have to sign it now," Johnny said between sips of coffee. "Look it over, show it to your lawyer, and mail it back to me."

Kerney said nothing and put the envelope aside. Through the café window tourists milled around the sidewalk, waiting to be called for the next available table. Across the street, a middle-aged man in baggy shorts and an oversized T-shirt videoed his wife and two bored-looking children as they walked along the Plaza.

Johnny put the cup down and gave

Kerney a sideways look. "You're not bailing out of the deal, are you?"

"No, but I'd like to meet the principal parties involved before I make a commitment."

Johnny made a thumbs-up gesture. "Hey, great minds think alike. We want you to come to the Bootheel for a couple of days in September before we start production."

Kerney was surprised: he'd expected Johnny to ask him to help get his DWI arrest dropped. "That might be possible," he said. "What would I be doing there?"

"We'll take a tour of all the locations before the actual filming begins. It's called a tech scout. The producer, director, cinematographer, and key members of the technical crew visit each site and do advance planning on what they'll need to shoot a scene."

"I thought you were the producer," Kerney said.

Johnny tapped his chest with a finger. "I'm an *executive* producer. That means, aside from coming up with the story idea, writing some stuff for the rodeo scenes, scouting out the Bootheel locations, getting my clients cast in the movie, and arranging for some product placement, I don't have much to do with the actual filming."

"And this tech scout thing would be done in two days?"

"Your part of it would."

"You do know that the town of Playas is now an antiterrorism facility," Kerney said.

"Yeah, but the governor arranged for us to use it."

"What days would you need me?"

"It can be on a weekend." Johnny pointed to the manila envelope next to Kerney's elbow. "I've added the tech-scout trip to your contract, along with a nice bump in your fee."

Kerney shook his head in amusement. "Even as a kid you always assumed that you'd get whatever you wanted."

"That's because I practice the power of positive thinking, Kerney. What are you doing later this morning?"

"Why do you ask?"

Johnny smiled and shrugged his shoulders. "I've got this DWI thing nipping at my heels and I could sure use a character witness."

Many ordinary citizens weren't shy about asking for special treatment from cops when they got in trouble with the law. But in this case Kerney wondered if

Johnny had added money to the consulting contract as a way to buy a favor. Although it smacked of attempted bribery, it fell legally short of the mark.

"That's not possible," he said flatly.

Johnny's lips tightened in annoyance. He hid it by dabbing his mouth with a napkin. "I just thought I'd ask."

"Let your lawyer handle it," Kerney said.

Johnny gave Kerney an easy, casual grin that didn't quite mask his irritation. "Yeah, I guess you're right. But I can't afford to be hobbled by legal stuff right now. There's too much I've got to do. We're less than three months away from filming. I need to be able to move fast, stay mobile."

"If it's your first DWI conviction, you'll have your license back in ninety days."

"That's what I'm talking about. This is no time for me to be without wheels."

The waitress came with the check. At the cashier's station Kerney paid the bill and left a tip. "I can't help you, Johnny," he said. "I'll be in touch about the contract."

"Make it soon."

Kerney left Johnny on the sidewalk looking completely disgruntled. But it didn't bother him one bit. Doted on and spoiled by his parents, Johnny had never been forced to take responsibility for his actions. A shot of reality might help him grow up.

Pissed off, Johnny watched Kerney's unmarked police cruiser turn the corner. All he'd asked Kerney to do was vouch for him with the judge. What was the big deal with that? He'd put money in the guy's pocket and gotten nothing in return.

Staying angry at Kerney wouldn't help him solve the immediate problem of losing his driver's license. The sports-channel rodeo deal had been finalized, but it would be weeks before he'd see any cash. There were cross-country business trips and client meetings that couldn't be put off, and he didn't have the scratch to hire a car and driver. Johnny decided his only option was to get the local lawyer he'd retained to request a continuance so he could stay behind the wheel. He walked across the street to the Plaza, sat on a park bench, flipped open his cell phone, dialed the lawyer's number, and told him what had to be done.

"We've already had one continuance," the lawyer said after hearing Johnny out.

"Get me another one."

"Do you have any chronic medical conditions?" the lawyer asked after a pause.

"Head traumas from getting kicked and

stepped on by horses when I rodeoed," Johnny said.

"Any physical proof of it?" the lawyer asked.

"I've got a dent in my skull and medical records at home."

"Go to the emergency room right now," the lawyer said. "Tell them you feel dizzy, disoriented, and have blurred vision. I'll call the court and reschedule your appearance."

"Can you have it put off until November?"

"Easily. I'll waive your right to the six-month rule. Sign a release at the ER so I can get a copy of your treatment record and forward it to the judge."

Johnny laughed. "It's that simple?"

"For now," the lawyer said, "but you'll still have to face your day in court."

"Whatever." Johnny disconnected, got directions to the hospital from a Hispanic cop on the Plaza, and drove to the hospital. He checked his watch. If Brenda was back at the hotel room when the docs were finished with him, maybe there would be time for a quickie before his meeting with the director of the film office.

He was about to rid himself of Brenda. Next week, while she was at work, he'd move out of her apartment into a sublet he'd rented. But until then he'd put her to good use.

In the ER Johnny faked a set of symptoms and gave the admitting clerk a history of his old rodeo injuries. After a thirty-minute wait he was screened by a nurse who took his vitals. Then a doctor examined his skull and took an X ray of the dent in the back of his head. After reviewing the X ray he shined a light in Johnny's eyes and had him read the letters on a vision chart.

Johnny deliberately messed it up.

"I don't see anything abnormal on the X ray," the doctor said. "But your symptoms are worrisome. Have you been under stress recently?"

"I've got a lot on my plate, Doc."

"I think we need more tests."

"Can I get it done in Denver?" Johnny asked. "I go home tomorrow."

"Will you make an appointment to see your physician right away?"

"I'll call his office as soon as I get back to the hotel."

"Are you driving?"

"My girlfriend is with me," Johnny replied. "She can drive."

"Okay. Make sure you see your physician."

After paying the bill by credit card and signing a release to let his Santa Fe lawyer get a copy of his ER chart, Johnny went back to his hotel room to find Brenda trying on a new pair of red running shoes.

"I found this great designer-shoe store near the Plaza," she said, bouncing up and down, pointing her toes so she could admire the new footwear, "and they had these in my size. How did it go in court?"

"I got another continuance."

"Your lawyer called."

"The guy here in Santa Fe?"

Brenda shook her head and pirouetted in front of the full mirror on the closet door, studying her shoes as she twirled. "Nope, Jim Blass in Denver. Call him back right away. He said it was important."

Johnny flipped open the cell phone, speed-dialed the number, and got put through to Blass immediately.

"I couldn't reach you on your cell," Blass said. "The call kept getting dropped."

"What's up?" Johnny asked.

"Your wife has filed a claim against the proceeds from your sports-channel contract. That means the money will be tied up until the divorce settlement is finalized, unless we can work something out."

"That bitch," Johnny said. "Did you talk to her attorney?"

"Yeah, I did. Seems you borrowed money from her right before you got married."

"Borrowed, hell. We used that money for our honeymoon trip to Europe. I paid her back."

"That's not what she says," Blass said.

"Fuck her," Johnny said. "What can you do?"

"Tell me the facts, Johnny. Did you pay her back the loan?"

Johnny's squeezed the cell phone in frustration. Sometimes he hated telling the truth. "No."

"How much?"

"Twenty-five thousand and change."

"I'll offer repayment to her from your contract proceeds," Blass said. "But don't expect a rapid response. Madeline is determined to make you suffer as long as she can."

"Push it along," Johnny said. "I need that money." He hit the disconnect icon and threw the phone on the bed.

"Bad news, baby?" Brenda asked as she cuddled up to him.

Johnny filled her in with a sanitized version of Madeline's latest legal maneuver.

She sighed sympathetically, shook her

head, and threw her arms around his neck. "I'd never do something like that to you," she said breathlessly. "Never, ever."

"I know you wouldn't, sweetie pie. But I was going to use some of that money to find us a bigger apartment. We need to get settled into our own place and see where our relationship is headed."

Brenda smiled gleefully at the idea, wiggled her rump, and slid her hand down the front of Johnny's trousers. "Could we get a condo downtown?"

"I don't see why not," Johnny said.

Looking over Brenda's shoulder, Johnny grimaced slightly at the thought of keeping up the charade with her. His sour mood quickly evaporated when Brenda unzipped his pants and dropped to her knees.

Police headquarters sat on the outskirts of the city at the edge of a business park, in an area that had experienced explosive growth over the past decade. To the southwest residential subdivisions, strip malls, apartment complexes, town homes, fast-food franchises, and trailer parks had filled up vast tracts of once-vacant land along a four-mile stretch of road that led to the municipal airport.

For a city that touted its romantic

charm, unique architecture, beautiful setting, and rich cultural and artistic traditions, the area had become Santa Fe's version of tasteless urban sprawl, featuring ill-proportioned faux-adobe pueblo and territorial-style buildings with no character.

Fortunately, few tourists saw it, so the city's reputation as a lovely four-hundred-year-old Spanish village at the foot of the Sangre de Cristo Mountains remained mostly intact.

In his second-floor office at headquarters Kerney read through the art-theft case files. The most recent rip-offs had occurred when two pieces, a small bronze and a miniature oil painting, had been found missing after exhibit openings. They carried a combined value of twenty thousand dollars.

Prior to that a ceramic sculpture and an unframed, signed photographic print had been taken from galleries with no security systems in place. Each item had retailed for over two thousand dollars.

But the rash of art thefts, as the morning headline reported, had all started with the theft of a woven Panamanian basket and a handblown glass vase, both valued in the thousand-dollar range. To date the total amount of the stolen loot exceeded twenty-six thousand dollars.

Kerney read the follow-up supplementals Detective Sergeant Ramona Pino and her team had prepared on the cases. Everyone in attendance at the gallery openings who could be identified on the video surveillance had been interviewed, but attempts to ID all the participants had failed. Statements taken from past and present employees, delivery persons, landlords, gallery owners, and customers who'd made purchases on the days of the thefts had yielded no creditable leads.

Pawnshops, flea markets, and art resale galleries had been visited, collectors of the various artists' works had been contacted, art appraisers had been telephoned, and experts consulted, all to no avail. They had no suspects, no real motive, and no physical evidence.

Using the new computer system Ramona and her team had analyzed the thefts, looking for a pattern. Other than the fact that they were clustered in the downtown area there wasn't much to go on. There was no consistency to the times and dates of the crimes, and nothing had surfaced from the fieldwork that could tie the thefts together. The detectives had checked into the possibility of insurance fraud, but all the gallery owners ran legitimate, profitable businesses. They'd visited nearby shops to learn if any suspicious persons had been seen hanging around before the thefts had occurred. *Nada.*

Feeling as stymied as the headline in the morning newspaper alleged his department to be, Kerney left his office and went looking for Sergeant Pino. Her office was empty and she had signed out to the field until midafternoon.

He returned to his desk and went through the paperwork again, hoping for inspiration. Were the crimes isolated incidents or connected? If the motive wasn't money, what was it? Had six kleptomaniacs with good taste in art suddenly descended on Santa Fe all in one month? He doubted it.

What were they missing?

Andy Talbot wasn't in love with Crystal Hurley, but he sure was having fun with her, at least most of the time. It didn't matter that she was slightly crazy and could get real bitchy, especially when she sank into one of her bouts of depression. When she was happy, no woman he'd ever known could match her, especially when it came to sex.

She had long legs, a tight ass, perfectly

proportioned tits, and hips with just the slightest bit of padding that felt like soft pillows in his hands.

Andy waited for Crystal outside the guesthouse where she lived on her father's Santa Fe hilltop estate, hoping today she'd come home from her noon workout at the gym feeling chirpy. If she was, it usually meant he could count on a quickie before heading off to work at the hotel where he tended bar from two to ten.

Eagerly, he watched her car come up the long driveway, only to be disappointed when she parked and walked past him without a glance or a word, her silky skin glistening with sweat from her workout, her moist brown hair tied up in a loose clump.

Andy followed her inside and watched silently as she ate a bowl of yogurt sprinkled with wheat germ, drank a bottle of water, and stared out the kitchen window as though he wasn't even there. She finished her meal, left the bowl on the counter for the housekeeper who came down from the main house to clean up every afternoon, and went off in the direction of the bathroom. Feeling sulky at being ignored, he plopped down in a living-room easy chair and listened to the sound of the shower through the closed bathroom door. With Crystal he never knew what to expect. One day she'd want him, the next day he was nothing more than an annoyance. Worse than that, her mood could change from minute to minute. Still, Andy was a complete sucker for her, would do anything she wanted.

She took some sort of prescription medication to control her mood swings, talked twice a week by telephone to a shrink who lived out of state, practiced yoga, meditated, and exercised religiously. But as far as Andy could tell, none of it made a difference when Crystal decided to tune out the world.

The sound of the shower stopped and after a few minutes Crystal padded into the living room in her bare feet with a towel wrapped around her torso. She nodded in the direction of the bedroom and dropped the towel on the floor. "Come on," she said without a flicker of emotion on her face.

Aroused and grinning with anticipation, Andy followed her down the hallway. In her bedroom she stripped him naked where he stood, put her arms around his neck, and curled one leg around his waist. He pulled her up by the buttocks and held her firmly while she rode him, staring into his eyes, breathing heavily into his face, her wet hair tangled against his cheek, until they climaxed in unison, both of them gasping in pleasure.

They stayed locked together for a moment, then slowly he lowered her to the floor. She patted his cheek, turned, and walked out of the bedroom.

As he dressed, the thought struck Andy that Crystal had never kissed him on the lips. Not once. He shrugged it off as a meaningless curiosity. He was a twenty-three-year-old bartender from Minnesota boffing a hot young heiress who made up her own rules as she went along, and he was having the time of his life.

After Andy left, Crystal slipped on a pair of thong panties, sat at the small desk in the corner of the living room, and called Benjamin Cohen, a semiretired New York City shrink who'd been her therapist for the past ten years.

"How are you feeling, Crystal?" Cohen asked after he'd picked up.

"Tense, and I just had sex and that didn't help at all. I've been taking things again."

"Tell me about it."

Crystal sighed. "Why? You'll just tell me to increase my medication, and I don't want to. It stops me from feeling horny."

"There is that," Cohen replied. "But let's talk about what you're really feeling."

Crystal giggled. "Guilty, but I'm not giving anything back."

"Care to tell me why?" Cohen asked.

Crystal sighed. "Because I don't want to."

"Sometimes, in the past, you've returned the things you've taken, or given them away as gifts."

She opened the locked desk drawer, looked at her new possessions, and caressed each of them. "These are too beautiful to give away. I'm going to display them in my Paris apartment. No one there will ever know I stole them."

"What else are you feeling?"

"Alive, euphoric, irritable, sexy, depressed. The usual stuff."

"Have you stopped taking your medication entirely?" Cohen asked.

"It turns me into a zombie."

"It helps to stabilize your mood."

"How boring."

"I think it would be best if you came back to the city for a time so we can talk about this in person," Cohen said.

"I can't stand New York. I'll never live there again."

"You need to think about what you're doing, Crystal."

"I hate it when you judge me."

"I'm judging you?"

"There's always that undertone, at least that's what I feel. Crystal doesn't need to steal. Crystal is a rich girl who can buy anything she wants. Crystal is so uncooperative and difficult. You don't say it, but it's there."

"Why have you decided to go back to Paris?" Cohen asked.

"Because Daddy's returning to Santa Fe next week and I don't want to see him. Besides, Paris is fun and sexy. The French are so accepting."

"Do you think Paris will ease your guilt?"

"Why not? I got a gun last week. A pistol. It's very small, so I can keep it in my purse."

"Whatever for?"

"Protection," Crystal replied. "Women get raped in Santa Fe all the time."

"You sound pleased about having a gun."

"In a strange way, I am. It gives me a feeling of control." She opened the expensive, imported crocodile handbag she'd stolen last year from a Fifth Avenue department store and took out the pistol, a small nickel-plated .22-caliber semiautomatic. It was Daddy's gun that he kept in a nightstand next to his bed. The weight of it felt good in her hand.

"Tell me some more about feeling in control."

"The world is a dangerous place." Crystal had never fired a gun. She wondered what the sensation was like.

"Mm-hmm."

"I'm not hiding anything," Crystal said defensively. There was a switch or something above the trigger. What was it? She flicked it back and forth a couple of times and decided it must be the safety catch.

"Are you thinking of hurting yourself?"

"Not yet."

"But soon?" Cohen asked.

Crystal pointed the gun at her reflection in the mirror on the wall behind the desk. "Maybe."

"I know a very good psychiatrist in Santa Fe, Dr. Candace Robbins. I think it would be wise for you to call and ask to see her immediately."

"So she can hospitalize me? No way."

"So you have someone to talk to face-to-face. Let me give you her name and number."

"I suppose I could call her."

"Good," Cohen said.

While Cohen paused to look up the name and phone number of the local shrink, Crystal pushed a lever at the top of the pistol grip and the magazine popped out. The bullets in it looked small, not dangerous at all.

She reinserted the magazine as she pretended to write down the shrink's phone number that Cohen gave her.

"I'll consult with Dr. Robbins," Cohen added, "and tell her to expect your call."

"Okay." Crystal disconnected, put the gun back in the handbag, and went into the bedroom to dress. Yesterday at the post office, when she'd picked up Daddy's mail, she'd seen an invitation for a preview of an art-and-antiquities show this evening.

Crystal decided she would go. Perhaps something would catch her eye. She shivered with anticipation.

Five minutes after Detective Sergeant Ramona Pino returned to her office, Chief Kerney stepped through the open door and sat in the chair next to the desk.

"Anything new on the art-theft cases?"

he asked. Pino's desk was unusually tidy, and the framed snapshot of Ramona and her boyfriend, a vice cop with the Albuquerque PD, taken while they were on vacation together last year, was missing.

"Not that I know of, Chief. I've been working a commercial burglary case today. Somebody broke into a construction trailer at a building site last night and took a couple thousand dollars' worth of power tools. We've got a suspect. All we've got to do is find him."

Kerney stretched his legs, crossed his feet, and nodded. "I'm sure you will. I've noticed a pattern to the art thefts that I wanted to mention to you."

"Are you talking about how more expensive items are being taken each time?"

Kerney smiled approvingly. Pino had a razor-sharp mind and great cop instincts. "Exactly. Do you think it's one person?" he asked.

"If it is, based on what's been boosted, I'd bet she's female, and not your ordinary garden-variety shoplifter either. It's all quality stuff, which shows a certain degree of sophistication and knowledge about art."

Kerney examined the bulletin board on the far wall of Pino's small office, where she'd thumbtacked photographs of the stolen art. "All the objects could have easily been hidden in a large tote or a handbag," he observed. "But is she stealing on impulse or is it planned?"

Kerney paused to see if Ramona got his drift. Planning a crime was not what a kleptomaniac would normally do.

"I think it's impulsive, Chief. But she seems to be putting herself at a greater risk of discovery each time out by stealing more expensive items."

"Do you think she has just been lucky?" Kerney asked.

Ramona settled back in her chair. "Yeah, and maybe not even aware of it."

"How so?" Kerney asked.

"Both galleries where the opening receptions were held have good surveillance systems. But when they arranged the exhibits, nobody thought to reposition the cameras. The bronze statue and the miniature oil painting were on display in blind spots within a few feet of the entrances. Easy in, easy out."

Ramona pulled two videocassettes out of a desk drawer. "We've been over these tapes a dozen times, looking for people who attended both openings, looking for anybody who might have disguised themselves, looking for any sign of suspicious behavior. We've had the gallery owners identify as many people as they could who were in attendance, and then we followed up with interviews."

"Did you check the mailing lists the galleries used to send out notices and invitations?"

Ramona nodded. "There was no overlap of names. But remember, these were public events, Chief. Besides the mailings that went out, there were ads in the newspaper and announcements on the radio. Plus, gallery hopping on a Friday or Saturday night is a Santa Fe tradition."

The telephone rang. Ramona picked it up, listened, said, "Okay, I'll be there in a few," and disconnected.

"Let's go with the theory it's a woman who's stealing for the thrill of it and unable to resist the impulse," Kerney said. "If she's true to form, she'll place herself at risk again, and I'm betting it will be at another exhibit opening or show."

"Why is that?" Ramona asked.

"Because she's stealing for the pleasure, not profit, and has upped the excitement for herself by doing it in plain view, surrounded by other people. There are six gallery openings tonight, if we include the preview of the art-and-antiquities show at the convention center. Let's put a detective at each gallery, and two at the convention center, which should have the biggest draw."

"Consider it done, Chief."

Kerney stood, pointed at Ramona, and tapped his chest with a finger. "We'll cover the convention center together."

"I'll set it up."

Kerney nodded and left. Ramona stared at the empty spot on her desk, where the photo of herself and the ex-boyfriend had once stood. The one consolation of finding out he would never get serious about their relationship was that she could once more work double shifts without feeling guilty about it.

She went looking for Detective Matt Chacon, who'd called while she'd been talking with the chief. He was in his cubicle at the far end of the bullpen, scribbling notes on a yellow pad.

Over the past several years Chacon's thin frame had filled out and he now sported a bit of a potbelly. He looked up from the tablet, smiled good-naturedly, and pulled the ever-present toothpick out of the corner of his mouth.

"What have you got?" Ramona asked.

"Dispatch routed a call to me from Dr. Candace Robbins, a shrink. Apparently there's a young woman named Crystal Hurley who might be suicidal."

"Might be?"

Matt consulted his notes. "Yeah. What Robbins knows she got from Hurley's primary psychiatrist, who called her from New York City. Seems Hurley has made several suicide attempts in the past and has been hospitalized twice for emotional problems. Hurley called her New York City shrink, a guy by the name of Benjamin Cohen, earlier in the day, and told him she had a gun and might — underline *might* — hurt herself with it. Robbins wanted to report that, based on what Cohen told her, Hurley might be a danger to herself."

"Has Hurley contacted Dr. Robbins?"

"Negative, although she was supposed to. I just got off the phone with Dr. Cohen. He says Hurley could be high risk. She's five six, one hundred fifteen pounds, brown and blue, age twenty-eight. She's been staying at her father's guesthouse in one of the those foothill mansions off Bishop's Lodge Road. Father's name is Robert. He's out of the country. I've got an address, and the phone company gave me

Robert Hurley's unlisted numbers. The housekeeper answered and said she had no idea where her employer's daughter was. It sounded like she didn't care either. I sent a uniform out to do a welfare check, and he reported nobody at home."

"Have you done a motor-vehicles records search?" Ramona asked.

"Robert Hurley owns a Lexus SUV and a BMW. There's nothing registered under his daughter's name. The cars could be garaged, as far as we know. There's no way of telling, according to the uniform who tried to make contact. He did note two different sets of tire tracks on the parking area near the guesthouse."

"What else did you learn about the woman?"

Matt shook his head. "Other than she's rich, has been living in New York City until recently, and is about to move to Paris, not much. Cohen wouldn't give an inch when I asked for more details about her psychiatric history."

"Is Hurley a danger to others?"

"Cohen doesn't think so."

"Does she have any friends or other family members in Santa Fe?"

"No, she grew up in Silicon Valley before the dot-com bubble burst, went to college in New York City, and until recently divided her time between Manhattan and Paris. Her parents are divorced, and her father built the Santa Fe house three years ago. As far as Dr. Cohen knows, this is the first time she's ever been here."

"How long?" Ramona asked.

"A little over two months."

"Get out an advisory with full specifics to all units, the county sheriff, and the district state police office. Make sure our shift commanders are apprised, and ask for close patrols at the Hurley residence through the rest of the day and night."

"Will do."

Ramona stepped away and Matt got busy writing the advisory.

After he had it finished, he contacted the New York State Department of Motor Vehicles, gave them Hurley's identifying information, and soon had a driver's-license photo of the woman on his computer screen.

From the neck up Hurley was a beauty. Her wide, round eyes and small nose gave her an innocent, schoolgirl look. Her smile showed a row of perfect white teeth above a dimpled chin.

Chacon printed the photo, made copies,

and put them in the shift commanders' cubbies for distribution. Then he called dispatch and gave them the advisory.

After a body wrap and a facial at a downtown spa, Crystal Hurley wandered through the jewelry shops on San Francisco Street, looking at watches, earrings, necklaces, and pins. Her urge to steal grew as she tried on some lovely pieces, but the clerks were much too attentive for her to risk it.

Frustrated by the lack of opportunity, she bought a single strand of turquoise and draped it around her neck. It went well with the white blouse, black slacks, and floppy straw hat she'd chosen for her outing.

She left the store and walked up the street to the Plaza, where a country-and-western band was playing an early-evening concert on the gazebo across the street from the Palace of Governors Museum. Under the portal of the museum a number of Indian vendors had their wares spread out on blankets. A stream of tourists wandered slowly past them, examining the Native American jewelry and pottery for sale.

Crystal listened to the band for a time as she watched the dancers in front of the gazebo two-stepping, twirling, and circle-dancing. Everyone in the crowd around her seemed to be having a good time, but Crystal found it all rather boring.

A smiling man with a ponytail, dressed in flashy cowboy boots and tight jeans, tried to pull her onto the dance area. She yanked her hand away, shook her head, and left the Plaza. Although he was cute and sexy, Crystal had a rule: only one lover at a time, and right now that was Andy.

The boutique hotel where Andy bartended was just off the Plaza. Crystal went inside and settled on a stool. Without needing to ask, Andy brought her a vodka on the rocks.

He grinned, leaned toward her, and whispered, "Can we hook up later?"

Crystal sipped her drink and studied Andy's face. He was the all-American boy, towheaded, blue eyed, square jawed, and forever eager to get laid. "We'll see," she said.

Andy squeezed her hand. "Come on."

"You're such a baby, Andy."

"I'm crazy about you."

Crystal finished the drink and stood. "Call me on my cell when you get off work."

"Where are you going?"

Crystal opened her crocodile handbag and put a twenty on the bar without replying. The glint of the gun inside the purse gave her a rush of excitement, and Andy's presence faded from her mind. The preview of the art-and-antiquities show at the convention center was about to begin and she didn't want to miss a minute of it.

She left before Andy could question her further and headed quickly in the direction of the center.

Santa Fe's convention center fell far short of the mark for a city that thrived on tourism. In fact, it was nothing more than a renovated public-school gymnasium located within a few steps of city hall. On the outside, the center had been fixed up to look like the real deal. But inside, the dimensions of the space gave away its architectural roots. Stairs from the lobby led to a partial mezzanine that looked down on the hall below and opened onto a few large meeting rooms off to one side. In the back, behind the stage, were kitchen facilities. Stark, small, and uninviting, the center failed to draw many conventions and was usually put to use for dances, regional trade shows, art fairs, and an occasional banquet.

Kerney stood on the mezzanine, watching Ramona Pino circulate among the booths that filled the hall. Petite, slender, and easy on the eyes, she blended in easily with all the well-groomed trophy wives and trust-funders.

There were sixty-five dealers set up on the convention-center floor, displaying a wide array of Western art, estate jewelry, rare books, collectible memorabilia, exquisite old Native American pottery, and antique Spanish colonial furniture.

After the doors had opened, people flooded in, some making a beeline to a particular booth, others wandering slowly down the aisles, pausing to examine a tray of jewelry, an oil painting, or a Navajo rug. Kerney left the mezzanine, wondering if he should have told Ramona to assign more detectives to the event. Given the size of the crowd, the two of them would have a hard time covering the floor by themselves.

He joined the throng, moving from booth to booth, stopping to glance at a pre-Colombian effigy pot, a nineteenth-century Apache woven basket, a Charles Russell pencil drawing, all the time watching the people around him.

It was a well-heeled crowd. Women in broomstick skirts wearing heavy turquoise-

and-silver jewelry cruised by. Gray-headed men in designer jeans and expensive boots trailed along. Flashy matrons with big hair, dripping with diamonds, chatted up dealers with Texas twangs.

He strolled down an aisle and squeezed past a cluster of people who'd stopped to look at a glass case filled with vintage wristwatches. Some of the dealers appeared watchful, while others seemed distracted by the crowds. All in all there were easy pickings for any good shoplifter in attendance.

Kerney stopped briefly at a display of intricately carved nineteenth-century wood chests imported from Mexico to watch a young woman at an adjacent booth put her handbag on the counter next to a stack of rare books. Dressed in black slacks and a white blouse, the woman wore a hat that hid her face. She picked up a book, studied it for a moment, put it back, and moved on.

At the end of the aisle he saw Ramona Pino eyeballing the woman and wondered if he'd missed something. He stepped into the aisle, jockeying his way past a few people to get behind the woman as Ramona closed the gap from the opposite direction.

The woman paused in front of a booth filled with landscape paintings. Ramona sidled up to her, gave Kerney a slight nod, and said, "Crystal Hurley?"

The woman's head snapped in Ramona's direction. "What?"

"Are you Crystal Hurley?" Ramona asked.

"What if I am?"

Ramona flashed the shield she held in the palm of her hand and put it quickly in the pocket of her slacks. "I need to speak with you," she said softly. "Please step away with me."

"I will not."

"You're not in trouble, Ms. Hurley," Ramona said reassuringly.

Hurley smiled. "I don't know what you're talking about."

Ramona held out her hand. Self-destructive or not, Hurley could be packing, and that upped the danger considerably. "Can I look inside your handbag?"

Hurley clutched it to her midriff, turned, and looked at Kerney, her blue eyes wide and frightened. Just then a woman stepped between Ramona and Hurley and a man jostled past Kerney, pushing him slightly off balance. Before he could react, Hurley bolted past him, knocked a woman to the floor, shoved a man into a display case, and ran down the aisle. People scattered as Ramona and Kerney forced their way through the spectators in hot pursuit. At the end of the aisle Hurley veered out of sight toward the lobby.

Kerney turned the corner in a crouch. Up ahead he spotted Hurley making for the exit. Ramona darted past him, caught Hurley at the door, and slammed her against it.

"Why are you doing this to me?" Hurley yelled as Ramona cuffed her.

Kerney covered the takedown with his weapon at the ready.

Ramona spun Hurley around. "Calm down," she said softly. "Everything will be all right. We're going to get you some help."

Kerney holstered his weapon and picked up the handbag Hurley had dropped on the floor. It contained a wallet, a cosmetic case, a nickel-plated .22 semiautomatic, and an old silver-and-turquoise Navajo bracelet with the dealer's tag still attached.

Kerney held up the bracelet. "She may also need a lawyer."

Hurley looked at the bracelet and then smiled seductively at Kerney. "I'll give you a blow job if you'll let me go."

"Not today, thank you," Kerney replied.

Ramona grinned at Kerney's response as she pushed Hurley out the door.

Three hours later Crystal Hurley sat in an observation room at the hospital, sedated and under guard, while Ramona and Kerney cleared all of the recent art-theft cases.

Ramona loaded the last of the evidence from the guesthouse into her unit and looked down on the lights of Santa Fe that shimmered across the plateau. "Do you think she's crazy?"

"Not crazy would be my guess," Kerney said.

"Then what?" Ramona asked, glancing around at the hilltop estate. "The woman has been given everything."

Kerney shrugged. "Not everything. Maybe she feels unloved. There's nothing worse than that."

Thinking about her ex-boyfriend and the emptiness she now felt about her personal life, Ramona stared off into the night sky and nodded solemnly.

Chapter Three

July and August were the busiest months in the summer tourist season and placed a heavy burden on the Santa Fe Police Department. Early in July, before things heated up, Crystal Hurley was arraigned on multiple felony charges, including carrying a concealed weapon, and entered a not-guilty plea. She paid a hefty cash bond, surrendered her passport, agreed to remain in the state, and underwent a court-ordered psychological evaluation. Immediately thereafter she entered a private psychiatric hospital for treatment.

If convicted on all counts Hurley faced the possibility of fifteen to twenty years in prison, although Kerney doubted such a sentence would be handed down. According to Ramona Pino, who was doing follow-up legwork for the prosecutors, Hurley's lawyers and shrinks were busy building a case based on their client's long-standing emotional problems.

Although in principal everyone was equal before the law, the scales of justice always seemed to tip in favor of those people with money, power, or influence. Kerney had seen it played out time and again during his law-enforcement career. Hurley's money might not buy her love, happiness, or peace of mind, but it could go a hell of a long way to lessen the legal consequences of her criminal behavior.

During the last weekend in July the annual Spanish Market was held on the Plaza. The largest exhibition of traditional and contemporary Hispanic arts in the country, it remained one of the few major events in the city that still drew the locals downtown. It had grown in size and scope over the past thirty-odd years, but from a policing standpoint the crowds and the congestion remained manageable.

For the major Plaza events Kerney put on his uniform and worked side by side with his officers. Throughout the weekend mariachi bands played, flamenco dancers whirled, politicians made speeches, processions circled the Plaza, arts-and-crafts people sold their wares, and folks lined up at the food booths, drawn by the spicy aromas of New Mexico cuisine.

August brought Indian Market, an event where upwards of a hundred thousand people converged on Santa Fe. To manage the congestion and chaos Kerney saturated the downtown area with all available officers. When time allowed, he would relinquish his command responsibilities to his deputy chief, Larry Otero, and spend an hour or two on foot patrol, relieving his supervisors for meal breaks or walking a beat through the hundreds of white tents that ringed the Plaza and spread down the side streets. It was a weekend of extra shifts for every officer on duty.

The population of Santa Fe more than doubled during Indian Market and stretched his department's resources to the limit. The number of sworn personnel Kerney had was barely adequate to cope with the resident population of Santa Fe, and the possibility of a disaster or major crime during Indian Market always worried him. Fortunately, the weekend wound down with nothing more than a few purse snatchings, several cases of heatstroke, some lost children safely returned to their parents, one shoplifting arrest, and a few fender benders.

In late August the mayor publicly announced that he would not stand for re-election in March. As the candidates lined up to announce their intention to run for the office, a stream of concerned, curious, and ambitious senior commanders sought Kerney out to question him about his plans. He made it clear to all that he would step down and retire, although he didn't say when. He needed to discuss it with Sara first, and not by telephone.

On a Friday morning Kerney took an early flight from Albuquerque to Washington, D.C., where Sara was to meet him at the airport. After he arrived, he spotted her outside the passenger screening area with Patrick at her side. His son, now three, had grown again and looked more and more like his mother each time Kerney saw him. The same strawberry-blond hair, eyes more green than blue, the same line of freckles across the bridge of his nose, and a smile that melted Kerney's heart.

Patrick broke away from his mother and ran to Kerney, who picked him up and gave him a bear hug.

"Can I have a pony?" Patrick asked, after Kerney smooched him.

"What does your mother say?" Kerney asked as Sara stepped up, gave him a kiss, stroked his cheek, and smiled her wonderful smile. She was wearing her Class A army uniform, which surprised Kerney. On the phone last night she'd said she was taking the day off.

Patrick raised four fingers. "I have to be this old."

"How old are you now?"

Patrick glumly held up three fingers.

"You'll be four soon enough," Kerney said.

Patrick shook his head, as though such a day was an eternity away.

"Don't pout," Kerney said. "Soon you'll be back in New Mexico and you can ride with me every day."

Patrick's eyes lit up. "Every day, forever?"

Kerney laughed. "How long is that?"

Patrick pondered the question seriously and spread his arms wide. "This much is forever."

"Forever it is," Kerney agreed with a laugh. "Are you working?" he asked Sara.

Sara nodded. "I'll tell you about it on the ride home."

In her SUV, Sara explained that she'd been called a few hours ago and told to report to her Pentagon boss at sixteen hundred hours.

"I don't know why," she added. "But my orders for embassy duty have been re-scinded. I'm to remain at the Pentagon until further notice."

"In the same job?" Kerney asked.

"God, I hope not," Sara said. For three

years she'd worked for a one-star general, a petty tyrant who'd given her nothing but grief. It was a distinct possibility that her orders had been canceled as a payback for standing up to him time and time again.

"So we're in limbo," Kerney said.

"For now. Have you officially resigned?"

"Not yet," Kerney replied. "The mayor asked me to stay on until the end of his term. I wanted to talk to you about it before I gave him my answer."

Sara sighed.

"What?" Kerney asked.

"It seems like reality is again interfering in our lives."

"I will retire, Sara. In fact, I've already announced it."

"Well, that's one piece of the puzzle."

"What are the other pieces?"

They'd reached Arlington, Virginia, where Sara and Patrick lived in the house Kerney had bought as an investment when Sara had started her tour of duty at the Pentagon. She turned onto the street that led to the Cape Cod–style cottage and pulled into the driveway.

"Will we ever get to the point where we can live together as a family?" Sara asked as she killed the engine.

Kerney avoided Sara's questioning look,

removed Patrick from his child's seat, hoisted him into the front of the SUV, and put him on his lap. The last thing he wanted was to start the weekend with an argument.

Sara put the SUV into reverse and smiled. "Don't worry, I'm not picking a fight. Patrick has a brand-new book he's been saving for you to read to him, and guess what? It's about a horse."

Patrick grinned and tugged Kerney's hand. "It's about a *pony*," he said emphatically, "not a horse. I'll show it to you."

Kerney opened the door. "Let's go, champ. I've *got* to see this book."

As Sara drove away, Patrick scooted toward the cottage, urging Kerney to hurry. He followed Patrick up the path, delighted by his smart, self-confident son and disconcerted about Sara's situation. Would new orders place her in harm's way, separated from Kerney and Patrick for the duration?

Except for Kerney's pending retirement all plans were now on hold. There was some solace knowing that at least he'd be free to be a full-time parent if circumstances required it. But the thought of not seeing Sara for an indefinite period of time was gut wrenching.

"Come on, Daddy," Patrick said.

Kerney smiled and hurried to his son.

Brigadier General Stuart Thatcher delighted in keeping subordinates off guard and anxious. He routinely called his staff in for impromptu meetings or one-on-one confabs without specifying an agenda, and took great pleasure in making them wait interminably outside his office.

To deal with the man, Sara tried hard to control her feisty nature but at times found it impossible to do so. With appropriate deference to his rank she would occasionally point out to Thatcher that she would be better prepared to meet with him if she knew in advance what he needed to talk to her about. The suggestion always brought color to Thatcher's cheeks.

Additionally, Sara had taken to asking Thatcher's secretary to buzz her when the general was ready to meet, so she could work at her desk rather than waste time cooling her heals outside his office. Although it raised Thatcher's ire, he couldn't fault her working instead of waiting.

How Thatcher had earned his one-star rank had always confounded Sara, until she'd learned he was a third-generation

West Pointer with a senior U.S. senator in his extended family.

Sara shared an office with three other officers. She sat at her cubicle desk and listened as her colleagues got ready to leave for the day. Twelve- to sixteen-hour workdays were not uncommon at the Pentagon. But when Friday came, everybody who wasn't scheduled for weekend duty bailed out as soon as possible.

On her desk stood a photograph of Kerney and Patrick astride a horse at the Santa Fe ranch. From the grins on their faces both of them looked like they were in heaven. Sara marveled at how much Patrick and Kerney were alike in personality, temperament, and looks. They had the same square shoulders, gentle strong hands, and narrow waists. They shared a dogged determination to do things well and a capacity to be bullheaded.

Two sides of the same coin, she thought with a smile.

She said good-night as her office mates filtered out, wondering how long Thatcher would keep her waiting. An hour later, after she had cleared out some routine paperwork, Sara's phone rang and she was summoned to Thatcher's office, where she found him sitting ramrod straight in his chair, hands clasped on the obsessively tidy desk.

Sara snapped to and said, "Sir."

Thatcher raised his egg-shaped head that was punctuated by a pointy nose, thin lips, and a seriously receding hairline. "You are to be held over at the Pentagon pending re-assignment."

"Sir, I am aware of that," Sara said, wondering if Thatcher had called her in to repeat old news simply as a way to jack her around.

Thatcher forced a smile and waved her into a chair. "Of course you are. But I've been asked to determine if you'll accept a TDY assignment in the training branch."

Sara sat. *TDY* meant temporary duty. "What would the job entail, General?"

"You'd serve as a member of a special project team tasked with preparing an advanced military-police-officer curriculum for reserve and National Guard units. It must be accomplished in six months."

Sara nodded, wondering why the training branch would be given a project that rightly fell under Thatcher's purview.

"However, if you choose, you could remain in your present position until your permanent orders come through. That would allow you to take your scheduled thirty-day leave next month."

"Sir," Sara said, "would it be possible for me to start on the TDY project after my return from leave?"

Thatcher almost sneered with delight. "I rather doubt it. The assignment has the highest priority. What shall it be, Colonel?"

Stone faced, Sara parried Thatcher's squeeze play. "If possible, General, I would appreciate it if you would query the training branch on my behalf to determine if I could begin the assignment after I return from leave."

Thatcher shook his head. "I'm afraid I need a yes or a no from you, Colonel."

Sara stood and snapped to attention. "With all due respect, you have my answer, General."

"I doubt your answer will be well received," Thatcher said. He looked decidedly pleased with the prospect of keeping Sara under his thumb for a while longer. "But I will pass your request along. You're dismissed, Colonel."

Sara saluted, did an abrupt about-face, and left Thatcher's office. He waited a few minutes before dialing the number of the aide-de-camp to the vice chief of staff, who was organizing the special team.

"General Thatcher here," he said when the aide answered.

"Yes, General."

"I'm calling about Lieutenant Colonel Brannon."

"Sir, will you hold for the vice chief?"

Taken aback, Thatcher said, "Of course." He'd had no inkling of the vice chief's personal interest in Brannon or the project.

Quickly, General Henry Powhatan Clarke came on the line. "What did the colonel decide, Stuart?" he asked.

"I believe Colonel Brannon would rather remain in her current position, sir."

"What makes you say that?" Clarke asked.

"She seems quite satisfied here, General."

Henry Powhatan Clarke knew better. As a four-star general recently installed as the vice chief of staff, he'd checked up on Sara Brannon without her knowledge. She'd been one of the best young officers to serve under him in Korea, winning the prestigious Distinguished Service Medal and a meritorious field promotion to her present rank. Under Thatcher, a man who should never have been allowed to pin a star on his collar, she was languishing, not being used to her full abilities.

"Did she turn down the assignment?" Clarke asked.

"Not in so many words."

"What exactly did she say?"

"She asked if she could take the TDY assignment after completing her leave. I told her it was unlikely."

"Did you, now? Well, you tell her I want her bright eyed and bushy tailed when she reports to the training branch *after* her leave is over."

"Yes, sir."

"Where in the hell did you get this notion she had to start the job immediately?"

"I believe that's what your aide told me, General," Thatcher replied.

"Negative, Thatcher. My aide made the call to you from my office, and he said no such thing."

"I must have misunderstood, General."

"Indeed you did," Clarke snapped. "When does Colonel Brannon start her leave?"

"In about two or three weeks, sir."

"Very well. Before she departs, make sure you've done her efficiency rating and forward a copy of it to me immediately. Understood?"

"Yes, sir."

"And let Colonel Brannon know ASAP

that she's good to go as the team leader of the TDY assignment."

The line went dead before Thatcher could respond. His hands were sticky with sweat. He dropped the receiver in the cradle, rubbed a hand through his buzz-cut hair, stared at the palm print on the desktop, wiped it dry with his shirtsleeve, and let the reality sink in that he'd screwed up big time with the new vice chief.

Sara eased to a stop in the driveway of the Aurora Heights cottage, killed the engine, and sat behind the wheel, trying to purge the last of her negative feelings about her meeting with General Thatcher before she went inside. She didn't want to start the weekend with Kerney ranting and raving about her boss.

She gazed at the small brick house with its pitched shingled roof, gabled second-story windows, and formal pilasters that bracketed the front entrance. She loved the house, loved the man and boy who waited for her inside, loved the fact that Kerney had bought it for her and Patrick. It was the first true home she'd lived in since the day she entered West Point.

Inside, she called out to Kerney and Patrick and got no response. On the kitchen stove a pot of spaghetti sauce simmered, one of Kerney's specialties he frequently fixed when he came to Arlington. She walked to the small enclosed back porch, heard the sound of Patrick's laughter, and looked out through the screen door to see father and son playing baseball. Patrick stood with a small plastic bat on his shoulder, watching Kerney chase down a large rubber ball that rolled across the lawn.

"Home run!" Patrick said.

"Home run," Kerney echoed, returning with the ball. He lobbed it underhand to Patrick, who swung and missed.

The last of Sara's snit about the meeting with Thatcher washed away as she watched her husband and son at play for another minute, before stepping to the bedroom to change out of her uniform. Last night, anticipating Kerney's arrival, she'd shaved her legs and taken a long soak in the tub. She dressed in a pair of shorts that accentuated her legs and pulled on a scoop-necked short-sleeve top that revealed the tiniest bit of cleavage.

In the kitchen Patrick and Kerney were at the table, reading *Pablito the Pony*. Sara nuzzled Patrick's cheek and stroked the back of Kerney's neck.

"Are you just now reading the book?" she asked.

"For the third time," Kerney said, glancing at Sara. "You look yummy."

"*Yummy* means good," Patrick announced as he turned the page.

"Can you hold that thought until later?" Sara asked.

Kerney grinned. "Easily. How did your meeting go?"

"Okay."

Patrick poked his finger on the book to get Kerney's attention. "This is where Pablito gets his hoof stuck in the fence, Daddy."

"Right you are," Kerney said.

"I'll get the noodles started," Sara said, "while you men finish reading."

The phone rang. Sara went to the living room and answered. Kerney paused, hoping it wasn't the Pentagon calling her back to work. She was still on the phone when he finished reading the story. He closed the book, sent Patrick off to his bedroom to put it away, and found Sara in the living room, her eyes dancing with excitement.

"Good news?" he asked.

"I'm staying at the Pentagon for at least six more months," Sara said, "in a new temporary assignment, with a new boss."

"What's the job?"

"I'm supposed to develop a military-police training course for reserve and National Guard units."

"How did you pull that off?"

Sara shook her head. "I don't know."

"Does this mean your leave is canceled?"

Sara snuggled up to him. "No way. We're still going to the Bootheel with you to play Hollywood cowboy."

Kerney grinned with relief, held her close, took in her scent. "Well, for now, that's another piece of puzzle solved."

"For now is good enough for me," Sara replied.

"I'm hungry," Patrick said, as he bounded into the living room and grabbed his parents by the legs.

After a great weekend with Sara and Patrick, Kerney returned to Santa Fe late Sunday night, caught a few hours of sleep, and arrived at work in time to convene an interagency planning meeting for the upcoming Santa Fe Fiesta.

Every year in September the city celebrated the Spanish reconquest of New Mexico with pageantry, religious services, music, dances, parties, and the public burning of Old Man Gloom. It was a time when a good number of the citizenry got drunk, started fistfights, brawled in bars, vandalized property, fought with spouses, drove under the influence, and occasionally shot or knifed each other. Additionally, the birthrate in the city always spiked nine months later.

Santa Fe's finest hated fiestas so much that many officers counted their years to retirement by the number of remaining celebrations they would be forced to work before they turned in their pension papers.

The meeting, held in the council chambers at city hall, brought together supervisors and commanders of all local, county, and state law-enforcement agencies, plus fire department, EMT, county jail, and hospital ER personnel. Working through the full agenda took the whole morning. Decisions were made on the streets to be closed and manned by uniformed personnel, where first-aid stations would be set up, how many personnel would be assigned to saturation foot and roving traffic patrols, the number of plainclothes, undercover, and gang-unit teams that would operate during the long weekend, and where DWI checkpoints would be established.

After setting SWAT command-and-control protocols for crowd and riot control, the meeting moved on to a discussion of what bars, liquor establishments, and convenience stores would be targeted for alcohol sales to underage drinkers, and how transportation to the jail and hospital would be coordinated.

Kerney brought the meeting to a close with a word of thanks and the announcement that he would be on vacation during the fiesta, leaving Larry Otero, his second-in-command, in charge. Because his pending retirement was now common knowledge in all the cop shops, the news was greeted with a lot of grins, head shaking, and friendly catcalls.

When the last of the group dispersed, Kerney stopped by the mayor's office and left word that he would stay on as chief until the new administration came into office. At the personnel office he picked up the application for pension forms that needed to be submitted at least sixty days in advance of his retirement.

Paperwork in hand, Kerney left the building. In six months he would become a civilian. For many cops retirement was a difficult milestone. But with Sara and Patrick in his life Kerney felt ready and eager for the future. He smiled at his good fortune as he walked to his unit.

In preparation for the tech scout Kerney read up on the history of the Bootheel, a part of New Mexico he'd never really explored. He also surfed the Internet for information and bought some maps of the area to study. In 1853, under the Gadsden Treaty, the United States bought from Mexico over twenty-nine-million acres along the border for a paltry ten million dollars. The land purchase stretched from the Rio Grande to the junction where the Colorado and Gila Rivers joined. The deal had been struck by the government on behalf of the railroad barons, who wanted a southern route to California. Thanks to political patronage a new international boundary was surveyed and the Bootheel was born.

Eventually, at the turn of the twentieth century, the railroad had been built not to California, but to the copper mines in Arizona. Just as eventually, some sixty years later, the tracks were abandoned and dismantled, thrusting the small towns that had grown up along the right of way into free-fall decay.

The night before the tech scout was to

start, Kerney drove to Deming, a small city on Interstate 10 west of Las Cruces, and stayed in a motel. Although he wasn't due to meet up with Johnny and the movie-people party until late in the afternoon, he'd come down early so he could poke around and take a quick tour on his own.

On a bright, cloudless Friday morning Kerney rolled into Hachita, one of the Bootheel villages devastated by the loss of commerce after the railroad had pulled out. An old locomotive water tank perched on tall steel pillars stood next to the raised rubble of the railbed, still visible under the weeds and shrubby bushes that had gained a strong foothold amid the rocks. Fronting the highway that passed by the settlement stood a low-slung white building that housed a café and store. Next to it was a garage that sold gas, and a boarded-up structure that, according to the sign above the door, had once been a food mart.

The café consisted of a half-dozen tables crammed into a narrow room. At one end a passageway led to the kitchen, and a small area directly behind the diner served as a grocery store of sorts, offering a few basics such as sugar, flour, bread, and canned goods, and a wider selection of snack foods and soft drinks. On the wall of the café were sport plaques and framed certificates that had been awarded to teenagers from the village who attended high school in Animas, some thirty miles distant.

At a window table in the empty café, Kerney ate breakfast. From the time it took to place his order and finish his meal, not one vehicle passed along the two-lane blacktop. The bill came to pocket change, and Kerney tripled the tip for the young woman who had served as both waitress and cook.

Back in his pickup truck he made a quick tour of Hachita, which sat almost squarely on the Continental Divide. In among the derelict buildings, broken-down trailers, and trashed-out, sandy lots filled with the skeletal remains of cars, trucks, and miscellaneous pieces of cannibalized heavy equipment were a few tidy, well-tended, occupied dwellings. Kerney figured no more than sixty people lived in the village proper.

Aside from the post office, a small, stuccoed structure with a pitched roof, the only other buildings of substance were an old brick schoolhouse now used as an occasional community center, and a Catholic church with a mortared stone vestibule

111

and bell tower that soared above white-washed adobe walls.

Beyond the village, at a distance much farther than the eye imagined, the raw and barren-looking Little Hatchet Mountains jutted up from the valley. The mining town of Playas, where the film company would be headquartered, sat due west on the slope of desert scrub hills, out of sight.

With hours to kill, Kerney turned south, away from Playas, and drove the state road that would take him to Antelope Wells, the most remote port of entry into Mexico along the entire international boundary. The chill of the early desert morning had long passed and the day was heating up. Kerney rolled down the windows to allow the sharp smell of dry air to wash over him, cruised down the empty highway at a leisurely pace, and let his gaze wander over the valley.

By western standards Kerney's two sections of rangeland outside Santa Fe hardly qualified as a ranch. Although it contained some good pastureland and live water, a great deal of it consisted of rocky soil that had been overgrazed and invaded by piñon and juniper woodlands.

Kerney had little knowledge of modern land conservation practices, so to get up to speed he'd enrolled in a series of weekend workshops on restoring western rangeland. Using what he'd learned, he had begun to institute changes on his ranch. Last year he'd cut, lopped, and bulldozed over a hundred acres of woodland that had intruded into a pasture. He would burn the piles later in the fall and reseed the acreage the following spring with cool-season grasses. With that accomplished he planned to create some swales at the lower end of a pond where an arroyo was forming, so the water could spread out slowly and allow the marsh grass and cattails to stabilize the banks.

What Kerney had in mind to do was only a start. He had a great deal more to learn about good stewardship of his land. But he'd met a number of smart, well-informed people he could turn to for advice and information.

Along the highway Kerney could see the effects of drought and overgrazing on parts of the valley. Vast acres of gray rabbitbrush and broom snakeweed stretched across the plain under thick stands of greasewood and mesquite. To the untrained eye the landscape looked lovely. But, in fact, it no longer resembled the open grasslands settlers had found over a hundred and twenty years ago.

At a pasture that had been brought back to life, Kerney stopped the truck and walked to the fence line. A rancher had restored the sandy soil as far as the eye could see with Indian rice grass, blue grama, little bluestem, burro grass, and a few varieties Kerney didn't recognize. In some places grass stood in waist-high clumps, seed tips waving gently in a slight breeze. Close to the faraway mountains a herd of cattle moved slowly across the valley in the direction of a stand of trees that signaled a water source.

Only the song of a blue jay on a nearby fence post and the lowing of a cow broke the silence. The growing sound of an engine drew Kerney's attention to the road and soon a noisy, rattletrap panel truck came into view, traveling at a high rate of speed. Headed north to Hachita, it passed Kerney without slowing.

Back on the highway, Kerney continued in the direction of Antelope Wells with the Big Hatchet Mountains guiding his way south, announcing the border and Mexico beyond. The road curved sharply at Hatchet Gap. Kerney came through the pass and saw a small flock of crows converging over the blacktop. On the center stripe, a quarter mile distant, he spotted what appeared to be the carcass of a large animal, perhaps a yearling calf. Kerney drew near and hit the brakes as soon as he realized it was a body facedown on the pavement.

He grabbed his first-aid kit from under the seat of his truck, ran to the body, and rolled it over. Blood bubbled from the smashed mouth and nose, and the skull had been crushed at the temple, exposing the cranial cavity. Teeth protruded through the lower lip, and Kerney couldn't force the mouth open. He ripped open the shirt, took a small penknife from the kit, probed for the soft spot beneath the trachea, and punched a hole in it. Bloody fluid gushed out, splattering Kerney's hands and face.

He dropped the penknife and started CPR, but it was too late. He sat back on his haunches and stared at the body. From what Kerney could make out from the mangled features and the clothing the victim had been a young man, maybe a teenager, probably Mexican, and most likely an illegal immigrant worker.

Had he been dumped out or accidentally fallen from the back of the panel van?

In the silence of the sun-drenched morning, as the crows circled noiselessly above, Kerney sat next to the body for a moment on the empty highway, thinking that he'd seen, in both war and peace, far too many dead people.

He got slowly to his feet and used his cell phone to call for police assistance and an ambulance. He got a tarp and some road flares from the toolbox in the bed of his truck, covered the body, and set out the flares. Above him the crows called out in protest as they floated down to the side of the road and pranced noisily back and forth, while Kerney kept them away with his silent vigil.

Forty minutes later an EMT from Hachita arrived on the scene, closely followed by a Border Patrol officer up from Antelope Wells. Kerney identified himself to the men, and the officer took his statement while the EMT inspected the corpse. Soon after, a state police officer from Deming appeared with an Animas volunteer fire department ambulance trailing behind. Two cowboys in a pickup truck, hauling a horse trailer filled with hay, stopped to watch the proceedings.

Kerney gave another statement to the cop, a senior patrol officer named Flavio Sapian, whom Kerney knew from his days as deputy chief of the New Mexico State Police. Sapian put out a radio bulletin on the panel van and took photographs of the dead man. He checked the roadway, the shoulder, and Kerney's truck for any sign of a collision before releasing the body for transport. As the ambulance pulled away and the Border Patrol Officer left, Sapian walked to Kerney, clipboard in hand.

"Does this happen often?" Kerney asked.

Sapian, a stocky man with a fleshy face and deep chest, waved at the cowboys as they drove off. "Not like this. Sometimes a rancher will find a body on his land, or the *coyotes* — the smugglers who bring the illegal immigrants across the border — will abandon them in the desert. But mostly that happens west of here, where the copper smelter is located. It's forty miles north of the border. The coyotes and immigrants use the flashing lights on top of the smelter stack as a beacon to guide them into the United States. They call it the Star of the North."

"Do you think the dead man fell or was pushed?" Kerney asked.

"It's hard to say," Sapian replied. "If he was riding in the panel van as you suggest, you'd think there would be skid marks or other evidence to indicate that something happened to cause the rear door to pop open and the victim to fall out. On the

other hand the coyotes pack their customers in trucks like sardines to maximize
their profits. The victim could have been
leaning against the door and it just gave
way."

"That may not be what happened,"
Kerney said as he walked to the spot where
the body had landed on the highway. "He
hit facedown, and the only bruising and
blunt-force trauma was on the front of his
head and torso. There's nothing here or on
the body that shows he either tumbled or
slid along the pavement."

"That doesn't prove murder," Sapian
said.

Kerney looked at Sapian. "You're right,
but homicide can't be ruled out either."

Sapian shrugged. "Maybe the autopsy
will tell us something."

"Yeah," Kerney said as he stared at the
bloodstained pavement.

"You did the best you could to save
him," Sapian said.

"He was just a kid."

Sapian nodded solemnly. "When I was
first married, I'd come home from work and
my wife would ask me how my day went.
Some days I'd just say that she didn't want
to know. Once she asked and I told her. She
doesn't ask that question anymore."

"There are days it just gets to you."

"I know that feeling, Chief," Sapian replied, eyeing Kerney's blood-splattered face, hands, and shirt.

"I look a mess, don't I?" Kerney said. "Is there anyplace nearby where I can clean up?"

"Not until you get to Hachita. But there's a ranch a few miles north of here. Sign on the highway says Granite Pass Cattle Company. I'm sure the owners wouldn't mind if you used one of their water tanks. I'll give them a call, if you like, so you don't get run off for trespassing."

"Who are the owners?"

"Joe and Bessie Jordan," Sapian replied. "An older couple, pretty much retired now. Joe's gotta be pushing eighty. Their manager, Walter Shaw, and their daughter run the operation."

Kerney smiled at the thought of seeing Johnny's parents and sister. "Joe, Bessie, and Julia."

"You know them?"

"You could say that," Kerney replied. "I'd appreciate it if you'd give them a holler for me."

A mile in on the ranch road the mesquite and greasewood shrubland gave way to open range that swept north and south along the flank of the Little Hatchet Mountains. Just off the road on the edge of a grassy pasture stood a rodeo grounds, complete with an elevated crow's nest. A sign on it read: JORDAN ARENA.

The arena, enclosed by sturdy railroad ties and wire, had chutes at one end, gates at the other, and electric light poles outside the perimeter. Not that many years ago ranch rodeo arenas were a common sight in many rural areas of the state. Once or twice a year ranch families and working cowboys would come together to socialize and show off their skills in friendly competition. Folks would back their pickups against the fence and set up folding chairs in the truck beds to view the action. Events usually consisted of team penning, wild-horse catching, team branding, team roping, and wild-cow milking.

Kerney was glad to see that Joe and Bessie Jordan were keeping the old tradition alive.

Behind the holding pens was a stock tank fed by a windmill. Kerney stripped off his shirt and stuck his head and arms into the clear water, raised up, and started scrubbing off the dried blood with his hands. His moist skin dried almost immediately in the arid heat of the day. He stuck his head in the tank again and splashed water on his chest, shoulders, and back. He came up for air and a voice behind him said, "Remember when we used to go swimming in the stock tanks on Daddy's Jornada ranch?"

He turned and looked at the woman who stood in front of a three-quarter-ton flatbed truck. "Hello, Julia."

"Hello, yourself," Julia Jordan said. "I understand you tried to save somebody who died on the highway."

Kerney nodded as he gazed at Julia. Although now a bit more full figured, she still retained her good looks, and her laughing eyes, which always seemed to be a bit mocking, hadn't lost any luster. Her long, curly hair, more gray than dark brown, cascaded onto her shoulders.

"I didn't help much."

"You look good with your shirt off," Julia said slyly. "Care to go skinny-dipping with me?"

"I don't think so."

Julia laughed as she glanced at Kerney's wedding band. "I'm not surprised. You always were the straight-arrow type."

Quickly, Kerney slipped into his blood-splattered shirt. "Was I, now?"

"My God, were you hurt?"

Kerney buttoned up. "No, it's not my blood."

"Do you have a fresh shirt to wear?"

Kerney nodded.

Julia stepped to the three-quarter-ton. "Good. Follow me home. My parents can't wait to see you. Mom's in the kitchen cooking up a storm for you. You were always the one friend Johnny had that Mom favored the most. Me too."

"Why didn't I know this back then?"

Julia grinned as she climbed into the three-quarter-ton. "I've often wondered that myself."

The drive to the ranch headquarters was a straight shot to low, grassy hills that rolled on toward the mountains. Four houses, all of them white pitch-roofed structures with screened front porches painted in green trim, sat in a large grove of shade trees within easy walking distance of a horse barn. A water tank, windmill, and feed storage bins stood behind the barn next to a large metal shop and garage. Everything about the place was spic and span. Even the heavy equipment parked outside the garage was lined up in a neat row.

Julia stopped in front of the largest

house in the compound, a long ranch-style home with a big picture window that looked out on the porch. She led him through the unoccupied front room, a comfortable space filled with art, books, and easy chairs, to a spare room, and left him there to change his shirt. When he returned to the front room, Joe and Bessie greeted him, both smiling broadly.

Bessie wiped her hands on her apron and gave Kerney a hug. She felt like a feather in his arms, so tiny now and stooped of shoulder. The top of her snow-white head barely reached his chest. Joe Jordan's handshake was hearty and firm. He also was white haired, but still ramrod straight and lean. Wire-rim spectacles sat low on the bridge of his nose, and his face was wind-burned a deep red, accenting the furrows of crow's feet at the corners of his blue eyes.

Julia stepped out of the kitchen holding a tall glass of water, which Kerney gratefully accepted and quickly drained.

"Since I found him on the ranch," Julia said with a grin, "can I keep him?"

"Not from the looks of the wedding ring he's wearing," Joe replied with a laugh as he herded Kerney into the kitchen.

At the kitchen table Bessie passed

around a platter of sliced cold beef, a basket of hot fresh biscuits, a bowl of sauce for the beef, a salad, and a pitcher of lemonade. She'd set the table with her best flatware and linen napkins.

Over lunch Joe questioned Kerney about the fatality on the highway. He answered but left out the gory details.

Joe shook his head as he cut a small piece of beef and dipped it in the dollop of sauce on his plate. "Those Mexicans are so damn poor, not even the fear of death stops them from crossing the border. A neighbor south of here found two dead bodies on his land just last year. A young woman and a middle-aged man."

"I guess it isn't a problem that's going away anytime soon," Kerney replied.

"Not in my lifetime," Joe said. "Best we can do is try to keep them off the ranch. Walt Shaw does a pretty good job of that."

The conversation switched to old times on the Jornada, and they reminisced and caught up. Kerney learned that Bessie had survived breast cancer, Joe had undergone a hip replacement, and Julia was divorced and now dividing her time between the ranch and her house in Tucson.

Kerney told them about Sara and Patrick. Only Joe and Bessie seemed genuinely pleased to hear him talk about his family.

Julia changed the subject as soon as politely possible. "Johnny says you're ranching up in Santa Fe," she said.

Kerney noticed the hint of a scowl cross Joe's face at the mention of his son's name. "Only in a small way," he replied. "I've partnered with a neighbor to raise and train cutting horses."

Joe nodded as he passed Kerney the platter of meat. "If you can pay the bills, there's no better life than ranching."

"True enough," Kerney said.

Bessie smiled appreciatively as Kerney forked another slice of beef onto his plate. "I can't resist your cooking," he said to her.

After lunch Julia took Kerney on a tour of the ranch headquarters, the sun hot against their backs, the ground warm underfoot. Under a shade tree in front of Julia's house, Kerney asked if she and Johnny were planning to keep the ranch in the family.

"It's all mine," Julia said. "That's why I'm here so much of the time now."

"Well, I guess Johnny has his own life to lead."

Julia leaned against the tree and laughed.

"It's not that, Kerney. No matter how much he makes, money runs through Johnny's fingers like a sieve. He's always been that way. Daddy has bailed him out financially time and time again and has never once been repaid. So the deal is, I get the ranch, Johnny gets his debts forgiven, and we divide up what's left equally."

"That sounds fair."

"Johnny doesn't think so. That's why he got the production company to film on location at the ranch. He figures the payment Daddy receives will change his mind about cutting him out of the ranch. It won't."

"I hope it doesn't cause you any problems."

Julia waved away Kerney's concern. "Johnny will move on to some other scheme. He always does. Come on, I want to show you my little casa."

The inside of Julia's house was done up in light, cool shades of beige and ivory upholstered furniture. A choice collection of Navajo textiles, including a large chief's blanket, were displayed on the living room walls. Kerney could tell that the house had been gutted and completely renovated. A stacked-stone fireplace divided the living room from the dining area, and the kitchen was ultramodern. A professional chef's stove beneath a copper range hood stood at one end of the room, surrounded by maple cabinets with black marble countertops. A large antique drop-leaf table sat in the middle of the kitchen.

Julia's master suite contained a king-size four-poster bed and a large Oriental rug that complemented the floral draperies. An alcove with a built-in desk served as a small office and reading area.

In the guest room on the opposite side of the house, Julia said, "Why don't you come back here after your meeting in Playas with those Hollywood boys and spend the night? I'll fix you a good meal."

"It's kind of you to offer," Kerney said, "but we're due to get an early start in the morning to scout all the locations."

"The first few stops are here on the ranch," Julia said, "at the rodeo arena and then on the route Johnny's picked for the cattle drive."

She stepped close to Kerney, rubbed his arm, and smiled coquettishly. "I promise to kick you out of bed in time for you to make it to work."

Kerney took Julia's hand off his arm and patted it. "It's a delightful invitation, but not a good idea, Julia. I'll see you in the morning."

She smiled to hide her disappointment, escorted Kerney to the front door, gave him a kiss on the cheek, and watched him walk to his truck. He cut a handsome figure in his jeans, long-sleeved cowboy shirt, boots, and hat. He was six foot one, square shouldered, blue eyed, and had a cute, firm butt and the most absolutely beautiful hands she'd ever seen on a man.

Both her ex-husbands had been studs in bed, but totally amoral, charming alley cats. She wondered why it had taken her so long to learn the difference between men and boys. She'd hoped to find Kerney in an unhappy marriage and susceptible to the possibility of an affair that might lead to something more. But so far it didn't look promising.

She waved as Kerney honked the horn and drove away, thinking that he'd be back for three weeks when the film started shooting. That would give her plenty of time to test Kerney's matrimonial fidelity.

Chapter Four

Kerney arrived in the town of Playas ahead of schedule and used his spare time to take a look around. What he saw amazed him. Although he knew Playas was a virtually abandoned, modern company town, it was quite another matter to see it.

The two-lane road into town was paved, and just on the outskirts were two churches, baseball fields, a swimming pool, and a recreation center. The road looped around a grassy knoll dotted with trees that formed the gateway to the town, where a single-story apartment building with a covered portal faced the parklike setting.

Beyond the town a sweep of low hills rose up, rock strewn, barren, and steeply sloped. Backed against them the town looked out at a dry, glistening white lakebed in a broad valley that stretched to the Animas Mountains. The word for *beaches* in Spanish was *playas,* and the dry lakebed looked exactly like a pristine sandy shore without any water.

Playas was a bit of suburbia transplanted in the middle of the desert. A raven flew overhead and Kerney thought that from a bird's-eye view, with its paved streets, Santa Fe–style houses, and modern commercial buildings, it could have passed for a bedroom community outside any major southwestern city. At ground level things didn't look so normal. On street after street abandoned, weather-beaten houses with cracked stucco, warped garage doors, faded trim, and blank windows looked out on weed-infested front yards peppered with dead trees and shrubs.

A few occupied houses stood out here and there with grassy lawns and shade trees in full green color. Cars were parked in driveways, front doors were cluttered with children's toys and bikes, and there were curtains in the windows. On a street at the top of a small rise the occupied houses were larger, lawns bigger, shade trees more numerous, and the views of the valley spectacular. Kerney figured it to be the neighborhood where the mining company honchos had once lived.

The commercial area of town contained buildings that had once served as a mercantile store, medical clinic, post office, bank, community center, and an indoor recreation complex. As a cop Kerney could see the endless possibilities for using Playas as an antiterrorism training center. It would serve perfectly for any number of training scenarios, such as massive house-to-house searches, SWAT-team helicopter incursions, bomb-squad disposal operations, hostage-negotiation situations, sniper training, and any number of high-risk police, fire, or medical emergencies. In many ways the town reminded him of a much larger version of Hogan's Alley, a self-contained, fully functional village on the grounds of the FBI Academy at Quantico, Virginia, which was used to train agents in crime-scene scenarios.

He made a mental note to talk to his training lieutenant about getting sworn personnel enrolled in the program once it was fully operational. He stopped at a sleek, stepped-back stuccoed structure with multiple entrances and a flat roof, where several semitrailers were parked. A group of men were unloading construction materials. On the lawn in front of the building two workers were planting a large carved wooden sign that read:

TOWN OF COUNCIL ROCK
MUNICIPAL OFFICES

131

Council Rock was the name of the fictional town in the screenplay, which meant that Playas was already being dressed up as a movie set.

Kerney approached the men who were installing the sign and asked where the production team was meeting. One of the men pointed across the way to the community center, which Kerney found to be locked. He looked through the glass doors. Two long folding tables sat pushed together in the middle of the hall, surrounded by chairs. There were plastic coffee cups, water bottles, soda cans, and documents on the table, but no one inside.

He hung around and watched a crew of men use portable scaffolding to attach new signs to the stepped-back building. Over the next twenty minutes they transformed three doorways into entrances to the Council Rock mayor's office, municipal court, and police headquarters.

Four black full-size SUVs pulled up to the curb in front of the community center. A dozen people piled out of the vehicles and walked quickly to the community meeting hall entrance. Kerney spotted Johnny Jordan in the middle of the pack, talking animatedly to a tall man carrying a thick three-ring binder and wearing chinos, athletic shoes, and a brand-new straw cowboy hat perched on the back of his head. He tagged along and got close enough to hear the two men exchange heated words about some proposed script changes.

Inside the community center the debate continued as the group took their seats around the tables. Unobtrusively, Kerney stood by the door and watched.

"I want that damn copper smelter in the film as the location for the climax of the chase scene," the tall man in the new cowboy hat said.

"The climax occurs at the rodeo arena," Johnny said, looking agitated. "We agreed on that when we finalized the script."

"We can change the damn script," the tall man said, as he flipped through the pages of the binder. "For Chrissake, that's what writers are for. I want the copper smelter for the climax. All that industrial stuff sitting in the middle of a desert is visually stunning. Plus, it makes a great juxtaposition between the cowboy culture and modern society."

"The brawl at the rodeo arena is the climax," Johnny shot back.

The tall man stared Johnny down. "Here's the way I see it: We keep the script as it is right through the scene where the cops scatter the cattle with police helicopters and the rancher hightails it off BLM land through the mountain pass. But instead of having the cops bust them later in the day at the ranch rodeo, we keep the pursuit going to the smelter, where the cops find the cowboys gathering up the strays. We'll have cowboys on horseback chasing cows in and out of the buildings, cops chasing cowboys on foot and with squad cars, and a brawl that ends in a standoff when the rancher decides to call it quits before anyone gets seriously hurt."

The tall man turned to a man with glasses on his immediate left, who was studying papers on a clipboard. "Costwise, can we do this?"

"If we drop the rodeo scenes completely, we can."

"I've got world-class champions signed on to this film, expecting to showcase their talents," Johnny said.

"Maybe they still can," Kerney said.

All eyes turned toward Kerney.

"Who are you?" the tall man asked.

"Kevin Kerney. I'm one of your technical advisors."

"Kerney's here for the cop stuff," Johnny said, looking flustered. "Not rodeoing."

"Let Chief Kerney talk," the tall man said, waving Kerney toward an empty chair. "I'm Malcolm Usher, the director."

Kerney sat at the table and nodded a hello to all before turning his attention to Usher. "It seems to me, you can show off their rodeo talents through some good old-fashioned cowboying. They can rope cows and cops, do some bulldogging and bronc riding, and cut out stock so that it's a combined rodeo, brawl, and police bust."

All the people at the table, including Johnny, waited for Usher's reaction.

Usher slapped the table with his hand and stood. "I love it. It's exactly what I had in mind." He patted the man with the glasses on the shoulder. "Get our stunt coordinator started working out the details. I want cows climbing over squad cars, knocking cops over, barreling through buildings, that kind of stuff. I'm thinking it will be a late-afternoon, early-evening shoot, just like we planned for the rodeo scenes. Probably two days. Schedule us to go back to the smelter tomorrow before sundown."

The man with the eyeglasses wrote down Usher's instructions on the clipboard. "We'll have to come to some agreement to lease the premises. But with the smelter shut down, I doubt the cost will be exorbitant."

"Good," Usher said as he closed his three-ring binder and looked at Johnny. "Let's you and I get together before dinner and sketch out the new scenes for the writers."

Glumly, Johnny nodded.

"That's it," Usher said. "Everybody back here at four a.m. for the tech scout. Charlie will give you your housing assignments, and our schedule for the next two days. For now, we'll all be crashing in the apartment building."

Usher left. Charlie, who turned out to be the man wearing the eyeglasses, read off the housing assignments, which had Kerney bunking with Johnny. Charlie told the group that meals would be served by the caterer in the mercantile building, and the tech scout locations would be passed out after dinner.

As the meeting broke up, Johnny introduced Kerney to the people in attendance. The group included the unit production manager, set decorator, transportation captain, construction coordinator, cinematographer, the assistant director, several other lighting specialists, and Charlie Zwick, the producer.

Zwick shook Kerney's hand and thanked him for his good idea.

"Yeah, thanks a lot," Johnny said sarcastically, after Zwick left the building.

"Come on, Johnny," Kerney said. "It was apparent that the director had already made up his mind to change the ending before I spoke up."

"You don't get it," Johnny snapped. "I'm trying to build public interest in rodeoing with this movie. Get people excited about the sport, make it a major ticket draw. Now that's not going to happen. Instead, filmgoers are just gonna see what they think are a bunch of neat horseback and cowboy stunts as part of a brawl."

Kerney pushed open the door and stepped outside. "I wasn't trying to thwart you."

Johnny took the cell phone off his belt and flipped it open. "It sure felt that way. I've got some phone calls to make. I'll see you later." Johnny hurried across the parking lot with the cell phone planted in his ear.

Kerney decided to let Johnny chill out before going to the apartment. He didn't want to face a contentious evening with Johnny ragging on him about not getting his way. It was a good two hours before dinner. He decided to drive to the smelter to take a look at the place that had inspired Malcolm Usher to change the script. Besides, he wanted to see the Star of the North that Officer Sapian had told him about.

The paved road from Playas to the copper smelter paralleled a railroad spur that connected with the main trunk line east of Lordsburg, a windblown desert town on Interstate 10 that served as the seat of government for Hidalgo County.

The valley widened a bit as Kerney headed south, deep into the Bootheel. To the west the Animas Mountains cut a broad, foreboding swath against the sky. To the east the Little Hatchet Mountains, drenched in afternoon sunlight, were buff gold at the peaks.

Farther southeast the Big Hatchet Mountains rose up, pointing the way to Mexico and the Alamo Hueco Mountains at the border, where, according to what Kerney had read, once a year in the spring buffalo came up from the Chihuahua Desert to forage. He thought it would be great to see that.

Under the greasewood and mesquite the tall valley grass was a thick pelt that signaled summer rains had arrived at exactly the right time. Otherwise the grass would be yellow and stunted, the sandy soil dried out and cracked.

The big sky, the mountains, the desert so deceptively serene, the scarcity of anything man-made in the valley, pleased Kerney and gave him hope that maybe ranching could hold on and survive for a few more generations.

Nine miles south of Playas all those thoughts passed from Kerney's mind. The smelter sat on the east side of the valley between two dry lakebeds with the Little Hatchets looming over the complex, dwarfing the towering smokestack. The gate was open, and Kerney parked in front of the administration building, where a sign directed him to a side entrance.

Inside, he found fully equipped offices, conference rooms, and a reception area devoid of people except for a lanky, middle-aged man dressed in a Western shirt, jeans, and boots, who was filling out paperwork at a counter in front of an enlarged, framed photograph of the smelter.

"Can I help you?" the man said.

"I'm with the film company," Kerney told him, extending his hand. "Name's Kevin Kerney."

"Ira Dobson," the man replied, shaking Kerney's hand. "I had a whole slew of you movie folks through here a couple hours ago."

"I missed the tour," Kerney replied.

"You didn't miss much," Dobson replied with a laugh. "About all I showed them was where we used to unload the copper concentrate, the building that houses the flash furnace, and the acid plant."

"Acid plant?" Kerney asked.

Dobson nodded. "Yep. We used to produce more sulfuric acid than copper. Time was, we shipped twenty-five tank cars of acid and up to forty semitruck loads a day. Most of it went to make fertilizer."

"Where did you get the water to run the acid operation?" Kerney asked.

Dobson studied Kerney more carefully. "Sounds like you know something about the process."

Kerney shook his head. "Not really. But I do know it takes water to make sulfuric acid."

"Lots of water," Dobson agreed. "We used two hundred fifty thousand gallons a day when the plant was running, just on acid production alone. At peak capacity our wells can produce four million gallons a day."

"That's a hell of a lot of water to pump out of the ground."

Dobson nodded. "The company owns or controls almost a half-million acres of land in the Bootheel, plus about seven thousand acre-feet of annual water rights. The day could come when the water may be worth more than the land."

"Do you run the show here?" Kerney asked.

Dobson chuckled. "Nope, I run the water system for the smelter and the town site. We've got wells spread up and down the valley. Some are used by ranchers who lease grazing rights from the company, some are for wildlife habitat. In the more remote areas we use solar power to pump the wells."

"The job must keep you jumping," Kerney said.

Dobson snorted. "At least I've got a job, for now. But once they tear this smelter down, I'll be looking for work."

"Is that going to happen anytime soon?" Kerney asked.

Dobson shrugged. "That depends. We've got some groundwater contamination issues to deal with, along with some other environmental cleanup problems. The lawyers are fighting it out with the federal and state regulators."

141

"Do you live in Playas?" Kerney asked.

"I sure do. Me and about fifty-some other folks, give or take a few. The deal is that when the town got sold to become an antiterrorism training center, the residents could stay. Some have been hired on as maintenance and upkeep personnel."

"Mind if I take a look around the smelter?" Kerney asked.

"Go ahead," Dobson said. "But keep out of those areas posted for employees only. That's most of the plant. But you can walk or drive around the perimeter, if the gates are unlocked. Watch out for rattlesnakes."

He opened a counter drawer and handed Kerney a packet of general information about the smelter. "There's some interesting stuff in there about the valley and the company."

Kerney thanked Dobson for his time and went outside. High above him the warning beacon on top of the smokestack flashed brightly in the afternoon sunlight. At nightfall, if Officer Flavio Sapian was right, the Star of the North would guide another group of illegal immigrants across the border. Kerney wondered how many Border Patrol officers were on station, ready to pounce on the coyotes who'd be hauling illegal human cargo into the

States. The Border Patrol was stretched tight from lack of funding, and the increase promised after 9/11 had never fully materialized.

Behind the administration building, at the end of a large, virtually empty parking lot, was the main employee entrance to the smelter, festooned with fading painted signs that promoted safety and noted 698 consecutive accident-free days at the plant. Parked near the entrance were several vehicles, including a panel van that looked like the one that had passed Kerney earlier in the day just before he found the dying Mexican lying on the pavement.

He couldn't be sure if it was the same vehicle, but it was a close enough match to make Kerney pull out Flavio Sapian's business card and call him on his cell phone.

"Have you been able to ID the victim?" Kerney asked, when Sapian answered.

"Negative, Chief. He had no papers on him at all. The body's en route to Albuquerque for an autopsy. Maybe his prints will ID him, but I doubt it."

"I'm down at the copper smelter south of Playas, looking at a vehicle that's similar to the one that passed me on the highway," Kerney said. "Same color, same make. You want the license plate number?"

"You bet I do. Read it off."

Kerney gave him the info and said, "Let me know if anything comes of it."

"Ten-four."

Sapian disconnected and Kerney continued his walk. He didn't know the first thing about copper smelting, but the handout Dobson had provided told him a lot. The flash furnace Dobson had mentioned once produced eight hundred tons of cast copper daily. In its heyday the smelter had operated around the clock, processing two thousand tons of copper concentrate every twenty-four hours.

Kerney eyed the buildings, many of them two or three stories tall. Several were connected by what looked like covered chutes or conveyers. To the north the rail spur ran to what appeared to be a loading dock abutting a storage silo. To the south a series of large steel storage tanks defined an area that Kerney took to be the place where sulfuric acid had been produced. Near the tall smokestack in the center of the complex stood another silo and the largest structure on the grounds, which Kerney figured held the furnace used to mold the copper castings.

He could see why Malcolm Usher, the director of the film, would want to use the smelter in the movie. The stark, utilitarian industrial complex rose out of the desert on a grand scale, in sharp contrast to the raw, knuckled mountains, the soapweed yucca flats, and the ruddy white soil of the dry lakebed, creating a visually stunning effect.

Back at the employee entrance the panel truck was gone and the administration building was locked. Near his truck a young diamondback rattlesnake slithered slowly across the pavement, soaking up the heat of the day, and disappeared under a boulder in a landscaped bed of crushed red rock that fronted the entrance to the building.

In late summer or early fall female diamondbacks laid their eggs, giving birth to upwards of two dozen young. As a precaution Kerney checked around his truck carefully before climbing on board and driving away.

Over twenty years ago Malcolm Usher had started his career directing country music videos, gradually working his way up the food chain. After a successful stint directing episodes for a number of sitcoms, he'd moved on to made-for-television movies, one of which had been nominated for an Emmy.

Usher had hoped the Emmy nomination would vault him into a shot at directing a feature film, and after waiting for two years he'd finally gotten the call. With this new movie Usher could advance his career. But after reading the script he'd realized the story line was just a little shy of the necessary ingredients for a successful feature film. He was determined to make it better.

In his apartment he sat at the dining table and looked at the digital photographs his cinematographer had taken of the smelter. The best location for the new scenes was next to the delivery dock by the rail spur, where ore cars and some heavy equipment were parked at the siding. From that vantage point the smelter and smoke-stack would form a perfect backdrop against the mountains.

Besides offering excellent visuals, the site provided easy access, which minimized the logistics of moving the equipment, live-stock, and cast and crew to the location.

He thought about Alfred Hitchcock's famous crack that actors should be treated like cattle, and snickered. Hitchcock had never made a Western, or he would have had his chance.

Pleased with his decision, Usher began mapping out the scenes. He was deeply engrossed in the process when Johnny Jordan knocked at the open door and entered, looking piqued.

"I don't like this change you're proposing, Malcolm," he said.

Usher glanced at his wristwatch. "You took your time getting here."

Johnny turned a chair around and straddled it. "And I've been talking to some people who don't like it either."

"Let me guess," Usher said. "Could that be your rodeo stars?"

Johnny nodded. "They hired on to do a cattle drive and a rodeo, not to be part of some dumb melee at the damn copper smelter."

Usher removed his reading glasses. "No, they signed on as *actors*, which means they do what the director tells them to do. If they don't like it, I've got stuntmen who can do the job just as well for a lot less money. In fact, Corry McKowen, my stunt coordinator, rode the pro circuit for five years. I'm sure he wouldn't mind getting a costarring credit on his résumé."

"Corry was a lightweight on the circuit."

"Maybe so, but he's no lightweight as a stuntman. Tell me now if you want to pull your cowboys off the film. Believe me, it's no big deal to replace actors who walk before shooting starts."

"I didn't say that," Johnny said, his brow creased with worry.

Usher held back a smile. Jordan might know a lot about rodeoing, but he didn't know squat about moviemaking. "Then work with me, Johnny. This could be the best damn Western fight scene in a film since John Wayne and Maureen O'Hara brawled with the homesteaders in *McLintock!* over forty years ago."

"That was a good movie," Johnny said grudgingly.

"Let's write the scenes together so that your boys get to show off their stuff in front of the cameras," Usher said.

Johnny nodded and edged his chair close to the table.

The apartment Kerney was to share with Johnny had two small bedrooms separated by a bath, a galley kitchen with an adjacent dining nook, and a living room furnished with a couch, one easy chair, a couple of end tables with lamps, and a wall-mounted television set. The groundskeeper who had been watering the lawn when Kerney arrived had told him the building had originally been used to provide temporary housing for visiting company employees and executives from the home office.

Johnny wasn't around, so Kerney dumped his travel bag in one of the bedrooms and went to the mercantile store to grab some dinner. A large motor home parked by the entrance had a sign painted on it that read:

WESTERN SCENE CATERERS
PURVEYORS OF FINE FOOD
TO THE FILM INDUSTRY

Inside the store, rows of cafeteria tables and chairs had been set up, and a buffet meal was available at a serving table filled with warming trays of food, drink urns, dinnerware, and utensils. Kerney chose the vegetarian entrée and joined two men at one of the tables, who introduced themselves as Buzzy and Gus.

In their early fifties, both men had an easy style about them that made Kerney feel comfortable and welcome. Over dinner he learned a good bit about the complexities of photographing a motion picture.

Gus, the key grip, explained that his job was to set up diffusion screens and large shades to modify light for the cameras, operate camera dollies and cranes, and mount cameras on vehicles and airplanes. Buzzy, the gaffer, supervised the lighting for each scene and ran the crew responsible for setting up the lamps and generating the power.

Kerney asked them if Usher's decision to change the ending of the screenplay was common practice.

"You ain't seen nothing yet," Gus said with chuckle. "Any good director puts his own stamp on a film. There will be dialogue rewrites, camera-angle changes, scenes that get dropped, altered, or added — the list goes on and on."

"We'll have most of it sorted out at a final production meeting once we've visited all the locations," Buzzy said. "That's when we'll know basically what stays and what goes."

"Don't the producers have a say?" Kerney asked.

"Not creatively," Gus replied. "Charlie Zwick will have his hands full dealing with production delays, weather changes, sick or ill-tempered actors, continuity problems, staying within the budget — you name it."

"Fortunately, Charlie and Malcolm have worked together before," Buzzy said, "so it should go smoothly."

After dinner with Gus and Buzzy, Kerney took a stroll through the empty, silent streets of Playas, past rows of dark, vacant houses. As daylight faded, streetlights in the dormant town flickered on, casting eerie shadows through an occasional dead tree. It felt almost otherworldly, as though some invisible catastrophe had annihilated the population of the town, leaving behind the houses as a mute testimony to the disaster.

He turned the corner on a residential street near a shuttered building that had once served as the town library, and caught sight of a roadrunner scooting around the rear end of a Motor Transportation Division patrol car parked in front of an occupied house.

Part of the New Mexico Department of Public Safety, the MTD primarily enforced federal and state safety statutes of commercial motor vehicles, including hazardous-material and drug-interdiction inspections. Although its officers had full police powers, most of the agency's resources were allocated to traffic safety, commercial vehicle over-the-road compliance, and drug trafficking.

Farther on Kerney passed another occupied house with a Hidalgo County sheriff's squad car parked outside. He was on the tail end of his walk, heading down the hill in the direction of the town center, when his cell phone rang.

"I've got information on that license plate," Flavio Sapian said after Kerney answered. "The vehicle is registered to Jerome Mendoza."

"Tell me about Mr. Mendoza," Kerney said.

"It's interesting stuff. Mendoza is an MTD officer assigned to the Lordsburg Port of Entry. Single, age twenty-eight, he's got a home address listed in Playas."

"I just passed by his house," Kerney said. "What's his connection to the smelter?"

"Unknown. I'm going to call his supervisor after we hang up."

"I suggest you hold off on that," Kerney said. "If Mendoza is involved in any wrongdoing, you'd be giving him a heads-up."

"Why wait?" Sapian asked. "As it stands, I have no evidence that proves a crime was committed, nor can I actually put Mendoza at the scene of the accident."

"I understand that," Kerney said. "But for now you might want to treat him as a person of interest, until you have a few more facts."

"Such as?"

"The victim's identity, for starters," Kerney said. "What if it turns up that Mendoza knew the victim? You'd look pretty foolish if you didn't have that information before approaching him. When will you know something?"

"Tomorrow," Sapian replied.

"That's soon enough," Kerney said. "If he's clean, it leaves his reputation intact, and if he's dirty, well, that's a whole different matter."

"I hear you, Chief," Sapian said. "Talk to you tomorrow."

Back at the apartment Johnny was nowhere to be found. Grateful for the solitude, Kerney read several chapters in the first volume of Gabriel García Márquez's planned autobiographical trilogy before rolling into bed. He wondered what kind of story Márquez might fashion about the town of Playas. Surely it would be filled myth and magic, enriched with intrigue and imagined dreams.

He was almost asleep when he heard someone pounding on the apartment door. Thinking it was Johnny, Kerney opened up, and two men in suits flashed U.S.

Customs agent shields and invited themselves inside.

"You're Kevin Kerney, right?" an agent with a hook nose asked as he closed the door behind him. He was fortyish, dark skinned, and spoke with a slight Spanish accent.

Kerney nodded. The man's partner, a blond-headed, blue-eyed, baby-faced man, made a quick inspection of the apartment and returned to the living room.

"He's alone," the man said.

Barefoot, wearing only shorts and a T-shirt, Kerney held up his hand to stop any further questioning. "If you know my name, you probably also know I'm a cop. Let me put some clothes on, and then we can talk."

Hook Nose nodded and said, "We'll watch, if you don't mind."

"Come along," Kerney said, "if that kind of thing turns you on."

In the bedroom Kerney fished his badge case and police credentials out of the pocket of his jeans and tossed them to Hook Nose before dressing. He looked them over as Kerney pulled on jeans and a shirt. Back in the living room Kerney asked to see some identification. Hook Nose was Supervising Special Agent Domingo Fidel. His partner was Special Agent Ray Bratton.

"Okay," Kerney said. "Tell me what this is all about."

"The man you found on Highway Eighty-one was an undercover officer," Fidel said, "who'd spent the last six months infiltrating an illegal-immigrant smuggling ring operating in this area. He was on his first solo run across the border from Mexico with ten aliens who'd paid two thousand dollars each to be brought across."

"He looked like a Mexican teenager to me," Kerney said. "Was he a fresh young recruit right out of your academy?" Many officers were assigned to undercover duty immediately after completing their training in order to reduce the risk of having their cover blown.

"Exactly," Fidel said. "He was supposed to bring his cargo up to a remote ranch road west of Antelope Wells and then walk them to a place where a vehicle would be waiting for him with instructions on his final destination. We couldn't stake it out because he didn't get the route information until just before he left."

"He'd made six previous runs," Bratton said, "with the coyote who heads up the operation. Each time the crossing took place at a different location."

"On those earlier runs he was sent back to Mexico after the crossings," Fidel added, "while the coyote finished the transport alone."

"So you don't know the final destination," Kerney said.

Fidel shook his head. "Or who the coyote is working with on this side of the border."

"We think they're using someplace in the Bootheel as a holding area for the illegals," Bratton said, "before moving them on to Tucson, Phoenix, and L.A."

"Playas?" Kerney asked.

"No way," Fidel said. "We've had people from Homeland Security through this town a dozen times, posing as part of the team that put together the purchase agreement to buy it for use as an antiterrorist training center. The people who live here are clean as a whistle."

"What kind of vehicle would be used to move the human cargo on this side of the border?" Kerney asked.

Bratton sank down on the couch and leaned forward. "It was always changed on each run. That's why what you saw could be important."

"You obviously know what I saw,"

Kerney said, "or you wouldn't be here."

"But where you saw the vehicle the second time could be important," Fidel said.

"The panel van at the smelter may or may not be the same vehicle," Kerney replied.

"But it was similar enough to catch your interest," Bratton said, "and it's owned by a state Motor Transportation officer, who just happens to moonlight on his days off as a security guard at the smelter."

"You did a background check on Mendoza?" Kerney inquired.

"On everybody who lives in Playas," Fidel replied. "All fifty-six of them. Mendoza enlisted in the army at eighteen and served as a truck driver. After discharge he got a job as a long-haul driver for an outfit in El Paso. Three years ago he joined the Motor Transportation Division as a recruit and went through the New Mexico Law Enforcement Academy. He was assigned to Lordsburg upon graduation and has been there ever since."

"Do you think he's your man?" Kerney asked.

Fidel eased himself down on the arm of the couch. "Unknown, but consider this: The smelter is a sprawling, huge plant, off limits to outsiders. It's run by a skeleton crew of ten employees who are just there to basically maintain it and deal with environmental cleanup issues. Can you think of a better place to warehouse illegals? There must be a dozen places in that smelter where you could hide people for a short time with no one the wiser."

"That makes sense," Kerney said, "but back up for a minute. Your undercover officer saw six different vehicles on his runs with the coyote. Didn't he get license-plate and vehicle information to you?"

"The plates were stolen from trucks in the States," Bratton replied, "and the vehicles were abandoned in Phoenix and L.A. All of them had been originally registered in Mexico under fictitious company names."

"Okay," Kerney said. "Now that I know all this, tell me why you're really here."

"Tomorrow Officer Sapian will call and tell you the body couldn't be identified. Because there is no probable cause that a crime has been committed, we'd like you to suggest that he close the case as an accidental death."

"That's easy enough to do," Kerney said. "What else?"

"Bratton here is going to join the film crew as an apprentice employee vetted by a theatrical stage employees' union. He'll be a gofer for the set decorator, or something like that. You'll be his contact. What he tells you, you'll pass on to me."

"What purpose does putting Bratton undercover serve?"

"We're after a network here, Kerney," Fidel answered. "One that has been way too successful at not getting caught. The coyote on the Mexican side is a former corrupt cop. Mendoza is a cop. There may be other officers involved that we don't know about. Maybe some Border Patrol officers are on the pad, looking the other way. Or some of the good citizens of Playas could be supplementing their incomes. I lost a nice young kid who was doing his job, and now it's personal. Somebody blew his cover, and I want the son of a bitch who did it, and the other son of a bitch who killed him."

"And Mendoza?" Kerney asked.

"He's under surveillance twenty-four/ seven starting now," Bratton said, "as are some of our own people."

Kerney walked to the door and opened it. "Did you roust me because you thought I might be a dirty cop involved in this scheme?"

"Think of it as a reality check," Fidel replied.

"It's your show."

159

"You'll do it?" Fidel asked, as he and Bratton stepped outside.

"Yeah, I'll help," Kerney said, "in spite of your bad manners."

Johnny Jordan and Malcolm Usher didn't finish working on the new scenes until after midnight. It was all good stuff, and Johnny had to admit to himself that the changes totally outdid the rodeo in terms of high-octane action. He watched as Usher sent the new material by e-mail to the screenwriter in California so some fresh dialogue could be worked up.

"I still think we could use the rodeo scenes," Johnny said, when Usher closed the lid to his laptop. "Maybe in a slightly different way."

"How so?" Usher asked, looking at Johnny over the rim of his reading glasses.

Johnny leaned back against the couch. "You've been talking about plot points all night long. How the film has to move the action along. So, I've been thinking about the opening scenes. Except for when the rancher chases the BLM officer and the sheriff's deputies off the land, there's not a lot of drama."

"The tension builds nicely," Usher retorted.

"Yeah, but where's the impact? The rancher stands down the cops, who go off to get a court order to force him off the federal land. Meanwhile, the rancher's daughter goes looking for her brother, who's on the pro rodeo circuit, and doesn't come back with him until the day before the cattle drive."

"How in the hell does a rodeo fit into any of that?" Usher asked.

"We do a scene where the daughter finds her brother competing at a rodeo," Johnny said. "Maybe he gets thrown and busted up at bit. He's short of cash and down on his luck. So is his buddy."

Usher raised an eyebrow. "You're talking Steve McQueen in *Junior Bonner.*"

"Yeah, a great movie. Anyway, the brother and his buddy agree to help out, because they don't have enough cash between them to pay their expenses and enter the next rodeo."

"And the rancher has issues with his son," Usher added, "because he never came back to take over the ranch."

"Just like it's in the script," Johnny said. "Except now the son comes home because he's broke, not because he wants to make amends with his old man."

"We'd need a real rodeo grounds to film it."

"There's a nice one just over the state line in Duncan, Arizona, a little more than a hour's drive from here."

"It might work," Usher said, "if we used tight shoots to film your boys, Tyler and Clint, saddle bronc riding, and edit in some crowd background noise and a booth announcer's voice to set the scene. We could put the girl at the arena railing with your Hispanic cowboys, Maestas and Lovato, to establish her presence, and then shoot a dialogue scene with her talking to her brother next to a horse trailer."

"Do you like the idea?" Johnny asked.

"Can we get the rodeo grounds?"

"For a song, guaranteed. It sits unused most of the year except for a short horse-racing season in the spring and a community rodeo in late summer."

Usher pushed the laptop away and reached for a tablet. "Are you up to pulling an all-nighter?"

Johnny laughed. "Hell, besides rodeoing, that's what I do best."

Chapter Five

Up and ready to go at four a.m., Kerney checked the second bedroom for Johnny and found it empty. At the mercantile building the caterers had breakfast ready and Johnny and Malcolm Usher were sitting together, chowing down on scrambled eggs and bacon.

With his breakfast plate in hand Kerney walked toward an empty table, only to be waved over by Johnny. He sat down with the two men, both of whom had circles under their eyes and slack looks on their tired faces. "Long night?" he asked.

Johnny managed a smile. "You could say that, but we got a lot of good work done."

Usher nodded in agreement.

"Why the early wake-up call?" Kerney asked Usher.

"We've got daybreak and early-morning scenes in the script," Usher replied. "We can't plan for them correctly unless we know what the light will be like at that time of day. The same applies to our evening and nighttime shoots."

"We may be doing the rodeo scenes after all," Johnny said.

"That's good news," Kerney said.

"If Charlie Zwick can find the money in the budget for it," Usher cautioned.

"Will that be a problem?" Kerney asked. If Johnny got what he wanted, maybe he'd stop bitching about his story idea getting all screwed up.

"I think we've worked it so it won't be," Usher replied.

Kerney nodded. "If you've got a minute, can I ask how you plan to use me on the film?"

"You've read the screenplay?" Usher asked.

"Several times."

Usher laid his fork beside his plate of half-eaten scrambled eggs and bacon. "Your job is to tell me what real cops would do. Anything that has to do with police procedure is your domain. If you see me planning to do something that's completely screwball, tell me or my assistant director. Examples might be how the police would position themselves or restrain somebody — that sort of thing. The fewer glitches we have when we're shooting, the smoother things will go."

"That sounds easy enough," Kerney said.

Usher downed the rest of his coffee. "But please don't get upset with me if I don't use every suggestion you make."

"It's your movie," Kerney said. "I'm not here to argue."

"How refreshing," Usher said, giving Johnny a pointed look. "Enjoy yourself, Chief Kerney. I think you'll find it fun to see how movies get made, although sometimes it can be real boring."

Usher left and Johnny leaned back in his chair and broke into a big grin.

"You look pleased with yourself," Kerney said.

Johnny drained his coffee. "If the rodeo scenes get overhauled the way Usher and I brainstormed them, I'm going to be a happy camper. Maybe you did me a favor yesterday after all. The more exposure my clients get in the film, the better the chances that I can get them bigger product endorsement deals and more acting jobs."

"Are you trying to becoming a movie mogul?" Kerney asked.

"I don't see why not," Johnny replied. "There's a lot of money to be made in motion pictures."

"Well, you've got your foot in the door," Kerney said. "But from what I've heard, making movies is a risky business."

Johnny dropped his napkin on the table. "It's no more risky than anything else I've done. Hell, you can't get anywhere if you don't roll the dice." He pushed his chair away from the table. "Our first stop is at the ranch. It's quite a spread. Old Joe has sunk a fortune into it. I can't wait for you to see it."

"I was there yesterday," Kerney said, "and had lunch with your parents and Julia."

Johnny's eyes widened in surprise. "Why didn't you tell me this before?"

"I haven't had a chance," Kerney said as he walked with Johnny out the door.

"Did the old man talk to you about me?"

Kerney shook his head. "No, he didn't."

"That's just as well," Johnny said with a laugh, "since he doesn't have much good to say about me anyway."

On the drive to the Granite Pass Ranch, Kerney sat in the backseat of an SUV with Charlie Zwick, the producer, who quietly wrote notes to himself. When Zwick put his pen away, Kerney asked what arrangements had been made for standby emergency personnel during the filming. Charlie explained that full-time medical services would be on-site and that the unit

166

production manager, Susan Berman, would coordinate with the local volunteer fire departments for ambulance services to be made available. Private security officers would handle all traffic and crowd-control issues.

They arrived at the Granite Pass Ranch road, where the day's work began. In the predawn light Kerney stood with the crew and listened as Usher sketched out what he wanted for two scenes that occurred early in the movie. The first one would be a shot of police vehicles on the road to the ranch house. Usher, his assistant director, a young man named Marshall Logan, and the cinematographer, a guy named Timothy Linden, talked about starting with an establishing shot that would show the police cars coming into view, and using a following shot as the vehicle passed by on the way to the ranch. They'd need a camera dolly and a crane to make it work.

As the first touch of pink coated the underbelly of the clouds on the eastern horizon, Usher had made his camera decisions and talked to his lighting specialists, Buzzy and Gus, about how he wanted the scene lit.

Interested to learn that exterior daytime shots needed artificial lighting, Kerney eavesdropped and found out that the angle and intensity of the sun created problems that had to be controlled in order to get the proper effect on film. In addition, lens filters might be needed to either heighten or dampen the sunrise effect.

While Usher was busy with Buzzy and Gus, Roger Ward, the transportation captain, staked out an area for the various equipment vehicles that would be brought to the location. He told Kerney at least a half-dozen trucks and the police vehicles to be used in the scene would be at the location several hours before the cast arrived, so the crew could set up.

After the art decorator and construction coordinator selected the placement for a wrought-iron ranch sign that would be erected, Usher did a three-sixty walk around the site. When the sun had fully crested the mountains, he assembled the group and asked if anyone saw problems that needed to be addressed.

"We're going to have problems with dust on this road," the photographer said.

"We can dampen it down with a water truck," Susan Berman, the unit production manager, replied.

"Maybe we don't need to do that," Usher replied. "The dust could be a nice contrast to the serenity of the opening shot. Emergency lights flashing, cutting through the haze. Sirens wailing. The morning sun cresting the mountains."

"They wouldn't approach with lights flashing or sirens wailing," Kerney said.

"Why not?" Usher asked.

"To retain the element of surprise," Kerney answered.

"So how would the rancher know the cops were coming?"

"The dust would give them away," Kerney answered. "Any rancher worth his salt always keeps one eye on the weather."

Usher grinned. "Excellent." He flipped through his shooting script. "Although I think we'll keep the flashing emergency lights for dramatic effect. But instead of the rancher hearing the sirens, he sees the dust cloud from the road and emergency lights as the cop cars approach."

"That would work," Susan Berman said, checking her script.

"Okay," Usher said, "let's run through everything we need here one more time and then move on."

What Kerney thought would take no more than a few minutes to accomplish took almost an hour. Usher's attention to detail was impressive, as was the amount of work that would be needed to get a one-minute scene on film.

He asked the art director, a portly, middle-aged Englishman named Ethan Stone, if such thoroughness was normal.

"With Malcolm it is," Stone replied in a clipped British public-school accent. "Some directors are far more freewheeling, of course. But no movie ever gets made exactly as planned. There are too many variables: cost, weather, equipment failure, the decision to improvise. You've seen *The Wild Bunch*?"

"Several times," Kerney answered.

"Remember the scene where William Holden attempts to free a member of his gang? Sam Peckinpah shot that on the spur of the moment and it worked brilliantly."

Ward, the transportation captain, waved everyone toward the vehicles. They were ready to move on.

"So, even with all this careful planning," Kerney said as he walked with Stone to the cars, "the actual filming can change."

"It's bound to," Stone replied with a chuckle. "But too much change will have Charlie Zwick tearing his hair out."

At the ranch headquarters the group was met by Julia Jordan. Joe and Bessie did not join them, although Kerney caught a quick glimpse of a figure standing at the living-room window inside their house.

Before Usher started working on the next location setup, the catering vehicle arrived, and everyone broke for coffee. Julia, who'd glued herself to Kerney's side, shook her head when he asked if Joe and Bessie were planning to come out and watch the goings-on.

"Dad wants nothing to do with this. It took Mom browbeating him for weeks to get him to let Johnny use the ranch in the movie."

"Why is that?"

"Dad doesn't like the fact that Johnny is using other people's money to pay back a tiny portion of what he's borrowed from him over the years. He doesn't think it's the same as paying the debt yourself."

Kerney couldn't think of a polite comment on such a grim assessment of the relationship between father and son. He watched Roger Ward take a folding card table and several chairs out of the back of a vehicle and set them up for Susan Berman and Charlie Zwick, who sat and busily got to work.

"Looks like you'll be here for a while," Julia said.

"All morning," Kerney said, handing her

his copy of the scouting location schedule. "Six different exterior scenes are to be filmed here, over a period of three days. For each sequence they have to map everything out and decide exactly what they need. Then they move on to the cattle drive."

Julia scanned the schedule. "My, don't you sound like an expert."

Kerney laughed. "Hardly." His cell phone rang. The screen flashed an unfamiliar number, and when he answered Flavio Sapian identified himself. "Hang on for a minute," he replied.

"The wife?" Julia mouthed silently.

Kerney didn't rise to the bait. "Will you excuse me?"

Julia frowned briefly, then grinned and stepped away.

"What's up?" Kerney asked.

"We can't ID the victim," Flavio replied, "but the autopsy revealed that he was heavily sedated on barbiturates at the time of death. The pathologist says the vic was definitely unconscious when he was thrown from the vehicle."

"I see," Kerney said as he watched Johnny gesture to Julia to join him. She waved and smiled winningly at Kerney before hurrying off.

"Plus," Sapian said, "he had ligature marks on his wrists, which suggests his hands had been tied prior to the time he was dumped."

"Anything else?" Kerney asked.

"According to the autopsy the victim wasn't a teenager, and probably not a Mexican national. The pathologist pegged him to be in his early to mid-twenties. Based on his dental work he was most likely either a U.S. citizen or a permanent resident. It seems like you were right, Chief, this was a homicide."

"A premeditated killing with an interesting twist," Kerney said.

"What twist is that?" Flavio asked.

"Why go to all the trouble to bind and drug the victim, only to throw him out of a moving vehicle to die in the middle of the road?"

"That makes sense if the killer wanted the body to be found," Flavio replied.

"Or to send somebody a message," Kerney added. "But what kind of message and who was it for?" The questions had been in Kerney's head since yesterday, and he'd yet to come up with answers that made sense.

"Well, Mendoza is my only lead," Flavio said. "I'll do a little more digging into his personal life before I approach him. Maybe something interesting will pop up."

"Good idea," Kerney replied. He disconnected, fished out the business card Supervisory Special Agent Fidel had given him, and dialed his direct line.

Over by the catering vehicle Julia and Johnny had hooked up with Ethan Stone, and the trio were walking in the direction of the barn. When the agent answered, Kerney gave him the gist of his conversation with Sapian, and suggested that Fidel should be the one to get Flavio to back off on his investigation. Gruffly, Fidel agreed, told Kerney to stay in touch, and disconnected.

Somewhat piqued by Fidel's attitude, so typical of federal officers who looked down their noses at local cops, Kerney put the phone away just as Malcolm Usher called him over. He asked a few questions about how cops would serve a court order to the rancher and, armed with the information Kerney provided, began talking to the cinematographer about the shots he wanted to use.

Johnny, Julia, and Ethan Stone had returned from the barn and were clustered around the construction supervisor, a man named Barry Hingle, who had the good looks and hard body of an actor.

Kerney joined them and listened as Stone told the man he wanted all the buildings to look weather beaten and dingy.

"Hardscrabble and impoverished best describes it," Stone said. "This must appear to be the ranch of a man who is barely hanging on."

"Daddy will absolutely hate that," Julia said with a laugh.

"Don't worry, my dear," Stone said. "It's all magic, smoke and mirrors. Barry and his crew will put every thing back as it should be once we finish."

"You'd better," Julia said teasingly.

Stone and Hingle moved away to inspect the buildings.

"Where's the old man?" Johnny asked Julia, his gaze locked on his parents' house.

"Dad is probably inside," Julia replied. "He doesn't get around as much as he used to."

Johnny squared his shoulders. "I'd better go see him." He marched off to the house and paused at the screen door to the porch for a long moment before entering.

"That should be interesting," Julia said as she rested her hand on Kerney's arm. "It always is when those two get together."

Kerney wondered why Julia seemed so pleased about the tension that existed between her father and brother. He studied her expression, looking for an answer. All he saw was the face of a self-indulgent, attractive middle-aged woman. Although her eyes danced and her lips smiled, it was surface charm. The thought occurred to him that she was very much like her brother: both were vain, lacked empathy, and craved excitement. He took her hand off his arm.

Julia reacted with a teasing smile. "Oh, was I being too familiar?"

"As a matter of fact you were," Kerney said.

"Come on, Kerney. We're old friends. Don't be so uptight."

"Old friends, and nothing more," Kerney replied.

Julia tossed her hair and gazed up at him. "Maybe we should change that."

"Not likely."

"Are you a happily married man, Kerney?"

"Indeed I am."

Julia giggled. "I've heard that line before." She kissed him on the cheek. "Let me know when you change your mind."

He watched her walk away, hips swaying

in tight jeans, her body toned and trimmed. Or was it that she'd been under a plastic surgeon's knife, maybe more than once?

Johnny Jordan stood in the front room of his parents' house, trying to force down the uneasiness that always overcame him when he was about to see his father. Except for the ticking of the ornate mantel clock above the fireplace, not a sound could be heard. On the bookcase that held his father's prize collection of books by novelists, biographers, and historians of the Old West stood the Cattleman of the Year Award his parents had jointly won some years back.

Johnny had shown up late to the award ceremony, drunk and in the company of a blond, buxom woman he'd picked up after finishing in the money at a California rodeo. He couldn't remember the blonde's name or even what she looked like. She'd been just another anonymous buckle bunny, one of the many women who made themselves available to rodeo cowboys after the events were over and the partying began. But he clearly remembered the disgusted look on his father's face when he'd walked in with his date.

He shook off the memory and pushed his uneasiness aside. Ever since the day he'd left home to become a rodeo cowboy, the old man had never given Johnny anything but grief about the way he lived his life, had never once shown any pride in Johnny's success and accomplishments. All he got from his father was criticism and some money when he needed it. Except for the games he had to play to get the old man to open his wallet, that suited Johnny just fine.

He stepped into the kitchen, and through the window he saw his mother in the backyard tending the flower beds that bordered a flagstone patio shaded by several large honey locust trees. He watched her for a minute as she carefully pruned a butterfly bush and put the cuttings in a neat pile at her feet. She'd slowed down considerably since Johnny had seen her last, and her face looked tired and drawn.

He rubbed his eyes, stifled a yawn, put on a big smile, opened the back door, and said, "How's my girl? Need some help?"

Bessie shook her head and removed her gardening gloves. "You wouldn't know what to do."

"I'd probably just make a mess of things," Johnny agreed jovially, surprised that his mother made no attempt to hug him. "Where is he?"

"He left before you arrived to meet up with Walt down at the old Shugart cabin," Bessie said. "That's where they'll be pasturing the cattle for your movie."

"Why doesn't he just leave that stuff to Walt?" Johnny asked. "After all, he pays the man good money to manage the ranch."

"Because he loves doing it," Bessie said, "and would probably die if he didn't get up and go to work every day, even if it's only for a few hours. It's bad enough that he can't ride a horse anymore."

"Is he still not talking to me?"

Slowly, Bessie lowered herself into a patio chair and looked at Johnny with sad eyes.

"What is it this time?" he asked.

"A woman named Brenda called for you here last night, and your father answered the phone. Why did you tell her your father had had a stroke?"

"I never said that. I said he wasn't getting around all that well. Brenda must have misunderstood. She's a flake. Half the time I don't even know what she's talking about. Don't worry, I'll set things right with him."

"You leave your father alone for now,"

Bessie said sharply. "He doesn't want to see you."

"All because of what some woman who doesn't know what she's talking about said? That's ridiculous."

"Do you really want your father dead?" Bessie asked.

Johnny knelt down and patted his mother's knee. "Come on, you know better than that."

Bessie pushed his hand away. "You never mean any of your little lies, and you always try to sweet-talk your way out of them. Until you show your father the respect he deserves, I'm not going to stand up to him on your behalf anymore."

She rose, reclaimed her gloves, and began snipping angrily at the butterfly bush with the pruning shears.

Johnny stared at his mother's back. She'd been his strongest ally in the family, the person he relied on to mend the broken fences between him and the old man. He wondered what he could do to fix things with her.

It had saddened Bessie that her children had produced no offspring, although she rarely spoke of it. Would it help to tell her that she had a granddaughter? A girl that Johnny had fathered ten years ago? He decided truth telling would only backfire and get him deeper in trouble. He had no pictures of the girl, hadn't seen her in years, didn't even know where she lived.

He watched as his mother pruned the shrub, the twigs of the butterfly bush falling haphazardly around her feet. Figuring out a way to placate her would have to wait. Right now, there was Brenda to deal with. He needed to sweet-talk his way back into Brenda's good graces. He wasn't about to head back to Denver when the weekend was over without a place to stay.

As he left the backyard, he dialed Brenda's number on his cell phone. Maybe if he told her his father had Alzheimer's, that would do the trick.

After lunch the team drove in a convoy on a ranch road that wound toward the mountains in the direction of the Shugart cabin, where, according to the location schedule, filming of the roundup and cattle drive would take place. Julia, who had invited herself along, positioned herself between Kerney and Susan Berman in the backseat of their vehicle. During the drive she kept her leg pressed against Kerney's while ignoring him and making small talk with Berman.

Over the course of the morning there had not been a lot for Kerney to do, other than watch Usher and his people in action. Johnny, who was riding in the lead car, had made himself scarce after leaving Joe and Bessie's house, walking back and forth in front of the barn, energetically talking to someone on his cell phone.

After a bumpy thirty-minute drive the caravan arrived at the Shugart cabin, which turned out to be a partially collapsed line shanty marked by two old cottonwood trees that had died from lack of water. Behind the cabin stood a windmill missing half a dozen blades. Sagging chicken wire hung on listing fence posts enclosed the site.

About a quarter mile west, in a holding pasture of untrammeled grassland intermixed with clumps of blue-green sage, a small group of men were building a corral out of railroad ties, wire, and large poles. They were using a backhoe with a front-end bucket to dig the post holes and set the heavy crossrails.

The pasture rose to meet a rocky, vertical cliff face in the mountains that was broken by a sheer, narrow gap. Here and there on a jumble of outcroppings, an occasional juniper had gained a foothold, showing up dark green against gray stone etched with thin, pale-pink fissures.

Usher assembled his crew in front of the cabin and immediately got down to business. Johnny, who now seemed fully reengaged in the process, eagerly joined into the discussion of how best to film the opening sequence of the cattle roundup.

Kerney left the group and walked across the pasture toward the men who were building the corral. He was halfway there when Julia caught up to him, obviously unfazed by his earlier rejection. Kerney wasn't sure what to expect from her. Would she be congenial or continue her seductive ways?

The day had heated up, and a fierce afternoon sun washed away the color of the grassland that waved gently in an intermittent breeze. High overhead a prairie falcon glided toward an inaccessible cliff shelf in the mountains, where some blackbirds set up an outcry and scattered into the sky.

"This is one of Daddy's grass-bank pastures," Julia said, as she matched Kerney stride for stride. "He burned two thousand acres three years ago, and it hasn't been grazed on since."

"It looks good," Kerney said, his eyes fixed on the vehicles parked near the work site. A panel van, very much like the one that had passed him on the highway, stood out among the pickup trucks. In such a sparsely populated area, where most folks drove pickup trucks, he wondered what the probability of spotting another panel van might be. Perhaps not entirely unlikely, but certainly interesting nonetheless.

At the corral Julia introduced him to Walt Shaw, the ranch manager. Under his cowboy hat Shaw had the face of a man who'd called the open range his office for a lifetime. Probably in his late forties, he had a wide mouth, a long, broad nose, and a blunt chin.

Over the noise of the backhoe he greeted Julia warmly, pulled off his work gloves, shook Kerney's hand, and smiled, showing a gap between his two front teeth.

"Where's my father?" Julia asked.

"Took off some time ago," Shaw replied.

"We didn't pass him on the road," Kerney said.

"Didn't go that way," Shaw said, nodding in the opposite direction. "He's two pastures south, where we're gathering the cattle."

"Are you building the horse corral for the movie?" Kerney asked.

"Yep, but we get to keep it after you folks

are long gone," Shaw replied. "Bought and paid for by Hollywood. Can't beat that, I'd say."

"No, you can't," Kerney said, looking at the four men who were busy setting posts. Two of them were the cowboys who had stopped at the accident scene on the highway. "Is this your permanent crew?" he asked.

"They're day hands I hired on for the job," Shaw said. "My two full-time wranglers, Kent and Buster, are busy gathering. We're planning to bring the cattle up here nice and slow."

Kerney nodded and asked if the slot canyon through the mountains was Granite Pass, and Shaw allowed that it was, noting that the smelter sat one valley over, due southwest of their location.

Ranch raised, Kerney knew better than to ask about the size of the spread, which was akin to asking how much money the Jordan family had in the bank. But he did ask Julia how close the ranch came to the Mexican border.

"About twenty miles," Julia replied. She went on to explain that the high country on the ranch was mostly leased state and federal land, while the valley land was all deeded property.

Behind Julia, twenty feet away, the two cowboys Kerney had seen yesterday were eyeing him and talking to their companions.

When Shaw turned to check on his crew, the men quickly broke off their conversation and got back to the job of securing a crossrail to a post.

With Shaw and Julia at his side Kerney walked to the corral, inspected the work in progress, and praised the sturdy construction to Shaw.

"It should still be standing here long after I'm gone," Shaw replied.

Kerney nodded in agreement as he admired the handiwork and made a mental note of each of the workers, whom Shaw introduced by first names only. The two cowboys Kerney had seen on the highway were Mike and Pruitt, and their coworkers were Ross and Santiago.

On the way back to the cabin Kerney commented to Julia about the panel van. "You don't see many cowboys driving one of those."

"That's Walt's," she said. "When the weather's good and the roads aren't muddy, he uses it as his portable workshop. Carts just about anything he might need in it: wire, pipe, tools, spare parts."

"I didn't see it at the ranch headquarters," Kerney said.

"He keeps it at the Harley homestead that Daddy bought about twelve years ago. Walt uses the old barn there for storage and repair work. It's centrally located and a lot more convenient than having to run back and forth to ranch headquarters."

"Has Shaw been here long?" Kerney asked.

"Almost twenty years," Julia replied. "He's like family."

"Does he have one of his own?"

Julia laughed liltingly. "He's a confirmed bachelor, although he has been known to flirt with the idea of marriage every now and then."

"With you?" Kerney asked.

Girlishly, Julia bumped him with her hip. "I knew you were going to ask me that. Walt gave up on that notion a long, long time ago."

Julia had resumed her flirting full bore, but it seemed so disingenuous Kerney decided not to take it personally. He quickened his pace, wondering what dynamics in the Jordan family could have caused such arrested development in the two offspring.

— During the remainder of the afternoon the crew moved from location to location, and the planning went smoothly until Charlie Zwick announced that actually filming a fifty-mile cattle drive would put the movie way over budget.

Quite simply, the problem was logistics. Johnny Jordan, who had done the initial location scouting, had assured Zwick that transporting equipment and personnel to the various sites on the ranch would be easy. In fact, some of the locations were barely accessible by four-wheel-drive vehicles. Getting the necessary equipment to the sites would be a slow, time-consuming process, add several days to the shooting schedule, and cost thousands of dollars in overtime pay.

Zwick explained all this to Usher as the production crew stood on a ledge looking down into the narrow canyon that cut through mountains. It had taken them a half hour to traverse the rough jeep trail and reach the overlook.

Usher nodded as he stood enchanted by the view. Below him the canyon walls were sheer and imposing, and the view toward the valley was vast and forbidding. He could visualize the cattle entering the canyon, pushed along by the cowboys, police vehicles streaming across the basin in hot pursuit, helicopters dropping low, stampeding the herd.

He turned to Zwick. "I *want* this location."

"I'm not suggesting we drop it," Zwick said. "But we could easily film the roundup and the cattle-drive sequences down in the valley near the cabin, and not have to move to three other locations that are difficult to reach at best."

"Dropping those locations would screw everything up," Johnny said hotly. "How in the hell can you film the roundup and the cattle drive in one place? It will look completely fake."

"Not necessarily," Usher said. "We can shoot the sequences from various directions. Use different angles, different shots. Focus on the actors, their horses, the cows. Believe me, on film it will look real."

"Or like some cheap B Western," Johnny replied.

Usher's jaw tightened. "On film it will be just fine. Let me worry about what the audience sees."

"I've got a say about what goes into this film," Johnny retorted, "and the shooting script calls for a fifty-mile cattle drive."

Usher pushed his new straw cowboy hat back on his head and smiled thinly. "And that's exactly what you'll get, done my way." He turned to Zwick. "We're finished here."

Johnny kicked a rock into the canyon and stomped off. Kerney glanced at the faces of the crew as they dispersed toward the vehicles. None of them seemed the least bit upset by Johnny's childish outburst.

At the vehicles Ethan Stone joined Kerney. "Not to worry," he said gaily as he slid into the front passenger seat and waved a hand in the air. "These little catfights break out all the time."

"That's good to know," Kerney said as he crammed himself into the backseat next to Julia, who'd kept up her tiresome coquettish behavior all afternoon. He'd decided she did it solely to entertain herself.

On the drive down the mountain a dust devil churned across the valley, lifting sand several hundred feet into the sky as it churned on its thin axis. Kerney tuned Julia out and turned his thoughts to Walt Shaw and his panel van.

Shaw seemed to be a good guy and solid citizen, but that was no reason to discount him as a person of interest in the Border

Patrol officer's death. However, Kerney decided it would be premature to point Shaw out to Agent Fidel as a possible second suspect until he learned more about the man. He would do some digging and if Shaw came up clean, he could drop the matter and avoid stirring up any unnecessary trouble for Joe and Bessie.

During the course of the afternoon the production team had traveled up and down the valley, and Kerney had learned a good deal about the lay of the land. With that, and what Julia had told him about the location of the Harley homestead, he felt fairly certain he could find his way to the barn where Shaw kept the van.

He'd come out to the ranch tonight, try to take a closer look at the van, and then decide on a course of action if one was needed.

They arrived at the copper smelter, the last stop of the day, right on schedule an hour before sunset. To the west the bare, blinding sand of the playas stretched like a ribbon on the desert floor, and the grim Animas Mountains sloped upward, craggy and inky black in long shadows that masked the eastern slope.

The warning beacon on the smokestack

blinked faintly in the glaring light of a hot yellow sun, and the metal roofs of the smelter buildings reflected the sun's glow in shimmering waves.

Usher and Johnny looked completely exhausted, and the remainder of the crew not much better. With bottled water in one hand and shooting scripts in the other, they followed Usher as he walked to the area he had chosen for the brawl between the cowboys and the cops. He stood on the rail spur near the ore delivery dock and explained what he wanted: cattle running loose among the ore cars, cowboys scattering as police cars careened over railroad tracks, vehicles overturning, cops on foot chasing mounted riders, cowboys roping cops — all of it to be filmed against the backdrop of the smelter and the mountains.

Fortunately for Kerney, Julia had elected not to accompany the production crew to the smelter. Freed from her company he gave his full attention to learning more about the intricacies of motion picture making, which in this sequence included some major stunts.

By nightfall the team had finished their work, except for Charlie Zwick, who continued talking on his cell phone to the mining company's corporate attorney as he negotiated the details for using the smelter in the film. He was still on the phone, talking to somebody else about preparing a location lease agreement, when the weary crew wandered into the old mercantile store for a late dinner.

Kerney had hoped to eat quickly and then get back out to the Granite Pass Ranch for a surreptitious look at Walter Shaw's panel van. But Susan Berman, the unit production manager, delayed his departure.

She'd approached him at his table with a slightly worried look on her pretty face, asked for a moment of his time, and explained that the county sheriff, because of staff shortages, had turned down her request to do background checks on all the cast and crew members before actual filming got under way.

Berman was a tiny, attractive brunette in her late thirties, no more than five two, with blue-gray eyes and a confident, businesslike demeanor.

"Since nine-eleven we've become much more security minded," she said as she sat with Kerney, "and because Playas is now being used for antiterrorism training, we have to satisfy the government that there are no criminals, insurgents, fanatics, or terrorists working on the film. Thank God, they haven't as yet told us to exclude hiring any bleeding-heart, progressive Hollywood liberals. That would totally shut us down."

Kerney laughed. "When would you need the information?"

"After the cast, extras, and crew hiring has been done. About a week before we start actual production."

"How many people?"

"Over a hundred," Berman replied.

"Get me names, social security numbers, and birth dates, and I'll have my department do a computer check for wants and warrants."

Berman smiled warmly. "That would be great. I'll fax the information to you in Santa Fe as soon as it's complete. Did you have fun today?"

Kerney nodded. "The complexity of making a movie seems staggering."

Berman laughed. "This is the mellow part of putting a film together. Wait until the cameras start rolling."

"How does Johnny figure into the filming?" Kerney asked.

"His participation will be limited, but we'll do our best to keep him happy. But as you saw this afternoon, it doesn't always work out that way. Do you know him well?"

"Yes and no," Kerney replied. "We go back a long way, but it's been years since we've had any close contact."

"Have you got any tips on how to deal with him?" Berman asked.

Kerney gave the question some thought as he looked at Johnny, who was sitting with Usher at another table. Usher was talking with his arms spread wide, as though he was framing a camera shot for Johnny to visualize. Johnny looked totally bored.

"I think Malcolm already has Johnny's number," he said. "Overwhelm him with technicalities and facts he knows nothing about while you stroke his ego — if you can stand to do it."

Berman stuck the three-ring binder under her arm and smiled appreciatively. "That's a no-brainer, Mr. Kerney. I started out in this business years ago as a script girl, and, believe me, I've got lots of experience feeding male egos."

Berman left and Kerney soon followed, saying good-night to Gus and Buzzy on his way out the door. The dark sky was awash with stars, and a cool, downslope breeze rustled through the trees. At the ranch property he swung south on a cutoff dirt track near the rodeo arena that paralleled a pasture fence line. He passed through two gates, a dry wash, and made a wrong turn to a dead end before finding his way to the barn where Shaw garaged his van.

Kerney parked behind the barn and sat in the dark for a few minutes to let his eyes adjust before he circled the structure on foot. Built from scrap slat boards, the barn had a pitched tin roof, no windows, and a padlocked double door. There was no way he could get inside without leaving behind clear evidence of a forced entry.

He was about to leave when he saw two sets of headlights approaching in the distance. He hid behind a stone foundation of a cylindrical water tank that stood next to an empty water trough and watched as the vehicles arrived and stopped in front of the barn doors.

In the glare of a pickup truck's headlights Walter Shaw got out of the panel van, unlocked the barn doors, and drove it inside. Then, with the help of the man driving the pickup, Shaw unloaded the contents of the van. When the chore was finished, he backed the van out of the barn and locked the doors. Shaw's helper climbed into the van and it traveled south into the valley.

Kerney waited at his hiding place until the red glow of the taillights disappeared from view. Following the men wasn't an option; he'd be spotted immediately. When the sound of the engine had faded completely away, he fired up the truck and drove in the opposite direction with the headlights off until he dropped over a small rise in the valley floor.

Back on the highway Kerney sorted through what he'd seen. Shaw had removed all his tools, equipment, and supplies from the panel van at a remote, secure location and then had driven away in the direction of the border. He could think of no legitimate reason to do that so late at night. Were Shaw and his helper engaged in smuggling? People? Drugs? Some other form of contraband? And who was Shaw's companion? A rancher? A hand? In the darkness Kerney had been unable to get a good look at the man.

He'd memorized the license-plate numbers of both vehicles. Using his cell phone, he called the regional dispatch center in Santa Fe, asked for a motor vehicle check on the van and pickup, requested an NCIC wants and warrant check on Shaw, and told the dispatcher to call him back on his cell.

As he made the turn at Hachita on his way back to Playas, a small airplane flew overhead out of the south, its anticollision beacons clearly visible in the night sky. The sight of the airplane made Kerney's excursion on the ranch all the more interesting. While he wasn't about to jump to any conclusions about Walter Shaw and his unknown companion, his misgivings had been raised. Tomorrow he would find an excuse to break away from the production crew and pay another friendly visit to Joe and Bessie at the ranch to see what more he could discover about their ranch manager.

Chapter Six

A cloud-covered sky veiled the mountains and hid the rising sun, and a stiff, moisture-laden breeze flowing up from Baja California carried a refreshing chill to the air that lingered until midmorning. Jackrabbits skittered across the empty streets of Playas, and a resident roadrunner stood frozen on its large feet for a long moment before it pumped its tail feathers up and down and trotted away.

Under the overcast sky the expanse of the valley yawned as far as the eye could see to the faint outline of the Animas Mountains, which hovered at the edge of the basin like a misty mirage. In the dull gray light the colors of the desert were muted and the sands took on a soft, pearl-white sheen.

The agenda for most of the day had the crew working on locations in and around Playas, which made for less traveling. By late morning the wind had subsided and the sun broke through the clouds, only to dim and fade as a gentle rainstorm moved across the hazy valley, creating a gray sky that bled yellow shafts of light through the patchy cloud cover.

The work for the day had nothing to do with police procedure, and consigned to the role of onlooker, Kerney followed the crew around from location to location as they discussed the specifics of what would be needed for each scene. Earlier in the morning Johnny had driven off to Duncan, Arizona, some seventy miles northwest, to arrange to use the rodeo arena on the county fairgrounds. As a result of his absence the work of the production crew seemed to proceed at a more rapid and relaxed pace.

Kerney used his time to talk to some of the town residents who'd assembled to watch the filmmakers. Those he spoke with knew about the death of the Mexican on the highway, and several people wondered if it meant that smuggling activity along the border was on the upswing. Kerney probed a bit deeper and learned that over the past six to eight months, border-related incidents had dropped. One man recounted stories of how half-starved migrants had once routinely wandered into town, and speculated that they now avoided Playas because it was an anti-terrorism training center. While the man's argument made sense, Kerney wondered if the fall-off in immigrants passing through the town was also tied to the smuggling operation Fidel's undercover agent had infiltrated.

A woman he spoke with criticized the Mexican government for handing out desert survival pamphlets to the illegals who were planning to cross the border, calling it nothing less than an attempt to flood the United States with undocumented workers. Her husband, an older man with a U.S. Navy anchor tattooed on his arm, thought the problem was tied to not having enough Border Patrol agents assigned to the Bootheel.

When Kerney asked about drug trafficking, he was told that the unmanned drones the Border Patrol had put into service to track aircraft crossing from Mexico hadn't reduced the number of nighttime flights by any significant degree. Rumor had it that large amounts of marijuana, cocaine, and heroin were still being flown in on a regular basis, off-loaded at remote locations, and trucked north.

Kerney wondered if his take on the death of Fidel's agent was all wrong. Was it possible that the murderers had had no intention to leave their victim in the middle of the highway with ligature marks on his wrists? Had he fallen out of the van, as Officer Sapian had suggested? And if so, did the driver fail to stop because he or she had seen Kerney rubbernecking at the side of the road almost within shouting distance of where he would find the dying agent, and didn't want to chance turning around to retrieve the body?

The more Kerney thought about it, the more he seriously questioned his initial analysis of the crime. Why would the killers deliberately dump the body of a man they knew to be an undercover cop on a highway to be found? Wouldn't it be better to simply make the agent disappear altogether and avoid becoming hard targets as cop killers?

Agent Fidel had told him a corrupt ex-policeman in Mexico ran the immigrant smuggling operation, possibly aided by some dirty Border Patrol officers. Bringing the feds down around his head by dumping the agent's body would be the last thing a coyote would want to do.

There were two ways to test the theory: either find and take statements from the people who were in the panel van, or inspect the rear door latch on the vans owned by Walter Shaw and Jerome

Mendoza, the motor transportation officer, to see if either was defective. Locating the smuggler's clients might be hard to do, but checking out the rear door latches to the panel vans shouldn't be difficult.

Services ended at the Baptist church on the outskirts of town, and the number of onlookers swelled, bolstered by ranch families and a few folks from nearby Hachita who'd come by to watch the happenings. One of the people was Ira Dobson, the water works manager Kerney had met at the smelter. He was dressed in his Sunday-go-to-meeting best: a pair of blue jeans with razor-sharp creases, a starched white long-sleeved Western shirt, and a pair of polished black cowboy boots.

"Have you signed up to work on the film?" Kerney asked.

"Not me," Dobson replied. "I've got enough to do without taking on any more responsibilities."

"I understand the Granite Pass Ranch borders the company's property," Kerney said.

"Pretty country," Dobson allowed. "It runs for a far piece along our eastern flank."

"Do you know the Jordans?" Kerney asked.

"Good people," Dobson said with a nod.

"Yes, they are," Kerney replied. "I grew up on a ranch outside of Truth or Consequences that neighbored their old spread."

"Then you know that Joe's a smart old boy. He's had me over for supper a number of times, mostly to pick my brain about water conservation. I'll tell you this: He may be long in the tooth, but he sure keeps up with the latest ranching practices."

"What has he done?"

Dobson described how Joe used solar power to pump water at his remote wells, covered stock tanks with evaporation barriers, used almost indestructible truck tires as water troughs in his holding pastures, and had protected several artesian springs in the foothills by fencing off the streambeds and restoring the riparian habitat.

"He's saved hundreds of thousands of gallons of water every year," Dobson added, "recharged the aquifer, and has reduced his pumping costs. He hasn't had to dig deeper wells, install larger pumps, or spend a lot of money on erosion stabilization. It's damn smart ranch management."

Dobson looked over at Usher and his team standing in the middle of the baseball diamond next to the empty outdoor swimming pool. "What are they going to be filming here?" he asked.

"A country music concert," Kerney replied. "Free to the first five hundred or so people who show up."

"Now, that I'll have to see," Dobson said, breaking into a grin.

"Do you know Walt Shaw?" Kerney asked. The motor vehicle and background check he'd asked for on Shaw had come back clean.

"Walt is as solid as a rock," Dobson said. "He showed up in the Bootheel about the same time I did. Grew up in Virden on the Gila River Valley near the Arizona border. It's a Mormon ranching and farming community. He once had kin living there, but they've all passed away. He owns a house he inherited that he uses as a getaway, mostly during hunting season. I spent a weekend with him up there tracking mule deer bucks in the Big Burro Mountains. Neither of us had a darn bit of luck."

Kerney had half a mind to ask Dobson about Mendoza, who worked as a part-time security guard at the smelter, but decided to leave that to Ray Bratton, the young Border Patrol agent who was scheduled to go undercover as a film-crew apprentice when shooting began. Instead, he talked about deer hunting with Dobson.

When Dobson finished reminiscing about a more recent, successful hunt, he made his excuses and left. If Kerney had his geography right, Virden was just a few miles east of Duncan, Arizona, where Johnny had gone to check out the rodeo grounds for the film.

Earlier, Johnny had called from Duncan with the news that the location was available and could be rented for the film. To fit in a change to the scouting schedule, Charlie Zwick had arranged for the caterer to pack sack lunches so the team could eat while they traveled to the rodeo grounds, which were about an hour away by car.

Kerney caught Usher's attention as he was leaving the ball field and asked if he was needed for the remainder of the day. In a hurry to move on to the next shooting-script location, Usher shook his head, thanked Kerney for his help, and said he would see him when filming got under way.

In his truck Kerney located Virden on a state highway map. A secondary road that branched off from the main highway to Duncan led straight to the settlement along the Gila River Valley. He decided to make a quick run past Mendoza's house to see if the panel van was there, before moving on to the Granite Pass Ranch and then to Virden.

At the house a man he took to be Mendoza was washing the Motor Transportation squad car in the driveway. As Kerney drove by, a younger-looking man exited the house and climbed into the driver's seat of the panel van parked at the curb. Kerney waved at the men and kept going, wondering who the young man was and whether or not he should just drop the whole thing and leave it all up to Agents Fidel and Bratton to figure out. The cop in him said no.

On the highway to the ranch Kerney thought about the Jordan family. Joe and Bessie came from frontier stock. Bessie's ancestors had arrived soon after the Civil War to take up ranching along the Rio Grande River near the military outpost of Fort McRae, now submerged under the waters of Elephant Butte Lake, a man-made reservoir built in the early twentieth century. Joe's grandfather had migrated west to El Paso in the 1880s and made his money in banking before buying a huge tract of land on the Jornada, east of the Caballo Mountains.

Joe had inherited not only the ranch but a majority ownership of the bank his grandfather had established in Truth or Consequences. Why had Joe sold both interests, taken a job as president of a savings and loan in Deming, and bought a ranch in the Bootheel?

Until now Kerney hadn't given it any thought. He'd been away from his boyhood home for so long, the comings and goings of people he'd known in his distant past hadn't concerned him. But in retrospect the question had importance. The Jordan family had been part of the social, political, and economic fabric of the Jornada for generations. What would have prompted Joe and Bessie to pull up stakes from a place where they had such deep roots?

Did it have something to do with Johnny or Julia? Kerney doubted it. Both had been long gone from home at the time of the move to the Bootheel, Julia finished with college and living on her own, and Johnny competing on the pro rodeo circuit.

At the ranch the gate was closed but unlocked and no one was around. As the son of ranching parents Kerney knew that Sunday wasn't necessarily a day of rest. There were simply too many chores that needed constant or immediate attention:

salt licks and feed to be put out, broken machinery to be repaired, cattle to be moved to new pastures, a calf with a broken leg that needed to be tended to — the list was endless. It wasn't all that unusual for a rancher to send the family off to church services, if he could spare them, and stay behind to get the work done.

He decided to drive to the new corral to see if Shaw had his day hands working. He arrived to find Joe Jordan supervising the men, who were nailing galvanized wire mesh fencing to the corral. Kerney was familiar with the product; he'd used it for his paddock at the Santa Fe ranch. It kept horses from damaging legs or hooves on the posts and cross poles and absorbed the animals' impact without cutting their coats or causing abrasions.

Shaw was nowhere to be seen, nor was his panel van. However, Bessie sat in Joe's pickup truck, reading a book. She saw Kerney, smiled, and motioned him over.

"Will you go and tell that husband of mine to stop working and take me to Las Cruces like he promised?" she asked.

"Where's Walt Shaw?" Kerney asked.

Bessie closed the book and put it on the dashboard. "I suspect he's in Virden. He tries to get up there once a month to check on his property. Normally, Julia fills in for him when he's gone, but she's on her way to Tucson to attend a bull sale tomorrow morning. But these boys have worked for us before and they certainly don't need any supervision."

Kerney tipped his hat. "I'll see what I can do, ma'am."

Bessie touched him arm before he could walk away. "Back when you and Johnny were young, I'd hoped he would go to college with you and Dale Jennings."

"I guess it wasn't what he wanted."

"What he *needed* was to be with friends who were steady and reliable and not so easily swayed by his shenanigans."

Kerney smiled. "That's kind of you to say, but I don't think anyone could have held Johnny back when he was feeling his oats."

"You're probably right," Bessie said, patting Kerney's hand. "Go tell Joe Jordan if he doesn't get over here soon, I'm going to Las Cruces without him."

"Yes, ma'am." He stepped off toward Joe, who was busy watching the hands stretch out a two-hundred-foot roll of wire.

"Is the boss getting restless?" Joe asked, as he shook Kerney's hand and nodded toward his wife.

"You could say that," Kerney replied. "She's threatening to leave without you. When does Walt Shaw get back?"

"Probably late evening. Why, do you need him for something?"

"I was hoping to get a tour of the water conservation measures you've put in place on the ranch. Ira Dobson told me a bit about what you've done, and I'd like to profit from your experience."

"I'd show you around myself," Joe said, "if we weren't going to town."

"Perhaps some other time," Kerney said. "It's generous of you to give Shaw the day off with so much work to do."

"Walt takes maybe a day a month to himself," Joe replied. "I'm not about to say no when he needs to get away."

"Will he stay on after Julia takes over the ranch from you?" Kerney asked.

Joe looked a little surprised by Kerney's question. "She told you that? Well, I guess it's no secret. She pretty much has taken over already, but I like to kid myself that I'm still in the ramrod of the outfit. Walt will stay on. Otherwise Julia would have to give up her place in Tucson, and she's not about to do that. She likes her city life too much to let go of it completely."

"Would you mind if I took a look around on my own?" Kerney asked.

"Not at all," Joe said. He paused to watch as the men cut a section of the wire fencing and began attaching it with brads to the post-and-beam corral. "Make yourself at home. Just remember to close the pasture gates behind you."

After Joe and Bessie left, the day hands took a break, hunkering down to smoke cigarettes and drink some water. The welcome coolness of the cloudy morning had given way to a blistering sun, which felt uncomfortable in the humid air left behind by the rain squall.

Kerney talked with the men for a time, and once they learned that he ranched on a small place up in Santa Fe County and had known the Jordan family all his life, they loosened up noticeably. Mike and Pruitt, the two cowboys who'd stopped on the highway after the border agent's body had been dumped, wanted to talk about the incident. Kerney obliged but kept his narrative of the event short.

He learned that the two men bunked together in a rented house in the town of Animas, and worked as stock haulers and heavy equipment operators when they weren't hired out on the area ranches.

He asked Mike, a muscular six-footer in his thirties, about the problem of illegal immigrants crossing the border.

"The government would have to post an army down here to stop them," he said. "We see the crap they leave behind everywhere. Backpacks, clothing, water bottles — you name it."

Pruitt, who had the upper body of a weight lifter and carried a few extra pounds around his waist, nodded in agreement. "Hell, if you had the time, you could track them cross country all the way to Deming."

"I didn't see much evidence of that when I was out here yesterday," Kerney said.

"They make a beeline for the smelter smokestack," Mike explained. "They call the warning beacon on it the Star of the North."

"I heard about that," Kerney said. "But you'd think with Antelope Wells close by, it would draw more people crossing the border through this ranch."

Mike shrugged. "I don't know why the coyotes don't use it that much. But if they did, Walt Shaw would run them off in a hurry. He doesn't let anybody on the ranch he doesn't know personally."

The men went back to work and Kerney left, heading south toward the barn where he'd seen Shaw and his unknown associate unload the van.

On the one hand Shaw's protectiveness about the ranch made sense; trespassers were never welcome on private land. On the other hand Shaw's desire to keep strangers off the ranch might serve the alternative purpose of keeping certain activities hidden.

At the barn Kerney took another look again for an entry point. But daylight made no difference and he found none. He studied the tire tracks left behind by the van and followed them south along the ranch road. Soon the valley widened and he came to a fenced pasture that held over three hundred well-fed Angus heifers and calves, along with a few bulls that had been separated from the herd into a smaller paddock. The herd was clustered around a water trough and a nearby solar panel on a metal stanchion that supplied electricity to a well pump.

Kerney passed through the gate, closed it behind him, and crossed the pasture. Drawn by the sound of his truck the cows raised their heads, got to their feet, lifted their ears, and followed behind in a slow trot until it became clear no feed would be set out.

Through another gate Kerney continued south. In the distance he could see the faint outline of a fence that ran east and west across the wide valley, which he took to be the ranch boundary. He stopped and consulted the maps he'd bought in Santa Fe as part of the research he'd done on the Bootheel. He located his position on a Bureau of Land Management map of New Mexico that showed all federal, state, local, tribal, and privately owned land in the state and saw that he'd crossed over into the Playas Valley.

He looked up from the map through the rear window and saw the faint beacon of the Star of the North twinkle on and off. He switched to another map that showed the immediate area in greater detail. Clearly marked on it, no more than three miles away, was a landing strip.

Previously, Kerney had paid the map symbol no mind. It was not uncommon for larger spreads in remote locations to have landing strips. Big ranchers frequently used small fixed-wing airplanes to check on livestock, inspect fence lines, access range conditions, or occasionally ferry in needed equipment and supplies.

He put the maps away and scanned the land in front of him. There was no evidence of human habitation on the valley floor or in the hills and mountains that bracketed the basin. There were no telephone poles, electric lines, or microwave towers that would require maintenance or repair, and there was no sign of a landing strip on the north side of the fence that cut across the valley.

Kerney put the truck in gear and followed the tire tracks in the ruts of the dirt path until he reached the fence, where the tracks swung toward Chinaman Hills, a low-lying, bleak rise that bumped out of the valley. Before he reached the hills, the tracks veered south again, passed through a gate, turned east, and took him directly to the landing strip.

Kerney got out of the truck and looked around. On the bladed, packed dirt surface he could see fresh tire impressions from the nose and main landing gear of a light aircraft. Multiple sets of footprints led him to the spot where the vehicle had been parked, suggesting several trips had been made back and forth to load cargo. Although he wasn't certain, Kerney didn't think the landing strip was on the Jordan ranch. He walked around the strip in a wide circle and found a rutted dirt road that showed no signs of recent traffic and cut east across the valley toward a windmill. He went back to the truck and drove along it until he came to a locked gate that barred his passage. He climbed over it and read the posted sign attached to the other side of the railing. The landing strip was on the Sentinel Butte Ranch.

Kerney had seen enough. He checked his watch. If he hurried along, he could still make the drive to Virden, snoop around for a bit, arrive in Santa Fe by midnight, catch a few hours' sleep, and get to work on time.

Back at the new horse corral Kerney spotted Shaw talking to the day hands and stopped for a little friendly conversation. Shaw greeted him cordially and asked if he'd enjoyed his tour of the ranch.

"I've never seen desert grassland look so good," Kerney replied.

"It's been a lot of hard work to bring the rangeland back to where it should be," Shaw said with smile, "and it never would have happened without the coalition."

Kerney asked about the coalition, and Shaw explained that the area ranchers had agreed to make grassland available to each other in exchange for creating land-use easements that prohibited subdivision.

"We get scant rain down here," he added, "and the monsoons that do come are fickle, putting moisture on one ranch and bypassing another. Grass banking allows us to move cattle to neighboring ranches where there's ample forage. How much of the ranch did you get to see?"

Kerney laughed. "Not a hell of a lot, given the size of the spread. I stopped near some westerly hills."

Shaw nodded. "Those are the Chinaman Hills on the Sentinel Butte Ranch. Joe tells me you're the police chief up in Santa Fe."

"Not for long," Kerney said with a grin. "I'm about to retire. This trip is sort of a dry run to see what it feels like to be a civilian again. I think I'm going to enjoy it."

"You'll be coming back down when they start filming the movie?" Shaw asked.

"With my family," Kerney replied. "We're going to make a vacation out of it."

"I'll look to see you then," Shaw said, extending his hand.

After a handshake and a good-bye Kerney left thinking Shaw continued to come across as a pleasant fellow with nothing to hide. But why had he come back to the ranch on a rare day off? Had one of the day hands called to let him know Kerney was poking around unescorted? If so, that meant it wasn't a chance encounter.

Shaw had hauled ass down from Virden in time to intercept Kerney and find out where he'd been. As before, he'd acted cordial and not in the least uptight. But then Kerney had played the innocent, had carefully omitted mentioning all that he'd seen, and had deliberately reassured Shaw that he wasn't into any kind of cop mode.

If Shaw *was* into something illicit, chances were good that he would backtrack on Kerney.

Where the ranch road curved out of sight of the horse corral, Kerney stopped the truck, got his binoculars out of the glove box, hustled up to a small rise, and stretched out in the tall bunch grass. Through the binoculars he could see the dust trail of Shaw's pickup heading south toward Chinaman Hills on the Sentinel Butte Ranch.

Chances were that Shaw would lose Kerney's tire tracks in a hard rock portion of the ranch road that curved around the base of Chinaman Hills. If not, so be it.

Eager to get to Virden, Kerney returned to his pickup and drove away. He'd never been to the settlement before and knew nothing about it. Although he was a native of the state and enjoyed exploring it, Kerney had yet to see it all and probably never would.

New Mexico was larger than the combined landmass of the United Kingdom and Ireland. Within its boundaries were the soaring southern Rocky Mountains, the bone-dry Chihuahuan Desert, the windswept high eastern plains that butted up against deep canyonland gorges, the stark, majestic northwestern Navajo Nation, and the tangled western Mogollon Plateau that rose to meet wild mountains of dense climax forests.

Over the years he'd ridden, hiked, backpacked, and camped from his boyhood haunts near the Tularosa to the high country above Taos, four-wheeled in the desert, and deliberately detoured to see isolated hamlets, ghost towns, and remote archeological sites. He looked forward to the time when he could show Sara and Patrick the wonders he already knew and discover new ones together. Johnny's movie would be their first opportunity to do that as a family.

As he left the Bootheel, the mountains receded and gave way to mesquite flats, playas of sand, and stretches of irrigated cotton fields that were startlingly green against the dun-colored terrain. He passed through Lordsburg, a dusty ranching and railroad community that drew its lifeblood from the interstate traffic with little to offer other than fast food, cheap motels, and self-serve gas stations.

Beyond the town the desert continued to dominate. Flatlands were interrupted by an occasional mesa or the knobby spines of low hills. In the distance barrier mountains rolled skyward, promising relief from the heat of the day. It was raw country, where monsoon rains ran over the hard-baked soil and spilled into deep-cut arroyos, the sun cracked the earth into spiderlike fissures, and harsh volcanic mountains stood, weathered and desolate, above the expanse of sand and scrub.

Soon after the cutoff to Virden the road dipped into a valley and revealed the narrow ribbon of the Gila River, the last free-flowing river in the state, barely discernible through thick stands of cottonwoods that bordered its banks. On the far side of the river Kerney could see a swath of irrigated fields that stretched along the bottomland. Contained by low brown hills the valley was a green carpet of hay- and cornfields, some of which were punctuated by bright orange pumpkins that had been planted in among the long, straight rows.

Fat cattle grazed along fence lines in mowed fields, and in the sky above a black hawk, clearly identifiable by the broad white band on its tail, swooped down toward the wooded stream bottom. Mountains rose up behind the hills, one peak soft as a rounded shoulder, another shaped like a citadel carved out of solid rock.

Virden consisted of several dozen tidy farms and houses that lined the roadway paralleling the valley floor or fronted several side lanes flanked by orderly rows of mature shade trees. The only business in the settlement was a quilt shop in a single-wide trailer that stood near an old abandoned schoolhouse with a rusty, hipped metal roof, boarded-up windows, and an overgrown playground containing a broken swing set.

Kerney cruised the area, looking for Shaw's van. He followed a farm road that led into the hills, where he found a derelict homestead and the hulk of an old tractor behind a locked gate posted with a No Trespassing sign. Back in the village he stopped on a lane where an older man was working on a truck parked under a shade tree in front of a house.

The man looked up from the engine compartment and nodded when Kerney approached. In his late sixties, he had a deeply seamed face and a semicircle of thin gray hair that crowned his bald, freckled head.

"Engine trouble?" Kerney asked with a smile.

"Busted thermostat," the man said. "You lost, or just passing through?"

"Poking around is more like it." Kerney extended his hand and told the man his name. "This is really an out-of-the-way, beautiful valley you live in."

The man put a screwdriver in his back pocket and shook Kerney's hand. "Name's Nathan Gundersen. If you like the quiet life, it's the right place to be. You looking to buy some property?"

"Is anything for sale?" Kerney asked.

Gundersen shook his head. "Not really. Folks here tend to hold on to what they've got."

"Do you know Walt Shaw?"

Gundersen leaned against the truck fender. "He grew up in these parts. What's your interest in him?"

"A friend of Shaw's told me that he came here and went deer hunting with him," Kerney said, "so I thought I'd check out the area before the season got started."

"Maybe they were hunting up in the mountains," Gundersen said, "but not down here. We don't allow it. The whole valley to the Arizona state line is posted."

Kerney shrugged. "I guess I must have misunderstood."

"Not necessarily," Gundersen said. "Walt owns a farm in the valley, about two miles down the highway toward Duncan. Little white house that sits just back from the road. He leases out the acreage and uses the place as a retreat of sorts. Don't see much of him. Comes here occasionally to check on things and stay overnight. During deer season he sometimes brings a friend along to go hunting in the mountains."

"He grew up in the valley?" Kerney asked.

"He came here as a foster child the state placed with an older couple. They adopted him and found out they got more than they bargained for."

"How so?"

"Let's just stay he had a hard time adjusting to our ways. He went straight from high school into the service and didn't come back much after that. His adoptive parents died in their sleep from carbon monoxide poisoning about fifteen years ago. A leak in the bedroom wall heater is what killed them. Walt inherited the property."

"I enjoyed passing the time with you," Kerney said. "Good luck replacing that thermostat."

"I'll get it done," Gundersen said as he pulled the screwdriver out of his pocket.

Kerney left Gundersen to his chore and went looking for Shaw's house, which he spotted without difficulty from the highway. There was no sign of activity and no vehicles parked outside, although a nearby barn could easily house the van. He cruised by slowly and continued a mile down the road before turning around for another pass.

Shaw kept his property in good repair: both the house and barn were freshly painted, and although there were several barren flower beds in front of the porch, the grounds were free of junk and the grass had recently been mowed.

Kerney decided a closer inspection of the house and grounds wouldn't be wise. Driving onto the property would raise the interest of the farmer on a tractor tilling a nearby field, or the woman across the highway hanging out the wash at the side of her house.

What he'd learned about Shaw from

Gundersen was interesting but added no weight to his suspicions. A couple of hours of research into Shaw after he was back in Santa Fe might give him a better handle on the man. He was particularly intrigued by the way Shaw's adoptive parents had died, and wanted to do a records search to see what kind of an investigation had been mounted and what the official findings had been.

Kerney left the valley wondering whether he'd be able to drop his cop mentality when he retired. He'd spent his career questioning motives, digging into dirty little secrets, unraveling crimes, probing for guilty knowledge, and holding people accountable for their wrongdoings.

Would he ever be able to step aside from the ingrained reflex he had to want to set everything right? He wasn't sure it would be easy, but he would damn sure try. Although, so far, he had to admit to himself that he wasn't doing a very good job of letting go.

All in all Johnny Jordan was pleased with how the scouting trip had gone. Usher loved the rodeo grounds location in Duncan, and they had worked out a sequence of shots based on the new material from the Hollywood screenwriter that gave Johnny's clients more lines and time in front of the cameras.

Besides that, the new scenes strengthened the backstory conflict between the rodeo cowboy and his father and, as Usher put it, contrasted the hard-living hedonism of the son with the rock-solid decency of the father. Usher likened it to the clash between Paul Newman and Melvyn Douglas in *Hud*.

Johnny also thought the brawl sequences between the cops and cowboys during the stampede at the smelter would be outstanding. About the only thing he didn't like was Usher's decision to cut some of the locations from the cattle drive.

After returning from Duncan, Johnny tried to get Usher to restore the cattle-drive scenes, but his pitch fell on deaf ears. He left Usher and his team, who were about to finish up for the day, went back to the apartment, and tried to call his mother at the ranch. When the answering machine clicked on, he hung up without leaving a message. He tried Julia's number, hoping he could recruit her as an intermediary to soothe Bessie's anger with him, and got no response.

He threw the cell phone on the couch

and decided it didn't really matter. He'd endured his father's cold rejection for years, hadn't been close to Julia since high school, and would probably never again need his mother's help to get money out of the old man.

He was on the verge of becoming a major player. Foreign distribution rights for the movie had sold for big bucks, and the sports-cable-channel rodeo deal was in the bag. Sponsors were warming up to the idea of signing his clients to advertising contracts, which would put a fifteen-percent commission in Johnny's pocket.

Entertainment-industry buzz about the movie had generated talks with a major network about the possibility of a spin-off series. It would basically be an updated version of the old *Stoney Burke* television drama of the early 1960s that starred Jack Lord and Warren Oates as two maverick rodeo cowboys vying to make it to the national championship and win the buckle. But now one cowboy would be Hispanic and the other a high-stakes poker player, and they'd spend a lot of time at rodeos in Reno and Las Vegas.

The positive reaction by the network bigwigs to his slightly twisted, fun-loving, rodeoing, poker-playing characters, which he'd thought up while watching the World Series of Poker on ESPN, convinced Johnny that he was going to make a killing in Hollywood. After all these years he'd finally found something he could do as well as ride. Rodeo was my first love, Johnny joked to himself, but now it's all going to be about residuals.

In an matter of weeks Johnny would be able to stop floating loans to himself by maxing out his credit cards, pay off the shyster who masqueraded as a divorce lawyer, and settle accounts with his soon-to-be ex-wife, Madeline. But until then he still needed Brenda.

After a series of telephone conversations Johnny had managed to convince her that his father's "stroke" had left him foggy headed and confused about his medical condition. Johnny figured he would stay with Brenda until just before filming began and then pack his bags and go.

Johnny picked up the cell phone and clipped it on his belt. Usher's meeting with the production team was about to start. He left the apartment and fell in behind Susan Berman, who was on her way to the community center where the group would convene.

She was a tasty-looking piece in spite of

her no-nonsense, all-business manner. He couldn't help but wonder what it would take to get her in the sack. He quickened his pace, caught up with her, flashed a big smile, and asked if she'd ever been to a rodeo.

"No, I haven't," Berman replied.

"Maybe I could get my boys together and put one on for you after the film wraps," Johnny said, feeling remarkably expansive.

"That would be unusual," Berman said, trying hard not to laugh at the man's unbelievable grandiosity.

"We could do a barbecue at the ranch with live country music, tubs of longneck beer on ice, and some good sipping whiskey. Do you know how to two-step?"

"No, I don't," Berman replied.

"I'll teach you," Johnny said.

Susan Berman arched an eyebrow. "Will you, now?"

Johnny smiled broadly. "Private lessons."

Susan smiled sweetly and quickened her pace. "That would be hard to pass up."

He watched her scurry ahead of him and grinned. Long ago, Johnny had tired of the easy pickings he found with the buckle bunnies. He liked women who showed a little spunk, put up a few barriers, and made the chase worthwhile. At first Brenda had acted that way, but in truth she was nothing but a gushy, gullible, tiresome chatterbox.

Experience had taught Johnny that aloof women were totally hot in bed. He followed along behind Berman and pondered the moves he could make, promising himself that he would have her before filming ended. He had months to wear her down.

Chapter Seven

Sara parked the rental car next to Kerney's unmarked police cruiser, carried a sleepy Patrick inside the house, and quickly put him to bed. As she tucked him in and kissed his warm cheek, he asked for his father.

"You'll see him in the morning," Sara said.

Patrick smiled. "Can I go riding with Daddy in the morning?"

"Daddy has to work tomorrow and you may have to go with him."

"Why?"

"To keep him company," Sara said as she gave him his favorite stuffed animal, a palomino pony with a bushy tail. "Now go to sleep."

Clutching the pony, Patrick turned on his side and closed his eyes.

Outside, the horses in the paddock gently whinnied as Sara opened the trunk of the car and removed the luggage. In the stillness of the night she could hear the sound of their hooves as they trotted expectantly along the fence. She crossed the pasture to the barn and gave each of the four geldings a horse biscuit and a nose rub before taking the luggage inside. In the living room she dropped the bags on the oversized sofa and walked into the adjoining study. She sat at the original mission desk that she'd inherited from her grandmother and looked out through a picture window onto the canyon below, where the ranch road crossed an arroyo and rose toward the house. From here she would be able to see the headlights of Kerney's pickup truck long before he reached the house.

She opened her briefcase and took our her laptop before speed-dialing Kerney's cell-phone number. The call didn't go through. Since leaving Arlington for the flight to Albuquerque, she'd repeatedly tried to contact him without success. Kerney was way overdue from his weekend trip to the Bootheel and it was unlike him to be unreachable. As Santa Fe police chief he was on call virtually all of the time, no matter where he was or what he was doing. Until now Sara had always been able to contact him without difficulty.

She couldn't help but wonder if he'd encountered some trouble on the road or had been caught up in an emergency at work. To ease her mind she dialed his direct office number and got no answer. With growing concern she called the regional emergency dispatch center and asked to be put through to him. The dispatcher advised her that he was not on duty and had last been heard from by telephone earlier that morning.

Trying hard not to sound like a worried wife, Sara asked the dispatcher to let Kerney know, if he made contact, that she was at the ranch.

"Is everything all right, Colonel Brannon?" the dispatcher asked.

"Perfectly," Sara replied. She thanked the woman, disconnected, and powered up her laptop.

Kerney had no idea she was about to leave Patrick in his care for the next two weeks. It would be a first for father and son, and she wasn't happy about springing the situation on him unannounced. Fortunately, Patrick was thrilled about seeing his father, although she doubted he had really taken in the fact that Sara would be gone for two weeks, the first time they'd been separated for more than a few hours. Even on the busiest days she had always managed to look in on him at the Pentagon day-care center.

She stared at the laptop screen for a long moment searching out the folder containing the case file that had led to her special orders. She would be out of the country for the next week, but her mind kept wandering back to Kerney. Where was he? What was he doing? What if he arrived home without checking in with dispatch, saw lights on inside the house, and assumed a crime was in progress?

She went from room to room and turned on all the exterior lights, hoping it would signal her presence at home. Had his truck broken down? Had there been an accident? Was he hurt and unable to call? The thought that he might be cheating on her surfaced in her mind, and she tried to dismiss it as absurd. Yet why else would he not be home or at work so late on a Sunday night?

It was an unkind, silly notion that she fought off as she returned to the study and forced her attention to the task at hand. In twelve hours she would be flying to Ireland on the hunt for George Spalding, an army deserter from the Vietnam War.

Two years ago Spalding had gone missing after Kerney had uncovered facts that revealed he'd faked his death in Vietnam and had been living in Canada under his ex-wife's maiden name for over three decades. At Kerney's request Sara had searched old military and CID records and uncovered evidence that Spalding had operated a gemstone-smuggling operation while in-country. When the pieces had been put together, it was clear that he'd funneled his ill-gotten gains to his father, who'd used the money to build a multimillion-dollar company that operated a string of luxury resort hotels. If Spalding's father hadn't been murdered by his second wife, none of it would have come to light.

Spalding, a graves registration specialist assigned to a military mortuary in Tan Son Nhut, outside of Saigon, had been targeted by army CID for possible smuggling activities, but the case had been dropped after Spalding faked his death. According to the army CID investigator, a retired chief warrant officer, the scheme had surfaced when a shipment containing the personal effects of dead soldiers was found to include a quarter of a million dollars in precious stones bought on the black market in Southeast Asia. Although he couldn't substantiate it, the investigator thought it likely that a number of similar shipments had slipped through undetected.

In her spare time Sara had dug into the

case. She tracked down and interviewed surviving members of Spalding's unit who had been implicated but never charged, and ran into a wall of silence. Forced to look elsewhere for evidence, she accessed quartermaster archives, looking for a paper trail that might point to the Stateside member of the ring responsible for intercepting the shipments, removing the smuggled gems, and selling them to unscrupulous dealers.

Fortunately, the Quartermaster Corps, which oversaw mortuary operations, carefully inventoried and documented the shipment of personal effects, and sign-off sheets showed the names of the personnel who'd conveyed the shipments from Tan Son Nhut and those who'd received them Stateside. Unfortunately, there were literally thousands of documents from a variety of sources to search through.

To simplify the process Sara concentrated only on those shipments Spalding himself had inventoried and sent from Vietnam. With that information in hand she compared it to the logs of the receiving authority, and one name surfaced that drew her attention: Thomas Loring Carrier, a junior officer who'd been stationed at the Ton Son Nhut mortuary with Spalding before rotating Stateside to take charge of a unit tasked with returning personal effects to family members.

Unwilling to jump to conclusions, Sara dug deeper into the paperwork. The forms used to ship and receive all personal effects required two signatures on both ends of the process: one to certify the contents, and one to attest to the form's completeness. On at least eight of the shipments that Carrier had authorized for release to next of kin, the handwriting of the signatures looked decidedly similar.

Sara sent the forms to an army forensic center for handwriting analysis and did a background check on Carrier. A graduate of a southern military institute, he had stayed in the service after Vietnam, rising to the rank of full colonel before retiring. Divorced with two grown daughters, he owned a house free and clear in the Virginia suburbs, had a high-six-figure mutual fund account with a large brokerage firm, drove a midsize SUV, and apparently lived within his means.

For the past five years Carrier had worked as a senior military analyst for a conservative think tank with close ties to the White House. According to a Pentagon insider Sara trusted, he was a close friend of an assistant deputy secretary of defense and had access to a senior national security advisor to the president. The policy papers he'd written for the think tank clearly supported the current administration's prosecution of the war on terrorism.

It took six months for forensics to get back to her with a report that Carrier had forged signatures on the documents she'd submitted for analysis. Even with that evidence in hand Sara had let the investigation slide. Without corroboration of Carrier's involvement in the smuggling ring, it would be impossible to prove, and Spalding was nowhere to be found. But all that had changed in the last two weeks.

Before he could be detained, Spalding had left Canada with cash, valuables, and negotiable assets in the high seven figures. After a failed attempt to find him, army CID investigators and the Canadian authorities developed a watch list of a select number of Spalding's known associates and close friends in the hope that one or another of them might eventually lead them to him. Those on the list had their bank, credit cards, brokerage accounts, and their foreign travel monitored, and their incoming telephone calls and e-mail traced.

Nothing had materialized until two weeks ago, when one of the targeted subjects, a French-Canadian woman named Joséphine Paquette, had bought an expensive seaside house on the coast south of Dublin with cash she'd deposited in an Irish bank.

A senior editor of a fashion magazine in Toronto, Paquette had been Spalding's lover for a time before marrying the scion of a Canadian brewery. When the marriage failed, an ironclad prenuptial agreement kept Paquette from tapping into her ex-husband's wealth. Although her income as a fashion editor put her in a high tax bracket, she had nowhere near the resources to pay for an expensive Irish property.

Before traveling to Ireland, Paquette had spent three days in France. Asked to backtrack on Paquette, Interpol reported that she'd received one telephone call at her Paris hotel from a number listed under the name of a Georges Bruneau. A records search revealed Bruneau to be a French citizen with a birth date exactly one year, one month, and one day different from that of George Spalding. Further investigation showed Bruneau's identity papers to be forged.

Spalding had made the classic blunder of

adopting an alias but keeping his given name and using a slightly different, but easily remembered, birth date. He had lived safely for years in Canada under his true given name and his wife's surname, but that was only because no one had been looking for him.

A quick visit by Interpol agents to Bruneau's residence, a furnished apartment in a working-class Paris neighborhood, showed that he'd moved out the day after Paquette left for Dublin.

A check of train and airline reservations confirmed Bruneau had traveled from Paris to London by rail and then flown from Gatwick Airport to Dublin, arriving the day before Joséphine Paquette had closed on the seaside house. Acting on an Interpol priority fugitive alert for Spalding, the Irish national police service, Garda Síochána — the guardians of the peace — started looking for Bruneau, and at the request of Canadian officials, they placed Paquette under surveillance.

Sara had been brought up to speed by a telephone call from Hugh Fitzmaurice, the Garda detective supervising the case. From Fitzmaurice she learned Paquette was in Dublin on a working holiday and writing a cover story for her magazine about Canadians living in Ireland. Spalding had not yet surfaced, nor had he made any attempt to contact Paquette.

Sara shut down the computer and stared out the window. Until last week she'd kept her speculations about Carrier to herself. But with Spalding now within range she'd bypassed her boss, who was known to be Carrier's friend, and taken the information directly to the vice chief of staff, General Henry Powhatan Clarke, a man she trusted and admired.

Clarke had raised an eyebrow when Sara brought up the possible involvement of Colonel Thomas Loring Carrier, USA, Retired, in Spalding's gemstone-smuggling ring.

"You do know that Tom Carrier is highly regarded by many ranking officers and senior administration officials, don't you?" Clarke asked.

"Yes, sir," Sara answered. She knew Clarke to be a tough, no-nonsense officer who didn't appreciate subordinates who wasted his time, tried to curry favor, or went outside the chain of command as she was now doing. Clarke glared at her for a long moment.

"Sir?" Sara asked, trying to evoke a response.

"All you have here is speculation about Carrier," Clarke said, tapping the report Sara had presented to him. On his uniform jacket he wore a Good Conduct Ribbon, awarded only to enlisted personnel. He'd earned it, along with a number of medals for valor, as an infantry sergeant in Vietnam before winning an appointment to West Point.

"Except for the forged signatures, that's true, sir," Sara said, "which is why I thought it best to ask for your guidance and direction in the matter."

"Who else knows about this allegation?" Clarke asked.

"No one, sir. But if the Irish authorities find, detain, and interrogate Specialist Spalding, that could quickly change, unless we have someone there to manage it properly."

Clarke's eyes narrowed. "Are you suggesting we try to find Specialist Spalding and muzzle him about Carrier before the Irish pick him up?"

"No, sir. I'm not. If Carrier is guilty, he should be held accountable, one way or another."

"In spite of the consequences that could befall you if you're correct?"

"Yes, sir."

"And if you're wrong about the colonel?"

"Then we'll still have brought to justice a wartime deserter and thief who smuggled black-market gems in the body bags of soldiers who died in service to their country."

Clarke turned in his chair and stared out the window. "Do you have a plan?"

"I propose that you place me on special duty and send me to Ireland to aid in the capture of Specialist Spalding."

Clarke turned in his chair quickly to face her. "Once you have him in custody, what will you do then?"

"Gather the pertinent facts, inform you, and await your orders, sir."

"What if I ordered you right now to cease all inquires into Carrier?"

Sara stared into the black hole she'd dug for herself and decided to speak frankly. "I would respectfully disagree with your decision, sir, and do as you request."

Clarke shook his head. "You're one gutsy officer, Colonel, I'll give you that. I have half a mind to send you packing with orders never to come to me again outside the chain of command."

Sara snapped to attention. "Sir."

"However, in this case, I believe you've exercised good judgment. You'll receive orders in the morning attaching you to my office for a top-secret courier assignment. You will go to Ireland, find Specialist Spalding, and take him into custody. I'll have my aide deliver the necessary diplomatic credentials, special orders, and travel authorization to you at your quarters."

"Thank you, sir. How much time do I have?"

"One week. If this plan of yours goes sour, Colonel, be prepared to wear those silver oak leaves on your collar until the day you retire."

"I understand, General."

"Report only to me."

"Yes, sir. Will you give General Thatcher a pretext for my absence?"

"He'll be told only that you've been placed on detached duty to my office. That should suffice."

The memory of her meeting with General Clarke faded from Sara's thoughts as she looked out the window at the star-filled night sky. Would finding Spalding and nailing Carrier amount to anything more than an exercise in futility? General Clarke had given her no guarantee that he would take any action against Carrier if she came through with the evidence. If he told her to hush it up for the good of the service, would her conscience allow her to do so?

She bit her lip and toyed with her West Point class ring, a nervous habit she'd yet to break completely. For the first time in history a woman graduate of the U.S. Military Academy had recently been promoted to the rank of brigadier general. Sara had long hoped to reach that rank herself, perhaps go even further. Now she wondered if she'd put herself on a path that would bury her in a career-ending, paper-pushing job with no chance for advancement.

She shut down the laptop and stared into the night. There was still no sign of Kerney. She wanted him to come home so she could tell him everything, knowing she could tell him nothing. Frustrated, she left the study, grabbed her travel case from the living room couch, and carried it to the bedroom, trying hard to clear her head.

In the walk-in closet she picked out a few of her more classy-looking skirts, slacks, and dresses to pack for her trip. If she was going to blend in with the crowd Paquette was writing about, she needed to look the part of a well-heeled American on holiday.

She folded and packed the clothes, her mind racing with visions of Kerney stranded on some lonely back road or, worse yet, mangled in some horrible traffic accident. She huffed with anger at the thought of him with another woman. It seemed no matter what passed through her mind tonight, it all felt gloomy or disastrous.

Kerney entered the canyon that led to his house, saw that the exterior lights under the portal were on, and didn't know what to make of it. Either he was being burglarized or an unknown person had decided to take up residence in his absence. He killed the truck headlights, popped open the glove box, grabbed his off-duty handgun, stuck it in his waistband, and glanced at the useless cell phone. A few miles outside Virden the battery had stopped functioning and wouldn't hold a charge.

He left the truck at the top of the hill just out of sight of his house and moved toward his police cruiser in a crouch, scanning the living room windows for any sign of activity. He cleared the inside of the sedan parked next to his unit before popping the trunk and removing his department-issued shotgun. With his eyes fixed on the house he quietly unlocked the door to his unit, dropped down for cover, put the key in the ignition, called dispatch, and reported a possible burglary in progress at his location.

"That's your wife, Chief," the dispatcher said, repressing a laugh. "She's been trying to reach you to let you know she's home."

"You're sure of that?" Kerney asked.

"Ten-four, Chief. I took the call from Colonel Brannon myself."

Kerney thanked the dispatcher, locked the shotgun and sidearm in his unit, and took a closer look inside the sedan. On the backseat was Patrick's dog-eared copy of *Pablito the Pony.* Inside the house he found Sara in the master bath, dressed in her nightie, brushing her teeth.

"Where have you been?" she asked, her mouth full of toothpaste. She rinsed out and gave him a steely-eyed, exasperated look. "I've been trying to call you for hours."

"My cell phone gave out," Kerney replied, "and I had a late start coming home."

Sara shook her head. "Well, if you weren't so obsessively punctual all the time, I never would have worried about you."

"You were worried about me?" Kerney asked, stroking her shoulder.

"More than I'd like to admit," Sara said as she wrapped her arms around Kerney and gave him a kiss. "Did you have fun?"

Kerney nodded. "The world of film-making is zany but highly entertaining. What brings you home so unexpectedly?"

"I'm off in the morning on a special assignment. Patrick is yours for the duration."

Kerney's expression turned slightly befuddled. "I don't have a sitter. I'm not prepared for this."

Sara smiled sweetly. "There really isn't an alternative, so you'll have to work it out."

"How long will you be gone?"

"A week," Sara replied. "But since I'll be starting leave so soon after I get back, Patrick might as well stay with you until then."

"You could have given me some warning," Kerney said, sounding a bit apprehensive.

Sara slipped past him into the bedroom. "I tried. I called here and called your office Thursday night and again on Friday morning, and I couldn't get through to you on your cell phone over the weekend to leave a message because the calls kept getting dropped."

"Cell phone reception in the Bootheel seems to be spotty at best. The film crew were all annoyed about it."

"Or maybe you had the phone turned off for some reason you'd rather not tell me about."

"What's that supposed to mean?"

Sara shrugged and set the alarm clock. "Nothing. Chalk it up to my overactive imagination. I'm just glad you're home and safe. I was worried about you."

"What kind of special assignment are you on?" Kerney asked.

"I can't tell you."

"Is it dangerous?"

"Not really. It's more along the lines of challenging." She fluffed her pillow, pulled back the duvet, and climbed into bed. "I'm up and out of here in five hours. Patrick will need his breakfast. He's recently become fond of blueberry pancakes."

"Blueberry pancakes," Kerney repeated as he leaned down and gave Sara a kiss. "Every day?"

Sara shook her head and yawned. "Vary the menu, but no fast food."

"Yes, ma'am."

Kerney gave her another kiss, turned out the bedroom lights, closed the door, and tiptoed into Patrick's room.

His son slept soundly with the blanket kicked down below his knees and his stuffed pony snug under an arm.

He pulled the blanket up to Patrick's chest and whispered, "I guess we'll have to learn how to bach it for a while, sport."

Sara woke at five in the morning to find Kerney's side of the bed empty. As she moisturized her face, put on a touch of eye shadow, and dressed, she could hear him rattling around in the kitchen. She made the bed, checked her travel bag, and joined him.

"There are no blueberries in the house," Kerney said with an apologetic smile. He handed her a mug of coffee and went back to mixing batter in a bowl. "Patrick will have to settle for apple pancakes."

Sara held the warm mug in her hands and took a sip. "That will do nicely."

"Will you be able to stay in touch?"

"I'll try." She looked out the French doors that led to the pergola-covered patio. Impending daybreak brightened a cloudless sky and in the gathering light the sweep of mountains behind Santa Fe slowly unveiled. Coming to the ranch always filled Sara with contentment. If she blew it on the Spalding case and was forced to take early retirement, at least she'd be able to live in a magical place with her family on a full-time basis.

The thought of having another child had been on her mind lately, and with her biological clock ticking it would be best to do it within the next year or two. She'd planned to raise the subject with Kerney after his retirement, but maybe she wouldn't have to wait that long if the Spalding affair blew up in her face. Still, she found no comfort in the notion that her career might end before she achieved her professional goals.

"You're very quiet this morning," Kerney said, as he searched her face with his extraordinarily blue eyes. "Are the wheels turning?"

Sara sighed and smiled. "I'm having a hard time getting motivated for the day ahead. Have you thought about who can watch over Patrick?"

Kerney shook his head. "I'll take him to work with me and call around to day-care and preschool centers. Can you tell me where you're going?"

Sara reached out and squeezed Kerney's hand. "Don't worry, I won't be in a war zone or anywhere near one."

She put her coffee cup in the sink, got her luggage from the bedroom, and went to check on Patrick. He was just waking as she knelt at the side of his bed and told him once again that he'd be staying with Daddy for a while.

Sounding a tiny bit anxious, Patrick asked how long she'd be away. Sara spread her fingers wide and asked him to count with her to fourteen.

"That's a lot," Patrick said when they'd finished, looking none too happy.

Sara rubbed his head and kissed his cheek. "The time will go fast and before you know it, I'll be home. Daddy's making pancakes for you. If you stop acting like such a sleepyhead, you can go see the horses after breakfast."

Patrick's worried look vanished as he hopped out of bed and made a beeline for the kitchen.

Minutes later Sara drove away in the golden early-morning sunlight. In the canyon a small antelope herd browsed on sage near a shallow arroyo. A motionless buck, clearly identifiable by his lyre-shaped horns, watched as she drew near and then bounded away in alarm, causing the herd to bolt up a narrow draw. The sight of the animals in full flight, white rumps flashing above their long slender legs, was lovely to behold.

She headed for the highway with child-hood memories of growing up on a Montana sheep ranch dancing in her head, thinking how wonderful it would be to raise her son in the country, never again live thousands of miles away from Kerney, and have a somewhat normal life.

By the time she reached the highway she was quarreling with herself. Should she keep to the path she'd chosen so many years ago? Or was it time to explore new possibilities, no matter what happened in Ireland? The questions remained unanswered long after her flight had passed over the mountains east of Albuquerque.

During her layover in Chicago, Sara called Kerney at his office for an update on how the child-care arrangements for Patrick were going.

"So far I've talked to five preschool directors," Kerney replied, "and they don't have any openings. I may have to settle for finding a sitter."

"Don't give up that easily," Sara said. "What's Patrick doing?"

"When he's not using my office as a playpen, he's busy charming my office staff. Right now one of the secretaries is reading *Pablito the Pony* to him."

Sara laughed. "It sounds like you have everything under control."

"Barely."

"Don't grumble, Kerney. You can do this. E-mail me tonight."

Sara worked and catnapped on the flight to Dublin. Fitzmaurice, the Garda detective, had faxed her some preliminary information on the house Paquette had bought with Spalding's funds. It was a protected structure, the Irish term for a building with historic significance, and as such could not be altered without permission by a local government planning commission. The house was located in a suburb of Dublin known as Dún Laoghaire. Fitzmaurice had thoughtfully circled the name of the town and scratched a note to her, saying that the name of the town was pronounced "Dun Leary." Included in the material he'd faxed was some general information about estate agent fees, stamp taxes on purchased property, and registry requirements.

From her window seat she watched the coastline of Ireland appear in the early-morning glare of the rising sun. Soon the plane was flying over rocky cliffs, wind-swept mountains, and stretches of farmland that rolled down to rivers and lakes. On the approach to the Dublin Airport the plane turned and banked over the Irish Sea, revealing the busy harbor filled with ships. The city spread out along the coast, cut by the River Liffey and buffered by green inland hills.

Sara had been to Ireland once before, on her honeymoon with Kerney. But they'd flown into Shannon and spent all their time in Connemara on the rugged western shore of the Atlantic Ocean, so Dublin was new to her. Against the backdrop of the bay and the hills the city looked intriguing, with its magnificent old buildings, beautiful squares, and stunning coastline.

Her diplomatic passport in hand, Sara quickly cleared customs and was met by Hugh Fitzmaurice, the Garda detective who was heading up the hunt for George Spalding. A middle-aged man with a full head of raven-black hair, blue eyes, and a long, broad nose, Fitzmaurice greeted her with an easy smile and hearty handshake.

"Welcome to the Republic of Ireland, Colonel," he said. "Is this your first visit?"

"It is to Dublin," Sara replied. "But I've spent some time in Connemara."

" 'Tis beautiful there, no doubt. Shall we stop at your hotel first or go straight to my office?"

"Why don't you brief me on the way to the hotel?"

Fitzmaurice nodded. "As you wish."

As he drove toward the city in the slow-moving traffic, Fitzmaurice filled her in on the status of the investigation. Garda were shadowing Joséphine Paquette everywhere she went, and the officers were keeping their eyes open for Spalding. Each person Paquette met, interviewed, or socialized with was being carefully checked for a link to Spalding. Her phone calls were being traced, her mail intercepted, and her credit card transactions monitored.

"We know from the French that Spalding didn't alter his appearance," Fitzmaurice added, "so we've shown his photograph around at banks, brokerage firms, area hotels, and guesthouses. He's not been seen."

"I've studied the Interpol file," Sara said. "He's cautious, but he has made some mistakes. Keeping his given name and using a slightly altered birth date for his new identity was a misstep. Making a phone call to Paquette from his Paris apartment was another slipup. I think he's eager to come out of hiding and may have discarded the Bruneau alias and taken on a new identity."

Stuck behind a lorry on a busy street,

Fitzmaurice sounded the car horn. "Perhaps it's time to bring Paquette in and have a go at her."

"Not yet," Sara said. "It could alert Spalding that we're hunting him. Is there anything going on with Paquette that looks promising?"

"Tomorrow she's to meet a builder at the house she bought with Spalding's money. The estate agent who sold her the property told us she wants to refurbish it while it's still vacant."

"Would she do that without consulting Spalding?" Sara asked.

Fitzmaurice eased around the lorry. "If she did consult him, it happened before we started our surveillance."

They were approaching the heart of the city along a wide boulevard jammed with traffic, headed toward a bridge that crossed a river. People hurried along the sidewalks past old storefront buildings, giving the street scene a vibrant air.

"Let's pay a visit to the builder after Paquette meets him," Sara said.

Fitzmaurice nodded. "And do you have any plans for today?"

"I'd like to review your case file and get an up-close look at Paquette."

"The file is waiting for you at my office,"

Fitzmaurice said as they crossed the bridge. He turned onto the quay and parked in front of Sara's hotel, a four-story Victorian building that looked out on the river.

"Would it be an imposition to have it dropped off at my room?"

Wondering if Brannon had some reason to avoid going to his office, Fitzmaurice gave her a questioning look, which she answered only with a smile.

"Not at all," he said. "You'll have it within the hour. Tonight Paquette is scheduled to attend an award ceremony for a Canadian writer. I've secured tickets for both of us."

"Excellent," Sara asked.

"Do you need help with your bags?"

"I can manage, thank you."

After Fitzmaurice drove away, Sara checked in at the reception desk, where she was greeted by a pleasant young man who told her all about the hotel's restaurant, spa center, and pub before handing her the room key. The room had a view of the River Liffey and was quite spacious, with a high ceiling capped by ornate cornices. Furnished with an overstuffed easy chair, small dining table, desk, a double bed, and a large armoire that hid a television, it had framed landscape prints on the walls and beige window drapes.

Sara unpacked, took a shower, and had just finished dressing when a Garda officer arrived with the police files. She sat on the bed, propped against the pillows with her legs crossed, and read the paperwork, until her body demanded physical activity and her head required her to stop thinking. She grabbed a tourist guide from the writing desk that had a map of the city center with points of interest highlighted and left for a walk.

Out on the street she strolled briskly to the O'Connell Bridge and turned to find herself in front of Trinity College, a wonderful campus that seemed both restrained and grand. Unwilling to stop in fear she'd become distracted for the rest of the day, she hurried on to Grafton Street, a pedestrian walkway filled with high-end shops, pubs, and milling tourists serenaded by street musicians playing fiddles, whistles, pipes, and guitars.

By the time she reached St. Stephen's Green, Sara was completely entranced. A beautiful park surrounded by stately buildings, the green was as manicured and inviting as any she'd known.

She circled the green and spotted the

hotel where Joséphine Paquette was staying. It was a truly elegant building, with a fancy ironwork entrance bracketed by two bronze statues of women holding what appeared to be torches above their heads.

Reluctantly, she retraced her way toward her hotel, feeling clearheaded and invigorated, thinking how wonderful it would be to come to Dublin on a holiday with Kerney and Patrick and spend time together seeing all that the city had to offer. In her room she checked for an e-mail message from Kerney and found an upbeat note from him, reporting that Patrick had been enrolled in a highly recommended preschool they'd visited over the noon hour. He would start in the morning.

With a smile on her face Sara went back to work and spent the rest of the morning combing through the various reports, trying to find anything that would get her closer to George Spalding.

In the afternoon Sara took a short nap, finished working on her notes, and walked to the Canadian embassy on St. Stephen's Green, where she presented her diplomatic credentials to a Royal Canadian Mounted Police liaison officer, laid out the facts of the case, and asked for a full and immediate investigation to be mounted in Toronto regarding Joséphine Paquette's current personal and financial status.

That evening Hugh Fitzmaurice, wearing a fresh suit, picked Sara up at her hotel and drove her a short distance through busy traffic to University College, where the award ceremony and reception for the Irish-Canadian writer was to be held in O'Reilly Hall.

"Did you glean anything from the file?" he asked as he braked for a car that cut in front of him on the motorway.

"This afternoon I telephoned estate agents and pretended to be looking for an Irish retreat in Dún Laoghaire. It's not often that seaside villas in the town come on the market, and they sell quickly at premium prices. I can't believe Paquette simply waltzed into Dún Laoghaire and snapped up a desirable house in a prestigious location by chance."

"The estate agent assured us that is exactly what happened."

"I don't believe it," Sara said, "no more than I believe Paquette would renovate the house without Spalding's approval and permission."

"You're suggesting Spalding made advance arrangements with the estate agent."

Sara nodded. "Of one sort or another. I'll know more in the morning. I've asked the French to search for any travel bookings Spalding may have made under his alias prior to Paquette's arrival in Paris."

Fitzmaurice gave her an appraising glance. "If he came to Ireland at some earlier time, your theory may well prove to be correct. What put you onto the idea?"

"For over thirty years Spalding lived his life as an established, well-regarded, wealthy man," Sara replied. "Surely he would want to replicate that lifestyle under a new identity."

"Why did he choose Dún Laoghaire?"

"The answer to that question was buried in the case material the Canadian authorities sent you. Among Spalding's property the Canadian Customs and Revenue Agency seized for tax evasion were two boats, an offshore sport-fishing boat and a sailboat."

Fitzmaurice's eyes widened. "Dún Laoghaire is a boat lover's paradise."

"Exactly. Spalding wants to live on the seashore in an English-speaking country where he can fit in, indulge in his hobbies, and travel around Europe as he wishes."

"Are you quite sure you're not an FBI

profiler?" Fitzmaurice asked as he pulled into a campus parking lot.

"Quite sure," Sara answered with a laugh.

They'd arrived early, Fitzmaurice explained as they crossed the campus to O'Reilly Hall, so they could spot Paquette and sit as close to her as possible. The university consisted of modern buildings surrounded by well-kept grounds with walking paths that led to classrooms, faculty office buildings, and common areas. At an ornamental lake near O'Reilly Hall a small group of well-dressed people had already started to gather, but Paquette was not among them.

The doors to the hall were opened for the audience, and Sara and Fitzmaurice took programs from ushers as they walked in. The writer being honored, Brendan Coughlan, was an Irish emigrant to Canada who'd written a number of contemporary novels set in Nova Scotia. According to the program notes Coughlan had been born and raised in County Clare, and his novels captured the essence of Irish characters living in a foreign land yet still haunted by the bloody history and partition of their native country.

Paquette showed up accompanied by an

older man and a middle-aged couple. In contrast to their quite fashionable clothes Paquette wore a designer dress that broke at her knees and had a revealing bodice. She wore diamond stud earrings and her hair was done up in a French twist that accentuated her long neck. She had an oval, pretty face with high cheekbones, and a petite figure with a tiny waist.

"She enjoys being flamboyant, doesn't she?" Sara said.

"It is attire perhaps more appropriate to a gala opening at the Abbey Theater," Fitzmaurice replied.

With Fitzmaurice at her side Sara followed Paquette into the hall, listening in on her conversation, which consisted of small talk about the beautifully decorated Georgian terrace house she'd visited while interviewing a Canadian celebrity, and the wonderful, perfectly presented dinner she'd been served at a restaurant owned by a young chef who immigrated to Dublin from Vancouver.

They sat behind Paquette in the packed auditorium and eavesdropped as she described to her companions her recent meeting with the evening's honoree, Brendan Coughlan. Paquette babbled on until the lights dimmed and the event began.

After some short introductory remarks by a faculty member, who praised Coughlan as a unique voice in Irish literature, the writer took center stage to rousing applause and spoke at length about his childhood and youth in County Clare, and how he'd found the magic and beauty of Ireland mirrored along the rocky coast of Nova Scotia, where the pure, deep sounds of Eire could still be heard among the many voices, memories, and dreams that had blossomed there.

He finished with a reading from his most recent work, and Sara decided she wouldn't leave Dublin without at least one of his novels in her bag.

When the award was presented to Coughlan, the audience gave him a standing ovation, which included thunderous clapping by Fitzmaurice. As people filed out of the hall, Sara lost sight of Paquette.

"Don't worry," Fitzmaurice said, "I've a man on her. She's off to a private reception for Coughlan, along with all the other glitterati who were here tonight."

"He's a brand-new writer to me," Sara said.

"You've not read him?"

Sara shook her head.

"Well, you should," Fitzmaurice said. "I

mean no offense, but you Yanks spend far too much time beating your own literary drums, and not enough time listening to other voices."

"None taken," Sara replied. "He's on my to-be-read list effective immediately. I think you would have come here on your own tonight if I hadn't asked to have a look at Paquette."

Fitzmaurice grinned. "You've caught me fair and square. I'm a big fan of Coughlan's work."

On the ride back to her hotel Sara's enthusiasm for Dublin waned a bit. The late-night traffic was awful, and some of the neighborhoods they passed through looked no more inviting than the typical urban sprawl found in any major city.

Fitzmaurice parked at the curb in front of the hotel, and through the open car window Sara watched a group of talkative young people hurry down the quay toward a pub where a laughing, cigarette-smoking crowd stood on the sidewalk in front of the entrance.

"I bet you're bored stiff with this assignment," she said.

Fitzmaurice shifted in his seat and looked at her. "It's been less than exciting, although I have enjoyed knocking around a bit with high society."

"Can you arrange to get me into Paquette's hotel room?"

"With or without the blessings of the court?" Fitzmaurice asked.

"Without, preferably."

"It's been on my mind to ask you," Fitzmaurice replied slowly, "why all the bloody secrecy about a Yank soldier who made a fortune smuggling and then went missing from Vietnam so many years ago?"

"Spalding's not the only target of the investigation," Sara answered.

"And would that target be some lofty member of your government?"

"You have a suspicious nature, Mr. Fitzmaurice."

" 'Tis because of you that I've taken to speculating. What would possibly bring a Yank colonel to our shores with a diplomatic passport to hunt down a lowly soldier? Am I now part of some clandestine military operation?"

Sara smiled. "You're making far too much of it. I would rather move cautiously until we have more of a fix on Spalding."

"Yes, you more or less said that before. But quite possibly, talking to Paquette could bring him into our sights."

Sara shook her head. "She could easily

deny doing anything more than having bought a seaside villa with Spalding's money. Once we pull her in for questioning, we will have played our hand."

"An offer of immunity might loosen her tongue."

"Let's wait," Sara said. "Can you get me into her hotel room?"

"Most likely I can," Fitzmaurice answered as he started the engine. "I'll let you know in the morning."

Sara opened the car door. "You're a prince, Detective Fitzmaurice."

"Not quite," Fitzmaurice said with a chuckle. "On my mother's side of the family we were never more than landless, impoverished earls."

On her second day in Dublin, Sara rose to a cheerless early morning, which didn't depress her in the least. Through her hotel-room window a low sky pressed down upon the city, and the still-dark buildings across the Liffey were soft shapes in the mist that had rolled in from the bay. Along the quay only a few people were out. Several university students toted book bags on their way to Trinity College, an early-rising couple were consulting their tourist guides, and a middle-aged man in a pinstriped suit hurried by with briefcase in hand.

Sara showered, dressed, and went outside, where a clearing sky and Detective Fitzmaurice greeted her. He nodded, reached into a pocket, and handed her a slip of paper with a number written on it.

"That's Paquette's room number," he said. "The housekeeper will leave the door unlatched exactly at eight-forty. You'll have ten minutes, and ten minutes only."

Sara smiled her thanks. "Are you sure Paquette will be gone?"

"According to her driver she'll be at a photography session with a Canadian model who's all the rage in Paris this year. One of my lads will be following along."

"Perfect," Sara said. "What about hotel security?"

Fitzmaurice smiled. "They'll be busy with more important matters."

"When does Paquette meet with the builder?"

"Late in the afternoon. We have time for breakfast. There's a small café on a side street next to the post office where the 1916 Easter Rising took place. They serve great bangers and eggs."

"Wasn't it shelled by a gunboat on the river and virtually destroyed?"

"Indeed it was. Have you been reading a

guidebook about our fair city?"

"I confess I have," Sara said with a smile.

Over breakfast Sara learned that Fitzmaurice was married to a school-teacher named Edna and that the couple had two sons, Brian, who lived close by and worked as a programmer for a software company, and their younger boy, Sean, who lived at home and was studying literature at Trinity College on a scholarship.

"He was at the award ceremony last night," Fitzmaurice said, "but I asked him to give me a bit of a wide berth, as I was working."

"You could have at least pointed him out," Sara said as she cut into one of the bangers. "Did he get his love of books from you?"

"And his mother," Fitzmaurice said with a nod. "She was quite interested to learn from Sean that I'd squired an attractive woman to the event under the guise of official business."

"You didn't tell her who you'd be with?"

Fitzmaurice laughed. "Of course I did, but Sean rightly made you out to be a stunning American beauty."

"Give him my thanks for the compliment."

"I will," Fitzmaurice said. "From the

ring on your finger I take it you're married."

"To a policeman, of all things," Sara replied.

Fitzmaurice slapped his knee. "Married to a peeler, are you? That's grand."

"And he's a third-generation Irish-American."

"Even grander," Fitzmaurice said, his smile widening.

For a while they talked about their lives and families and by the time the meal had ended, Sara found herself feeling that she'd made a new friend. On the way to the car Fitzmaurice, who'd adamantly refused to let her pay for breakfast, announced that he was so taken by her descriptions of the Southwest that he'd already decided to start planning a holiday to New Mexico.

He dropped her off a block from Paquette's hotel, and Sara timed her entrance to give herself three minutes' leeway to find her way to the room. She crossed the richly appointed lobby and took the elevator to the third floor, where she found the hallway empty expect for a housekeeping cart, and the door to Paquette's room ajar.

It was far more elaborate than Sara's room, although not much bigger, with windows looking onto St. Stephen's Green, a thick carpet with a subtle Oriental design, and embossed fleur-de-lis wallpaper. By the window was a chaise longue next to a rosewood table with a reading lamp. An arched camelback sofa faced a huge armoire that opened to reveal a television, DVD player, and compact stereo. Between the oversized bed and the chaise longue stood a small round dining table with fluted legs and two matching chairs. Against the wall opposite the windows, under a Chippendale-style mirror, was a writing desk with satinwood inlays and finely tapered legs.

Paquette was a very tidy person. Her shoes were in an orderly row on the closet floor under garments arranged neatly on hangers, her toiletries and makeup had been put away in the bathroom cabinet, the duvet on the bed had been pulled up and smoothed out, and the papers on the writing desk were organized in stacks.

Sara quickly searched through drawers, clothing, and luggage, putting everything back in its proper place, before turning her attention to the writing desk. She checked the wastebasket and then fanned through the paperwork, which was all work related, before powering up Paquette's laptop. It was password protected, so Sara shut it down, closed the lid, and pushed it back to its original position. The edge of a piece of hotel stationery slipped into view. She pulled it out. On it was a string of numbers.

Sara wrote the numbers down, checked her watch, and saw that she was out of time. Back at the car she gave the paper to Fitzmaurice.

"It's definitely a telephone number," he said.

"How quickly can you check it out?"

"Promptly. The government agency that regulates communications is just a short distance away, and they have access to all landline and mobile telephone records."

"Good. While you're doing that, I'll go back to my hotel and call the French. They should have researched Spalding's previous travel bookings by now."

Fitzmaurice waved the notepaper at her before putting it his shirt pocket. "You may be onto something here."

"Let's hope so," Sara replied, flashing a smile.

An hour later Fitzmaurice sat with Sara in her hotel's restaurant and filled her in.

"The telephone number belongs to a George McGuire," he said with a knowing shake of his head. "It's for a mobile phone bought here in Dublin under a prepay plan that was purchased three months ago. Records show that a number of text messages from that number were sent to Paquette's computer, several as recent as two days ago, but no voice calls have been made."

"When did he open the account?" Sara asked as the waitress brought coffee for her and hot tea for Fitzmaurice.

Fitzmaurice read off the date from his notes. "Of course, he used a fictitious mailing address on the mobile-phone contract and paid in cash."

Sara grinned. "That date coincides with the information I got from the French authorities. According to Spalding's travel bookings he was in Ireland during that time, supposedly on holiday, and he stayed for six weeks. What will it take to get access to Paquette's e-mail account?"

Fitzmaurice added milk to his tea and stirred it. "A writ from an agreeable judge, which I think we can get by attesting that Paquette used illicitly gotten gains provided by a known fugitive to purchase property on his behalf. I have a detective on his way to the registrar of deeds and titles to pull the paperwork so we have the necessary documentation."

"When will you be able to secure the writ?"

"By day's end, I would hope." Fitzmaurice leaned back in his chair, crossed his legs, and smiled broadly. "But there's also another avenue we can pursue that may surely get your blood racing. If you're right about Spalding wanting to settle here permanently, free to come and go as he pleases, he might well have either started or completed the process to claim Irish citizenship by virtue of descent. To accomplish it the documents would need to be in perfect order, but it would be well within the realm of possibility for him to do it."

Sara leaned forward. "I'm all ears. Explain to me how it would work."

"Anyone born outside Ireland can qualify for citizenship by submitting proof that at least one grandparent was born in Ireland. It requires making an application and including all the necessary birth, marriage, and death certificates to support the claim. Once everything has been confirmed, the applicant is entered into the Irish Register of Foreign Births and is eligible to apply for an Irish passport."

"How can we find out about this?" Sara asked.

"Foreign-birth citizenship applications must be made through an Irish embassy or consulate in the country where the person resides," Fitzmaurice said. "Inquiries have already been made to our French and English embassies, asking if a George McGuire has applied, and we're querying all the others through the Department of Foreign Affairs. But remember, Spalding may not have started the process. He could be still at the point of trying to find someone willing to sell, for an agreeable sum of money, a dead grandparent's name he could use, or paying an intermediary to do it for him."

Sara smiled at an elderly couple who nodded a greeting as they trailed the hostess to an empty table. "Now that we know about Spalding's earlier visit, shouldn't we do a search of birth-certificate requests made during the time he was here?"

Fitzmaurice finished his tea. "Yes, of course, but it may be a while before we learn anything. Requests for birth certificates can be made either through the Registrar General's Office here in the city, or directly to one of the county offices."

Sara motioned for the waitress to bring the check. "How many counties are there in Ireland?"

"Twenty-six in the Republic and six in Northern Ireland. But the records of Irish ancestors born in the north before 1922 are kept by the Registrar General's Office, which is nearby. We'll make a quick stop on our way to Dún Laoghaire and ask them to get cracking on it."

Sara signed the charge slip and stood. "Although a hint of a brogue is in your voice, sometimes you sound more British than Irish."

"Do I, now?" Fitzmaurice said with a chuckle as he walked Sara through the lobby. "I suppose it's because I come from one of those Anglo-Irish families that embraced Catholicism and drew Oliver Cromwell's ire. In his zeal to transform Ireland into a Protestant colony of the British Empire, he either reduced us to poverty or drove us into exile. It's taken us a few hundred years to work our way back into polite society."

Sara laughed. "As far as I'm concerned, you're excellent company to keep, Hugh Fitzmaurice."

"As are you, Colonel Sara Brannon, although it pains me to know so little of your real reason for being here."

"I'll try not to cause you any trouble," Sara said as she slid into Fitzmaurice's unmarked Garda car.

Chapter Eight

The short drive from Dublin to Dún Laoghaire reminded Sara of the sprawl of large American cities where suburban towns and once rural villages, now surrounded by commercial and residential development, had been absorbed and become virtually indistinguishable from one another.

Granted, there were differences between Dublin and the States: The architectural styles of the spreading residential subdivisions paid homage to a Georgian, Palladian, Victorian, and Irish cottage heritage, and in many cases the houses were smaller and squeezed onto tiny lots. There were lovely old buildings scattered about in parkland meadows cut by cobblestone drives, and the new commercial buildings had a distinctly European minimalist flair. The Irish Sea, the coastal hills, and the remaining open space soothed the eye, but there was construction everywhere. Roads, subdivisions, shopping centers, and business parks were eating away at the edges of the intact village centers and gobbling up the land.

When Sara mentioned this to Fitz-maurice, he railed against the development, pointing out that the old family-run bakeries, fish-and-chips takeaways, butcher shops, grocery stores, and ice cream parlors were nigh on gone, swept aside by fast-food franchises, gimmicky tourist enterprises, and big-box shopping malls with huge car parks that catered to the relentless consumption of a nation gone mad with consumerism.

"The whole bloody Republic is being turned into an Irish theme park," he added with a huff.

Sara smiled sympathetically but said nothing. Fitzmaurice sounded just like Kerney complaining about the changes in Santa Fe and northern New Mexico. If the two men ever had a chance to meet, she thought they would hit it off immediately.

They arrived in Dún Laoghaire, which, according to Fitzmaurice, had been a sleepy village in the early nineteenth century until the railroad arrived and a harbor had been dredged to accommodate mail ships that crossed the Irish Sea to Holyhead in Wales. Now it was not only a popular day-trip destination for tourists staying in Dublin, but also home to the largest ferry crossing to and from the UK, a retreat for the wealthy who maintained vacation homes in the area, and a bedroom community for people who worked either in the city or in the resort towns that ran along the southeast coast.

The area promoted itself as Dublin's Riviera, compared itself to Naples, Italy, and had no industry other than tourism, which was offered up, as Fitzmaurice put it, to all those gullible people who came looking for the charm of Old Eire while turning a blind eye to the neighborhoods where the poor resided and street gangs roamed.

From the road the villa Paquette had bought looked like nothing more than a cottage painted a soft pastel blue. But from the end of the line of houses that followed the curve of the bay, Sara could see that it extended four stories down a cliff face to a rocky beach and a slipway where pleasure boats rocked gently against a pier. Terraced gardens of palm trees and brilliant flowers flowed down the cliff almost to the shore.

The view across Killiney Bay was stunning, with low hills and a distant mountain sheared off at the top standing on a headland under a gunmetal cloud bank.

"It's glorious," Sara said.

"Certainly a place where one could settle in and live comfortably," Fitzmaurice replied.

Sara laughed at Fitzmaurice's sarcasm. "Let's make sure Spalding doesn't get that chance."

The storefront office of the auctioneer and estate agent who'd handled the sale of the villa was closed. A note attached to the door said that the agent, a man named Liam Quinn, was off showing property and would be back in the afternoon.

Fitzmaurice tried Quinn's mobile telephone number, got no response, and left a brief voice message asking him to ring back when he returned to the office.

"While we're waiting for Quinn to call, let's ask around for Mr. Spalding at some of the hotels, guesthouses, and inns," he said.

Working from a tourist guide of area accommodations, they stopped at the few downtown hotels before widening their search to self-catering apartments, short-term rental units, and bed-and-breakfast establishments. Just as they were about to give up canvassing and head off for a quick lunch, the estate agent rang Fitzmaurice on his mobile and said he was on his way back to his office.

"Let's hope he has something to offer," Fitzmaurice said as he clipped the phone to his belt. "Otherwise we'll need at least two more days and many more officers to query every innkeeper and hotelier in the area."

"Have you met or spoken to Quinn before?" Sara asked.

Fitzmaurice shook his head. "No, I sent one of my detectives around to see him."

"So he doesn't know you're a peeler."

Fitzmaurice's eyes lit up. "Are you thinking we should present ourselves as prospective clients?"

Sara nodded. "Let's string him along and see where it leads."

"You're a gifted schemer, Lieutenant Colonel Brannon."

Sara laughed. "With a willing accomplice, Detective Inspector Fitzmaurice."

Fitzmaurice found a car park within easy walking distance of Quinn's storefront office and they passed along a street of two- and three-story stone buildings with brightly painted trim work that housed retail shops featuring Irish crystal, linens and woolens, posters and prints, Celtic jewelry and trinkets, and souvenir T-shirts and hats, all geared to the tourist trade.

Although the architecture and landscape

were different, the area reminded Sara of the shops on the Santa Fe Plaza, where the store clerks assumed all their customers were from out of town. Kerney and Fitzmaurice, strangers living two continents apart, were right to complain about theme-park mentality and crass consumerism. It was everywhere and it sucked.

Liam Quinn greeted them with a smile and a hearty handshake when they entered his office. In his mid-thirties, he had a ruddy complexion, red hair cut short and brushed forward, and a narrow nose that ended abruptly above thin lips. He wore a white shirt and striped tie, a light wool tweed sport coat, and dress slacks. The office was nicely furnished with an antique desk and an old-fashioned wooden chair on casters, a credenza with a desktop computer, printer, and fax machine on top, several comfortable easy chairs, and a round conference table with four matching straight-backed chairs. One wall featured flyers with photographs and descriptions of available properties. Hung on the opposite wall were several framed posters of area attractions.

They sat at the conference table, and Fitzmaurice, who had introduced Sara as his wife, took the lead.

"We've fallen in love with those Italian-style villas on Coast Road," he said. "Surely someone might be tempted to sell."

Quinn shook his head. "They rarely become available. I had a gentleman stop by earlier in the summer asking for the same inquiry to be made on his behalf, and it all came to naught."

"Yet a resident we spoke to said one had sold recently."

"Yes, to a client of mine," Quinn replied, looking quite pleased with himself.

"To the gentleman you mentioned?" Fitzmaurice queried.

"No, to a woman. She's hired a builder to refurbish it completely, once the planning council approves the architect's plans. It's a protected property, and nothing can be done until then. But I have other properties equally as charming you might wish to consider."

"But nothing on Coast Road?" Fitzmaurice asked.

"Sadly, no," Quinn said, with a shake of his head.

"That's too bad," Fitzmaurice said. "I suppose it's all a question of timing, isn't it?"

Quinn nodded in agreement. "The villa

came on the market unexpectedly and I had a ready buyer."

"A woman, you say?"

"Yes."

"Tell us about the gentleman who inquired about the villa earlier in the summer."

Quinn cocked his head and gave Fitzmaurice a sharp look. "What is this about?"

Fitzmaurice took out his Garda credentials, laid them on the table, and passed a photograph of George Spalding to Quinn. "Is this the gentleman in question?"

Quinn shifted his gaze from the photograph to Fitzmaurice and then to Sara.

"Please answer the question," Sara said.

"Yes."

"What name did he use?" Sara prodded.

"George McGuire."

Fitzmaurice plucked the photograph from Quinn's hand. "We know he purchased the property in Joséphine Paquette's name, yet you said his inquiries came to naught."

Quinn's ruddy complexion deepened. "There is nothing improper about purchasing property to benefit another person."

Fitzmaurice smiled as he slipped his

Garda credentials into his pocket. "It's just as you say, indeed. You've a keen sense of right and wrong, Liam. A very fine quality in an estate agent. But why did you lie to us?"

"I merely maintained a confidence. Mr. McGuire wished to preserve his anonymity by having the deed registered in Ms. Paquette's name. He wishes to move to Dún Laoghaire without drawing attention to himself. That is not so uncommon as you might think. Some of the wealthy have an obsession with privacy."

"Why didn't you tell the police about McGuire?" Sara asked.

Quinn tugged at the collar of his shirt. "It didn't seem to be of any consequence."

Fitzmaurice glanced at the framed photograph on Quinn's desk of a woman holding a chubby-cheeked infant. "Is that your family, Liam?"

Quinn nodded.

"It must be difficult to make your way as an auctioneer and estate agent and a family man running a business all on your own in such a competitive market. As I understand it, independents such as yourself constantly risk being either driven out of business or absorbed into the big national estate companies."

"It's been a very good spring and summer for sales," Quinn replied stiffly.

Fitzmaurice leaned forward across the table. "Made even more profitable for you by a sum of money in your pocket not reported to the taxman?"

Quinn stood up. "I resent that."

"Sit down, Mr. Quinn." Fitzmaurice waited a beat for Quinn to comply. "What if I were to tell you that McGuire is an international fugitive who used ill-gotten gains to buy the villa?"

"I know nothing about that."

"Of course not," Fitzmaurice said, staring hard at Quinn. "The thought never entered your mind that McGuire might be attempting to hide criminal assets."

"It is not my responsibility to determine the source of a client's wealth," Quinn replied sharply.

"I'm sure we can clear this up easily to everyone's satisfaction," Sara intervened with a smile. "Tell us about your dealings with Mr. McGuire."

Quinn's stormy expression cleared slightly. "He came to me three months ago asking about the villas. I'd just begun negotiations with an elderly gentleman who wished to sell his property by private treaty at the end of the summer rather than at auction. McGuire paid me a ten-thousand-euro commission in advance to secure the property."

"How did the money come to you?" Sara asked.

"He gave me a bank draft the very next day, along with written authorization to make an offer above the fixed price if necessary."

"Go on," Sara said.

"When the contracts were drawn up by the solicitor, Mr. McGuire returned, signed them, and paid the ten-percent deposit after renegotiating the closing date, which he asked to have put off because Ms. Paquette would be unavailable until a later time. Since it was a cash purchase without the need for a secured mortgage, the seller agreed."

"How did you keep in contact with McGuire?" Sara asked.

"I have his mobile number." Quinn stood, took an address book from a desk drawer, and read off the number, which didn't match with the one Sara had discovered in Paquette's hotel room.

"Where did he stay while he was here?" Sara asked.

"He stayed on his motor yacht at the marina," Quinn replied as he watched

Fitzmaurice dial his mobile phone. "Who are you calling?"

"A detective to come and take your written statement," Fitzmaurice replied, "which will then be carefully checked for truthfulness."

Outside Quinn's office Sara turned to Fitzmaurice. "Do you think he knew Spalding's money was dirty?"

"He probably suspected it, at the very least," Fitzmaurice replied, "as we have every reason to believe that Spalding bribed him to remain silent about certain particulars."

"Well, the one thing we know for certain is that Paquette agreed to Spalding's scheme long before she rendezvoused with him in Paris. What do you know about boating and motor yachts?"

"Except for a few nautical terms not a blessed thing," Fitzmaurice answered.

"Nor do I," Sara said as they walked toward the car park.

The Dún Laoghaire Marina, situated yards away from the ferry terminal to Wales and the rapid-transit rail station to Dublin, was a modern facility catering to all types of leisure boats, from small sailing dinghies to large yachts.

Sailboats and motorboats filled the marina, masts rising from the decks, sails furled, hulls gently knocking against the crisscross pattern of walkways where the boats were moored. In the bay a small regatta of boats in full sail cut through the waves past an old stone pier with a red-domed lighthouse and headed out to sea. In the distance the Holyhead ferry steamed toward Wales, smoke billowing from the stack. The ferry terminal adjacent to the marina was a stark contemporary structure with a circular upper story that seemed to have been deliberately designed to look like an airport conning tower. It matched perfectly with the steel-and-glass architecture of the nearby rail-station ticket office that spanned the tracks below.

At the marina office a young man named Bobby Doherty, who had the wind-burned face of a sailor and an anchor tattooed on a forearm, searched through recent berthing records.

"I remember him," Doherty said, as he flipped through papers. "He has a new Spanish-built Rodman Fifty-six, with twin Volvo engines and three cabins. He berthed here two or three times."

"A very expensive boat that is, then?" Fitzmaurice asked.

"It cost him half a million euros, if it cost him a penny," Doherty said.

"And you're sure this is the man," Fitzmaurice said, poking his finger at the photograph of George Spalding that he'd placed on the counter.

"Yes, Mr. McGuire," Doherty said, glancing at the photo. "He tied up on the Q berth, where we put the larger visiting boats."

"Did he sleep onboard his boat while he stayed here?" Sara asked.

"Of that I can't be sure," Doherty said as he handed the records to Fitzmaurice. "One of the night-watch crew could better answer that question."

Fitzmaurice scanned the papers and passed them to Sara. Spalding had berthed his boat, *Sapphire*, three times at the marina on dates that corresponded nicely with his recent travels to Ireland, and had paid in cash. They'd missed him by five days.

"Do you know for certain that Mr. McGuire owns the boat?" Sara asked.

Doherty shrugged. "He could have hired it. Many people do that when they come here on holiday."

"Who could tell us if it was a hired boat?" Fitzmaurice asked.

"Either the Registrars of Shipping or the Irish Sailing Association," Doherty said. "Both keep excellent records of ownership, and you may want to ask after Mr. McGuire at the National Yacht Club. On his first visit he asked me to direct him there."

"What time does the night watch start?" Fitzmaurice asked.

"Johnny Scanlan comes on duty at eighteen hundred hours," Doherty replied.

Fitzmaurice handed Doherty a business card. "Have him stand by for us at that time."

Doherty nodded. "Have we had a criminal in our midst?"

"It's a family emergency," Sara said. "How do we get to the yacht club from here?"

"Easily done," Doherty said, and he rattled off directions that took them directly toward the lighthouse with the red dome.

Fitzmaurice parked in front of the National Yacht Club. The entrance consisted of a six-panel double door with a semicircular pediment window above. It was enclosed by a wrought-iron fence and a gate bracketed by two tall, ornate light stanchions. In spite of the Georgian touches the building had the look of a low-slung French château. Two polished brass plaques on either side of the door announced that it was indeed the National Yacht Club and that the building had historical significance.

After Fitzmaurice showed his credentials at the reception desk, they explored the public rooms while waiting for a club official to come talk to them. In a large gallery comfortable chairs and couches were arranged to give a view of the bay through a series of tall windows. Oil paintings of sailing ships in hand-carved gilded frames adorned the walls. In the separate dining room the tables were set with crystal stemware and silver flatware. The adjacent bar was an inviting, intimate cove of dark paneling and polished mahogany. There were few people about, but as they returned to the front room, a smiling older man with a neatly trimmed gray beard and mustache, and wide-spaced brown eyes below a bald, round head approached, introduced himself as Diarmuid O'Gorman, the commodore of the club, and asked if he could be of assistance.

Fitzmaurice displayed his Garda credentials and showed O'Gorman Spalding's photograph. "We're trying to locate a Mr. George McGuire and we understand he may have visited the club early in the summer."

O'Gorman nodded. "Yes, I spoke with him myself. He was keenly interested in becoming a member. A very pleasant gentleman. Is he in some sort of difficulty?"

"Not at all," Fitzmaurice said. "A family matter requires his attention."

"I'm afraid I can't help you. He left with a membership application and a promise to return after he settled into a house in Dún Laoghaire. He said it might be some time before he would be ready to put himself forward for admission, and that he would be traveling until then."

"On his motor yacht?" Sara asked.

"Yes, but he's planning to purchase a racing dinghy, a sport we're particularly active in. We've hosted two world championships in recent years."

"Did he say where he might be going after he left Dún Laoghaire?" Sara asked.

"He mentioned wanting to complete the yachtmaster ocean training scheme."

"What is that, exactly?" Fitzmaurice asked.

"It certifies a skipper to operate a boat beyond coastal and offshore waters," O'Gorman replied. "The training must be offered by an approved ISA organization."

"The Irish Sailing Association?" Sara asked.

"Exactly," O'Gorman said. "They would be able to tell you where and when he completed the course, if indeed he has done so."

With directions from O'Gorman in hand they left the yacht club and found their way to the headquarters of the Irish Sailing Association. Housed in a mansion along a quiet street, the two-story brick building was surrounded by lush grounds, a wrought-iron fence, and a low ornamental hedge. Set back from the road and partially hidden by large shade trees, the mansion's entrance was topped by a neoclassical entablature supported by two Greek Revival columns.

Inside they spoke with Mary Kehoe, who managed the daily operations of the association. A pleasant-looking woman in her forties, Kehoe had a small, pointed chin, bluish-green eyes, hair that was as raven black as Fitzmaurice's, and a gangly figure.

"We're trying to locate a Mr. George McGuire to inform him of a family emergency," Fitzmaurice said as he settled into a chair in Kehoe's office. "He owns or has hired a motor yacht named *Sapphire* and may have had some recent dealing with your organization."

"Yes, of course, Mr. McGuire," Kehoe said, rising from her desk. "We've assisted him in a number of ways. Let me get his records."

When Kehoe left the office, Fitzmaurice flashed a big grin at Sara. "Are you starting to get the scent of our prey?"

"What if he's on the high seas and staying far away from land?" Sara asked.

Fitzmaurice grimaced. "Well, at least we won't have to waste our time canvassing every bloody hotel and inn from Dún Laoghaire to Wicklow."

Kehoe returned with a folder, sat at her desk, put on a pair of reading glasses, and slowly began to page through it. Fitzmaurice's eyes lit up as though he were a cat about to pounce, and for a moment Sara thought he was getting ready to rip the documents out of the woman's hands. Instead, he settled back and tried hard not to look impatient.

"We have his completed ISA membership application," Kehoe said, placing it carefully to one side and studying the next batch of forms. "Also his coastal and offshore certificates of yachtmaster training, both the shore-based and sea-based courses, his international pleasure-boat operator certificate, and his application for a certificate of identity and origin."

One by one Kehoe neatly arranged the papers to keep everything in order.

"Mr. McGuire owns the *Sapphire*, then?" Fitzmaurice asked.

"Indeed he does."

"What is a certificate of identity and origin?" Sara asked.

"It's used in conjunction with the ship's registry," Kehoe explained as she handed the paper to Sara, "to ensure yacht owners have free movement throughout the European Union. It may be helpful, especially if Mr. McGuire is at sea, as it contains his ship's radio call sign and his registered sail number."

Aside from what Kehoe had noted, the one-page form contained a trove of new information. It required Spalding, aka McGuire, to list his nationality, place and date of birth, passport number with the date and place of issue, and home address, along with specific details about his boat, right down to the builder, the model, the engine number, tonnage, the date and place of sale, and where the boat had been built.

According to the document McGuire

was an Irish national born in Boston who'd been issued his passport in Dublin over a year ago. He'd bought *Sapphire* from a dealer in Northern Ireland soon after that.

Sara gave the form to Fitzmaurice, who scanned it eagerly. "When did McGuire take his yachtmaster courses?" she asked.

Kehoe paged back through the documents. "He finished his coastal courses eleven months ago and his offshore training this past July."

"He lists a home address in Galway," Sara said.

"Yes," Kehoe replied, "but the information is outdated."

"How do you know that?" Fitzmaurice asked.

"Mr. McGuire came by several weeks ago to let me know he would be moving to Dún Laoghaire in the next few months and until then would be living on his motor yacht."

"Do you recall anything else he said to you?" Sara asked.

Kehoe nodded. "He was planning a voyage around Ireland after he completed his shore-based yachtmaster ocean-training scheme."

"Where would he take such training?" Fitzmaurice asked.

"There are any number of certified training centres," Kehoe said, looking at Fitzmaurice over her reading glasses. "Of the commercial centres the closest course offering is in Bray."

Fitzmaurice fished out Spalding's photograph and slid it across the desk to Kehoe. "Just to confirm, this is Mr. McGuire?"

Kehoe picked up the photograph and adjusted her glasses. "Indeed it is. Charming man. I hope his family troubles won't be devastating to him."

"His father died," Sara replied, "and his presence is needed to help settle complex issues regarding the estate."

"How sad."

Sara nodded solemnly in agreement.

"May we have a copy of your records?" Fitzmaurice asked.

"Yes, of course," Kehoe replied.

"Also, if you could furnish us with a list of the organizations who offer the yachtmaster training schemes, that would be lovely."

After Kehoe left to make copies and gather the information, Fitzmaurice turned to Sara. "Apparently, our George is well on his way to establishing himself as a charming and agreeable member of the Dún Laoghaire yachting set."

300

"If he has put out to sea on a cruise around Ireland," Sara said, "what are our chances of finding him?"

"Hit or miss would be my guess. I'll ring up the Coast Guard and ask them to start looking." Fitzmaurice glanced at his wristwatch. "If we're going to keep vigil while Paquette meets with the builder at the villa, we need to leave straightaway."

On the drive to the villa Fitzmaurice kept one hand on the wheel as he called the Irish Coast Guard to get a search under way for Spalding's yacht, and then made another call to the passport office in Dublin. He was still on the phone when he parked the car down the street from the villa.

When he finished the conversation, he turned to Sara and said, "Passport records show that Spalding, either under the name of Bruneau or McGuire, has spent seven of the last twelve months in Ireland."

"Did you get the exact dates?" Sara asked.

Fitzmaurice rattled them off from memory as Sara wrote them down.

"Interesting," Sara said, scanning the paperwork Kehoe had provided. "From what Kehoe gave us, soon after Spalding bought *Sapphire,* he started coming back to Ireland to take the coastal and offshore land- and sea-based training classes. To qualify he spent almost four months in class or at sea. To get his ocean certificate he needs to log another six-hundred-mile, nonstop trip. I bet that's what his voyage around Ireland is all about."

"There's no need to be checking marinas and yacht clubs for him if he's at sea," Fitzmaurice said.

"We don't know that."

"You're right, of course," Fitzmaurice said.

"How far are we from Bray?"

"A few kilometers."

"Telephone this number." Sara read it off. "It's for a company called Celtic Sailing. They offer the yachtmaster ocean certificate course."

Fitzmaurice punched in the numbers, put the phone to his ear, listened, and shook his head. "Closed for the day. No matter, I'll have an officer find the owner and arrange for us to interview him."

He made the call, put the phone on the dashboard, and said, "It may interest you to know that Spalding paid for his passport application with a cheque from a Galway bank. Quite possibly he's moved his assets there. I'll query the bank in the morning. With any luck we may be able to trace his current movements through his cheque and credit-card transactions."

Fitzmaurice stopped talking when a builder's van rolled to a stop in front of the villa, and a stocky man with gray hair, holding a roll of blueprints, got out and waited by the side of his vehicle. He wore work boots, blue jeans, a plaid shirt, and had a bit of a potbelly. Joséphine Paquette arrived shortly afterward in her hired car, accompanied by her driver. While the driver waited, Paquette talked briefly to the man at the front of the van, who quickly unrolled the blueprints on the bonnet of his vehicle and pointed to something that made Paquette nod in approval. The builder smiled, rolled up the blueprints, and followed Paquette into the house.

A half hour passed before they came out, Paquette talking and gesturing with her hands while the builder scribbled notes on a clipboard. Finally she waved a good-bye, got into the waiting car, and left.

The man walked to his van, sat in the driver's seat with the door open, and continued to make notes.

"Here we go, then," Fitzmaurice said as he got out of the vehicle.

Together they approached the man, who looked up from the clipboard to find Fitzmaurice's Garda credentials under his nose.

"A few moments of your time, if you please," Fitzmaurice said with a smile.

A brief conversation with the builder, a man named Brendan McCarrick, confirmed Sara's theory that Spalding could not possibly have left the renovation of his villa solely in Paquette's hands. Twice over the course of the previous week Spalding and Paquette, posing as an unmarried couple, had met McCarrick and an architect to discuss in detail the interior changes and improvements they wanted, which had to be made in accordance with the Protected Structures Act.

Once it had become clear to Spalding that McCarrick wouldn't be able to start work on the refurbishments until the local planning council had approved the architect's plans, Spalding had left Paquette in charge of seeing to the final details.

That afternoon McCarrick and Paquette had done a last walk-through to finalize all the construction specifications, before he sought permission from the planning council to proceed.

Without being specific Fitzmaurice advised McCarrick not to count on the project going forward. As they drove away from the disheartened builder, Sara asked Fitzmaurice about the Protected Structures Act.

"It's a fairly new law," Fitzmaurice replied as he pulled into the visitors' car park at the Dún Laoghaire Marina, "that requires planning permission to make any substantial change to either the exterior or interior of buildings deemed to be worthy of architectural conservation. My semi-detached suburban home, which I hope you may soon see, hardly qualifies. It is both a mercy and a pity. We can do what we like with it, but protected status does rather boost the value," he ended with a chuckle.

They followed a pathway that skirted the marina, looking for Johnny Scanlan, the night-crew worker, and came upon him at the fuel dock, where he was topping off the tank of a sleek-looking powerboat. When he'd finished and the skipper had pulled away, Fitzmaurice approached and flashed his police credentials.

"Doherty said you'd be coming to see me," Scanlan said, with a thick brogue that reminded Sara of the villagers she'd met on her honeymoon in Connemara.

"Have you seen this woman?" Fitzmaurice asked, holding up a photograph of Paquette.

"I have," Scanlan replied as he put the fuel hose in the cradle. "She came looking for the *Sapphire*, Mr. McGuire's boat, one evening no more than a week ago. Spent two or three hours on board before leaving. I saw her walking toward the rail station."

"Did Mr. McGuire sleep on board his yacht during his stay?" Sara asked.

Scanlan locked the fuel hose to the pump. "Yes. I'd see him most evenings, or notice his lights on late into the night."

"Did anyone visit him besides Paquette?"

"None that I saw."

"Did he have any crew members?" Fitzmaurice asked.

Scanlan shook his head. "With a boat like that you don't need a crew."

"Did he say where he was sailing?"

"No, but the way he provisioned his boat before he left, I'd say he was planning a long cruise." Scanlan eyed the fuel-pump gauge and recorded the amount of petrol he'd delivered to the speedboat. "Is that it, then? I've got work to do."

"Thank you," Sara said.

On the way to the car Fitzmaurice's

phone rang, and after a brief exchange with the caller he told Sara the owner of Celtic Sailing would meet them at his pierside business establishment in fifteen minutes. The phone rang immediately again and Fitzmaurice broke into a smile when he took the call.

"Just a minute, luv," he said, winking at Sara, "let me ask her. My wife wants to know if you're still beguiling me."

Sara smiled. "Tell her I am doing no such thing."

"The good colonel refuses to take any responsibility for her flirtatious ways," he said with a twinkle in his eye. He paused to listen and then turned to Sara. "Would you be up to having a late meal with us?"

"That would be lovely," Sara replied.

Fitzmaurice glanced at his wristwatch. "Give us two hours, luv," he said to his wife before disconnecting.

At the Bray pier Desmond Phelan, the owner of Celtic Sailing, waited for them under the shop's Boats for Hire sign. In his thirties, Phelan was a small-boned man with light-brown hair, a wide forehead, and an aquiline nose. Inside the shop two young boys, no more than four and six years old, sat on stools at a customer-service counter, drawing pictures on scraps of paper.

Phelan told the boys to stay put and led Fitzmaurice and Sara to a small back room that served as both office and a storage room. He nodded at the photograph Fitzmaurice placed before him on his cluttered desktop.

"George McGuire," Phelan said. "A genial fellow, quite the eager student. I couldn't imagine why a Garda would come to my house at suppertime to ask me to talk to you. I surely didn't think it had anything to do with Mr. McGuire."

"We need to locate Mr. McGuire," Sara said, "to inform him of a family emergency. Do you know where he might be?"

"On the water this fine evening in a smooth sea. You should be able to reach him by marine radio."

"When did you last see him?"

"He sailed this morning."

"Going where?" Sara asked.

"He didn't say. He came down from Dún Laoghaire five days ago and retained me to tutor him on celestial navigation techniques so he could prepare for his yachtmaster ocean certification, which requires making a passage without the use of electronic aids. He did the shore-based classwork in the mornings and then we went out later in the day for his practice exercises."

"Was he planning to do his qualifying trip for his certification right away?" Sara asked.

Phelan perched on the corner of the desk. "He said nothing to me about it."

"How did he pay for your services?" Sara asked.

"By credit card."

"Could we see the charge slip?"

"Of course."

Sara stood on the Bray pier looking out at the horseshoe bay while Fitzmaurice made phone calls on his mobile to learn if the writ had been approved to access Paquette's Internet account, and to arrange for a detective to speak to the solicitor who'd prepared the conveyancing documents for the sale of the villa. A paved promenade ran along the shoreline just behind a rock barrier where waves lapped at a slender ribbon of beach. A hilly spit of land rose up at one end of the bay, and the quiet sea, as pale gray as the evening sky, seemed to absorb the fading light.

At Sara's back pitched-roof buildings crowded Bray's waterfront high street. The shoreline curved toward the spit of land where a new residential development stood and the houses, all with matching red tile roofs in an Italianate style, climbed up the hillside to take in views of the bay.

Phelan had said it was a fine evening with a smooth sea, and indeed it was so. Sara wondered where Spalding might be out on the water. Was he anchored in some nearby cove or at an offshore island? Or cruising slowly southward in St. George Channel? She was less than a day behind Spalding now, but catching him remained no easy matter. They could probably reach him by ship to shore radio, but doing so could easily raise his suspicions.

Fitzmaurice motioned to her, and she walked back along the pier to the car where he waited. He told her the solicitor would be interviewed first thing in the morning and the order to inspect Paquette's Internet account and e-mail records had been served.

"Do we have her picked up?" he asked.

"I'd rather wait until we know Spalding's exact location," Sara replied.

"I've put in a query to his credit-card company," Fitzgerald said. "We'll have him the next time he uses it."

On their return to Dublin, Fitzmaurice avoided the motorway and drove through the coastal towns of Shankill, Killiney, and Dalkey until they reached Dún Laoghaire.

Sara fell silent, gazing out the car window at the glimpses of the sea and the plots of pastureland that dotted the inland side of the coastal hills. Along a winding, narrow road bordered by hedgerows they passed by granite cliffs covered in yellow shrubs, huge estates on promontories overlooking the water, and a seaside park along an inlet with rock outcroppings and tall trees that were dark green against the backdrop of gray sky and water.

In the towns they passed by weathered cut-stone churches with towering spires, an old castle with high turrets and parapets, and rows of Victorian and Georgian houses behind stone walls on finely tended lawns.

Although Fitzmaurice had said nothing about taking her on an impromptu Cook's tour, Sara appreciated his thoughtfulness and said so as they drove through Rathfarnham, a suburb of the city nestled against the foot of the Dublin Mountains several miles south of St. Stephen's Green.

So this is his semidetached, she thought, as Fitzmaurice pulled to a stop in front of a two-story modern town house in an established subdivision. It had brick facing on the ground floor, a plastered exterior wall above with several windows that looked out on the street, and a pitched, shingled roof with shallow eaves. A common lawn in front of the building had separate walkways leading to the two ground-floor entrances.

Fitzmaurice pointed to his side of the semidetached before killing the engine. "Here we are, then," he said. "Clan Fitzmaurice's castle, wherein the lady of the house awaits along with my infant son, should he be home from university."

Sara climbed out of the car. "It's sweet," she said.

Fitzmaurice shut the door and locked the car. "And within a very short distance of a real castle, where my grandfather worked as a groundskeeper when the Jesuits owned it. Sometime back they found secret tunnels at the castle, one of which runs to the golf course where I spend many pleasant afternoons slicing balls into the rough. We have megalithic tombs on the mountaintops and are home to the abbey where Mother Teresa of Calcutta first entered the religious life."

"History is all around you," Sara said as they walked toward the house.

"That it is," Fitzmaurice said with a laugh. "We also are home to the first McDonald's drive-through in Europe, for which, of course, we are eternally grateful."

"Is that true?" Sara asked.

Fitzmaurice nodded and grinned. "We're planning to raise a statue to Ronald Mc-Donald on the town green to commemorate the historical event."

Edna Fitzmaurice met them at the door. Green eyed, with laugh lines at the corners of a broad mouth, she was a tall full-figured woman dressed casually in jeans and a short-sleeve pullover top.

"So you are the woman who's kept my husband from hearth and home," she said, after greeting Sara warmly. "Come inside and tell me how he's been misbehaving."

In the living room Edna sat with Sara on a couch facing a fireplace, while Fitzmaurice opened a bottle of wine at the sideboard in the adjacent dining room. The small living room, comfortable and inviting, had scaled-down furnishings that created a feeling of spaciousness, and built-in shelves filled with books. From the kitchen came the aroma of roasting lamb with a hint of garlic. Footsteps on the stairway from the second floor announced the arrival of Sean Fitzmaurice, who rushed into the room and smiled at Sara with a toothy grin.

"Finally we get to meet," he said, shaking her hand. "At the award ceremony I was warned to stay away. Garda business and all that. Are you really an American army officer?"

Sara smiled back at the boy. "I am." No more than nineteen or twenty, Sean had his father's wide shoulders, large hands, and blunt fingers, and his mother's eyes and mouth.

"Leave her alone, Sean," Fitzmaurice called out as he carried in the wineglasses. "The colonel is a married woman. Wife and mother, to be exact."

After a glass of wine Sara helped Edna put the finishing touches on dinner, while Sean and Hugh set the table. Father, mother, and son were convivial company. Edna had bought the lamb — done to perfection — from a butcher who raised and slaughtered his own sheep on a farm in County Roscommon. A bowl of fruit topped off the meal, and it was then that Sean asked her if she'd read the works for which Brendan Coughlan had been honored at the National University.

"I have not," Sara replied. "But he's now on my personal short list of writers to read."

Sean nodded with great seriousness.

"He has a lyrical flair and a wonderful way of describing characters and settings. Did you ever hear of Finley Peter Dunne, a late-nineteenth-century Irish-American journalist?"

Sara's eyes widened in surprise. For an American Studies class at West Point she'd written a research paper on Dunne, a Chicago columnist who had created a comic Irish saloonkeeper named Mr. Dooley, a character with strong anti-imperialist tendencies who tenaciously criticized the Spanish-American War.

"Did you know he was great friends with Teddy Roosevelt, in spite of his opposition to the Spanish-American War?" Sara asked.

Sean beamed with pleasure. "I did. What was Mr. Dooley's given name?"

Sara laughed. "I don't remember."

"Martin," Sean replied. "And the customer who most often had to endure Dooley's social commentary was named Hennessy."

"That's right," Sara said. "Did you know that before he moved to New York City, Dunne wrote articles on women's issues for the *Ladies' Home Journal* magazine?"

Sean nodded. "He was one of the most popular muckraking reformers of his day."

"How did you come to discover him?" Sara asked.

"I'm reading Irish-American Literature at Trinity," Sean replied. "Do you know Thomas Flanagan's works?"

"I'm afraid not," Sara said with a shake of her head.

"You're missing one of America's great writers. He wrote a trilogy set here that reads like the work of a native son. Would you like me to write the titles down for you?"

"Yes, please."

"Enough about books," Fitzmaurice said as he pushed his empty fruit bowl away, "otherwise we'll be sitting at this table long into the wee hours of the night."

After the table had been cleared, Sean retreated to his room to study, and Sara helped Edna scrape and stack the dishes in the galley kitchen. As they stood at the sink, Edna turned to her and said, "I do hope you don't think I invited you over to see if my husband was planning to take you away on a dirty little weekend."

"I think he'll be glad to see the last of me," Sara replied with a smile.

"You're welcome in this house anytime you decide to return."

Impulsively, Sara hugged Edna as

though she were an old and dear friend.

Fitzmaurice arrived to find the two women chatting like magpies, which continued over coffee in the living room. When he was finally able to suggest that it was time to take Sara back to her hotel, she reluctantly agreed.

She left Edna on the front stoop with thanks for a scrumptious meal and a promise to visit again, then climbed into Fitzmaurice's car and waved good-bye.

Fitzmaurice started the engine, beeped the horn, and drove away. "The text messages Spalding sent to Paquette's computer don't help us one bit," he said. "They were all about small changes he wanted the builder to make to the architect's blueprints."

"That's it?"

"Afraid so." He glanced at Sara. "I think we need to agree upon a plan of action in the morning. I can't keep the number of people assigned to the case working any longer than that. Orders from the higher-ups."

"Okay," Sara said. "We'll figure something out in the morning."

At the hotel she thanked him for the wonderful evening, complimented him on his delightful family, and took the lift to her room, wishing Kerney and Patrick had been with her to meet Clan Fitzmaurice.

It was eleven p.m. in Dublin, and four in the afternoon in Santa Fe, but Sara was too drained to call Kerney or even check her e-mail for messages. She got ready for bed, her thoughts firmly fixed on Spalding and what to do about catching him come morning.

Chapter Nine

As Brigadier General Stuart Thatcher saw it, he'd risen through the ranks because he was objective, ambitious, and maintained a healthy skepticism about other people's motives. Accordingly, he was constantly on guard for any sign of disloyalty from his subordinates or any outside threats to his authority.

On Friday, as he was about to leave the office at the end of the day, a memo from the vice chief of staff had been hand-delivered by his aide, advising Thatcher that Lieutenant Colonel Sara Brannon had been tasked to carry out a special courier assignment effective immediately. The memo contained no specifics as to the whys or wherefores, nor had Thatcher been consulted on the matter. His authority had been undermined, and he was desperate to know why.

Officially there wasn't anything Thatcher could do about it other than defer to the vice chief. Still, he fumed that Clarke had not even given him the courtesy of a call about needing Brannon for a special detail. Because Henry Powhatan Clarke was clearly Brannon's mentor and protector, Thatcher couldn't help but wonder if hidden motives were in play.

Since her arrival at the military police directorate, Brannon had caused Thatcher nothing but trouble. It had started with her assignment to revise sexual-assault criminal investigation protocols and procedures, which she'd turned into an indictment against the army for failure to prosecute offenders and adequately protect victims.

Her findings had reached the halls of Congress, and it had taken a concerted effort to keep the situation from becoming an embarrassment to the service while preserving the careers of several ranking, highly connected officers. Fortunately, Thatcher's second cousin, U.S. Senator Howard Ballard Rutledge, chairman of the Senate Armed Services Committee, had buried Brannon's report under the provisions of the National Security Act. But from that moment on Thatcher had kept a watchful eye on Brannon and her work, reviewing it in exhaustive detail.

Thatcher had hoped to quash Brannon's chances for promotion by holding her back from accepting a plum temporary duty assignment with the training branch, and giving her a less than exemplary efficiency rating prior to her departure from his command. But General Clarke had outmaneuvered Thatcher and quashed his plans.

He wondered what Clarke and Brannon were up to and had spent the last two days discreetly trying to learn the nature of Brannon's assignment. People he could usually rely on for information had professed no knowledge, and all his attempts to tease out any particulars from collateral sources failed.

Alarmed and convinced he was a target of some scheme hatched by Clarke and Brannon to ruin him, Thatcher decided to uncover the threat on his own and counteract it. Late Tuesday evening, after the personnel in Brannon's section had left for the day, he exercised his authority to conduct a security audit of her workstation and began going through her files, paperwork, and notes in minute detail, searching for anything that would confirm his suspicions and reveal the nature of the plot against him.

In the top drawer of Brannon's desk he found a file containing computer printouts of her outgoing telephone calls. Some time back Brannon had placed a number of calls to the Quartermaster Corps and the army forensic lab. He knew of no reason for her to do that. Additionally, over a considerable period of time, Brannon had also telephoned the Royal Canadian Mounted Police. One call had been made the day before Clarke had cut her special orders. What was that all about?

Thatcher decided to dig deeper and began dialing the numbers. Within short order he had duty officers at the Quartermaster Corps and the forensic lab scrambling to locate any documents or memorandums to or from Brannon. Then he phoned the Royal Canadian Mounted Police and spoke to a supervisor, who told him his department routinely kept in contact with Brannon regarding the status of an army deserter named George Spalding.

"What is the current status of the case?" Thatcher asked.

"Spalding is still at large," the officer replied. "But based on a close watch list of one of Spalding's known friends, we now have reason to suspect that he may be in Ireland."

"Was this information shared with Colonel Brannon?" Thatcher asked.

"Yes, the colonel was advised."

Thatcher thanked the officer and hung up. Well over a year ago the Spalding case had been transferred from Brannon to army CID. Yet Brannon had continued to follow up on the investigation without his knowledge or authorization. What was she up to and why all the secrecy?

He called back the duty officers and told them to concentrate on looking for specific information to or from Brannon that pertained to the Spalding investigation.

Within the hour Thatcher hit pay dirt. Long after the case had been transferred, Brannon had requested a handwriting analysis on documents she'd requested from the Quartermaster Corp which showed that Thomas Loring Carrier had, during the Vietnam War, forged signatures on personal-effects release forms.

Brannon had obviously targeted Carrier as a member of the smuggling ring Spalding had operated in Vietnam, which was completely incredible to Thatcher. Tom Carrier was no common criminal. A born-again Christian and a great American, Carrier had the ear of important people in the president's inner circle. Brannon's assumptions about him were simply scurrilous.

Had Brannon sidestepped him because

of his friendship with Carrier and taken her unfounded suspicions to General Clarke? If so, why now?

He ran a hand through his thinning hair. He didn't like Brannon. She was an officer who subtly challenged his authority in ways that avoided outright censure, who had a pattern of consistently maneuvering behind his back, and had no allegiance to the command ethics of the army.

Thatcher tapped his fingers on the desktop. Brannon had been tasked by Clarke on a secret assignment one day after she'd learned from the RCMP that Spalding might have surfaced in Ireland. Could it be that was where Clarke had sent her?

Clarke had to know of Carrier's ties to the White House, how he'd been a media point man to sell the administration's handling of the war on terrorism. Had Clarke authorized the mission to find evidence that could embarrass the commander-in-chief by raising questions about a man closely associated with his war policies?

Thatcher smiled. As far as he could tell, he wasn't a target after all, and foiling Lieutenant Colonel Sara Brannon's mission for General Henry Powhatan Clarke might win him his second star. If he played

his hand well, the result would be decidedly less pleasant for Brannon and Clarke.
His smile widened in anticipation of the
debt of gratitude Tom Carrier would owe
him and the good days that loomed ahead.

In the morning Sara met Fitzmaurice in
the hotel lobby. On the way to the car he
gave her an update on the overnight activity. Spalding had made no new credit-
card purchases, his boat hadn't been
spotted by the Irish Coast Guard, and
Paquette had spent the evening clubbing
with friends before retiring late to her
hotel room.

"Is that it?" Sara asked.

"We've dropped surveillance on her,"
Fitzmaurice said as he opened the car door
for Sara. "But I've arranged for her hired
driver to keep us informed of her where-
abouts. All on the QT, of course."

"Good."

Fitzmaurice settled behind the steering
wheel and handed Sara a file folder. "We
have been able to determine the specifics
of Spalding's Irish citizenship claim based
on the passport information we got during
our visit to the Irish Sailing Association.
He was granted citizenship by virtue of descent under the name of George McGuire,

but the supporting documentation of his Irish-born grandparents was forged."

Sara scanned the report.

"Also," Fitzmaurice said, "we accessed the records of the mobile-phone account Spalding established under the name of McGuire. He's been using it to communicate with the Dún Laoghaire solicitor who handled the conveyance of the villa. A detective spoke to the solicitor early this morning and learned that Paquette has signed a legal document that will transfer the property to Spalding at the end of the year by private treaty. Paquette stands to receive payment of half a million euros for the property. A far cry from the full value of the house, but a tidy sum nonetheless."

"So Paquette is looking forward to a very profitable payday," Sara said.

"In squeaky clean cash." Fitzmaurice put the key into the ignition but didn't start the engine. "The text messages he sent to Paquette's computer are interesting. He gave her very specific instructions on the type of countertops, appliances, and fixtures he wanted installed in the kitchen and bathrooms at the villa and a color scheme for the walls of each room. Apparently, he's planning to settle permanently in Dún Laoghaire, as you suggested, and live a long and happy life as George McGuire."

Sara closed the file. "What else?"

"He's made several recent calls on his mobile to a London telephone number, one of which was placed just before he left Bray on his boat. We've asked the London authorities to find out what they can and ring us back."

"I wonder if he sailed to England," Sara said.

"He could get to Wales in a matter of hours," Fitzmaurice replied. "Or, according to the Coast Guard, he could not be at sea at all, but cruising along the mouth of some inland waterway."

Sara looked out the windscreen of the car. People hurried along the quay, shops were opening, lorry drivers were queuing up at curbside to make deliveries, buses rolled by. Sunlight dappled the Liffey, the blue sky was tinged with green, and the tourists were in short sleeves, anticipating a warm, clear day.

"Do you have a plan?" Fitzmaurice asked.

Sara let out a small sigh. She'd hoped to get to Spalding by working around Paquette and leaving the smallest possible footprint of her participation in the investigation. "Has there been any fresh communication between Spalding and Paquette?"

Fitzmaurice shook his head. "Not as far as we know."

Sara bit her lip. If she waited for Spalding to surface or make another misstep, it could be days before he could be brought to ground, and time wasn't on her side. "Let's have a talk with her."

Fitzmaurice turned over the engine and laughed. "That's a fine plan, Colonel Brannon. One I heartily endorse."

Sara touched Fitzmaurice's shoulder. "Wait a minute. Let's think this through. Where is she now?"

Fitzmaurice glanced at his watch. "On her way to an appointment with a Canadian artist who is about to have a major show at a gallery in the Temple Bar district."

"Can we have her picked up without arousing her suspicion?"

"A subterfuge of some sort? Is that necessary? We have sufficient cause to question her."

"Which would surely put her on guard," Sara countered. "If we approach her as a suspect, she could immediately go on the offensive and either request a solicitor or ask to contact the Canadian embassy."

Fitzmaurice eyed Sara. "And you wouldn't want that." Sara shook her head.

"I could arrange for a detective to approach her about a theft of items from her hotel room."

"That would work. But I would prefer to meet with her somewhere other than your office."

"Dublin Castle would do nicely," Fitzmaurice replied.

"Isn't it a big tourist attraction?"

"One of the most popular in the city. The former police yard and armory on the castle grounds house Garda offices, including the drug unit. There are several belowground rooms that are equipped for interviews and interrogations."

Sara laughed. "So we'll have Paquette thrown into the castle dungeon."

"Not quite," Fitzmaurice said with a smile as he pulled out into the crush of morning traffic. "But with a bit of embellishment it will give you an excellent tale to tell once you're home in the States."

Sara asked how far it was to the castle, and Fitzmaurice replied that it was no more than a biscuit's throw away. When they arrived, he gave Sara a few minutes to look around, pointing out an old Norman tower with tall battlements that housed the

Garda Museum; the circular gardens, with their serpentine footpaths amid lush grass, resting on the site of the dark pool — *dubh linn* — that had given the city its name; the Gothic Revival chapel; the state apartments; and the viceroy's coach house that, from the outside, looked much like a small castle but now served as an exhibition and conference center.

"Originally," Fitzmaurice said, as he led Sara to a brightly plastered building that bordered the circular garden, "the castle sat along a river. But the old moat was filled in and it's an underground river now that flows into the Liffey."

"This is an amazing place," Sara said as she followed Fitzmaurice inside the Garda Carriage and Traffic Building. They walked down a long hallway, past offices where uniformed officers manned desks, to a suite of rooms that housed the drug unit. There Fitzmaurice introduced Sara to a detective named Colm Byrne and explained that he had need of an interrogation room.

Byrne, who had the look of a young tough who could street-fight with the best of them, gave Sara the once-over from head to toe.

"You've come up in the world," he said to Fitzmaurice with a toothy grin. "Circulating with a much better class of people now, are you?"

Fitzmaurice smiled jovially. "I'm still knocking the north side riffraff's heads together as need be, Colm, and if you keep drooling on the good colonel's shoes, I'll soon be adding your name to my list."

Byrne threw back his head and laughed. "I want none of that. The interrogation rooms aren't in use. Take your pick."

The underground rooms had one-way mirrors that hid small viewing areas where digital video equipment was set up to record interviews and interrogations. The walls were a neutral beige and the rooms were well lit. The only furniture consisted of rectangular office tables and several straight-backed chairs.

"Perfect," Sara said.

"Soon you'll have Paquette in hand," Fitzmaurice said, "which may put you in close reach of Spalding. But who are you really after?"

"Is it that obvious?"

He perched on the end of the table and studied Sara's face. "Yes. You've skirted around Paquette until it has become absolutely necessary to confront her, you've relied on me as your intermediary to make it seem as though the investigation has been conducted completely independent of any involvement on your part. Except for being introduced to Colm Byrne, you have avoided all possible contact with Garda personnel other than myself. I'm half convinced that soon you'll be asking me to delete all references in my reports of your presence in the Republic and your participation in the investigation."

Sara shook her head. "I have no need to do that, and to ease your mind, I'm not setting you up."

"Since I am an Irishman and a peeler, and therefore doubly suspicious both by disposition and training, normally I wouldn't believe you." Fitzmaurice rose to his feet and smiled. "But I do. However, you've severely limited my ability to assist you."

"The person I want is outside of your reach," Sara said.

"Fair enough, but when all is over, I expect to be told the truth, in the strictest confidence, of course, with no mention of it to be made in my official reports."

"Fair enough," Sara echoed. "How much time do we have before Paquette is picked up?"

"About a half an hour, more or less, I would say."

"Then let's go over all the facts and information we have before she gets here."

Fitzmaurice opened the folder he'd been carrying and sat at the table. "I have a statement from Paquette's driver you might find interesting, as well as a report from the Royal Canadian Mounted Police that came in overnight, addressed to you, about Paquette's rather precarious current employment and financial situation."

Joséphine Paquette listened as Hayden LaPorte, the Canadian artist she had just finished interviewing, prattled on, mentioning for the third time that the Canadian ambassador to the Irish Republic would be attending the gallery opening of his one-man show on Friday night.

Bright overhead lights glared against bare walls where paintings were stacked, waiting to be hung. One of them was a large triptych of a band of Inuit, moving camp across the frozen tundra in a snowstorm, a work that captured the harsh beauty of the Arctic. The gallery was uncomfortably cold in spite of the warm September day and the bright interior lights, as though a hundred or more Dublin winters had seeped through the stone walls and created a permanent chill that would never go away. The triptych only served to heighten the effect.

LaPorte, a stocky, bearded, nervous, distractible man in his sixties, hadn't been easy to interview, but Paquette had managed to keep him on track by stroking his ego and directing the conversation back to his work as an artist.

When LaPorte stopped talking, Paquette smiled, closed her notebook, stood, and smoothed her skirt, a Jean Muir creation, silky brown with a slightly flared hem at the knee, which she'd bought on a one-day shopping trip to London. "I've taken far too much of your time."

LaPorte nodded absentmindedly, stared at the empty walls, and sighed. "So much to do."

After assuring LaPorte that she and the freelance photographer she had hired would see him at his opening, Paquette stepped outside into the warmth of the day. Her waiting car was parked on the narrow cobblestone street, in front of a yellow building where a vendor stood behind a ground-floor window selling coffee to a man with several bundles under his arm.

As she stepped toward the car, a young, pleasant-looking man in a business suit approached her and displayed police credentials.

"Ms. Joséphine Paquette?" he asked.

"Yes?" Paquette replied.

The man introduced himself as a Garda detective and told her that valuables had been reported stolen from her hotel room.

Paquette stiffened. "I've been robbed?"

"So it seems," the detective replied, "but fortunately we've recovered a number of items which need to be identified by you."

Paquette searched the man's face for any sign of deception and saw none. Still, she was wary. "How did you find me?" she demanded.

"The doorman at the hotel knows your driver. I contacted him by mobile and he gave me your location."

"Must I do this now?" Paquette asked.

The detective smiled. "Yes, if you wish your possessions returned in a timely fashion. It will only require a few minutes of your time. If you'll accompany me, we'll have you on your way shortly."

Paquette glanced over the detective's shoulder at her driver, who leaned against the car door. When she caught his eye, he quickly dropped his head and lowered his gaze. During her many years as a journalist Paquette had learned to read behavioral signs, and her cheerful, chatty Irish driver seemed decidedly ill at ease.

"Of course," she said with an amiable smile. "I'll be glad to help in any way I can. But may I follow you in my hired car? I have an appointment I dare not be late to."

"I've arranged to have your driver follow me," the detective replied as he touched Paquette on the arm and pointed at his vehicle.

As far as Paquette could tell, there was nothing to worry about. But a twinge of anxiety surfaced, and she had to force it down as she got into the unmarked Garda vehicle.

At Dublin Castle the detective guided her to a building on the grounds that sat perpendicular to the coach house with its mock Gothic façade. Across the gardens and behind the state apartments Paquette could see the turquoise-blue cupola that rose above Bedford Hall. Two days ago she had attended a luncheon for benefactors of a Canadian-Irish arts guild there in the Erin Room.

Inside the Garda offices she was taken down a flight of stairs to a room where a very attractive woman sat at a table studying some papers, which she quickly put away in a folder. As the detective left, the woman stood, smiled at Paquette, gestured at an empty chair, and said, "Please, sit down."

Paquette noted the woman's attire as she sat at the table. She wore dark, taupe gabardine pants by Calvin Klein paired with a lightweight V-necked Ralph Lauren cashmere top.

"You don't sound Irish," Paquette said.

The woman laughed. "My father was an Irish diplomat, my mother is Norwegian, and I spent most of my youth growing up in the States. I get teased about my Yank accent all the time. May I call you Joséphine?"

"Of course," Paquette said. The woman neither looked or acted like a police officer. Aside from her clothes, her strawberry-blond hair had been cut and shaped by an expert stylist, and she was obviously very knowledgeable about using makeup that complemented her lovely green eyes and creamy complexion. She wore a pair of gold hoop earrings mounted with single small diamonds that looked custom made. All in all she appeared extremely high maintenance.

"I'm Sara. Thank you for coming."

Paquette smiled in return. "I understand

you have some items stolen from my hotel room you want me to identify."

"In a moment. But first, can you recall any recent encounters with people who might have approached you to do something for them that seemed unusual?"

"Such as?" Paquette asked.

"Leave a package at the hotel for another guest, or perhaps give you money and ask you to buy something for them?"

Paquette shook her head. "No. Do criminals pick the people they plan to rob that way?"

"Frequently. They'll use any number of ploys to target potential victims. Have you had occasion to make expensive purchases that might have drawn attention to yourself?"

"I went clothes shopping in London for a day and overindulged a bit. But I'm far too busy here in Ireland working on a cover article for my magazine to do much in the way of supporting the local economy."

"Yes, I understand you're a fashion-magazine editor. That must be a very exciting profession."

Paquette smiled. "It has its entertaining moments. Can you tell me what was stolen from my room?"

"So, you've not been asked by anyone to

do a special favor, nor have you made a large purchase that might have drawn attention to yourself?"

"No," Paquette replied. "Can we get on with this?"

Sara slipped a photograph out of the folder and placed it before Paquette. "Do you know this man?"

Paquette's gaze jumped from the photograph to Sara's face. "That's George," she said quickly. "Why are you asking me about him?"

"And what name is he using now?"

"Now?"

"Yes, Joséphine, now. We know you met him in Paris."

"I knew him as George Calderwood in Canada, but the police told me his real name was Spalding and that he was an American army deserter and a tax dodger."

"Now, Joséphine," Sara said gently. "Tell the truth, don't you also know the name he's using now?"

Paquette answered without hesitation. "He legally changed it to McGuire. He said it was his mother's maiden name. He even showed me his Irish passport to prove it."

"But the funds he gave you to buy a villa for him came from an account under the name of Georges Bruneau."

Paquette nodded. "Yes, Mr. Bruneau, his personal accountant. George said they joked about having the same Christian name."

Sara stood, put her hands on the table, and leaned toward Paquette. "An amusing coincidence. Life is full of funny things like that no one can explain, isn't it? But surely you can tell me how you came to agree to help a known fugitive purchase a house under your name."

Paquette looked nonplussed. "Fugitive? George's legal problems have all been resolved."

Sara sank back in the chair and studied Paquette silently for a long moment, unsure if the woman had simply rehearsed a story or was telling the truth as she knew it.

"Are you sure you're a Garda detective?" Paquette asked.

"Do you have something to hide from the police that would make you ask that question?" Sara retorted.

Paquette shrugged. "Not at all. But you're wearing expensive American designer labels from recent collections, and I don't know too many police officers who dress in such nice outfits."

"I'm glad you like it," Sara said with a

smile. "I picked it up in New York City. With the euro strong against the dollar, the United States is a shopper's paradise for Europeans looking to go on a weekend clothes-buying spree."

Paquette nodded. It made sense. The fashion trade journals had reported on the phenomenon several times since the dollar had plunged in value against the euro and the pound, and a diplomat's daughter probably didn't have to live solely on her police salary.

"Tell me why you believe George's legal problems have gone away," Sara asked.

"Is he still wanted?"

"Yes, by your government for income tax evasion and flight to avoid prosecution, and by the United States Army for smuggling and desertion."

Paquette sighed. "He told me that he'd reached a settlement agreement with Canadian revenue officials and that the matter of his military service had been resolved."

"And you believed him?"

"Not without proof," Paquette retorted. "He had legal papers and official documents from both Canadian and American government agencies."

"What kind of documents?" Sara asked.

"Dishonorable discharge papers from the U.S. Army and a tax payment agreement from the Canadian government. It was all there in black and white."

"Didn't you think it strange that if his legal problems were behind him, he would want you to buy an Irish seaside villa for him in your name?"

"He said he wanted to move on with his life and start over in Ireland without drawing any attention to himself."

"How did George arrange for you to meet him in Paris?"

"He sent a letter to me at work asking for my assistance."

"Do you have that letter?"

"No."

"Why didn't you call the police when the letter arrived?"

"I saw no reason to doubt him. He wrote that he was no longer in trouble with the law and could prove it to my satisfaction, if I was willing to help."

Sara rose, walked to Paquette, and looked down at her. "How could he have possibly known when you would be traveling to Ireland?"

"I didn't think to ask him that."

Sara stayed silent for a moment, letting the tension build. "Explain to me why

George would buy the villa under your name and then hire a solicitor to prepare a conveyance to transfer the deed to him by the end of the year."

For the first time during the interrogation Paquette's composure wavered. Her mouth tightened and she gave Sara a stormy look. "If he's still a criminal, why don't you just go arrest him and ask him these questions? I've done nothing wrong."

Sara walked behind Paquette's chair and looked at her in the one-way mirror. "I wonder what a polygraph would tell me."

"Would you not stand behind me, please," Paquette said.

Sara stayed put. "You could avoid further difficulties by telling me now how much George promised to give you if you went along with his scheme."

Paquette craned her neck to look at Sara. "It's not a scheme. I simply agreed to help out a friend."

"I'm confused, Joséphine. If this was all on the up and up, why would you pose as George's lover when the two of you met with the architect and builder?"

Paquette looked away. "I did no such thing. They must have formed a mistaken impression about our relationship."

Sara patted Paquette gently on the

shoulder. "That could well be the case. People make faulty assumptions about others all the time."

"Which is exactly what you're doing with me," Paquette said pointedly as she looked at her wristwatch. "I really must go."

"Not yet." Sara moved to the table, sat on it, and smiled down at Paquette. "I'm still a bit confused."

"About what?"

"Your secret meeting with George on his yacht at the Dún Laoghaire Marina."

"There wasn't anything secret about it."

"Then why was it the one and only time since you've been in Dublin that you didn't use your car and driver?"

Paquette nodded and paused an extra beat. "I needed some time by myself without having to listen to my driver's incessant chatter."

Sara reached for the folder and thumbed through it. "Your driver, Martin Mullaney, told us that you informed him early in the day you wouldn't be needing him that evening. It doesn't appear that your need to take a break from a chatty driver was all that spontaneous."

"Believe what you like. I'm telling you the truth."

Sara sighed and plucked a sheet of paper

from the folder. "Joséphine, everything we've learned points to the fact that George is paying you to be his intermediary."

"I've been helping out because he's been spending most of his time cruising on his yacht."

"We know that your magazine is about to be sold," Sara said as she scanned the paper, "and your chances of staying on as the editor are slim to none. We know that you've been actively job hunting for the past three months and have had no offers. We also know you are strapped for cash and carrying a lot of debt."

Sara returned the paper to the folder. "The point is, no matter how often you tell this story, we can show that you have colluded with a known fugitive and that money was your motive. You can be charged as an accessory."

"I have nothing more to say."

"What do you think could happen to a person who did something like this?"

Paquette put her hands on the table and clasped them tightly together.

"People make mistakes," Sara continued as she returned to her chair. "I understand that. Now is your chance to set things right. I'll listen to anything you want to say."

"Where would that get me?" Paquette asked.

"It could be very advantageous to you. Once we have George in custody, we'll learn the truth about your involvement and any chance you have to extract yourself from this situation will be gone."

Paquette picked some imaginary lint from her pleated silk Louis Vuitton blouse and shook her head. "I feel so stupid."

"Don't, Joséphine." Sara leaned forward and smiled sympathetically. Although Paquette probably didn't know it, she'd just admitted guilt. "George Spalding has spent a lifetime using people. He's a master at it. You are simply one of his victims."

Paquette smiled weakly in return.

"Why don't you tell me everything," Sara said.

"If I do, will I be arrested?"

"Not if you give a full and truthful account," Sara replied, sidestepping the fact that the half a million euros Paquette expected to receive at the end of the year had just evaporated.

Paquette took a deep breath and started talking. When she finished, Sara had all the particulars of the scheme, but most important she now knew that Spalding would be at the villa tomorrow afternoon to have one final look at his new home before starting his qualifying cruise for his ocean yachtmaster certificate.

She cautioned Paquette to cooperate fully with the Garda in all possible ways, made her surrender her passport, and turned her over to the detective waiting outside the door.

Within a minute Fitzmaurice stepped into the room with a big smile spread across his face. "Well done," he said. "You got her to lie to you right from the outset. It's all been recorded on digital video and sent to the server. I made a diskette copy."

He tucked it into the chest pocket of his suit coat. "A detective will take her written statement. We'll keep a close watch on her from now until tomorrow afternoon."

"Are you smiling because you think I should have questioned her sooner rather than later?" Sara asked.

Fitzmaurice shook his head. "Not at all. She never would have broken unless you had the facts at your disposal."

"Then why the big grin?" Sara asked.

Fitzmaurice laughed. "Because I had no idea you were the product of an Irish diplomat's marriage to a Norwegian shipping heiress, *and* a Garda detective authorized to grant foreign citizens immunity from prosecution."

Sara grinned and handed Fitzmaurice the passport. "I said nothing about a shipping heiress. You're a terrible embellisher, Mr. Fitzmaurice. She almost had me there. Did you really want to arrest her?"

"No, but now I'm more convinced than ever that you're a far cry from an ordinary lieutenant colonel."

"You just won't quit, will you?"

Fitzmaurice shook his head. "Is it time for us to start uncovering and freezing Mr. Spalding's assets?"

"Is that possible?" Sara asked.

"Indeed so," Fitzmaurice replied. "His bank in Galway serves only private clients, and it is justifiably concerned that it not be a party to any illicit dealing. The rumours of that may not be good for business, and a scandal in the courts might frighten off prospective clients. I've asked for a writ from the court under the Proceeds of Crime Act. It should be signed shortly and then we can be on our way to Galway. We'll travel by helicopter."

On the flight to Galway, Fitzmaurice gave Sara a short history of the Garda Criminal Assets Bureau. The bureau had been established in 1996, after drug dealers murdered Veronica Guerin, an investigative reporter who'd exposed the extent of drug trafficking in Dublin and the wealth of the drug lords who controlled it. The public outcry that resulted from her death had led to the creation of the bureau, which was given the authority to identify, freeze, or confiscate assets and other wealth derived directly or indirectly from criminal activity.

During that time Fitzmaurice had been an undercover narcotics officer working the tough, drug-ridden north-side Dublin neighborhoods, and he had participated in the investigation that brought Guerin's killers to justice.

"That was back when I was still young enough to do that type of work," Fitzmaurice said. "Some days I would go home wondering if Edna and the boys would still be there when I arrived. I rarely saw them."

Sara nodded sympathetically, her thoughts suddenly riveted on Kerney and Patrick. The emptiness that came from seeing Kerney so infrequently often weighed on her, and the unhappy prospect of being separated from Patrick for two weeks only served to enlarge that feeling.

Fitzmaurice read her gloomy expression. Sara quickly hid it with a forced smile.

" 'Tis hard on family life, this work we've taken on," he said.

Sara nodded. "Yes, it is. Will we have full access to Spalding's bank records?"

"Indeed," Fitzmaurice replied, noting Sara's shift away from private thoughts. He understood completely. When family worries gnawed at the back of one's mind, it was always best to focus on the work at hand. "The order allows a search through all records bearing the name of George Spalding and any of his known aliases."

They flew into Galway City and in the distance Sara could see the banks of the river fed by Lough Corrib, which was apple green in the distance, ringed by fields and wetland thickets.

She remembered her day in the city with Kerney; visiting the museum at Spanish Arch, walking the nearby pedestrian streets, wandering in and out of the shops, gazing at the many medieval buildings, and listening to the Irish folk tunes played by buskers for spare change.

She recalled Kerney's amazement at the fast-flowing rivers and waterways that coursed through the city, the lush green of the surrounding countryside, the delicate blue sky that turned the bay silver. The thought of that lovely time together with him cheered her.

After landing they were driven to the bank by a uniformed officer. In a sixteenth-century building on the corner of one of the pedestrian streets, the bank was beautifully preserved, with an arched window front and decorative stone carvings above the ground floor.

Inside, they were met by the bank's solicitor, a tall man with a mustache who wore standard corporate attire: a dark suit, white shirt, and a conservative necktie. He inspected the order and escorted them to an upstairs room where two revenue officers from the Criminal Assets Bureau waited, seated at a table with desktop computers. Introductions were made and after Fitzmaurice politely dismissed the solicitor, work promptly began.

As the computer files were accessed it became apparent that Spalding, using the alias of Calderwood, his ex-wife's maiden name, had been a client at the bank for a number of years, long before Kerney unmasked him. Millions of Canadian dollars had flowed into his original account from Swiss and offshore banks, converted first into Irish punts and later to euros when

Ireland switched to the new currency.

From the original account the money had then flowed into various investment portfolios managed by a wholly owned subsidiary of the bank. At that point the audit trail became murky until well after nightfall, when the revenue officers linked a hedge-fund account to the new accounts Spalding had opened under his Bruneau and McGuire aliases.

During a short break for a meal of fast food takeaway one of the revenue officers had fetched, Fitzmaurice leaned back in his chair and flipped through a stack of hard-copy investment records.

"He's been electronically siphoning off profits from his investments for years," he said, "and sending the funds out of the country. It all looks on the up and up. The paperwork is in order, taxes on the earnings have been paid, and the money deposited into a numbered Swiss account."

"Can we identify the owner of that account?" Sara asked.

"Yes," Fitzmaurice replied, "but not until tomorrow morning when the Swiss bank opens. Do you have a particular person in mind?"

Although Fitzmaurice's tone was mild, his eyes were watchful as he sat slightly forward in his chair, poised and waiting for her reply. Over the past three days he'd been more than patient with her, never once asserting the authority he could rightly have claimed over the investigation. Instead, he had done all in his power to help her and for that he deserved an honest answer. She wrote down a name on a slip of paper and handed it to Fitzmaurice.

Fitzmaurice's eyes lit up. "Thomas Loring Carrier. I take it that this is the gentleman who is beyond my reach."

Sara nodded.

Smiling broadly, he slipped the paper into his shirt pocket and turned to the revenue officers. "Let's gather and compile the evidence we need."

"What will you do with it?" Sara asked.

"Present it to a judge and ask for Spalding's assets to be frozen and the villa and the motor yacht to be seized. That should put a damper on his plans to start a new life here."

For the next hour the revenue officers printed hard-copy information from the bank's mainframe files, while Sara and Fitzmaurice entered it into evidence. After the material was boxed and carried away by the revenue officers for further inspection, Fitzmaurice presented a list of the seized records to the bank's solicitor on their way out the door. The man looked none too happy to receive it.

Outside, they hurried across the dark street through a light rain to a waiting Garda vehicle that would take them to the airport for the return flight to Dublin.

"Were I to do a computer search on Thomas Loring Carrier, what might I learn?" Fitzmaurice asked as he slid into the backseat next to Sara.

"Enough to confirm your suspicions about my assignment," Sara answered.

"Why did you tell me about Carrier now?"

"Because I may need you to cover my back," Sara said.

"Exactly who might I be protecting you from?"

Sara carefully considered her response before she answered. "They think of themselves as patriots," she said.

"Ah," Fitzmaurice said with a knowing nod. "We had our fair share of those during the Troubles."

Each day that passed with no word from Sara made Kerney more anxious and worried about her. Patrick, who missed his mother badly, intensified Kerney's unspoken concerns by constantly asking where she was and when she would return. Sara's absence had shaken Patrick and made Kerney realize that up until now he'd been a sorry excuse for a parent.

Clearly, Sara was the linchpin in Patrick's world and Kerney the absent father seen only occasionally. That point had been driven home to him midmorning when he'd been called to Patrick's preschool. A mean, bossy kid had pushed Patrick down and kicked him during playtime. Patrick had thrown a tantrum and tried to run away. When Kerney got there, he found his son teary eyed, sullen, and miserable, demanding his mother, wanting to go back to his real home, his real school, his real friends.

Kerney took Patrick home immediately and tried to soothe him, but it wasn't until after lunch, when he suggested an afternoon ride, that Patrick broke into a smile. After Kerney saddled up Hondo, a gray gelding, and put Patrick on the saddle in front of him, his son's spirits lifted enough for him to start in again about wanting his very own pony. By the time they reached the pond, fed by a natural spring, surrounded by marsh grass and cattails, Patrick seemed to be over his preschool

ordeal. In the coolness of the cloudy afternoon, with a slight breeze tinged with
enough humidity to promise rain by evening, Kerney dismounted and led Hondo
up a hillock, with Patrick still in the saddle
clutching the pommel. At stone ruins that
looked out at the Sangre de Cristo Mountains, knife-edge sharp in a shaft of sunlight that cut through the cloud bank, he
tethered Hondo to the thick branch of a
cedar tree.

"Do I have to go back?" Patrick asked as
Kerney lifted him out of the saddle.

Kerney studied his worried son's face
before he set him down. "To preschool?"

Patrick nodded somberly.

"Only for a few more days."

"I don't want to," Patrick said stubbornly.

The look on Patrick's face almost broke
Kerney's heart, and he made a snap decision. "Okay, you don't have to go back
there."

"Ever?" Patrick asked, his eyes bright-
ening.

"Ever," Kerney replied as he ruffled his
son's hair and unclipped his cell phone
from his belt. Patrick smiled and scrambled gleefully to the top of the low stone
ruins. With one eye on his son Kerney

called Deputy Chief Larry Otero and told him that he was starting his vacation effective immediately and wouldn't be back until after he returned from the Bootheel.

"You deserve it, Chief," Otero said.

"It's more that my son deserves a father," Kerney replied.

After a short but fruitless search for arrowheads and potsherds at the ruins, which were purported to be the site of a Native American sweat lodge, Kerney rode, with Patrick in front of him, to the barn, where he unsaddled Hondo, put him in the paddock, rubbed him down, and fed him some oats. Then, as a treat, Kerney fixed strawberries and ice cream for Patrick and spent an hour reading to him until it was well past his nap time. When Patrick's head drooped and his eyelids fluttered and closed, Kerney carried him to his bed.

In the study Kerney checked his e-mail. There were still no messages from Sara, which, since he still didn't know where she was or what she was doing, left him with a growing sense of alarm. He fired off a note to her, saying all was well at home but that he really needed to hear from her, and went to check on Patrick. The events of the morning had worn him out and he was fast asleep, but his face was clear of worry. Kerney closed the door quietly and went to the kitchen to clean up the lunch dishes, marveling at the resilience of the young, wishing some of it would rub off on him so he could rebound from his present funk.

Upon their late-night arrival in Dublin, Fitzmaurice received a message informing him that the calls Spalding had made to London were to a very expensive, independent personal escort named Victoria Hopkins, who operated out of a flat in St. John's Wood and advertised herself on the World Wide Web as a "courtesan of distinction." Inquires made of her neighbors by the police revealed that Hopkins was traveling in Wales and due to return home tomorrow.

"Apparently," Fitzmaurice said after he filled Sara in, "yachting isn't Spalding's only preferred leisure-time activity. I would imagine he's anchored in a lovely cove somewhere near Holyhead, rocking the boat — so to speak — with his for-hire courtesan right now."

"Can you arrange for overnight surveillance on the villa in case Spalding arrives early?" Sara asked.

"Consider it done," Fitzmaurice replied

as he eased to a stop in front of Sara's hotel. "And I'll alert the Coast Guard and ask them to be standing by so that he can't slip away to sea."

"Perfect," Sara said as she opened the door. "You really have been a prince, Detective Fitzmaurice. I appreciate all that you've done."

" 'Tis the company I've been keeping, Colonel," Fitzmaurice said with smile. "Till the morning, then."

In her room Sara kicked off her shoes, read her e-mail, and immediately called Kerney.

"Everything is fine," she said when he answered. "I'm safe and sound, and there's nothing for you to worry about. How is Patrick? How are you?"

"All is well here," Kerney replied. "But we've been missing you a lot."

"Me too," Sara said. "Tell me what the two of you have been up to."

After the call Sara sat for a long time trying to figure out why Kerney had sounded a little strained behind his cheerfulness. He'd told her about his daily horseback rides with Patrick, his plan to take him to the Albuquerque zoo, and how Patrick loved to help him in the barn when it was time to feed the horses. But he'd skirted around her questions about Patrick's adjustment to the Santa Fe preschool.

It wasn't like Kerney to hold things back from her. She wondered if he'd deliberately avoided discussing some difficulties Patrick might have experienced. The thought stayed with her long after she set the alarm clock, turned off the light, and went to bed.

Chapter Ten

With the *Sapphire* anchored off the coast of Llanddwyn Island just south of Holyhead, George Spalding was spending a lovely morning after. As always, Victoria Hopkins had been a delight. In her early thirties, she was tall with long dark-blond hair, classy features, naturally perfect breasts, and a slender, fit body.

The evening before, after several hours belowdeck, they had lolled on the fly-bridge, sipping wine and watching terns fishing in the bay and sandpipers wading along the rolling dunes sprinkled with spiky beach grass at the edge of the rocky coastline. At the topside barbecue Spalding had fixed Victoria a dinner of grilled marinated chicken and chard, spinach, and beetroot leaves wilted to perfection in olive oil with a touch of garlic. They talked until a chill in the air forced them once again belowdeck, where Victoria gave him a long kiss and told him to wait for her in the master cabin. A few minutes later she came out of the head dressed as a provocative schoolgirl, wearing an unbuttoned white shirt that exposed a good deal of her breasts, a tie loosened at the collar, a short plaid skirt, and white stockings with a touch of lace that showed at her thighs. With her hair in braids and a pout on her mouth, she told Spalding she had been a bad girl who needed a spanking. It had been a memorable after-dinner treat.

Whenever Spalding availed himself of Victoria's services, he always specified the schoolgirl role-play as part of the package. It was a total turn-on, in and of itself well worth the thousand euros a day, plus expenses, Victoria charged for her services. But aside from the naughty, playful sex Spalding also appreciated Victoria's charm and sophistication. She was university educated, well read, conversant in the arts, and an excellent companion.

She was still asleep in the master cabin when Spalding went on deck. Dawn had yet to break on the horizon, the night sky shimmered with stars, and a pale quarter moon hung above him. He'd awakened from a sound sleep much earlier than usual, prompted by his eagerness to see his villa again. For far too long he'd lived as a transient in ratty furnished flats and apartments, moving from place to place across Europe until he was sure the U.S. Army and the Canadian cops were no longer actively looking for him.

He'd carefully kept a low profile while he invented a new identity, had been cautious with how he used his money to avoid drawing attention to himself, and had exhaustively researched where he wanted to settle down and start anew. It had all been worth the effort. Now the time was drawing near when he could once again have a normal life, come and go as he pleased on the Continent, travel the seas, and enjoy himself to the fullest.

The boat rocked gently in the tidal current as Spalding sat in the cockpit and looked out the windscreen. For a moment he thought back to his time in Vietnam, the Tan Son Nhut mortuary, and the smuggling ring he'd put together. All of the guys in the ring, including Tom Carrier, had been patsies, only interested in having ready cash waiting for them so they could buy new cars, chase skirts, or keep getting high once they got back to the States. They'd accepted without question his accounting of the profits, never realizing that Spalding's father was the Stateside "gem dealer" in the scheme who skimmed fifty percent of the proceeds off the top. In a few short years he and his father had become rich men.

Spalding heard footsteps and swiveled in the pilot's chair to find Victoria, with her hair still in braids, standing a few feet away wrapped in his terry-cloth robe.

"Can't sleep?" she asked with a smile.

Spalding shook his head. "You must have energized me."

"Turn on the lights."

Spalding flipped a dashboard switch and the cockpit lights flickered on. Slowly, Victoria opened the robe. She was naked except for the black seamed nylon stockings and the garter belt he'd given her as a present.

"Isn't it lovely?" she asked.

"You're a bad girl to wear such naughty things," Spalding said sternly.

"I know." She let the robe drop to her feet. "I shan't do it again."

"Turn around."

She handed him an unwrapped condom. "Are you going to punish me?"

"Mind your elders and turn around."

Shivering slightly in the cool air, Victoria turned and bent over to be spanked.

Ten minutes before Sara was due to meet Fitzmaurice outside the hotel, a knock came at her door. She opened up to find two men, one of whom flashed a Department of State special agent shield.

"Colonel Brannon," the man said, "I'm Daniel Withers, with the Bureau of Diplomatic Security assigned to the American embassy, and this is Major Stedman, assistant military attaché. You are to come with us."

"What's this about?" Sara asked, eyeing the two men. Withers, a man nearing thirty with a receding hairline and a dimpled chin, nodded at the major, who wore civvies.

Stedman stepped forward and handed Sara a paper. "The deputy secretary of defense has ordered your immediate return to the Pentagon, Colonel. You are to cease all current activity and accompany us to the airport for a flight to Washington."

Sara read the order. It was original and authentic, most likely delivered overnight by courier. She looked at the major. No older than Withers, he had an intelligent face and close-set, baby-blue eyes that gave nothing away.

"Let me see some identification, Major," Sara said.

Stedman fished out his military ID and gave it to Sara. He was a Marine officer, but what else? She guessed he was with the

Defense Intelligence Agency, which routinely assigned personnel to embassy duty.

"May we come in, Colonel?" Stedman asked, smiling affably.

Sara handed him back the DEPSEC order and his ID. "I see nothing in the order that authorizes you to take me into custody, Major."

"No, ma'am," Stedman replied. "Our orders are to see you safely on your way home."

"Very good, Major," Sara said, "then you can wait in the hall while I pack."

"We have orders to stay with you until your departure, ma'am," Stedman said, pushing his way into the room. Withers followed, closed the door, and stood in front of it with his arms crossed.

So much for not being in custody, Sara thought grimly. She kept her composure in front of the two men and started packing. She passed by the window, hoping to spy Fitzmaurice on the quay waiting for her, but he wasn't there. She wondered if some senior foreign service officer from the U.S. embassy was sitting in the Garda commissioner's office at that very moment, arranging to have the Spalding investigation disappear completely.

While Stedman and Withers watched,

she pulled clothes off hangers and stuffed them into her bag, emptied her toiletries from the bathroom into her kit, and dumped papers into her briefcase, her mind racing. The orders from DEPSEC had apparently left General Clarke out of the loop. She was to report directly upon her return to Thatcher's boss, the provost marshal general, who also commanded army CID. That meant Clarke hadn't shut down the operation and quite possibly didn't even know it had been canceled.

How had the mission been compromised? Had she made a mistake by telling Fitzmaurice about Carrier? Outside of General Clarke he alone knew that Thomas Loring Carrier was a target.

Sara took another quick look out the window. There was still no sign of Fitzmaurice. She decided to trust her instincts; there was absolutely nothing duplicitous about the man. That left General Thatcher, her petty, childish tyrant of a boss, who was Carrier's good friend and second cousin of a powerful senator.

She stood at the desk, blocking Stedman's line of sight as she packed up her laptop. She knew that as soon as she walked out the door, the room would be searched and cleaned by experts, who would leave nothing behind. When Withers glanced away, she slipped the disk containing Spalding's file under the waistband of her slacks. Somehow she had to get it to Fitzmaurice and hope that the Garda bosses would let him do his job in spite of any pressure from Washington.

"It's time to go, Colonel," Stedman said.

"I'm ready," Sara said as she put the laptop in her soft leather briefcase and picked up her room key.

"You can leave the key here," Withers said as he opened the door. "We've already checked you out of the hotel."

"How very thoughtful," Sara said. No doubt Stedman's cleaners would return the key to reception after removing any trace of her from the room.

As she stepped outside the hotel with Stedman in the lead and Withers following behind, Sara spotted Fitzmaurice rolling to a stop at the curb. Perhaps he hadn't been ordered to stand down by his superiors after all. She caught his eye and nodded slightly at a black, right-hand-drive Jeep Grand Cherokee with Diplomatic Corps plates. He glanced at the vehicle and gave Sara a quick nod in return.

Stedman and Withers hustled Sara into the car and drove her away. To avoid telegraphing the tail she didn't dare look back to see if Fitzmaurice was following. Instead she spent the time during the short drive to the airport trying to figure out a way to pass Fitzmaurice the Spalding disk without arousing attention.

At the airport Stedman parked in a restricted zone next to the terminal, and the two men walked her to a check-in area on the upper level, where Withers gave her a ticket. Their diplomatic passports allowed them to bypass security, and they entered a long, wide corridor filled with shops, eateries, and stores that led to the departure gates.

Sara stopped in her tracks and looked at the flight information on the ticket. She had an hour before boarding time. Stedman touched her elbow as she glanced around, hoping to spot Fitzmaurice.

"We'll take you through U.S. Customs now," he said.

"What's the hurry, Major?" Sara replied. U.S. Customs ran a preclearance operation at the airport, and once she stepped across the line, she would technically be on American soil, which meant Fitzmaurice would be unable to easily follow.

"No hurry, ma'am," Stedman replied.

"Would you mind if I bought a book to read on the flight?"

Stedman glanced at Withers, who shrugged in reply. "Go right ahead, Colonel."

In a nearby bookstore crowded with travelers buying newspapers, magazines, and paperbacks, Sara browsed while her watchers stood at the entrance and kept her in view. At the new release section she picked up a copy of Brendan Coughlan's latest novel, *The Dory Shed*, which he'd read from at O'Reilly Hall, and placed the Spalding disk inside it. With the book under her arm she paged through other fiction titles, including a recently reissued edition of *The Year of the French*, by Thomas Flanagan, the writer Fitzmaurice's son, Sean, had so highly praised. Mentally, she counted off the minutes, and was about to lose hope that Fitzmaurice would show, when a man jostled past her in the narrow aisle.

"Excuse me," Fitzmaurice said, in a normal speaking voice.

"No harm done," Sara replied with a smile, as she very deliberately put the Coughlan novel back on the shelf face out.

Fitzmaurice reached for it. "Is it not a good book then?"

"Not my cup of tea," Sara replied. "It's

about some Irishmen living in some dreary place in Nova Scotia."

She turned away, went to the counter, and paid for the Flanagan book. Fitzmaurice stepped up behind her with *The Dory Shed* in his hand.

"Have a safe flight," he said with a smile as she was about to leave.

"Smooth sailing to you," Sara replied.

Just west of Dublin, within the confines of an eleven-kilometer wall, is the largest enclosed city park in Europe. Fitzmaurice had played in it as a child and, as an adolescent, had courted comely lasses under its trees and on the greens.

Seven hundred hectares in size, Phoenix Park, once a hunting preserve of a duke, was a popular destination for Dubliners seeking relief from the crowded streets, the noisy traffic, and the tourists that inundated the city from May to September. Aside from a zoo and flower garden the park also contained the official residence of the Irish president, the residence of the United States ambassador, and Garda Headquarters.

Called in by Deputy Commissioner Noel Clancy, Hugh Fitzmaurice settled into a chair in front of Clancy's desk and smiled at his old friend.

"Am I here to be caned for some misdeed, Commissioner?" he asked.

"Nothing like that, Hugh," Clancy replied with a laugh.

Almost totally bald and with a round, chubby face, Clancy had just celebrated his thirty-ninth year with the Garda. Twenty-five years ago, as a sergeant in the Criminal Investigation Bureau, he'd taken Fitzmaurice, then a new detective with five years in uniform service, under his wing and had shown him the ropes. For the next fifteen years Fitzmaurice, who was perfectly content to remain a detective, had worked for Clancy until he'd been promoted out of criminal investigations into upper management.

"You won't be too long with me, then, will you?" Fitzmaurice said, glancing at his watch. He had two hours to get to Dún Laoghaire before George Spalding was due at the villa.

Clancy shook his head. "An American diplomat paid the commissioner a visit this morning, asking if we'd be so kind, should we happen upon him, to quietly turn over to them this George Spalding fellow you've been searching for."

"Was any reason given?" Fitzmaurice asked.

"Supposedly, it's a matter concerning their national security and thus very hush-hush."

"I very much doubt that is the case," Fitzmaurice replied.

Clancy lifted his head and stared down his nose at Fitzmaurice. "Explain your reasoning."

Fitzmaurice gave Commissioner Clancy a quick summary of the investigation, including the information about Thomas Loring Carrier on the computer disk Sara Brannon had passed to him at the airport bookstore before being whisked away by the two American embassy staff members for a flight to the States.

"I did my own computer search on Carrier last night," he added. "He is a well-connected, staunch supporter of current American foreign policy and a saber rattler for the war on terrorism. Revealing him to be a member of a smuggling ring during his service in Vietnam would be an embarrassment to both the Pentagon and the White House."

"International affairs of state do not fall under our purview, Hugh," Clancy said.

"No, sir, but arresting criminals does."

Clancy leaned back in his chair. "Indeed. But is there sufficient reason to believe that the allegation about Carrier is well founded?"

"I have no reason to doubt Colonel Brannon," Fitzmaurice replied. "Am I to do as the Yanks ask, and help them clean up their sticky little mess?"

"I see no need for that," Clancy said. "We have to consider the Canadian authorities, after all. They have as great a claim on Spalding as the Americans. Take Spalding into custody, interrogate him, but do not charge him without my authorization."

Fitzmaurice smiled as he pulled himself out of the chair.

"Find a way if you can," Clancy added, "to make it appear that circumstances beyond our control made us unable to comply with the wishes of the Americans."

"I'll make it so."

Fitzmaurice left Garda Headquarters in a hurry and headed down the motorway to Dún Laoghaire. When he arrived at the villa, the officer on station reported the Coast Guard had spotted Spalding's boat forty-five minutes out. Fitzmaurice took a deep breath and relaxed. It gave him just enough time to put into play the scheme he'd worked up after leaving Clancy's office. He sent the officer down to the slip along the beachfront to keep watch for Spalding, called the Canadian embassy, and spoke to Ronald Weber, the Royal Canadian Mounted Police liaison officer.

"Surely you're acquainted with the George Spalding case," Fitzmaurice said.

"I am," replied Weber. "An American army officer requested our assistance in gathering information regarding one of his known associates."

"Well, I've a bit of a sticky situation. Apparently, the Yanks now want us to seize up Spalding and surreptitiously turn him over to them."

"Do you know where Spalding is?" Weber asked.

"We not only know where he is, we know where he's hidden the vast fortune of ill-gotten gains your government would very much like to recover. It occurred to me that if the Americans spirit Spalding away, you may never hear of him again."

"That would be unacceptable," Weber said.

"However, if you were to participate in the arrest, I think it would be impossible for us to comply with their wishes."

"Where are you now?" Weber asked.

"Close by," Fitzmaurice replied. "But

first, would you be willing to disavow any knowledge of what I've just told you?"

"You've told me nothing."

"Excellent," Fitzmaurice said. He gave Weber directions to the villa and said, "Be here in thirty minutes."

After he rang off, Fitzmaurice stood on the cliff and scanned the bay with binoculars. The balmy late-summer day had drawn a vast number of boaters to the water, and leisure craft of every imaginable type were cutting through the gentle waves.

Not at all sure what type of boat he was looking for, he lowered the glasses and thought about Lieutenant Colonel Sara Brannon. He feared that only trouble awaited her upon her return to the States.

George Spalding cut the engines and swung the wheel to turn the boat. When *Sapphire* eased against the slip and came to a full stop, he moored the yacht fore and aft. For a long moment he stared up at the pale-blue villa and the steep, terraced gardens that stepped down to the narrow spit of shore. From dockside it was hard to imagine that Dublin was so close at hand. Here he'd have seclusion, quick access to the city, and, as George McGuire, the freedom to roam throughout the European Union as he pleased without fear of discovery.

He imagined a very good life ahead. When the house was ready, he'd apply for membership at the yacht club, buy a sweet racing dinghy, and, starting next year, spend his summers sailing in the bay. But in the short term, after he qualified for his final sea master's certificate, he'd be busy with the house.

The builder had promised it done by the time the gloomy Irish winter set in, and Spalding planned to furnish it with the best that money could buy. He walked up the stone steps to the seaside entrance and unlocked the door. Inside, the musty smell of neglect greeted him. The previous owner had lived in it for fifty years without modernizing the interior. The bare wooden floorboards were scuffed and nicked, the large windows that faced the bay were covered with grime, and faded strips of wallpaper hung loosely below the crown molding that bordered the ceilings.

Spalding passed through the rooms, making mental notes of what kind of furnishings to look for, thinking it might be wise to hire an interior decorator after he returned from his qualifying cruise around

Ireland. He heard footsteps on the staircase and turned to see a friendly-looking, smiling man reach the landing.

"Mr. McGuire," the man said, "a moment of your time, if you please."

"Who are you?" Spalding demanded, as a second man came up the stairs.

"Detective Inspector Fitzmaurice. And this is Inspector Weber of the Royal Canadian Mounted Police. Walk slowly in my direction with your hands in plain view."

Spalding didn't move. He could feel his stomach twist into a knot, his hands get clammy.

"There are police officers outside," Fitzmaurice said. "It would be foolish not to do as I say."

"How did you find me?" Spalding asked as he stepped toward Fitzmaurice and Weber.

"Now, that's quite the tale to tell," Fitzmaurice replied as he turned Spalding around and cuffed him.

During the flight from Dublin, Sara prepared herself as best she could for a worst-case scenario. With the stop-loss program in effect, implemented to keep all career active-duty personnel from leaving the service, she knew it was unlikely she would be allowed to resign her commission or apply for early retirement.

Although the special orders she'd received from General Clarke protected her from any official reprimand, there were many other ways the civilian brass could exact a pound of flesh, including the depressing possibility of being posted to a job normally held by an officer of lower rank. It was a surefire way to signal to the general staff that an officer's career was over.

She deplaned at Ronald Reagan Airport, where an army captain in uniform met her outside of customs and drove her directly to the Pentagon.

"You can leave your luggage in the vehicle, Colonel," the captain said as he parked in a restricted zone near the entrance, "and I'll have it delivered to your quarters."

"Fine," Sara said, knowing full well her luggage would be searched, the Garda's initial surveillance reports would be confiscated, and the Spalding case file on her laptop hard drive would be permanently erased. But she'd deliberately made no case notes while in Ireland, so that would limit what the search revealed. As she followed the captain into the building, she wondered if she would be interrogated before the hammer fell on her. Instead, she was escorted to the office suite of Major General Bernard von Braun, the provost marshal general of the army. Predictably, von Braun kept her waiting in the outer office for twenty minutes.

Sara did her best to quell her growing anxiety, but when she was ushered into von Braun's presence and found General Thatcher there, looking smug and self-satisfied, she lost all hope of salvaging her career.

She snapped to, and von Braun kept her at attention as he stared her down for a long minute. He had a large, protruding lower lip that gave his expression a permanent scowl, and a long, pointed chin. Finally, he gave her the bad news. Her orders to the training branch had been rescinded, her leave was canceled, and she was to report to Fort Belvoir for a five-day orientation course in an intelligence-gathering initiative designed to analyze real-time combat-patrol reports of insurgent activities.

"From Fort Belvoir you will be deployed as part of a tactical survey team to Iraq," von Braun said, "and attached to a brigade. You are to report to Fort Belvoir on Monday morning. Until then I'm granting you immediate leave so you can put your affairs in order."

"Permission to speak, sir," Sara said.

"Go ahead."

"Upon deployment, am I to have command of the tactical survey team?"

"No, you are not, Colonel," von Braun replied. "You will serve solely as a senior analyst. General Thatcher has arranged to have your personal items packed and ready for you to remove from the premises."

"Sir, I request relief from this assignment and permission to either resign my commission or apply for early retirement."

"Denied, Colonel," von Braun snapped, "and for the record, be advised that your investigation of George Spalding has been classified as top secret. Any breach on your part of the National Security Act will be cause for disciplinary action. Do I make myself clear?"

"Yes, sir." Sara glanced at Thatcher, who couldn't control the pleasure that danced in his eyes. The tin soldier had won, and she didn't have another damn thing to lose except her pride. She snapped her gaze back to von Braun. "Permission to speak, General."

"Go ahead."

"Never mind," Sara said. "I think I've

been bullied enough for one day."

Von Braun's face turned beet red. "Dismissed," he thundered.

Sara did an about-face and left. At her cubicle she got an ice-cold reception. Officers she'd worked with for three years averted their eyes or looked down at their desks as she walked by. She checked her cubicle to make sure all personal items had been removed and looked through the packed cardboard box to see if anything was missing. All her files had been taken away and the cabinets and desk drawers were empty.

Carrying the cardboard box, she left without saying a word. At the end of the hallway a civilian employee met her and took her to personnel, where she was officially cleared from the Pentagon and received her new orders. Outside the personnel office General Clarke's aide caught up with her at the elevators. A congenial man by nature, he seemed morose, almost despondent, when he asked if she had a few minutes to meet with the general.

She followed along, wondering what additional bad news would be dropped in her lap. The general came around the desk when she entered his office and asked her to sit, something he rarely did with subordinates. He arranged himself in a facing leather chair, the big window behind him providing a clear view of a Pentagon parking lot, and sadly shook his head.

"Nasty business," he said through tight lips.

"Yes, sir."

"I did my best to stop this, Colonel."

"There's no need to explain, sir."

"There damn well is," Clarke replied gruffly. "You were following my orders."

"You made me aware of the risks, sir."

"I want you to know that your new assignment was my doing. But before you jump to any conclusions, understand this: If I hadn't intervened, you were going to be buried under Thatcher's thumb for the next two years and ground into mincemeat. One way or another you would have been cashiered from the service with the loss of all benefits. The Iraq assignment gets you out of here and gives you the chance to retire with honor once you have your twenty in."

"At this point I could care less about that, sir."

"Understood, Colonel. You are not alone in your feelings about the current conduct of military affairs in our country. I've been asked to hang up my soldier's suit and retire. I'll be leaving at the end of the month."

"Sir, if you'll excuse me, that sucks."

"Yes, it does." Clarke smiled. "You would have made a fine general officer, Colonel. But unfortunately, like me, you're one lousy bureaucrat."

"Its been an honor to have known you, sir, and to have served with you."

"Likewise, Colonel." Clarke stood. "When you get to Iraq, you'll be assigned to Slam Norton's brigade. You won't have to worry about any political booby traps with him. He's a good man, a stud officer, and a first-rate leader. Do your job well and he'll make sure you'll get a decent posting when you rotate back home."

Sara got to her feet. "Thank you, sir."

"Be careful and stay safe, Colonel," Clarke said, as he stepped forward and shook Sara's hand.

"Yes, sir, thank you, sir."

Clarke's aide, who had waited for her in the outer office, took Sara through security, and she caught the Metro with her thoughts in a jumble. What should she do with the Arlington house? Rent it? Put it on the market? There wasn't time to do anything. Kerney would have to deal with it.

What would she tell Kerney? *Sorry, but*

I'm going to Iraq and I can't tell you what I did to screw things up. What should they do about Patrick? What would be best for him? What would the upheaval do to him?

She got off the Metro at the Arlington station, carrying the cardboard box, feeling that her world had fallen into ruins around her feet. She wasn't about to let herself cry, although she could feel the wetness stinging at the corners of her eyes.

Because of Sara Brannon, Hugh Fitzmaurice would forevermore think of the interrogation rooms at Dublin Castle as the dungeon. It was there that Spalding waited under the watchful eye of an officer while Fitzmaurice brought RCMP Inspector Weber up to date on the investigation. Weber, an old-school peeler who paid attention to detail, took his time going through the book of evidence Fitzmaurice had assembled.

"What about the Swiss account Spalding has been siphoning money into?" Weber asked when he'd finished.

"Colonel Brannon thought it might belong to Carrier," Fitzmaurice replied. "But in fact the account is owned by Spalding's ex-wife. Which means, of course, it could rightfully belong to your government."

"Excellent," Weber replied, his gray eyes smiling. "I'll start the process with the Swiss to learn the particulars. Will you be bringing charges against Spalding?"

"I'd like to use that possibility as a bargaining chip with him," Fitzmaurice said. "If your embassy made an official request to Garda Headquarters not to do so, it would most probably be granted without delay."

"How can you be sure?"

"I'll make a telephone call."

Weber stroked his chin. "What if the embassy also asked for an expedited extradition hearing on Spalding?"

"We could help to hurry it along."

"How much time can you give me?" Weber asked.

"I am obligated to inform Interpol and the Americans that Spalding is in custody, but I can dawdle about it until the end of the day."

"I'll start the ball rolling," Weber said, eyeing Fitzmaurice speculatively. "You're going after this Carrier fellow, aren't you?"

"It seems a reasonable thing to do."

When Weber left, Fitzmaurice dialed Deputy Commissioner Noel Clancy's private line and said, "On behalf of the Canadian government and with their assistance,

I've taken George Spalding into custody."

"Well done," Clancy replied. "Have you informed the Americans?"

"I've nary had time to catch my breath. The Canadians would be most pleased if we didn't bring charges against Mr. Spalding. It would serve to hasten his extradition. Their embassy should be calling soon to discuss the matter."

"How unfortunate for the Americans that the Canadians became involved. Very good. I'll inform the commissioner and recommend he take a decision promptly. How long will it be before you catch your breath?"

"Surely not before the end of the day," Fitzmaurice replied. "I've yet to interview Mr. Spalding."

Clancy chuckled. "You would have made a grand politician, Hugh Michael Fitzmaurice."

"I am deeply offended by that remark, Commissioner," Fitzmaurice replied.

Clancy laughed and rang off.

Fitzmaurice put the telephone in the cradle, picked up the thick evidence book, and went to the interrogation room where Spalding waited. He was, at best, a nondescript-looking man, what the Yanks would call a good-old-boy type. A bit

387

fleshy in the cheek, he had a wide nose that sloped down to a broad chin, and a bit of loose skin at his Adam's apple.

Fitzmaurice dropped the evidence book on the table with a thud and sat across from Spalding. "Where to begin," he said amiably. "Let's start with the crimes you've committed in Ireland."

"I want a solicitor," Spalding replied.

"Yes, of course, but first allow me to inform you of the bill of particulars which will be presented against you. The courts are particularly harsh, when it comes to punishment, on those who launder money."

Spalding blinked. "What money?"

"Those many millions you've secreted away over the years in a Galway bank."

"You must be mistaken."

"Ah, George, don't make it hard on yourself." Fitzmaurice patted the evidence book. "We've uncovered the money, and the court will rule very quickly to freeze your assets. You'll soon be penniless."

Spalding stared silently at his hands for a few moments.

"Then, of course, there are the additional charges of illegal entry into the country, forgery, conspiracy to commit fraud, and a number of lesser indictments."

Spalding slouched in his chair.

"This must be depressing for you," Fitzmaurice said. "There you were, about to put all your troubles behind, get on with a new life, and it all vanishes like a puff of smoke. Unfortunately, I'm afraid things will be much worse for you when we turn you over to the Americans."

"What are you talking about?"

"The Yanks want you to disappear, and because you are a wartime deserter from the United States Army technically still under the control of the military, I imagine they can easily do it without any fanfare."

"Disappear?"

Fitzmaurice shrugged. "I can't be totally sure of it, but that's my distinct impression. They've asked for you to be released to them under their National Security Act."

Spalding looked completely nonplussed. "National security? That doesn't make any sense."

"It has something to do with a member of your smuggling ring, Thomas Carrier."

"I don't know who you're talking about."

Fitzmaurice took out the information on Carrier he'd downloaded from the Internet and handed it to Spalding. "This may refresh your memory. He's quite highly regarded by the current Washington administration."

Fitzmaurice continued talking while Spalding read. "Were it not for Carrier, you would not be in such a pickle. As I've reflected upon it, apparently the Americans wish to avoid any unpleasantness you might cause them by seizing you up and holding you incommunicado in some military prison."

Spalding stared at him with worried eyes.

"And I daresay," Fitzmaurice added, as he took the documents out of Spalding's hand, "from what I know about the new laws your government has passed, it may well be that you shall never again see the light of day as a free man."

"How do I know you're not just making this up?"

Fitzmaurice stood and reached for the evidence book. "I'll have the Americans here in ten minutes."

Spalding waved his hand nervously to stop Fitzmaurice from leaving. "Wait. I haven't violated any national security laws. I was an enlisted man who worked in a mortuary in Vietnam, for Chrissake."

"I know that. But what you did as a foolish young man in Vietnam over thirty years ago now has political implications no one could have predicted, and a far heavier burden than what the law normally allows rests squarely on your shoulders. Surely it is by no means fair. But there may be a way out of it."

"What way?"

"Perhaps we can avoid giving you over to the Americans."

"How?"

"Should you agree to admit to the crimes you've committed in Ireland, Irish law would take precedence, which means that neither the Americans nor Canadians could attempt to extradite you until your case here is settled."

Fitzmaurice returned to his chair and sat. "That could take a good bit of time, which you and your legal counsel — you will certainly need the services of a barrister as well as a solicitor — could use to an advantage. However, you need to know that I alone will decide if your case goes forward to the courts or if you are to be quietly given over to the Yanks."

"What do you want?" Spalding asked.

"Your free and willing confession, and all that you know about Carrier's involvement in the smuggling ring."

Spalding nodded.

"Very good." Fitzmaurice pressed a hidden button on the underside of the table to signal that it was time to start the digital recording. "Let's begin, then, shall we?"

Spalding made his voluntary statement with little need for prompting, and by the end of the very long session Fitzmaurice had not only a full confession but a detailed accounting of Carrier's role in the smuggling operation.

He turned Spalding over to an officer to be officially charged, called the American embassy to report the capture of George Spalding, and then drove to Garda Headquarters, where he presented himself to Deputy Commissioner Clancy and made his report.

"Why did you charge Mr. Spalding without my authorization?" Clancy asked.

"Not to have done so would have raised too many questions."

"We have promised the Canadians swift approval of their extradition petition."

"Surely the Garda solicitor could sympathetically wring his hands, complain bitterly about the mistake made by a lowly detective inspector, and promise to rectify the situation promptly."

"You know that can't happen," Clancy

snapped. "Spalding's solicitor will immediately file against the extradition petition. And the Yanks are all too likely to nobble the Canadians, who are well used to bowing to the Americans. What are you up to, Fitzmaurice?"

"Nothing at all, Commissioner. By the way, I did call the Yanks as you requested. I think it likely that they, too, will be seeking Spalding's extradition, which should confuse the situation nicely. If we let the Canadians and Yanks fight it out, we can sit on the sidelines while Irish justice runs its course and avoid being accused of playing favorites."

Clancy sighed. "You may be right. It does give us a way out of a worrisome situation."

"Is there anything else, Commissioner?" Fitzmaurice asked.

"Consider yourself censured for insubordination," Clancy said. "Now get yourself home and give my best to Edna."

"I will indeed. Good night to you, Noel."

"Just walk away, then," Clancy grumbled, suppressing a smile.

Outside, Hugh Fitzmaurice relaxed. He'd done what he could to make it impossible for the American government to bury the political embarrassment of

Thomas Loring Carrier's criminal history under the cloak of national security. For Sara Brannon's sake he hoped he had succeeded. He patted his suit jacket pocket, which contained a video of the Spalding interview he'd burned on a DVD disk. He'd made it just in case he might need a bit of insurance if and when the politicians started braying and carrying on.

Minutes after an unsettling telephone call from Sara, Kerney made airplane reservations on a flight out of Albuquerque that would take him and Patrick to Washington, D.C., by way of Chicago. With a two-hour layover they would arrive shortly after midnight eastern time.

He needed to call Sara back and let her know when to expect them, but was reluctant to do so until he could sort through his thoughts and feelings. Her announcement that she would be shipping out to Iraq in ten days had thrown him for a loop. When he'd asked what in the hell had happened to cause such a radical change in plans, she'd shrugged the question off, talking instead about how she wanted Kerney to come to Arlington to help her with all that needed doing before she left. Decisions about the house and its contents had to be made, arrangements for Patrick had to be decided upon, and a myriad of small pressing matters required attention.

He'd asked her for more information about the sudden turnaround of events, but she resisted talking about it. All he learned was that she would be temporarily assigned to Fort Belvoir, Virginia, for a week of training before she shipped out, but didn't know if she'd be confined to the post or allowed to make the daily commute from home.

In spite of Sara's best efforts to sound composed Kerney had hung up more worried about his wife than he'd ever been. Something bad had happened to Sara. He knew it from what she didn't say and the way she'd sounded. Her words had been rushed, the pitch of her voice unusually high, her tone tense.

He tried to figure it out. Did it have something to do with her special overseas assignment? Because he knew nothing about it, he could only guess. But having her orders rescinded, her leave canceled, and given short notice that she was about to be sent to a war zone made Kerney think the two events were connected.

He let the reality of the situation sink in and decided to let go of his indignation and give Sara his full support. She didn't need to have him bitching at her about something she couldn't control. He called her with the flight information, trying his best to sound cheerful.

"I'll pick you up," Sara said.

"There's no need. We can take a cab from the airport."

"I want to. We're not going to have much time together for a while."

"Do you have any idea how long you'll be gone?" Kerney asked.

"Six months, but it could be extended."

"You need to tell me what's going on, Sara."

"Not now, not on the phone."

Ten hours later Kerney carried a sleepy Patrick up the jetway at the Washington airport, where an exhausted-looking Sara met them outside the passenger boarding area. She scooped Patrick into her arms, gave Kerney a kiss on the cheek, and hurried them out of the airport, asking Patrick, as they walked to the car, rapid-fire questions about his time in Santa Fe with his daddy.

Never had Kerney seen Sara so agitated, which convinced him that whatever had happened to her was major. He was determined to learn the specifics but knew he'd have to wait until she was ready to talk about it.

At the house Sara disappeared with Patrick into his bedroom. After a decent interval Kerney looked in on them to see if everything was all right and found them asleep on the small bed, Patrick under the covers, Sara curled up beside him. In the master bedroom he discovered Sara had already begun to prepare for her deployment. Freshly laundered, neatly folded combat fatigues were on top of the dresser, highly polished boots were lined up on the floor, army-issue socks, underwear, belts, and caps were spread out on the bed next to two empty duffel bags.

Sara had left her orders on the kitchen table. Kerney looked through them and learned nothing more than what he'd already been told. He wondered if he'd misjudged her situation. Perhaps the new assignment was based solely on the requirements of the service during wartime.

He sat at the table and thought about it. Sara didn't rattle easily. Was she simply as dismayed as he by the disruption of their plans? He suspected those feelings played into it but couldn't shake off his intuition that something had gone wrong at the Pentagon.

He checked on his wife and son again. The sight of them cuddled asleep on Patrick's bed made all his resentment about the military bureaucracy and his growing fear for Sara's safety rise to the surface again.

The next day Kerney and Sara avoided any serious discussions until Patrick, who was delighted to be back home, took his afternoon nap. Earlier, Sara had already decided to tell Kerney everything, army regulations be damned. He had a right to know, not only because he was her husband and completely trustworthy, but because he was the reason the Spalding case had surfaced in the first place.

While Patrick napped, they sat at the kitchen table and Sara laid out the facts, starting with her suspicions of Thomas Carrier's participation in the gemstone smuggling ring, who he was, her subsequent hunt for Spalding in Ireland, and how it had all ended badly when she'd been pulled off the investigation, called back to the Pentagon, and royally reamed by the provost marshal general.

"Jesus," Kerney said, taking her hand.

"I asked to resign my commission or be allowed to retire," Sara said, reading the anger in Kerney's eyes, "but my requests were disallowed. They've got me for the duration, Kerney, and there's nothing I can do about it. I could be court-martialed for telling you all of this."

His jaw tight, Kerney lapsed into silence. Finally he said, "This is ludicrous."

"I know."

"These guys deserve to be brought down."

"There's still a slight chance that could happen," Sara said.

"How?" Kerney asked.

Sara thought about Hugh Fitzmaurice. Although she'd been able to pass him a copy of the Spalding file, there was no guarantee he'd be able to use it to expose the cover-up. "It's best if you don't know."

"Why?"

"Because I've told you too much already." Sara leaned close to Kerney and stroked his cheek. "Let it go. I'm not going to slink around with my tail between my legs. I fell apart yesterday, but except for wanting to inflict great bodily harm on a few people, I'm okay now. I'll pull my tour of duty, come back home, and you can get me pregnant again."

"Are you serious?"

Sara nodded. "I've been dreaming about a daughter. She's a sweet, lovely little girl."

Patrick's arrival in the kitchen ended the

conversation, but from the grin on Kerney's face Sara could tell that her suggestion of adding to the family had been met with enthusiastic approval.

By the end of the weekend they'd made decisions to sell the house, move what Sara wanted to keep to the Santa Fe ranch, donate everything else to a local charity, and dispose of her vehicle. During the week that followed, Sara and Kerney did their best to keep the family rituals intact. After reporting to Fort Belvoir, Sara had been granted permission to commute, so during the day Kerney took care of Patrick, did the household chores, and made all the necessary arrangements.

Not surprisingly, the pending changes did not sit well with Patrick, in spite of their repeated attempts to reassure him that while Mommy had to go away again, they would all be together soon. As the days passed, he became more grumpy, bossy, and whiny, and one night after dinner he refused to take his bath. When Kerney picked him up to carry him off to the tub, Patrick hit him with his fist and burst into tears.

That night they talked about Patrick, and Sara suggested it might be best to send him to stay with her brother and his wife on the ranch in Montana until she returned from Iraq.

"He'd have his older cousins to play with, and his grandparents nearby," she said.

"What kind of father would I be if I let that happen?" Kerney replied hotly. "I've shortchanged him enough as it is. Up to now our ranch has been a place where he comes to visit Daddy, ride horses, and take family vacations." He stabbed his finger at the floor. "This has been his only true home, here with you. Now that's about to permanently change. I won't have him shunted off to relatives."

Sara took in the raw look of self-recrimination on Kerney's face. For some reason he'd put himself under a microscope and come up sorely lacking as a parent. "What happened in Santa Fe, Kerney?"

"Patrick got pushed around by a bully at the preschool. When I got there, the worst of it was over, but all he wanted was you, his real home, and his real friends."

"Oh, Kerney, of course he would want his mother," Sara said. "He's only three."

Kerney shook his head. "It can't be that easily rationalized, and I can't stand the thought of you in Iraq and Patrick in

Montana. I'd feel terrible. He stays with me. I'll call Johnny Jordan in the morning and tell him I won't be going to the Bootheel to work on the movie."

"Maybe the two of you should go," Sara said.

Kerney looked away and stared stubbornly out the living room window.

"It might help the both of you keep your minds off things," she added.

"Not possible. Besides, who'd care for him while I'm working?"

"I'm sure the film company provides tutors for the child actors and nannies for the children of the stars. I'd be a lot happier knowing the two of you were off having some fun. Do it for me."

He switched his gaze from the window to Sara. "You can't be serious."

She met his stubborn blue eyes with a smile. "I am. And when you get back from the Bootheel, buy Patrick his pony."

Kerney's eyes softened. "Are those my orders?"

"If you please."

The week ended in a rush. Movers came to pack and box, the realtor showed the house to prospective buyers, and a charity sent a truck for the donations. Kerney sold Sara's SUV to a dealer and rented a car for their last two days together. On Friday morning they got up early and Kerney drove her to Fort Belvoir, where he and Patrick spent a hour with her at the hospitality center before she had to leave for her final block of instruction and then a flight to Baghdad.

He watched her crisply walk away, smile over her shoulder, throw a kiss, and wave. He threw a kiss back, smiling as brightly as he could, holding on tightly to Patrick's hand to keep him from running after her. He thought about roadside bombs, mortars, rocket-propelled grenades, snipers, and shrapnel, and prayed that no harm would come to her.

Patrick cried and tugged to free himself from Kerney's grasp. He picked him up, wiped the tears away, and hugged him tightly. "It's just you and me again, sport," he whispered in his son's ear as Sara disappeared from view.

Patrick sniffled and wrapped his arms tightly around Kerney's neck.

Chapter Eleven

The morning after his interrogation of George Spalding, Hugh Fitzmaurice prepared his reports and submitted them to the district court. At the proceeding later in the day the judge denied Spalding bail and remanded him, at the request of the prosecution, to Cloverhill Prison.

Feeling pleased about it all, Fitzmaurice took the afternoon off and spent the remainder of the day on the putting green at the Rathfarnham golf course near his house, until it was time for Edna to come home from work.

After a lovely weekend capped by a leisurely Sunday motor trip to visit his sister and her family in the town of Trim, Fitzmaurice returned to work on Monday to find that the Spalding case had been turned upside down. Someone had retained a top-flight Dublin solicitor to represent Spalding. The solicitor had visited with the attorney general on his client's behalf and asked that the charges be dropped, arguing that Spalding's confession had been coerced and subterfuge had been used to compel him to make false accusations against Thomas Carrier.

Fitzmaurice also found out that other cunning machinations were afoot. The Americans and the Canadians had joined forces and proposed to the minister of justice that if the extraditions were expedited, Spalding would be allowed to plead guilty to desertion from the U.S. Army, sentenced to thirty days incarceration in a military stockade, and then immediately handed over to Canadian authorities.

But the crowning bit of news came when Noel Clancy told him that a petition to the judge would be made that very Monday morning asking for the proceedings to be closed, which, under Irish law, effectively barred any written publication or public broadcast of the particulars surrounding the case.

"It seems we've been dealt a cold deck of cards," Clancy had said.

"Or the Americans have sweetened the pot by offering to outsource a thousand or more jobs to a wholly owned Irish subsidiary to keep the Celtic Tiger roaring," Fitzmaurice replied.

"You have a very pessimistic view of the world."

"No," Fitzmaurice said, "it's just politics I don't like."

"Well, let it go, Hugh. You've done your job and now it's in the hands of the politicians, whether you like it or not. Don't go off and dig yourself a pit to fall into."

At his office that morning Fitzmaurice placed a call to Sara Brannon to inform her of the situation, only to be told that she'd been reassigned and was no longer at the Pentagon. After completing a summary report on the Spalding case he faxed the official notification of Spalding's capture to Interpol, the Royal Canadian Mounted Police, and the Pentagon, before leaving to visit Cloverhill Prison.

Located in Clondalkin, five miles south of the city on the bank of River Camac, Cloverhill was a modern facility that housed over four hundred inmates. Inside he met with the assistant governor of the institution and asked to see Spalding's visitor records. According to the sign-in roster the solicitor representing Spalding had visited him last Saturday, accompanied by another man, one Major Stedman, a United States Marine Corps officer attached to the American embassy.

When Fitzmaurice asked if there might be any surveillance video of the solicitor and the Marine officer, he was escorted to a closed-circuit monitoring station and shown a clip of the two men registering at the visitors reception area. Major Stedman was one of the men who'd bustled Sara Brannon off to the airport.

He left the prison feeling both angry and dispirited, and the next day he went about his job trying to sort out what, if anything, he could do on his own to stop the cover-up. All of his reports and supplemental information had been sealed by the court, and he was obligated to let the matter drop. But surely there had to be a way to get around it. He had DVD copies of Spalding's and Paquette's interrogations, but he needed to hit upon a scheme that would allow him to put them to use without making a target of himself.

On Wednesday he had an idea that took him to Spalding's motor yacht. He searched it, and the following morning he took a page from Spalding's book of tricks and, using an alias, bought an inexpensive mobile phone with prepaid minutes. On St. Stephen's Green he stood across the street from Paquette's hotel, slipped one of the forged documents he'd found hidden on the motor yacht into an envelope, addressed it to Paquette, sought out a young lad passing by, and asked him to deliver it to the hotel bellman.

"What's in for me, then?" the lad asked in a distinct Irish brogue that left no doubt of his Dublin roots.

"Ten euros," Fitzmaurice replied. "Here are five for you now. Tell the bellman to delivery it straightaway and give him this fiver for his trouble. You'll have your second five when you report back to me that it's done."

The young boy took the envelope, stuffed the bills in his pocket, and gazed up at Fitzmaurice with mischief in his eyes. Before he could dart away ten euros richer, his job left undone, Fitzmaurice grabbed him by the scruff of the neck, opened his jacket, and let him take a good long look at his holstered handgun.

"You do not want to be skipping off without doing your little task, now, do you, my lad?" he asked pleasantly.

The wide-eyed boy gulped, shook his head, ran across the street clutching the envelope, and disappeared into the hotel. Within a few minutes he came back into view, returned for his fiver, and took off down the sidewalk toward Grafton Street.

Fitzmaurice waited a decent interval before dialing Paquette's mobile number.

"Did you get the document?" he asked when she answered.

"Who is this?" Paquette replied.

"That's not important. Did you get it?"

"Yes."

"I have all of the remaining forged papers George Spalding used to convince you to help him. If the Garda comes calling again, I'm sure you could make use of them."

"How much do you want?" Paquette asked.

"Money isn't at issue. A favor would suffice."

"What kind of favor?"

"Simply tell all that you know about George Spalding's recent adventures in Ireland to a journalist. He will call you later in the day on your mobile and arrange to meet you."

"Why should I trust you?" Paquette asked.

"Would you rather I destroy the papers?"

"No, don't do that."

"Very well, then," Fitzmaurice said. "If you handle this as I ask, you'll have sufficient proof of your innocence to avoid having any charges being put forth."

"Why are you doing this?"

"It serves a larger purpose," Fitzmaurice replied. "Are we agreed?"

"Yes."

"Good. You'll receive the remaining documents from the journalist after he's met with you."

At noon Fitzmaurice stood outside Davy O'Donoghue's Pub on Duke Street and waited for John Ryan, an investigative reporter for the largest newspaper in Ireland, to make his appearance. An eccentric by nature, Ryan was hard to miss as he came strolling down the street with his full beard and shock of thick, curly hair badly in need of a trim. He wore a double-breasted suit and carried the ever-present, prized walking stick his grandfather had won in a game of cards from the famous Irish dramatist Sean O'Casey some eighty or more years ago.

"Why are you loitering about in front of O'Donoghue's," Ryan asked as he drew near, "when you should be inside with a pint in your hand waiting for me?"

"To resist temptation," Fitzmaurice answered. "You know I can't drink while on duty."

" 'Tis an insufferable rule you are forced to live by. What scandalous information do you have for me today?"

"A story to match your considerable journalistic talents."

Ryan laughed and waved the walking stick at the entrance. "Well, in we go, then. There's not a moment to lose."

Davy O'Donoghue's didn't cater to the tourists or the up-market types who worked in the city center, but to the true working-class denizens of Irish pubs who ate their lunches at the bar or at the small tables jammed together at the back of the narrow room that would forever smell like stale cigarette smoke, even though such unhealthy behavior had now been banned in all drinking premises throughout the Republic. In defiance of the law O'Donoghue occasionally lit up a cigar while standing behind the bar, much to the delight of his clientele, who would quickly follow suit. The pub was one of the few city-centre drinking establishments that had escaped becoming a tourist stop on the famous Dublin pub crawl.

Amid the clamor and the clatter, with their elbows knocking against those of nearby diners, Ryan listened and ate lunch while Fitzmaurice talked. After he put aside his plate and drained his pint, Ryan said, " 'Tis a very interesting story, but certainly not front-page news without proof that this Spalding fellow pointed the finger at Carrier as a member of his smuggling gang. Is there nothing Paquette can tell me about this Carrier chap?"

"She has no knowledge of him," Fitzmaurice replied. "But she's a starting point that would allow you to ask questions about the highly unusual way in which this case has unfolded."

Ryan held up his empty glass for a refill, and the bartender gave him a nod in return. "Which would be greeted in return by nothing more than official denials, protestations of ignorance, invocations of court orders barring disclosure of information, and the like. I don't doubt what you've told me, Hugh, but I see no way to pursue it without more evidence in hand."

Ryan paused to accept his fresh pint from the bartender. "Using only Paquette as the gambit to expose all the diplomatic maneuvering and skullduggery you've told me about simply won't work. What you've given me will result in nothing more than a wee story buried in the back pages of the front section of the Sunday edition."

Fitzmaurice put his hands palms down on the table. "You won't do it, then?"

Ryan saluted Fitzmaurice with his pint and took a swallow. "You know there's not a peeler or a judge in the Free State who could make me reveal an anonymous source of information. Not even you could do it when you tried, and we go back to the days when we were lads playing football in the alleys on the north side of the Liffey."

Fitzmaurice laughed. He knew it to be so. The only possible way to get John Ryan to reveal his sources would be to take away his drink and lock him up in a hospital detoxification ward. "You've not answered my question."

Ryan set his pint down and leaned forward. "Did you record Spalding's confession that implicated Carrier and make a copy for yourself?"

Fitzmaurice nodded. "You know me well, John Ryan."

"Did you use a video camcorder or a tape recorder?"

"A camcorder, of course."

Ryan held out his hand. "Let me have the disk with the video file on it."

"I can't just give it to you. Noel Chancy would know in a instant that I am your source."

"Is the confession on the Garda server?"
"Yes."

Ryan smiled, took out a business card, wrote on it, and pushed it toward

Fitzmaurice. "Take the DVD to a city branch library where no one knows you, use one of the computers, and send it to the Web address on the back of the card."

Fitzmaurice picked up the card and waved it at Ryan. "This is all well and good, but how does one explain the sudden appearance of a Garda interrogation video on the World Wide Web?"

"Are the Garda computers harder to crack than the Pentagon's? A sixteen-year-old-boy in Norway ran riot in the U.S. military computers earlier this year, and from what the newspaper's technology reporter tells me, the U.S. government still doesn't know how deep the boy penetrated. So I should think we have more than adequate cover and deniability. In this particular instance I would imagine that some college student viewed the video while probing the Garda computers during a cyber visit, decided it was a worthy and interesting example of his technical wizardry, and put it on the Web for all to see."

"Hackers often get caught."

Ryan nodded. "Many do, but not all. I've made use of a few of them in the past with excellent results. Are you game?"

"You'll start with Paquette?"

"Of course. She's the entrée to the story.

If the video shows what you say it does, my exposé in the Sunday edition will be picked up by every television newsreader in Europe and North America within the day."

Fitzmaurice took the documents he'd promised Paquette out of his suit coat pocket and handed them to Ryan. "Call her on her mobile, and when you've finished meeting with her, give her these. Her number is attached."

Ryan nodded, glanced at his watch, drained the last of his pint, and stood. "You've given me a lot to do, otherwise I'd stay for another."

"You do your best work when you're sober, John."

"Now, that's a disquieting thought," Ryan said merrily. "Thanks for lunch. Don't tarry. I need that video file sent along promptly."

"I'll see to it."

Fitzmaurice paid the bill and made his way out of O'Donoghue's. From their earliest days together as schoolboy chums and neighborhood hooligans, John Ryan had never once lied to him or broken his word. His only worry was Deputy Commissioner Noel Clancy, who had a keen eye for his shenanigans. If pressed, he'd plead ignorance, of course, and hope that Noel would be secretly pleased by the unusual and highly regrettable circumstances that were about to unfold.

At the branch library he sent off the video file to the Web address Ryan had given him. On his way back to the office he sailed the DVD out the car window and into the Liffey.

It was a pleasant, clear early Sunday morning when Fitzmaurice's doorbell rang. He looked out the window to see Noel Clancy waiting at the door. Dressed in his Garda uniform, he had a stern look on his face and held a rolled-up newspaper in his hand.

Fitzmaurice slipped outside, thankful that Edna was upstairs in the tub taking a soak with the door closed and Sean was away for the weekend hiking the Twelve Bens mountain range with his older brother.

"Good morning to you, Noel," he said with a smile. "Have you been called into work today?"

"Have you seen this?" Clancy said, slapping the Sunday paper against Fitzmaurice's arm.

"Aye, I have."

"Jesus, Mary, and Joseph, what have you gone and done?"

"Not a thing, and I'll ask you not to be accusing me falsely."

"The commissioner has been getting calls from every bloody politician in the government about this. They all want answers, Hugh, and so do I. How did the interrogation video get onto a blog?"

Fitzmaurice shrugged nonchalantly. "Hackers?"

"How did John Ryan learn about Joséphine Paquette?"

"Again, I'm without an explanation. Would you like me to go around to her hotel and talk to her?"

"She returned to Canada yesterday."

Fitzmaurice shook his head sadly. "Bad luck that. I'll speak to John Ryan about it."

"That's already been done," Clancy said. "He's claiming Paquette came to him voluntarily with the information about Spalding, and the blog was not of his doing."

"Well, there you have it," Fitzmaurice said with a straight face.

"I'm putting you on desk duty until this situation is resolved by way of an official inquiry. Report to my office first thing in the morning."

"As you wish," Fitzmaurice said. "But this time, Commissioner, I would gratefully appreciate it if you didn't have me shredding old documents in the basement. It's very bad for my allergies."

Clancy almost smiled at Fitzmaurice's nonchalance. He was indeed a gifted rapscallion. "You could retire and avoid any unpleasantness."

Fitzmaurice shook his head. "I've done nothing wrong and have no plans to retire until Sean finishes university."

"Are you going to Sunday Mass?"

"As a good Catholic should. Will I see you there?"

"Not today."

"Will we be holding George Spalding now that the facts have come to light in the press, or be giving him over to the Yanks?"

"He stays put at Cloverhill. The minister of justice will soon be announcing that in the matter of George Spalding all Irish and international laws will be adhered to without fail."

"Isn't that a grand thing, seeing justice served?"

Finally, Clancy smiled. "Indeed it is."

Chapter Twelve

During the afternoon on the day Sara left for Iraq, Kerney spoke by phone with Susan Berman, the unit production manager for the movie, and explained he would be unable to honor his consultant contract unless child-care arrangements could be made for Patrick.

"That's no problem, we've hired a nanny for some of the cast's children."

"Okay, good. There's another problem, though. I'm going to be a day late getting to Playas. It's a family matter."

"What's wrong?"

"My wife's been deployed to Iraq unexpectedly."

"I had no idea your wife was in the military. Of course you can delay your arrival. If I'm not around when you get here, ask for Libby. She's the nanny. Including Patrick there will only be five children in her care, so he should get a lot of attention."

"Good," Kerney said, "he'll need it."

"This must be very hard on you."

"Yes, it is."

He spent the rest of that afternoon wrapping up little details; dropping off a change-of-address form at the post office, arranging for a lawn service to keep the grounds of the Arlington house tidy until the property sold, notifying utility companies where to send final bills, and meeting with the real estate agent to give him a house key.

The agent assured him the house would sell quickly and at a handsome profit. Kerney didn't doubt him; real estate values had skyrocketed in the D.C. area over the last three years and the resale market was strong.

On Saturday the movers came to take everything away and put it into storage until Kerney and Patrick returned from the Bootheel. After they departed, Kerney and Patrick took a number of boxes filled with usable castoffs and nonperishable food to a local charity. Then they went back to the house to clean it up.

Patrick seemed to welcome the activity and pitched in as best he could. Once all was in order, Kerney spread out Patrick's sleeping bag on the bare living-room floor and gave him his stuffed pony.

"You need to take your nap, son."

Patrick looked around the empty room. "Everything's gone."

"To our Santa Fe home," Kerney said. "That where we're all going to live from now on."

"Will Mommy be there?"

"Yes, but not right away. I'm going to need your help with the horses."

The thought of the horses cheered Patrick slightly, but he still looked unhappy as Kerney tucked him in. After he fell asleep, Kerney sat on the front stoop and called his old and best friend Dale Jennings, who'd been hired as a wrangler for the movie. He gave him a heads-up about Sara's deployment to Iraq and his delayed arrival in Playas.

"Damn, if that isn't bad news," Dale said with a heavy sigh, concern flooding his voice. "Seems we both have wives who are in a fix."

"What's up with Barbara?"

"She had an emergency appendectomy three nights ago, and I had to bow out on the movie job. We're not going to Playas."

"Is she all right?" Kerney asked.

"She's healing up nicely but sore and cranky," Dale replied. "The girls went down to Las Cruces this morning to enroll late in their fall classes at the university, so

I'm chief cook, bottle washer, and nurse until Barbara gets back on her feet."

"Give her my best," Kerney said, trying to sound upbeat, although the thought of missing out on Dale's company in the Bootheel wasn't a happy one.

"I sure will. Tell Sara we'll be praying for her and thinking about her."

"Thanks." Kerney hung up, feeling a bit depressed. With Sara in Iraq, Kerney's enthusiasm about the movie had waned, and now that Dale wouldn't be there, the whole idea was even less appealing. But he'd promised Sara he'd take Patrick and go, so he would do it.

On Sunday morning, after spending the night in a hotel near the airport, Kerney and Patrick flew home to New Mexico. Usually a good traveler, Patrick was hyperactive and irritable during the flight. Not even *Pablito the Pony* or any of his favorite toys held his attention for long.

At the ranch Kerney decided the best medicine for his son would be to wear him out. They spent the remainder of the day cleaning out stalls, laying down fresh straw and sawdust, rearranging the tack room, and clearing manure from the paddocks. It was slow going, with Patrick taking frequent breaks to give biscuits to the horses and getting brief rides around the paddock on Hondo's back while Kerney led the horse by the halter.

"I want to go see Mommy," Patrick said as Kerney plucked him off Hondo and carried him to the house.

"Mommy has to work in a place where children can't go," Kerney said. "She can't be with us until the army sends her home."

"Fourteen days."

"Is that what Mommy said?"

Patrick nodded. "The last time she went away."

"That's a long time."

Patrick pouted unhappily.

"She'll be gone a little longer than that."

"No," Patrick said emphatically, as if to make it so.

After dinner Kerry saddled up Hondo and took Patrick for a ride to the railroad tracks. They got there just in time to watch the excursion train that ran from Santa Fe to the village of Lamy pass by. The tourists riding in the old carriages waved, smiled, and pointed at the cowboy and his son on horseback. The engineer tooted his horn as the train rumbled by at ten miles an hour over the spur line.

Patrick loved trains. He waved back at the passengers until it passed out of sight and, on the ride back to the ranch, didn't ask once about Sara. It gave Kerney hope that Patrick would adjust to living with him.

That night, long after Patrick was asleep, Kerney turned on the television news and listened with growing interest as a local weekend anchor reported a breaking story out of Dublin. George Spalding, a U.S. Army deserter and international fugitive now in custody, had named Thomas Carrier, a retired colonel with close ties to high-ranking defense officials and senior White House aides, as a member of a smuggling ring that had operated during the Vietnam War.

As the news anchor talked about how the story had been leaked, a video clip from the blog was shown, and Kerney got his first look at George Spalding. Except for a touch of self-importance in the way he held his head and moved his mouth, he was nondescript in every way.

On the Sunday-morning television news show panels Carrier was a hot topic. Spokepersons from the White House and Department of Defense distanced the administration from Carrier. Opposition party leaders called for an investigation. Legal analysts discussed complex judicial issues. Spin doctors predicted the controversy would either fade away or cause irreparable damage to the credibility of key government officials.

Kerney wondered how the story had surfaced. Sara had hinted that it might go public, but she'd refused to say how. He worried that the brass would put her in their crosshairs again.

The morning they were to leave for the Bootheel, Kerney woke up dreaming of rows of flag-draped caskets. He shook off the sensation as best he could, checked his e-mail for a message from Sara, and found a short note. She'd arrived safely, reported to her brigade, been assigned a billet, and had immediately started working. She'd write again within the week when she had time.

He fired off a quick note in return and went to the kitchen to fix Patrick a breakfast of apple pancakes. There were still no blueberries in the house.

As they drove into Playas, Patrick stirred in the car seat and looked around eagerly. With a full movie crew in town Playas was a beehive of activity. The baseball field on the edge of town had new bleachers, lights, and a bandstand for the filming of the country-music benefit concert. Behind the nearby community swimming pool a parking lot had been established for a fleet of trucks and trailers, with a separate area cordoned off for cast and crew vehicles.

In the village center all the buildings looked occupied and prop vehicles were parked along the streets. The area had been dressed with lampposts, street signs, and parking meters. Several of the residential neighborhoods had been spruced up and there were rows of houses made to look inhabited with fresh coats of paint, curtains in the windows, and landscaped front yards complete with flower beds.

Dozens of people were out and about. Some were unloading props, others were building flats, and a long line of extras was queued up at the back of a wardrobe trailer.

Kerney parked and walked with Patrick past a dozen or more makeup trailers, motor homes, prop trucks, light- and sound-equipment vehicles, and a small fleet of transportation vans used to take the cast to and from locations.

The old mercantile building where the tech scout team had taken meals had been turned into an office. Desks and chairs were scattered around the large room and large bulletin boards on rollers were plastered with assignment sheets, shooting schedules, inventory documents, and memos.

Kerney checked in with a production assistant, who told him that Malcolm Usher and a crew were on location at the Jordan ranch. She gave him his housing assignment and directed him to the location of the child-care center. It was in a house on the hill where the mining company managers had once lived.

Libby, the nanny, was a pleasantly plump, young-looking woman with soft brown hair and a calm manner. She immediately took charge of Patrick and introduced him to her four other charges, three girls and a boy who ranged in age from two to five. Patrick eyed his new companions warily for a minute before making a beeline for a toy train set that sat on a pint-size table.

Kerney watched Patrick settle in, and by the time he left he felt that his son was in good hands and among friendly children. At the apartment he and Patrick had been assigned — a far cry from the house Johnny Jordan had promised to provide — he dumped the luggage and left for the Jordan ranch.

First he'd check in with Susan Berman and then see if he could find out if Ray Bratton, the young Border Patrol officer, had begun his undercover assignment as an apprentice set dresser. As he drove the empty highway, the events of his earlier trip to Playas flooded into his mind: the dying Border Patrol agent he'd found on the highway to Antelope Wells, the mysterious airplane that had landed south of the Jordan ranch, Walter Shaw's late-night trip to the old barn on the Harley homestead, and the beacon light on the shut-down copper smelter that guided smugglers and illegal aliens across the Mexican border.

Kerney had some questions for Agent Bratton. Had the feds developed any more evidence against Jerome Mendoza, the Motor Transportation officer who lived in Playas? Had they identified the man Kerney had seen driving away in Mendoza's van?

He thought about Walter Shaw, the ranch manager at the Jordan spread. The cursory background research he'd done on Shaw had been inconclusive. He'd turned the task over to Detective Sergeant Ramona Pino for follow-up and had heard nothing back.

Rhetorically, he wondered if he should just drop the whole damn thing and let

Agent Bratton deal with it. It wasn't Kerney's case or even within his jurisdiction. He should forget about it and give his full attention to Patrick.

Kerney knew he couldn't do that, no matter how tempting. He still carried a shield, a law enforcement officer had been murdered, and those responsible for the crime remained at large. With that locked in his mind he turned off the highway and headed down the dirt road past the rodeo grounds, toward the Jordan ranch.

From a distance Walter Shaw stood in front of his house at the Jordan ranch and watched Julia flirt with Barry Hingle, the construction supervisor for the movie. The two were off by themselves, away from the cast and crew that had assembled around the director at the cattle-guard entrance to the ranch headquarters. Julia leaned against Hingle, talking, touching him on the arm, laughing and smiling. Shaw wondered if she'd screwed him yet.

At one time Shaw would have been jealous, but that was many years ago, before he'd come to realize that she was nothing but a slut. Once, he'd hoped to marry her — for the ranch, not for love, although sex with Julia was outstanding.

Shaw's plans for marrying Julia had been quickly discarded when he'd come upon her straddling a hired hand in her pickup truck at the Shugart cabin. When Shaw had ridden up, she had stared at him with her eyes wide open through the rear window of the truck as she bounced up and down on the cowboy's lap, her lips thin and her teeth bared like those of an animal pouncing on its prey.

Out of convenience Shaw still slept with Julia now and then, when she was between new bedroom talent. But he kept his emotional distance as he would with any feral animal.

From time to time he toyed with the idea of killing Julia and her parents. But he could never hit upon a strategy that promised to give him legal control of the ranch once they were dead, not with Johnny still in the picture.

Shaw had been successful in the past when it came to murder. As a child he'd bounced from one foster home to another, until Ralph and Elizabeth Shaw had adopted him at the age of twelve and turned him into an indentured servant on their Virden farm. Over the next six years Elder Ralph and Sister Elizabeth recited the glorious teachings of the Mormon church while they worked him day and night during the summers, and every early morning, evening, and weekend during the school year.

When spiritual instruction and honest labor failed to keep him in strict bounds, they employed corporal punishment. Two or three times a week he paid for an ill-advised remark or look with a beating.

At eighteen, unconverted to the faith, mean, and filled with hate, he graduated at the bottom of his high-school class, escaped into the navy, and spent the next six years on an aircraft carrier. After his discharge he worked on a ranch outside of Willcox, Arizona, before taking the manager's job with Joe and Bessie, where he bided his time for a while.

Every year the residents of Virden celebrated their Mormon ancestors' trek to the Gila River Valley after being forced to flee Mexico in 1912 because of the revolution that made Pancho Villa famous. During one such celebration, while the villagers were at the annual picnic, Shaw sneaked into Elder Ralph and Sister Elizabeth's house, found their last will and testament leaving everything to a Mormon clinic in El Salvador, destroyed it, and loosened the gas line to the bedroom wall heater.

They were dead by morning, and after a lengthy probate hearing, Shaw inherited the farm and immediately leased out the land. Although the money from the lease-hold agreement gave Shaw a steady income stream, with land prices skyrocketing it was far from enough to buy a good-sized ranch of his own, even if he sold the farm outright. But soon he would never again be somebody's hired hand.

As he watched Julia and Hingle, Shaw decided she hadn't screwed him yet. She was still playing her cunning little seductive game with him, acting enchanted by everything Hingle said, as though he alone could delight her. It was such bullshit the sight of it almost made Shaw laugh.

His attention switched when he saw Kevin Kerney get out of his truck on the other side of the fence and walk toward the movie types clustered at the cattle guard. They were surrounded by cameras, lights, electrical equipment, and some metal frames covered in a black fabric that were used to shade sunlight.

The damn cop was a snoop. When he'd been down here last, Kerney had taken a solo tour of the ranch. Shaw had back-tracked on Kerney and found evidence that he'd been to the barn at the old

Harley homestead and tromped around the landing field on the Sentinel Butte Ranch. Shaw didn't like people butting into his business, and although he had no reason to believe the cop was onto him, he was wary nonetheless.

He watched Susan Berman, the pretty woman who always had a notebook or clipboard in her hand and a harried look on her face, break away from the group, greet Kerney, and give him a manila envelope.

The two chatted for a time and Shaw lost interest. The stock had been gathered at the Shugart cabin for the cattle-drive movie scenes, and the horse wranglers for the film company would be trucking in the remuda this afternoon. The new corral was finished, and Shaw's day hands were hauling feed to the site in preparation for the arrival of the horses. It was time to check and see how far along they were with their chore.

He pulled himself into the cab of the truck and headed south, kicking up dust on the ranch road and wishing Hollywood would just pack up and go away. He had a shipment arriving soon and he didn't like the idea of transporting contraband with a movie crew and a police chief parked under his nose.

When Susan Berman rejoined Malcolm Usher, who was running over the setup for the establishing shot of the ranch, Kerney paused to look around. As promised, Ethan Stone, the set designer, had turned Joe and Bessie's pristine ranch headquarters into a hardscrabble, weather-beaten movie set. The exteriors of the houses and the barn were painted a dingy, sun-bleached gray, and a rusted water tank and an old windmill had been planted squarely in front of Joe and Bessie's house along with two large, dead evergreen trees. The construction crew had added a rickety porch to the front of the house with a roof that seemed about to collapse. Several old, wrecked vehicles that looked like they'd been hauled down from vacant lots in Hachita were scattered around, and a pile of scrap metal had been dumped next to the barn.

There was no sign of Joe, Bessie, or Johnny, but Kerney noticed that Julia and Barry Hingle were looking pleased with each other. He smiled at the prospect that Julia might have found someone more receptive to her advances.

He opened the manila envelope. It was from the SFPD and inside were the NCIC wants and warrant reports on the cast and crew that his department had run. The name of one crew member, a transportation driver named Hoover Grayson, was circled. He had an outstanding warrant from Grady County, Oklahoma.

A sealed business envelope addressed to Kerney was attached to the paperwork. It contained Detective Sergeant Ramona Pino's memo on her further findings regarding Walter Shaw. The deaths of Shaw's adoptive parents had been ruled accidental, and no autopsies had been performed. Shaw owned the Virden farm free and clear, which consisted of the house, barn, and ten acres of land. With six years in the navy he'd been given a general discharge and denied reenlistment after being busted in rank twice by summary court-martial. Both times he'd gone AWOL and been arrested by the shore patrol for fighting.

On her own initiative Pino had researched Shaw's juvenile record. As a teenager he'd been picked up in Duncan, Arizona, for shoplifting and released to his adoptive parents after pleading guilty and paying a fine. Child welfare reported that he'd been in seven different foster homes before his adoption placement with Ralph and Elizabeth Shaw, and that he had been removed from most of the previous placements because of incorrigible destructive behavior.

Financially, Shaw wasn't well off. He had some money in the bank, but not much, and the value of the Virden farm wouldn't cover the median cost of a Santa Fe house.

Kerney put the memo back in the envelope, stuck it in his shirt pocket, dialed Santa Fe dispatch on his cell phone, and asked them to confirm the warrant on Hoover Grayson out of Grady County, Oklahoma.

Ten minutes later dispatch called back. The warrant was valid. Grayson was wanted on two counts of residential burglary. Kerney got a physical description of the man and went looking for him. He spotted him sitting in the cab of a truck, reading a magazine.

Kerney passed by without stopping. When he was out of Grayson's sight, he called the Hidalgo County sheriff, Leo Valencia, and gave him a heads-up.

Kerney knew and liked Valencia from meetings of the New Mexico Sheriffs and Police Association. He had a no-nonsense approach to policing, little tolerance for incompetence, and a quick wit.

"Are you sure about this guy Grayson?" Valencia asked.

"As much as I can be without confronting the man," Kerney replied.

"I'll have to confirm the outstanding arrest warrant myself and get a copy."

"Of course."

"Give me your exact location."

"The ranch headquarters of the Granite Pass Cattle Company off the Antelope Wells highway."

"Joe Jordan's place, where they're making that movie?"

"That's right," Kerney said.

"What in the hell are you doing down there?" Valencia asked.

"Trying to break into motion pictures, Leo. I've got to find something to do after I take my pension."

Valencia chuckled. "Isn't there some retired Chicago cop who's a big star now? The guy who plays an NYPD detective on a TV crime show."

"Yeah," Kerney replied. "He's my role model."

Leo laughed in disbelief. "Okay, Mr. Budding Movie Star, what are you *really* doing down there?"

"I'm the law-enforcement technical advisor for the film."

"Sounds like easy duty. Okay, hang tight. We'll come for Grayson if it checks out. But if it doesn't, I may pay you a visit anyway. I've always wanted to see how movies get made."

"I'll arrange a screen test for you," Kerney said. Valencia declined the offer and disconnected.

While Kerney waited for Leo's arrival, he watched Usher fine tune the exterior shots of the ranch. The cameras were equipped with a video feed, and Usher stood behind a table loaded with monitors and quietly asked for minor adjustments. He and the crew seemed to be well in sync, and he soon told an assistant director to start filming. Everyone fell silent and the cameras rolled: one on tracks that moved straight in on the ranch house, while a second camera panned from the ranch house to the barn.

What had taken an hour to set up was over in a matter of minutes, and the crew got busy readying the next shot, which called for the ingenue playing the rancher's daughter to rush out of the house and speed away in a pickup truck.

If Kerney remembered correctly, it was the scene that had been added to the shooting script to show the daughter hurrying to find her rodeo cowboy brother and tell him about their father's trouble with the feds.

The ingenue, a striking redhead with a thousand-watt smile, did several run-throughs before Usher was satisfied. Kerney couldn't see the necessity for it and wondered what he was missing. They all seemed pretty much the same to him.

Just as filming started, two Hidalgo sheriff's units with lights flashing came into view on the ranch road and wheeled to a stop at the cattle guard.

"Cut!" Usher hollered, looking totally pissed.

The ingenue froze on the porch step, and all eyes turned toward the police cruisers. Kerney, who'd stayed within striking distance of Hoover Grayson, stopped him with an armlock as he scrambled out of the truck, and put him facedown on the ground.

"Shit," Grayson said.

Kerney put his knee down hard on Grayson's back to pin him. "Don't move," he ordered.

"Good work, amigo," Valencia said as he reached Kerney with his chief deputy at his side. "You're not over the hill yet."

"Thanks for the vote of confidence."

Kerney pulled Grayson upright. Leo cuffed him, fished out Grayson's wallet, made the ID, and read him his rights.

"Mind if I stick around and watch for a time?" he asked as his chief deputy led Grayson to his unit.

A red-faced Usher arrived before Kerney could respond. "What's this about?" he demanded. "What did he do?"

"Residential burglary," Leo answered. "Two counts."

"Are you planning to arrest anyone else?" Usher asked sharply.

Over Usher's shoulder Leo scanned the faces of the cast and crew. "I don't know. Does somebody else *need* arresting?" he asked innocently.

Usher stared at Valencia for a long moment. Leo had a round face and a walrus mustache that made him look like Pancho Villa — an asset with both Anglo and Hispanic voters, he'd found. He gave Usher a toothy, election-day smile.

Usher glanced at Kerney, who was trying hard to keep a straight face. "No," he said as his irritation vanished. "That's enough reality for one day."

"Sorry for the inconvenience," Leo said.

Usher returned to the shoot and the two men stood at the fence by the cattle guard and watched Hollywood magic being made.

"Aside from trying to intercept drug shipments and chase coyotes smuggling migrants across the border, are the feds up to anything else in the Bootheel?" Kerney asked.

"There's been a big upswing in cigarette smuggling," Leo replied. "Counterfeit brands out of Asia. They cost two bucks a carton wholesale and get sold for ten times that. The feds had an investigation going for a time in El Paso, but it petered out."

"Who ran the investigation?"

"Hell if I know," Leo said. "Alcohol, To-bacco, and Firearms, I'd guess."

"That's all you know?"

Valencia gave Kerney a sideways glance. "That's it. Are you onto something?"

Kerney hitched his boot on a fence railing. "Just trying to stay well informed."

"That's a good thing to do." Leo eyed the production crew as they set up equip-ment for the next shot. When they fin-ished, Usher reminded everyone how the scene had been blocked out, and then watched it on the monitors as the young actress did a run-through. Just as they were about to start filming, the drone of an airplane overhead interrupted the take.

Everybody relaxed and stood around, waiting for the plane to pass by.

"So this is how it's done," Leo said.

"It's not very glamorous, is it?" Kerney replied.

"Maybe if they blew something up, it would be more interesting."

"I'll pass along your suggestion."

Leo laughed, thanked Kerney for his help, and left. After filming ended for the day and everyone returned to Playas, the arrest of Hoover Grayson had people buzzing. For a time Kerney's popularity soared as he answered questions about the bust. When he finally broke away and went to get Patrick, he found his son playing cheerfully with his new companions. They had dinner with the cast and crew, and much to Kerney's relief, Patrick's good mood held throughout the evening. Long after Patrick had gone to bed, Agent Ray Bratton knocked on the door.

"How's it going?" Kerney asked as the young man stepped nervously inside.

"The only criminal activity I've seen so far is a few of the crew members smoking pot."

"You're just getting started," Kerney said, motioning at the couch. Stiffly, Bratton sat on the edge of a cushion. "Is this your first undercover assignment?"

"Yeah. How did you know?"

Kerney settled into the easy chair that faced the couch and smiled warmly at Bratton. "Just a guess. How long have you been with the agency?"

"I'm three months out of the academy. They sent me here from Laredo, Texas, on special assignment. I go back when it's finished."

"Did you know the murdered agent?"

"No."

"Have you learned anything more about Mendoza, the Motor Transportation officer, and his van?"

"Mendoza checks out clean. But Agent Fidel still thinks he might be our guy. Mendoza had a cousin staying with him for a week, when you were down here last. The guy's name is Paul Rangal. He lives in San Diego and works as an apprentice machinist at the naval shipyards. We took a close look at him. *Nada*."

"Are you looking at anyone else as a suspect?" Kerney asked as he got up.

"Agent Fidel thinks Ira Dobson, the guy who manages the waterworks for the town and the smelter, may be involved."

"Fidel still thinks the smelter may be being used as a safe house for smuggled illegals?"

"That's his theory," Bratton replied.

Kerney walked Bratton to the door. "Good luck with it."

Bratton smiled. "Thanks. I'll keep you informed."

After Bratton slipped outside into the night, Kerney thought about what he'd just heard. It made sense to use an undercover rookie agent, assuming he'd been well coached and adequately prepared, to bust up a smuggling ring. Cop shops frequently used novice officers in such roles. But Bratton seemed completely out of his element and totally uncomfortable in his assignment.

Why would the Border Patrol bring in a second fresh-faced rookie after the first one had been killed? That didn't make any sense, especially if the smuggling ring included dirty cops. The circumstances called for experienced investigators to be working the case.

Kerney realized that he actually had very little specific information about the case — he didn't even know the murdered agent's name. The more he thought about it, the more he questioned why Fidel had asked for his assistance.

Could it be Fidel was playing him? There was no compelling need for Bratton to pass information to Fidel through him. Bratton could easily reach Fidel directly by cell phone without drawing attention to himself.

The night of his meeting with Fidel the agent had managed to get Kerney to help short-circuit Officer Sapian's investigation. Then he had kept the murder covered up and the victim's identity hidden from everybody, including Bratton. Kerney found himself wondering if the dead man on the highway was actually a cop at all.

He went over his conversation with Bratton one more time. Fidel had the kid concentrating primarily on Mendoza and Dobson as suspects, in spite of no hard evidence to support it. None of it made any sense.

Kerney decided to check into Agent Fidel's operation a bit more thoroughly before cooperating with him any further.

An early call had Kerney up long before dawn. Reluctantly, he woke Patrick, who had no desire to get out of bed, and after they were dressed the two of them went outside into the chill of the desert night, where the sky was a flat dark slate. Under a big tent in the mercantile-building parking lot a long line of people was queued up for the buffet breakfast. It seemed that the size of the film company had doubled overnight. He checked the call sheet for the day and discovered that several street scenes, requiring a large number of extras, were scheduled to be shot by the second camera unit, while Usher continued filming at the Jordon ranch.

He looked around for familiar faces and saw Buzzy and Gus, the gaffer and the key grip, hurrying off toward loaded equipment trucks. None of the leading or featured actors was present at the picnic tables inside the tent. Kerney assumed they were either breakfasting in the privacy of their custom motor coaches or preparing for the day's work in the wardrobe or makeup trailers.

He was about to take Patrick to the nanny when Johnny Jordan came up behind him.

"This must be your son," Johnny said, reaching out to rub Patrick's head, which earned him a quizzical look. "Good-looking kid. Where's your wife?"

"This is Patrick," Kerney said, although Johnny clearly didn't care what his son's name was. "Sara couldn't make it."

"That's too bad. I wanted to meet her." Johnny plopped down on the bench next to

Kerney. "I hear Dale had to bail out because Barbara got sick."

"Emergency appendectomy, but she's going to be fine. Where have you been?"

"L.A.," Johnny replied, looking pleased with himself. "I drove all night to get here. I've got big things happening, Kerney. Couple of deals in the works. Can't tell you about it yet, but I'm moving to Hollywood after we finish the picture."

"So you're going to be a movie mogul."

Johnny grinned. "Something like that." He was full of nervous energy, thumping the heel of his boot against the bench leg as he talked. "The talent in L.A. is incredible, man."

"I'm sure lots of creative people live there."

Johnny chuckled as he scanned the people in the breakfast buffet line. "I'm talking about the women, Kerney. They're unbelievable. Have you seen Susan Berman?"

"No. What can you tell me about Walt Shaw?"

"Why? Did you have a run-in with him?"

Kerney shook his head. "Have you?"

"Nope. My parents swear by him, and for a time I thought he and Julia were going to be a serious item, but I can't tell you more than that."

"Where are Joe and Bessie?"

"Off at their cabin in Ruidoso for the duration, and I'm glad they're gone. The last thing I need is to have the old man bitching at me about how much he dislikes seeing his ranch turned into a movie set. He's getting a chuck of money out of it, plus some improvements to the ranch, which you'd think would make him happy."

"I guess," Kerney said noncommittally, thinking back to Julia's comment about all the money Johnny had borrowed from Joe over the years and never repaid.

Johnny got to his feet and flashed one of his patented smiles. "Gotta go."

Prepared to give full value for his consultant services, Kerney spent the morning on location at the ranch and soon realized that he had little to do. At sunrise the shot of the police cruisers speeding down the ranch road, with emergency lights flashing through a haze of dust and a brilliant dawn breaking over the mountains, was captured on film in one take. At the ranch headquarters Usher got the initial confrontation between the rancher and the police out of the way and then ordered multiple takes of emotional interactions between the leads.

Kerney had sometimes seen military or law-enforcement technical advisors listed in movie credits and had wondered why the films were so inaccurate. Now he knew. In moviemaking action and drama trumped authenticity every time.

After a catering truck arrived with lunch, Kerney sought out Susan Berman and asked if there was anything she needed him to do for the rest of the day.

Berman flipped through some papers in a three-ring binder. "Not really. You'll be a cowboy in the cattle-drive sequence, but we don't start filming at the Shugart cabin until the day after tomorrow. I do know Malcolm wants you nearby when we're shooting at the smelter, and he may have some technical questions for you during the courthouse sequence scheduled for next week."

As if she'd read his mind, she said, "If you'd like to spend some time with your son, I can always reach you on your cell phone in case you're needed."

"I'd like that very much," Kerney replied.

When Kerney arrived to pick up Patrick, he found the door to the house open and the playroom empty. He called out for Libby and Patrick and got no response.

Through the kitchen window he spotted Libby reading a book to the other four children as they sat on the backyard lawn under a shade tree, but there was no sign of his son.

"Where's Patrick?" Kerney asked as he stepped onto the patio.

Libby got to her feet. "He went to use the bathroom just a few minutes ago."

Kerney searched the bathrooms, found them empty, and went through every other room of the sprawling house looking for Patrick. By the time he'd finished, Libby and the children were inside.

"How long has he been gone?" he demanded.

"No more than three or four minutes."

Kerney circled the house. Behind the backyard it was all desert. Cactus, creosote, and fluff grass peppered the chaparral slope of the low hills, and rock-strewn, sandy arroyos flowed down from brushy mountain hogbacks. How far could a three-year-old wander in five minutes?

Driving up, he hadn't seen Patrick on the street, but he checked around the adjacent houses anyway, yelling his son's name as he ran, his heart pounding in his chest. He entered the chaparral, zigzagging to cut Patrick's trail, hedgehog cactus thorns biting at his legs. A startled Gambel's quail rose up from the underbrush, sounded a sharp *quit quit* in alarm, and fluttered away. He cut across an arroyo, looking for a sign. There were the distinctive four-point-star tracks of roadrunners everywhere, and long, thin lines of snake trails etched in the sand, but no footprints.

Kerney stopped, gathered his breath, bellowed Patrick's name, listened, and took a long look around before running with his head down, eyes scanning the ground, until he reached the wide mouth of another arroyo that curved toward the valley floor. There, two hundred yards from the house, he found tiny shoe prints in the sand. Up ahead he saw Patrick sitting on a boulder with tears streaming down his face.

"Are you all right?" Kerney asked as he reached his son and pulled him into his arms.

Patrick sniffled and nodded.

"Did you hear me calling for you?"

"Yes."

"Why didn't you answer, sport?"

Patrick rubbed his nose. " 'Cause you sounded mad at me."

It kicked Kerney in the gut that Patrick didn't know every tone of his voice. "I'm not mad," he said. "I was worried about you. What are you doing out here?"

"I was looking for you," Patrick replied.

"Well, here I am, okay?"

"Okay."

With Patrick in his arms Kerney turned to see a half-dozen men fanned out behind the row of houses, coming in his direction. He whistled, waved, and held Patrick above his head for all to see. The men stopped and waved back.

"What are they doing?" Patrick asked.

Kerney lowered Patrick to his chest, kissed him on the cheek, and started back toward the house. "Looking for you."

"I wasn't lost, Daddy," Patrick said.

"I know you weren't. But no more of this, champ. You stay with Libby and the other children. Okay?"

Patrick nodded. "I saw a big snake. It curled up and rattled its tail."

Kerney's legs turned to stone and he stopped in his tracks. "Did it bite you?"

Patrick shook his head. "Nope."

Back at the house Kerney thanked the men who had started to search for his son and accepted Libby's apology. She promised that Patrick would never be out of her sight again.

He told Libby that Patrick would be

with him for the rest of the day, put him in his car seat, and drove away. "How about some ice cream?" he asked.

Patrick's face lit up and he kicked his feet. "Ice cream," he echoed, apparently without the slightest inkling that he'd panicked his father almost beyond belief.

Chapter Thirteen

Surrounded by a windswept desert broken only by the silhouette of the Florida Mountains to the east and the Tres Hermanas to the south, Deming sat sun blistered under a yellow, dust-filled morning sky. A town of modest homes ringed with patches of grass, house trailers on scrub acreage, and a main commercial strip that paralleled the interstate and the railroad tracks, Deming drew its lifeblood from travelers and truckers, and blue-collar retirees seeking the sun and affordable housing.

Billboards cluttered the sides of the highway, advertising lodging, fuel, and food. Warning signs advised travelers that the interstate would be closed during severe dust storms. Not at all an uncommon event, Kerney figured, given the amount of grit from a stiff breeze that covered the windshield of his truck.

He drove the main strip to get his bearings. There were a few older buildings that harkened back to the town's founding as a railroad stop in the late-nineteenth century, but for the most part the strip consisted of stand-alone gas stations, automotive repair shops, mom-and-pop businesses, eateries, and moderately priced motels.

Kerney had left Patrick behind in the care of the nanny, and he didn't feel good about it. But he was determined to find out what he could about Agent Fidel's undercover operation. Maybe he'd learn enough to let him step aside from it completely and give Patrick more attention.

Following Officer Flavio Sapian's directions, he took the main street east toward the Florida Mountains and followed the road that led to Rockhound State Park. He made a hard right at an intersection and bumped down a gravel road to a 1960s ranch-style house, where Sapian's state police cruiser was parked under a tin-roofed carport.

He pulled into the driveway and stopped in front of the house, shaded to the south by a row of tall poplars. Under the trees a trampoline and a swing set occupied a swath of green grass. Beyond the trees stood an old railroad boxcar that probably served as a storage shed.

Kerney tooted his horn and Sapian stepped out the front door. Off duty, he wore jeans, boots, a long-sleeved Western shirt, and a faded, sweat-streaked baseball cap. He got into Kerney's truck and the two men drove away.

"Your phone call took me by surprise," Flavio said. "I thought the Border Patrol was handling the death of that Mexican you found on the highway. Why are you still involved?"

Kerney ran it down for him, leaving nothing out. He concluded with his misgivings about Fidel's undercover operation. "I just want to know if things really are as they seem," he said.

"So that's why you asked me to set up a meeting with the agent in charge of the Deming Border Patrol Station."

"Exactly. How well do you know him?"

"His name is Steve Hazen and he's good people," Sapian answered. "Been here five, maybe six years. If he can tell you anything, he'll play it straight."

"That's what I like to hear."

The station, located just outside of Deming on the highway to the border town of Columbus, was a modern brick building with a sloping metal portal that covered the entrance. Shrubs and trees planted along the front of the building softened the monotonous façade, and an American flag waved from the top of a pole that towered over the building.

Inside, Steve Hazen invited them into his office. A heavyset man in his forties with wide shoulders and a thick neck, he had a military-style haircut that showed the bumps and ridges of his deeply tanned skull in full relief. His shipshape office contained all the personal and professional memorabilia some cops loved to display. Framed family pictures, official citations, university degrees, and recognition and award plaques from civic organizations lined shelves and filled walls.

Highly arched eyebrows gave Hazen's face a persistent quizzical expression. He held up a coffee mug that read # 1 DAD in big red letters. "Can I get you some?" he asked.

"No, thanks," Kerney answered.

"Not for me," Sapian said.

"Flavio said you have some questions." Hazen motioned to a table next to a tall bookcase that held volumes of government documents. "Take a load off and fire away."

The men pulled out chairs and sat. "What can you tell me about the under-cover operation at Playas?" Kerney asked.

Hazen smiled. "Domingo Fidel's little feint. He said you might not fall for it."

"Feint?"

"Yep," Hazen replied. "Eight months ago we got a contingent of National Guard soldiers from a Lordsburg unit assigned to assist us apprehend illegals crossing the border from Columbus west to Antelope Wells. Soon after that human trafficking volume picked up in the Bootheel, especially in those areas manned by the troops. We believe some of the soldiers have been taking bribes from the coyotes. The undercover agent you found dying on the highway was supposed to make his maiden run north of the border to a safe house, which we think is located outside of Lordsburg. Somebody ratted him out and he was killed."

"Are you saying Officer Mendoza is clean?" Kerney asked.

"He is," Hazen replied. "But Fidel has put the word out that he's dirty and is using you and Bratton to convince our target suspects that we're looking for the wrong people in the wrong place. By now every National Guard trooper on the line has heard scuttlebutt about the Playas operation."

"Why the charade?" Flavio asked.

"Since we've tightened up the corridor crossings in El Paso, the smuggling networks have shifted west to the more dangerous desert and mountain zones. We're not just after coyotes and soldiers on the pad. We want to shut down this operation on both sides of the border before the Bootheel turns into a sieve like southern Arizona."

"Why did you keep the undercover agent's identity secret?" Flavio asked.

"Because we think he was only suspected of being a cop," Hazen replied. "Confirming it would have blown the operation completely."

"What about the van I saw on the highway?" Kerney asked.

"Found abandoned in Phoenix. We matched the tires on it to tracks in the desert."

"Agent Bratton is in over his head," Kerney said. "I suppose Fidel wants it that way. Put the rookie out there with no training or guidance, give him a lot of misinformation, and let him flounder around for all to see. But why drag me in on it?"

Hazen smiled. "You and Sapian were doing too good of a job. Fidel had to coopt you, so he borrowed Mendoza as a target and fed you a line of bull to get you to back off."

"He could have just leveled with me."

Hazen smiled and shrugged. "It was his call."

Kerney didn't smile back. Although he'd been played by Fidel for a good cause, he still didn't like being used as a patsy. "Okay, enough history. What's the status of the investigation?"

"Sorry, I can't tell you that."

"Do you or any other federal agency have any other interdiction operations under way I should know about? ATF? DEA?" Kerney asked.

Hazen shook his head. "Nope. Why do you ask?"

Feeling unnecessarily exploited, Kerney decided not to voice his suspicions about Walter Shaw. "Just curious."

"Can I tell Agent Fidel that you'll continue to assist him?"

Kerney pushed back his chair. "I'll play along. What was the dead agent's name?"

"Roberto Sisneros."

Kerney stood and shook Hazen's hand. "Thanks for your candor. Tell Fidel that he can expect to hear from me about his little game playing the next time we meet."

Hazen laughed. "I'll pass it along."

Johnny Jordan stood at the barricade to the Playas access road. Traffic had been closed so an aerial camera could film an overhead master shot of the town. A few steps away Susan Berman was talking to the second unit director and his cameraman. When the plane passed overhead, cars on the streets had to be moving, pedestrians had to be walking about, and kids had to be playing in the ball field or riding their bikes on the sidewalks.

Up at the village dozens of extras were standing by, waiting for their cue. Johnny was astonished at the effort it took to get a fifteen-second bird's-eye view of townspeople going about their normal lives.

He glanced over at Susan Berman. Last night she'd turned down his invitation to drive to Deming for dinner at a Mexican restaurant, but he hadn't given up on her. Three weeks in Playas without a woman just wouldn't cut it.

After the plane took off from the Playas airstrip, the pilot made a few practice runs before the actual shooting began. Then it was all over in a matter of minutes. Johnny turned to see his sister's car approaching the barricade. He walked to her, and she stopped on the pavement.

"I hear you're playing house with Barry Hingle," he said with a grin and shake of his head.

"Have you seen Kerney?" Julia asked.

Johnny hunkered down at the side of the car. "Not since yesterday. What's up?"

"I just heard his wife got sent to Iraq."

"No shit? He didn't mention it to me. Have you come to comfort him?"

"Is that all you can think about?"

Johnny laughed. "Don't kid a kidder, Sis. I was there when you first started twitching your hips at all the boys."

"And you were the first to take advantage of it."

"Those were the days," Johnny replied.

Julia stuck her tongue out. "Do you know where Kerney is?"

Johnny shook his head. "Did he have a run-in with Shaw?"

"If he did, Walt didn't say anything about it to me. Why do you ask?"

"Kerney pumped me for information about him. Except for telling him that Shaw was once your lover, I really didn't have much to say."

Julia put the car in gear. "You're such a jerk, Johnny."

Johnny leaned in and kissed Julia on the

lips. "Are you ready for the cattle drive? We start shooting it tomorrow."

"It should be fun."

Men removed the barricade from the road. Julia waved ta-ta with her fingers, smiled, and drove away.

During the next three days Kerney had little time to think of anything other than herding cattle back and forth for the cameras along a ten-mile stretch of the Jordan ranch. Johnny's rodeo cowboys, and the character actor who played the rancher bedeviled by the BLM officials, all knew how to sit a horse, as did Johnny, Julia, and the locals hired as extras. But the ingenue was a complete disaster on horseback. Although she'd taken riding lessons in preparation for her role, she bounced in the saddle like a raggedy doll whenever her mount broke into a canter.

When her stunt double took over, things went fine. However, several scenes with dialogue required the young woman to be mounted. She had a hard time controlling her horse and jerked the reins every time it moved, making it shy and turn away from the camera. After several failed attempts Usher shot the scenes with her dismounted.

As a circle rider Kerney ate dust on the perimeter of the herd. He wondered if he'd feel self-conscious when cameras started rolling, but he was far too busy prodding cattle back into the fold to pay any attention to them. Fortunately, he had a sound cutting horse with a good mouth named Lucky who did most of the work.

On the second and third mornings there were predawn calls for wardrobe and makeup. All the working hands, stuntmen, and actors exchanged their costumes for identical outfits that were a bit more grungy, and then had their faces smudged and dirtied to make it look like they'd been driving cattle for days. The real cowboys from the area ranches who'd hired on for the movie got a big kick out of it.

Two of the cowboys were Kent Vogt and Alberto "Buster" Martinez, who worked full-time at the Jordan outfit. Vogt, a cheerful, talkative man in his late thirties, loved movie trivia.

During one break Vogt reined in his mount next to Kerney and said, "Did you know Steve McQueen filmed most of *Tom Horn* just across the state line in the Coronado National Forest?"

"I didn't know that," Kerney replied.

Vogt pushed back his cowboy hat to reveal a white forehead above a rosy brown, tan face. "Did you see that movie?"

"I did, a long time ago."

"Well, I played the boy sitting on the fence who got bushwhacked. My fifteen seconds of fame."

"No kidding?"

Vogt nodded. "This will be my second time being in a movie. Ain't that a hoot?" He flicked a rein gently against his horse's neck. The animal turned smoothly and trotted away in the direction of Buster Martinez.

Grim and reticent, Martinez was the complete opposite of Vogt. Although Kerney didn't recognize him, the MVD report had listed Martinez as the owner of the pickup truck that had arrived behind Shaw's panel van at the barn. Kerney had watched Shaw and Martinez drive south toward the Sentinel Butte Ranch where he later found the landing strip and signs of a recent cargo drop.

Kerney's attempts to draw Buster out had gone nowhere. Pushing fifty, Martinez had an oval face with small, narrow eyes that made him look like he was always squinting. He had a beautiful saddle, obviously custom made, with silver conchos on the cantle, a horn embellished with a sterling silver cap that bore his initials, and fenders tooled in a basket weave pattern. It had to have cost at least three or four thousand dollars new. Kerney wondered how a working cowboy could afford such a luxury.

During the next break he sought Martinez out at the new corral, where he was feeding his horse some crushed oats.

"That's a fine-looking saddle," Kerney said as he dismounted.

Martinez, who was inside the corral, grunted and nodded in reply.

Kerney climbed over the top railing, stepped up to the horse, and ran his hand over the padded seat. The craftsmanship was high quality. "Handmade, I bet."

"Yeah, it is." Martinez took his horse by the reins.

On the seat by the horn was the saddlemaker's name, Matt Thornton.

"Does it have a wood tree?"

Martinez nodded.

Where did you get it?" Kerney asked.

"Up in Nevada."

Kerney shook his head and smiled at Martinez. "It's sweet."

Martinez swung into saddle and pointed at the corral gate. "Get that for me, will you."

Kerney opened the gate and Martinez trotted his horse out of the corral toward Walter Shaw, who was about a hundred yards away on a nice-looking sorrel gelding, harrying a cow back into the herd. Martinez reached Shaw just as the cow scampered into the fold, and the two men paused to chat.

Although he couldn't be certain, Kerney had the strong impression that he'd agitated Martinez. Why would admiring the man's saddle get him riled? Most working cowboys were pleased to show off their prized tack. Martinez's behavior made Kerney all the more curious about him. He dialed his office and asked to be put through to the investigation unit.

Detective Matt Chacon took the call. Kerney described the saddle and asked him to track down the maker in Nevada.

"Sure thing, Chief," replied Chacon, who had never been on a horse in his life. "I know what a saddle horn is, but what's a cantle, fender, and tree?"

"The cantle is the back of the saddle seat," Kerney replied, "fenders are wide pieces of leather along the stirrup leathers, and the tree is the frame of the saddle. Have you got all that?"

"I wrote it down, Chief," Chacon said.

"Good. I want as many facts as you can get. Who the buyer was, when it was bought, how much was paid, and the type of transaction. Leave me a message after you run it down."

"Ten-four."

Over a bullhorn one of Susan Berman's production assistants ordered the cast and extras to report for a wardrobe and makeup check. Kerney mounted and rode to a tent to be looked over to make sure he was appropriately scruffy for the cameras. Far in the distance he could see Malcolm Usher and a camera crew on the cliff overlooking Granite Pass. Two other cameras were in place at the mouth of the pass, one on tracks with a boom and the other on a crane. A fourth camera, mounted on a truck, would parallel the cattle as they were driven toward the pass.

Up the valley a ways and out of sight, helicopters, squad cars, and stunt men were standing by, ready to roll into action for the exciting chase scene into the pass. High above Granite Pass a small plane with an onboard camera circled. It would capture the arrival of the squad cars and whirlybirds.

After getting his face smudged Kerney helped separate the herd into two groups.

Usher wanted some of the cattle stampeded by the approaching police helicopters and cruisers as they entered the pass. According to a crew member Kerney talked to, all the cameras would be rolling simultaneously, and if everything went okay, there would be enough raw footage in the can to edit the sequence to a final cut. But the chances were good, the man added, that Usher would want to shoot the sequence twice.

Trampled by thousands of hooves over three days, the rich grassland pasture Julia Jordan had bragged about now looked pale yellow and used up. The cattle Joe Jordan had rented out for the production were dust covered, thirsty, and cantankerous. In the strong afternoon sun heat waves quivered up from the ground, made more visible by the dust that swirled in the air. The mouth of Granite Pass revealed a narrow rocky trail that wedged and wound along the cliff face toward the Playas Valley.

Johnny joined up with Kerney as he trailed behind the cattle moving toward the pass. "Are you ready?" he asked, grinning from ear to ear.

"Have you ridden through the pass?" Kerney asked.

"Twice."

"There's bad footing in there," Kerney

said, "and mesquite and cactus on either side just waiting to jab man and beast. These cows are going to go every which way on that trail."

"Don't get throwed off that horse," Johnny said.

"Isn't that what you used to do for a living?"

Johnny threw back his head and laughed. "More often than not."

The man with the bullhorn began a countdown. Johnny spurred his horse and veered away to flank the herd on the side where the dolly camera had been positioned. Suddenly, the sound of helicopter rotors and police sirens filled the air and spooked the lead cows into a slant away from the pass. From that point on every working hand forgot about the movie as they ate dust and tried to keep the cattle from scattering.

Kerney entered the pass at the rear of the herd. Pressed tightly together, the cows were clambering over the rocks, crashing through the brush, stumbling against the canyon walls. Some stragglers turned for the valley. Kerney hit them on their snout with his lasso, but only one animal retreated toward the herd. The rest thundered past him to safety.

He pushed Lucky forward, reached out, and slapped a cow on the rump with his coiled lasso. The cow broke right and Lucky cut him off, pivoting and digging with his rear legs, sticking to the animal like a burr in its tail.

Kerney worked the stragglers until the sound of the helicopters and police sirens faded away. He glanced skyward. The choppers were leaving the valley. Behind him the police units were at a full stop.

Johnny's horse threw dirt as he reined in next to him. "That's it," he said. He pointed at the cliff above the pass, where one of the crew stood waving everyone off. "We're done."

Kerney looked up the trail through the pass. A bottleneck of frightened cows bawled and kicked in frustration. "Not yet. We need to turn those cattle around, get them out of there and watered."

"Let the working hands do it," Johnny said.

Kerney gave him a long, hard look, re-membering the day years ago when Johnny had left him out on the Jornada in the fierce afternoon heat, fixing fence ten miles from nowhere, and never returned.

"What?" Johnny asked.

"Do you always leave a job unfinished?"

Kerney didn't wait for a reply. He spurred Lucky forward and spent the next hour helping the hands untangle the cattle and move them back into the valley. Johnny was long gone when the work was done.

By sunset the temperature had cooled down nicely and a refreshing breeze washed across the Bootheel. At the Playas apartment Kerney turned off the air conditioning and opened all the doors and windows. Weary from three days in the saddle, he pulled off his boots and sprawled on the couch. On the living room carpet Patrick was busy building an airplane out of a Lego set borrowed from the nanny's treasure trove of toys.

Realizing that he'd forgotten to check for messages, Kerney speed-dialed his cellphone voice mail. Matt Chacon had called, but instead of leaving any information, he'd asked for a call back. Kerney got Chacon on the phone.

"There was no saddlemaker named Matt Thornton in Nevada, Chief," Chacon said, "so I did an Internet search and found him in Arizona. That saddle was stolen out of his shop a year ago. It has a retail value of forty-five hundred dollars. Whoever took it must have added the sterling-silver cap with his initials to the saddle horn. Do you have a suspect?"

"Possibly," Kerney said. "Did you confirm the theft?"

"Yes, sir. It was entered into the NCIC computer system the day after it was stolen. The thief got into the workshop by breaking a rear window. He took only the saddle, and it wasn't even the most expensive one there."

"Where is Thornton located?"

"In Duncan, Arizona. He does custom saddles for clients all over the country. You want his address and phone number?"

"I do."

Kerney scribbled down the information, thanked Chacon, disconnected, and watched Patrick circle the living room, airplane in hand, making a buzzing engine sound with his lips.

Duncan was only a few miles away from Virden, where Shaw had his farm. Martinez had helped Shaw unload cargo from a plane at the Sentinel Butte landing strip. Were they trucking it to Virden? Did Martinez spot the saddle at Thornton's workshop during one of their runs and go back to steal it? Or had Martinez bought the saddle from a fence or at a pawnshop in Nevada?

At the very least Kerney was fairly sure Martinez knew the saddle was stolen property. But he would need to tie Martinez to the theft in order to gain enough leverage to tease out an answer to the bigger question: What in the hell had been off-loaded from that plane?

Patrick crashed into the couch cushion next to Kerney and put the airplane on the armrest. "I want to read *Pablito the Pony*."

Kerney rubbed his son's head. "Go get it."

Patrick scooted to his bedroom, came back with his book, and settled on the couch. When Kerney reached for the book, Patrick shook his head. *"I want to read it to you,"* he said.

"Okay."

Patrick opened the book to the first page. "This is the story of Pablito the Pony," he said, "who lived on a ranch."

"Very good," Kerney said.

Patrick smiled and turned the page. "Pablito was a pretty pony."

"Don't you mean pinto?" Kerney asked.

Patrick corrected himself and continued to pretend to read as he looked at the pictures and told Kerney the story. When he finished, he closed the book, gave Kerney a pleased look, and said, "The end."

"What a good story," Kerney said, "and you read it very well."

"I know."

Kerney sent Patrick off to brush his teeth and change into his pajamas. Through the open door he heard Johnny Jordan talking to someone.

"Come on," Johnny said, his words slightly slurred, "have a drink with me."

"No, thank you," Susan Berman replied.

Kerney stepped outside. Johnny stood halfway down the walkway with a whiskey bottle in his hand, blocking Susan Berman's passage.

"I like a woman with spunk," Johnny said. "One little drink."

"Let me pass, Mr. Jordan," Susan said sharply.

"It doesn't sound like the lady is interested," Kerney said as he walked toward Johnny.

Johnny turned and squinted. "There's my old amigo." He waved the bottle. "How about you and me and Susan here having a little drink together?"

"You're drunk, Johnny. Leave Ms. Berman alone and go to bed."

Johnny laughed. "Are you giving me a lawful order?"

"You could say that."

Johnny shot Kerney a dirty look, took a swig from the bottle, and stepped out of Berman's way. As she passed by, she smiled and mouthed a silent thank-you in Kerney's direction.

"I thought you were a pal," Johnny said.

"Drunks don't have friends."

Johnny gave him a surly look. "Seems you and me just don't get along anymore."

"I'll see you in the morning, Johnny."

Kerney turned and went back to the apartment. Patrick, dressed in his pajamas and about to burst into tears, sat frozen on the couch.

"Where were you, Daddy?" he asked.

"Just outside for a minute, champ."

"I thought you went away just like Mommy."

"Never." He pulled Patrick off the couch, nuzzled him, and carried him to the bedroom. "Mommy and I will always be with you until you're grown up."

The call sheet for the next day didn't have Kerney's name on it. The scene at the copper smelter had been pushed back to rest the stock. In the morning he spent an hour after breakfast with Patrick before heading off to Lordsburg to seek out Leo Valencia. He sat in Leo's office at the

Sheriff's Department and told him about Buster Martinez and the stolen saddle.

Leo rubbed his walrus mustache with his fingers and said, "Interesting." He picked up the telephone and asked for a records check on Martinez. "Either Martinez is a real dumb thief, or he bought the saddle not knowing it was stolen."

"I'm hoping he's dumb," Kerney said. He handed Leo the background information on Walter Shaw. "Several weeks ago I saw Walter Shaw and Martinez drive toward a landing strip on the Sentinel Butte Ranch. Soon after, a plane traveling from that direction passed overhead. I inspected the landing strip and it showed evidence that cargo had been unloaded."

Leo's eyes widened. He read the report on Walter Shaw and grunted in disappointment. "There's nothing here that tells me Shaw is a bad guy. Of course, that doesn't mean anything. What do you want to do?"

"Talk to the saddlemaker and show him Martinez's photograph. Ask around in Virden to learn if Martinez has ever been seen up there. Try to discover if there is a pattern to Shaw's visits to his farm. If the two of them are moving product, I'm guessing he's using his property to warehouse it."

Leo pulled himself out of his chair. "I'll go with you to make it official. We'll take my unit."

They picked up Martinez's records on the way out the door. He had a DWI conviction and one arrest for battery against a household member, which had been dropped when the victim refused to press charges.

Leo bypassed the cutoff to Virden and drove straight to Duncan through desert breaks that hid the Gila River from view. There wasn't much to the town. The mountains beyond were uninviting shadows in the distance. Railroad tracks bordered the main highway, which ran through the river valley toward some low-lying westerly hills. Along the main strip were a smattering of local businesses and a much larger number of vacant buildings with fading signs and chipped stucco exteriors. An old Korean War–era air force jet mounted on a tall arched pedestal overlooked the town from the knob of a small hill. Below, house trailers, manufactured homes, and pitched-roof cottages sat on dusty, dirt-packed lots sheltered by occasional trees. Only a glimpse of the shallow valley could be seen as it spread toward humpback mountains.

From the main strip a hand-painted billboard planted on the side of the road directed them to Matt Thornton's saddle-making establishment. A quarter mile off the pavement on a gravel road, they arrived at a tree-shaded house and adjacent shop. Surrounded by a lawn, it was a cool, inviting oasis, but no one was there to greet them.

At a local eatery Kerney asked the proprietor, an older woman with dyed blond hair, if she knew where Thornton might be. She told him Thornton was the president of the Greenlee County Rodeo Association, and if he wasn't in his shop, he'd most likely be at the county fairgrounds and racetrack just outside of town.

The access road to the fairground was lined with trees and the entrance gate stood open. Matt Thornton was in the office behind the rodeo arena and covered bleachers. A shade under six feet tall, he had curly graying hair and a droopy mustache that almost matched Leo's in size.

"What can I do for you, gents?" Thornton asked, eyeing the shield and sidearm clipped to Leo's belt.

Leo made the introductions and after handshakes all around, he showed Thornton the driver's license photo of Buster Martinez.

"Have you ever seen him in your shop?" he asked.

Thornton studied the picture. "Yep. He's been in once or twice, but not for a while. Who is he?"

"Possibly the man who broke into your shop and took the saddle you reported stolen late last year," Leo replied.

"I'll be damned. Have you got my saddle back?"

"Not yet," Kerney said. "When did you last see him?"

"Now that I think of it, before the break-in at the shop. In fact, I was finishing the saddle at the time."

"Do you know Walt Shaw?" Kerney asked. "He grew up in Virden."

"Can't say that I do. I've only been here ten years. Came down from Wyoming to get away from the harsh winters."

"I'll let you know when we have your saddle," Leo said. Outside the office he chuckled. "Don't you just love dumb crooks?"

"I do," Kerney replied.

They made their way to Virden, past deep green fields, pastures, and the lush river-bottom bosque that lounged against a spate of rocky hills. Kerney had Leo slow down as they passed Shaw's farm.

"I didn't get many votes in this part of the county," Leo said. "Folks around here like their politicians conservative. Where do you want to start?"

Kerney pointed his thumb over his shoulder. "At Shaw's neighbor behind us."

Leo made a U-turn and stopped at the farmhouse where Kerney, on his earlier trip to Virden, had seen a woman hanging wash on a clothesline. Before they could gain the porch steps a man and woman stepped out the front door. Both in their late middle-age, the man was lean and blue eyed with lips that sagged at the corners. The woman, round in the torso with a sharp face, directed her attention to Leo. "How can we oblige you, Sheriff?"

Leo touched the brim of his cowboy hat. "I have a few questions, ma'am. Can I have your names?"

"Isaac and Priscilla Klingman," the man said grudgingly, casting a wary eye at Leo. "What is this about?"

"We're trying find a fellow who may have stolen a saddle from Matt Thornton over in Duncan." Leo handed Mr. Klingman Martinez's photo. "Do you recognize him?"

"Isn't Arizona out of your jurisdiction?" Klingman asked as he scanned the photo.

"A bit. Does he look familiar?"

Isaac Klingman shook his head and handed the photo to his wife. "I've never seen him," she said.

"Who leases the Shaw land?" Kerney asked.

"I do," Klingman replied. "Can't get him to sell it to me."

"Do you have use of the barn?"

"Shaw keeps it locked up tight. I don't go near it, or the house. That's the deal."

"Have you ever seen a white van parked outside?" Kerney asked.

"Yep, but not for long. After it pulls in, it gets put away in the barn. Stays there until he leaves."

Leo took the photo back from Klingman's wife. "Until Shaw leaves?"

"Can't say that I know who comes and goes all the time. Sometimes it's Shaw, sometimes not. There's another man who shows up about twice a month driving the van. Comes in the evening, so I've never gotten a good look at him. Parks in the garage and then leaves after an hour or so. Heads west on the highway."

"How long has this been going on?" Leo asked.

"A year or more. Maybe two."

"Can you remember the last time you

saw the panel truck?" Kerney asked.

Kingman shook his head.

"I remember," his wife said. "I was driving back from town and it was stopped on the side of the highway with a flat tire. I didn't get a good look at the driver, but Nathan Gundersen's truck was parked behind it."

"When was that?" Leo inquired.

"A week ago last Thursday, the evening our ladies' quilting society meets."

"Gundersen lives down the road." Isaac Klingman nodded to the left, eager to be rid of his visitors. "Maybe he can help you. Turn in on the second lane. His house is the third one on the right."

"Thank you," Leo said.

Klingman grunted.

Gundersen wasn't home, but Kerney spotted his pickup truck parked on a farm road that cut through the pastureland toward the river. He had the tailgate down and was encouraging a six-month-old calf up a ramp into the bed of the truck. He nodded in recognition at Kerney as he tied the calf to a side railing, dropped the ramp, and closed the tailgate.

"What brings you back here with the sheriff? Is it about Walt Shaw?"

"Not exactly," Kerney said. "That calf looks sickly."

"It is," Gundersen replied. "The vet thinks it's influenza, but he can't come out until tomorrow, so I'm taking the patient to him. Don't understand it, though. The calf was vaccinated along with all the others." Gundersen glanced at Leo. "What can I do for you, Sheriff?"

"I understand you recently stopped to help a man driving a white van with a flat tire."

"Can't say I was any help at all."

Leo held out the photo of Martinez.

"That's him, all right," Gundersen said.

"Was that a week ago last Thursday?" Kerney asked.

Gundersen nodded. "I'd say so. Are you a police officer too?"

"Yes, I am."

Gundersen pulled off his gloves. "Sure had me fooled."

Leo put the photo in his shirt pocket. "Did anything unusual happen when you stopped to help?"

"He wasn't a very pleasant fellow. When I pulled up behind him, he scowled and waved me off before I could even get out of my truck. Sent me on my way without so much as a word."

"Were you able to see inside the van?" Kerney asked.

"No." Gundersen turned his gaze to the calf. "If you gents don't mind, I'd better be off to the vet's. I don't want to lose this youngster."

They watched Gundersen drive away. In a nearby holding pen the mother cow lowed miserably for its departing calf. "All we've got is circumstantial evidence," Leo said. "Not enough to arrest Martinez or get a search warrant for Shaw's barn. Do we pull Martinez in for questioning?"

Kerney nodded. "I think I know where to find him."

The day had turned uncommonly humid. Kerney looked at the sky. A line of squalls was building to the south, broken by a daunting sun fueling a gathering wind. It could be storming fiercely in the Bootheel, dropping hailstones the size of quarters. Or clouds of dust could be whipping across the flats without so much as a drop of rain hitting the ground. "Let's go," he said.

All night, Buster Martinez had worried about the Santa Fe cop's interest in his saddle. He'd read somewhere that cops could get information about stolen merchandise from a computer back East in some government office that kept national records. Hopefully, Buster had thrown Kerney off base by telling him he'd gotten the saddle in Nevada. If push came to shove, he'd say that he bought it off a guy for cash money at last year's National Pro Rodeo Championship Finals in Las Vegas. He'd been there during slack season and could prove it.

At the Shugart cabin Martinez and two day hands, Ross and Pruitt, loaded cattle into stock trailers the film company had hired to move fifty head to the copper smelter. They'd trailed the animals up from an adjacent pasture where the herd had rested overnight. According to one of the truck drivers the cows would be used in a scene at the copper smelter sometime soon. A big holding pen had been thrown up where the animals would be fed and watered until needed.

Except for the heavily foraged, harshly trampled grass, the soft cow pies surrounded by fly swarms that littered the land, and the numerous tire ruts in the ground, all signs that a movie had been filmed in the valley were gone. Above Martinez's head the sky crackled with thunder and a lightning flash cut through the thick cloud bank that had settled over the valley. Suddenly, the light drizzle changed to a torrent of hard, howling, windblown rain that pelted Martinez's face.

He dismounted, lashed the last of the cows up the ramp into the stock trailer, slammed the tailgate closed, and turned to see Ross and Pruitt riding at a hard gallop, making for the safety of the partially standing wall of the old line shanty. As he remounted to join them, car headlights lurched over the crest of the ranch road. Through sheets of rain he could see the light bar on the roof, the five-pointed sheriff's star on the door.

Martinez hesitated. Were the cops coming for him? He could think of no other reason for them to be here. Under another lightning flash he held his horse in check and waited until the squad car drew near. He saw Kerney's face through the windshield, saw him curling his forefinger at him in a come-here gesture, and the thought of going to jail again made him bolt. Getting arrested and locked up on a DWI for one night had been bad enough. He spurred his horse toward Granite Pass.

Behind him he heard the sound of the squad car in pursuit. The hard rain beat against the packed earth, pooling and running into the draw that led to the pass. Martinez pushed his mount into the draw, forced it up an incline, and clattered it into the rocky canyon mouth. The sound of the engine receded and he turned in the saddle. The squad car stood snout up on the lip of the draw, wheels spinning, digging to gain traction. But behind the car, riding Pruitt's dapple gray, came Kerney, head down, low in the saddle, at a full gallop.

Martinez gave his horse free rein. Rainwater gushed down the cliff face, submerging the narrow trail. The horse stumbled on a rock, pitched, recovered, and wheeled into a mesquite that sent it spinning. Martinez clamped tight with his knees, kept pressure off the bit, and let it come to a stop. Twenty feet down the trail Kerney sat watching him on Pruitt's soaked and dirty dapple gray.

"Can you hear me?" Kerney called out over the roar of the storm.

"I can," Martinez yelled back, blinking hard to keep the hammering rain out of his eyes.

"Do you have a weapon?"

Martinez raised his hands to show that he did not.

"Would you like to stay out of jail?" Kerney asked.

"What do I have to do?"

"Let's get out of this storm and we'll talk," Kerney said.

Martinez nodded and approached. "I didn't steal my saddle."

"Of course you did," Kerney replied with an easy smile. "But if you cooperate, that saddle may buy you your freedom."

Chapter Fourteen

With the saddle in the trunk of the unit and Martinez cuffed and behind the cage in the backseat, Leo and Kerney returned to Lordsburg. The storm had passed, leaving behind a misty drizzle under a low sky, the sweet smell of moist air, and standing water in the streets.

Kerney's attempts to draw Martinez out during the ride were met with stubborn silence.

"I told you I didn't steal the saddle," Martinez said as they pulled to a stop at the Sheriff's Department near the courthouse.

Kerney glanced over the front seat at Martinez. "Then why did you run?"

"Because I don't like jails. Are you charging me with a crime?"

"Right now, we just need to gather some facts," Kerney answered. "If you cooperate, it shouldn't take long. Maybe you bought the saddle because it was too good a deal to pass up. Maybe you didn't actually know it was stolen, but in the back of your mind you wondered if it might have been."

"You said that I stole it."

Kerney got out and opened the door to the backseat. "Because you ran. It made you look guilty as hell."

Martinez stepped onto the pavement. "Like I told you, I got scared about going to jail."

Kerney uncuffed him. "That's perfectly understandable."

Inside, Leo guided them to a cramped, tiny room used for interviews and interrogations. It contained an old video camera on a tripod, a narrow table, two metal folding chairs, and a half-dozen sealed cardboard file boxes stacked in a corner. From the dust on the table it was clear the room hadn't been used for its intended purpose in a long time.

Kerney pulled out a chair. "Make yourself comfortable, Mr. Martinez. I'll be with you in a minute."

"Where are you going?"

"We've got to log the saddle into evidence. First things first. Would you like some coffee?"

Martinez nodded.

Kerney closed the door and went looking for Leo, who was in his office with the saddle on his desk. "He wants coffee."

"I'll have it brought in," Leo said. "You gave him a ready-made out."

"Deliberately. He's not going to admit guilt easily. I want him to feel free to tell me his story. How quickly can you run a financial history on him?"

"It's in the works." Leo picked up the phone and asked his secretary to take Martinez a cup of coffee.

"I'll start without it," Kerney said. "Get me what you can as soon as it comes in."

Martinez looked a bit more relaxed when Kerney returned to the interview room. He had his legs stretched out under the table and a mug of coffee in hand.

Kerney sat back in his chair and smiled. "Tell me how the saddle came into your possession."

Martinez nodded, took a sip of coffee, and put the mug on the table. "I bought it off a guy in Las Vegas last December. He'd had a bad run at the tables and needed the money."

"Where did you meet him?"

"In a diner off the strip. The guy came up to me at my table and asked if I'd be interested in a great deal. Took me outside to the parking lot and showed me the saddle. I bought it on the spot."

"How much did you pay for it?"

"A thousand."

"That's a lot of money to be carrying around."

"I got lucky at the craps tables."

"Who was the guy?"

"Just another cowboy in town for the pro rodeo finals. He said he was from Utah. I don't remember his name."

"Can you describe him?"

"Tall, maybe your size but younger." Martinez paused and thought for a long moment. "Oh, yeah, he had a crooked nose. You need to look for a tall man with a crooked nose."

"What kind of vehicle was he driving?"

"I think it was a Dodge truck. Extended cab. He had the saddle in the backseat."

"That's helpful information. Do you know if he was competing in the rodeo? If so, that could narrow our search."

Martinez shook his head and reached for the mug. "He didn't look like a contestant."

"Was anyone with you at the diner who saw the man?"

Martinez tensed his shoulders, pulled his hand back from the mug, and gave Kerney a hard look. "No. Why didn't you ask me all these questions at the corral when you made such a big deal out of admiring my saddle?"

Kerney smiled reassuringly. "I had no reason to question you then, Mr. Martinez."

"Yeah, but that didn't stop you from thinking I was some sort of criminal because I've got a custom-made saddle."

"If you had told me all this at the ranch instead of trying to flee, we could have avoided inconveniencing you."

Martinez drained his coffee and wiped his mouth on the sleeve of his shirt. "You cops always think the worst of people."

"Unfortunately, that's often the case. I've a few more questions about the truck the man was driving. Whatever you can recall could help us find him."

Martinez said the truck was black in color. He said it had a chrome rear bumper. He said the truck had a diesel engine. He recalled hearing it when the cowboy drove away.

Kerney wrote it all down.

Leo stepped into the room, gave Kerney a folder, and left. Kerney scanned the information. Martinez owned a manufactured home on an acre of land in Hachita that he'd bought outright over a year ago, and was making monthly payments on a top-of-the-line new four-wheel-drive pickup truck. He had two bank cards and a gasoline credit card, and the monthly transaction records showed that he paid the balances in full regularly.

All in all, Martinez had been living quite well over the past several years, an unusual circumstance for someone in a traditionally low-paying occupation.

Martinez leaned forward in his chair. "What's that you're looking at?"

"Just some additional information about the saddle," Kerney lied. "Did you know it's worth almost five thousand dollars?"

"That much?"

"Yeah," Kerney said as he scanned Martinez's credit card purchases. "It was taken from a saddlemaker's shop in Duncan, Arizona. Ever been there?"

"I've passed through it once or twice. Not much there worth stopping for."

"That's what I hear." Kerney stood and waved the file folder at Martinez. "Now that we know who the rightful owner is, the saddle has to be returned. I'm afraid you're out the thousand bucks you paid for it."

Martinez shrugged and smiled. "Easy come, easy go. Like I said, I bought it with money I won gambling."

"I'll tell the sheriff to cut you loose. If

you like, you can wait in the reception area. I'll give you a ride back to the ranch."

"No jail?"

"That's right." Kerney patted Martinez on the arm. "You're a free man."

He escorted Martinez to reception and then dropped in on Leo.

"That was quick," Leo said from behind his desk. "Did he confess?"

"I didn't even try to take him that far." Kerney handed Leo the gasoline-credit-card transaction report. "Look at the dates of his gas purchases. Every two weeks he fills up his tank, drives to Phoenix, Ruidoso, or Albuquerque, and then gasses up again for the return trip home on the same night. What kind of ranch hand does that kind of traveling, especially at night during the week? Or has the kind of money to buy a house outright?"

"None that I know of." Leo brushed his mustache with a finger. "He's making deliveries. But what kind, and why to Phoenix, Ruidoso, and Albuquerque?"

"I don't know."

"So why not lean on him?"

"Because it would only tip our hand. If his pattern holds, Martinez will be on the road again soon. I'm betting another plane will be landing at the Sentinel Butte Ranch any day now. If so, we can take down Martinez, Shaw, and the supplier all at once."

"You're talking about a stakeout."

Kerney nodded. "It needs to be put in place as soon as possible."

Leo scratched his chin. "I don't have the personnel to mount an operation like that."

"The state police should be willing to help out. I'll talk to Chief Baca in Santa Fe."

Leo nodded. "Do you want in on it?"

"Yes, I do," Kerney said. "Let me know the plans."

On the trip back to the ranch, with his freedom no longer in question, Buster Martinez became less apprehensive and a bit more talkative. He embellished the story about the tall cowboy with the crooked nose, suddenly remembering the man had told him that he was on his way to a new ranch job in Texas. It was obviously pure fabrication, but Kerney pretended to swallow it, and thanked Martinez. By the time they hit the Jordan ranch road, Buster had graciously agreed to treat his encounter with the police as nothing more than a misunderstanding.

They found Walter Shaw outside the barn. The movie set had been struck and the ranch headquarters, now restored to its original condition, looked neat as a pin. Martinez's expression clouded with worry as Kerney explained the events of the day to Shaw. He licked his lips and averted his eyes from Shaw's gaze.

"Ross and Pruitt told me what happened," Shaw said amiably when Kerney finished. He patted Martinez reassuringly on the shoulder. "I'm glad it got straightened out. Can't afford to lose a good hand like Buster."

Martinez lowered his head and smiled weakly.

"I understand completely," Kerney said. "That's why I wanted to make sure you knew he wasn't in any trouble."

"I appreciate that," Shaw said with a tight smile. "What made you think the saddle was stolen?"

"Remember the Oklahoma teamster working on the movie who was arrested at the ranch?"

"Yeah, I heard about that."

"He had two outstanding burglary warrants, so the sheriff took a hard look at him as a possible suspect in recent unsolved property crimes. The saddle popped up on a list of stolen items circulated by Arizona authorities."

"So when you saw the saddle, you called the sheriff," Shaw said.

"Exactly."

"Well, no harm done."

"I'm glad you see it that way."

Kerney left the two men standing in front of the barn. Shaw's aplomb had been almost convincing, but anger had flared in his eyes. At the very least Martinez was in for a tongue lashing and some hard questions from Shaw. Kerney wasn't worried about what Martinez might say; it was Shaw who concerned him. Shaw had to know that he was under suspicion. What he might do about it remained unknown, but the next move was his to make.

After Kerney passed out of sight, Shaw grabbed Martinez by the shirt and pulled him into the barn. "What did you tell him?"

"Nothing." Martinez yanked himself away from Shaw's grip.

Shaw slapped him. "Don't lie to me, you stupid turd. Did you steal that saddle?"

"I didn't steal nothing, for Chrissake."

Shaw grabbed him by the throat. "Tell me exactly what happened." Martinez coughed, his squinty eyes bulged. Shaw eased up. "Talk."

"It was just about the saddle. Where did I buy it. When. Who sold it to me — that kind of stuff. I told him what he wanted to know and they let me go."

Shaw released his grip and Martinez heaved for breath. "Did he ask you anything about me?"

Buster shook his head.

"Say anything about the landing strip?"

"Nada."

"Did you steal that saddle?"

Martinez rubbed his neck. "I didn't, *palabra de honor.*"

"Your word doesn't mean shit," Shaw said. "Get out of here and go back to work."

Eyes lowered, Buster left the barn and slogged his way through the mud to the corral where Pruitt had put up his horse. Shaw ran possible scenarios about Kerney's actions through his head. Everything pointed to a probe that went far beyond the theft of a mere saddle. But so far Buster appeared to be Kerney's only target. That might work to Shaw's advantage.

He stepped outside, closed the barn doors, and watched Buster hose the mud off his horse. As he walked to his truck, Shaw chewed over ways to ensure Kerney would come no closer to the truth.

★ ★ ★

The storm had shut down film production for the day and the town of Playas was quiet. Kerney checked the call sheet on the bulletin board. He was listed as an extra for an exterior shot in the morning, to be filmed in front of the community center. Kerney read the script revision that had been posted for the scene. None of the changes applied to the extras.

He stopped at the apartment and called Andy Baca at state police headquarters, who agreed to provide manpower and equipment for the stakeout. Then he powered up the laptop and found an e-mail from Sara. She was hard at work safely inside the Baghdad Green Zone, creating something called "actionable intelligence." Although she couldn't, for security reasons, go into detail, it had to do with collecting and analyzing real-time battlefield information on insurgent and terrorist activities.

Kerney wasn't reassured. He doubted such work could be accomplished solely in the air-conditioned comfort of a fortified, heavily guarded facility in a war-torn nation.

He wrote back, keeping it lighthearted and chatty. He told her how well Patrick was doing and about his three-day stint in the saddle, chasing cattle on the Jordan ranch. He wrote about Barbara Jennings's emergency appendectomy that had caused Dale to stay home. He mentioned the upcoming country-music benefit concert, scheduled to be shot at the Playas ball field in two nights. He left out the fact that he might be on a stakeout during that time.

He signed off with love and kisses and drove to the nanny's house, his thoughts still on Sara. Was she in some remote village, training combat ground troops on how to make uplink satellite intelligence reports from the field? Or with an infantry company, transmitting real-time intelligence on enemy activity during a firefight?

From his tour in Vietnam, Kerney knew firsthand about insurgency and guerrilla warfare. There were no rear areas or safe havens, no clearly defined enemy, no easily identified threat thresholds. He wanted Sara home now, and his heart ached at the thought of some disaster befalling her.

He sat in the truck for a moment and forced himself to clear away worrisome thoughts before he went to get his son. Back in the truck he put Patrick on his lap behind the steering wheel and told him he could drive. Grinning, Patrick clutched the wheel with his tiny hands while Kerney navigated through some of the empty residential streets. After a few slow go-rounds he put Patrick — who was very pleased with himself — in the car seat and headed for the copper smelter. There he found Kent Vogt at a portable cattle pen, feeding the stock.

Over at the rail spur and loading dock of the smelter, Barry Hingle and his construction crew were busy building ramps to be used to send police cars careening through the air, and a special-effects crew was rigging a flatbed railroad car to receive one of the airborne vehicles.

"This is going to be something else when they film it," Vogt said as he joined Kerney and Patrick at the truck. He nodded at the penned up cattle. "Ten tons of beef on the hoof meets ten tons of cop cars. I can't wait to see how they do it."

"You're not part of it?" Kerney asked.

"Nope, the stunt riders get to have all the fun. Something about liability and insurance. I get to help chase down the cattle after they been scattered to hell and gone." Vogt lifted his head toward the mountains behind the smelter. "I figure it will take Buster, Pruitt, Ross, and me a full day to round them up. That's if Buster ain't sitting in a jail cell in Lordsburg."

Kerney laughed. "Word sure travels fast. Buster's a free man."

"But without that fancy saddle, I bet," Vogt said with a grin.

"True enough." Kerney let Vogt's observation pass without further comment. In a land with so few people it was never wise to say too much about an individual's friends, neighbors, or coworkers until you knew what bound them together or split them apart.

Chuckling, Vogt put his gloves on and returned to his chore. After showing Patrick the cows Kerney took him to watch the movie people at work. Every few seconds the beacon on the tall smokestack pulsated, flashing its warning light into the sky. Come nightfall it would guide refugees, migrants, smugglers, and perhaps a fanatic or two across the border.

If Kerney had guessed correctly, within days a plane would lock on to the beacon and land at the Sentinel Butte Ranch. He wondered what cargo it would bring.

Back in Playas, Johnny and his rodeo cowboys were sitting in the ball field bleachers, drinking long-neck beers and listening to the country music star rehearse with his band. He was one of those vocalists who strummed a guitar for show and sang in husky, testosterone-laden tones that appealed to the buckle-bunny crowd.

Kerney watched Johnny drain his beer, say something to his companions, and walk to the bandstand where Susan Berman stood with a stopwatch in her hand timing the music. He put his arm around Berman's waist, grabbed her free hand, and tried to get her to two-step with him. Susan pushed him away, stopped the music, and gestured for him to leave. The rodeo cowboys hooted derisively and slapped their legs. Johnny returned to his pals laughing like a fifteen-year-old who'd just carried off a bold dare.

At dinner under the tent a publicist passed out an announcement about the filming of the benefit concert sequence. Free tickets to the concert had been given to area residents, and in two nights over seven hundred locals would fill the bleachers and the ballpark infield. Filming would start at dusk.

Kerney called Leo Valencia with the news.

"There won't be a soul at home in the Bootheel," Leo said.

"Exactly. It's the perfect time to fly in

contraband. What do you have in the works?"

"I just got back from the Sentinel Butte Ranch. We'll have a team of eight on the stakeout, including you, me, two of my deputies, and four state police officers. Two will be in a chopper, a pilot and a sniper.

"We'll use four-by-fours and ATVs on the ground. Two teams will be situated east and west, one at the windmill by the gate, the other in Chinaman Hills. You'll be with me to the south in an arroyo. The chopper will be with us. All equipment and personnel will be under camouflage netting, and we'll have a waning crescent moon that will add to our concealment."

"When do we go on-station?" Kerney asked.

"Traveling by convoy could draw too much attention, so I'll be moving people into position in stages, starting in the afternoon. We'll be the first on-site, the chopper last. Everybody in place before sundown."

"Sounds good."

"Be at my office at two o'clock the day after tomorrow."

"See you then."

In the morning Kerney pulled his stint

as an extra in a crowd scene of angry citizens protesting the revocation of the rancher's federal grazing permit. It took Usher three takes to get it right. Before Kerney could leave the set, Susan Berman asked to speak with him privately. She had dark circles under her eyes from too little sleep and seemed weighed down by the thick three-ring binder she clutched in her arms. Being overworked and tired made her no less attractive.

"Normally, I can hold my own with the alley cats in this business," she said, "and I really don't want to impose on you, but is there some way you could convince Johnny Jordan to stop hounding me?"

"Tell me what's been happening."

Berman sighed. "The man simply won't take no for an answer, and now it's at the point where he's interfering with my work."

"I saw the little prank he pulled yesterday at the ball field."

Berman winced and nodded. "It was so childish."

"Yes, it was. Can't you bar him from the set?"

"No, he's an executive producer and has every right to be here."

"I'll talk to him."

Berman touched Kerney's arm and smiled. "Thank you."

Kerney went looking for Johnny and learned he was on his way to the Duncan fairgrounds with his cowboy clients for the filming of the rodeo scenes. He arrived back in Playas late that afternoon. Kerney was there to meet him when the vans and trucks carrying the cast and crew rolled in.

With a pleased grin he slapped Kerney on the back and, in a rush of words, said, "You should have been with us, amigo. We got some really great shots in the can. Usher says that once it gets edited into a montage, it's gonna be better than what Peckinpah did in *Junior Bonner*, and that was one great rodeo flick."

It was typical Johnny. His drunken attempt last night to seduce Susan Berman was a thing of the past, to be forgotten and forgiven.

"We need to talk," Kerney said as he led Johnny away from the cast to the rear of one of the equipment trucks.

"Why so serious?" Johnny asked.

"You're getting out of hand with Susan Berman, and you need to leave her alone."

Johnny grinned. "Why? Do you want her for yourself?"

"I'll forget you said that. Just ease off,

Johnny. You're making her very uncomfortable."

Johnny smirked. "Roll your own, amigo. Berman is number one on my hit list and I aim to nail her."

"What does it take to get you to listen? Stop coming on to Susan. She isn't interested in you."

"Look," Johnny said, "if you need to get some action from the ladies while your wife is overseas, that's cool with me. Just find somebody else to shag. There's some tasty talent here."

"Don't get personal, Johnny."

Johnny glared and struck a cocky pose. "You want personal? I've got a DWI hanging over my head in Santa Fe because you wouldn't do a damn thing to help me out. Now you come around all puffed up with an attitude because of a skirt you want to jump on. What a joke. You've always been a loser when it comes to women, Kerney. I bet you were the only guy in our high school crowd who didn't get into my sister's pants."

"You're unbelievable." It made no sense to explain to Johnny the concepts of family loyalty, respect for women, or true friendship. Without thinking he slugged Johnny hard under the left eye.

Johnny hit the deck and bounced against the bumper of the truck. Slowly, he staggered to his feet and shook his head to clear away the cobwebs.

Kerney rubbed his unclenched fist. "I wasn't going to do that. Now do I have your full attention?"

Johnny closed his eye and gingerly touched his face. "If you want Susan Berman that bad, she's yours."

"Good. You might want to put an ice pack on that eye before it swells up."

That night, after Patrick had been tucked into bed, Kerney sat on the lawn outside the apartment. At the ballpark the stadium lights were on, and a crew was busy putting the finishing touches on the set for the concert sequence. Crickets chirped and a slight breeze slid through the trees, bringing the faint yelp of a distant coyote. He felt a tap on his shoulder and turned just as Susan Berman sat down by his side.

"Did you really punch Johnny in the face?" she asked with a smile.

"Did he tell you that?"

Susan nodded.

"I refuse to admit any wrongdoing whatsoever."

Susan laughed. "Why did you do it?"

"It was the only way I could get him to listen."

She leaned forward slightly and searched Kerney's face in the dim light that cascaded up from the ballpark. "You're a good man, Kevin Kerney, and if your marital circumstances were different, I wouldn't mind at all having you as my champion."

She kissed him on the cheek, said goodnight, and hurried toward the ball field.

Warmed by Susan's compliment and ladylike expression of interest, Kerney sat quietly for a moment before retreating to the apartment. At the kitchen table he opened the laptop and surfed the Web, looking for the latest news from Iraq. Five more soldiers had been killed in combat. It brought back memories of the dead and dying Kerney had seen in Vietnam. Sara's face flashed through his mind with images of her killed or maimed. It made him shudder.

Slowly, the images swam away. With his fingers poised over the keyboard Kerney considered what to write to his beautiful wife. He thought about the long, elegant line of her neck, her flashing green eyes, the freckles on the bridge of her nose, the graceful way she moved. Suddenly, with an unaccustomed ease, he found himself composing a love letter.

★ ★ ★

The next day, after dropping Patrick off at the nanny's, Kerney rendezvoused with Leo in Lordsburg. At five in the afternoon he was on-station at the Sentinel Butte Ranch with Leo, sitting in a brand-new four-wheel-drive sheriff's unit bought and paid for with Homeland Security funds. With the engine off to avoid the possibility of detection the temperature inside the vehicle had to be a hundred degrees. The open windows and camouflage netting provided some relief, but with no breeze the heat was relentless.

Behind the steering wheel Leo sucked down bottled water from a cooler and talked by radio to the teams. The Chinaman Hills duo had been in position for an hour and the team at the gate and windmill was setting up. The state police helicopter, last to arrive, was twenty minutes out.

Kerney dismounted the vehicle and swept the landscape with binoculars. The spot Leo had picked was a good one, with line of sight to the hills, the ranch gate, and the landing strip. Kerney concentrated on Chinaman Hills. The team had set up low on the eastern slope at the mouth of a small box canyon. Virtually invisible in daylight, they would be impossible to see come nightfall.

Kerney raised the glasses to the summit of the cinnamon-brown hills. Above it the Star of the North on the top of the smokestack winked weakly in the light of day. The wind-scoured hills, dotted with cactus, cleaved by the runoff of occasional torrential storms, showed no signs of trails leading down from the spine. At midslope a barbed-wire fence spanned the length of the hills. Where runoff had undercut the soil, several fence posts, no longer anchored in the ground, dangled, suspended in the air by the wire strands.

He swung to the east and scanned the ranch gate. The second team's vehicles were lined up behind the windmill. Once the netting was in place, they, too, would have excellent concealment.

To the southeast the Big Hatchet Mountains topped out, gray in the harsh light of a hot sun well beyond its zenith. The limestone uplift pressed against the sky and tall, scattered pines crowded the summits of the highest peaks. Juniper and piñon clung to the lower drainages on steep cliffs, and at the base, on the valley floor, cattle browsed among the bunchgrass and desert shrub.

He trained the binoculars on the high country, looking for the Continental Divide Trail that started at the border and ran all the way to Canada. Because of the distance he couldn't make it out.

Kerney returned his attention to the stakeouts. He figured it would take each team, including the chopper, which would need time to power up, three to five minutes to reach the landing strip. That was worrisome. A good pilot in a small plane could be airborne by then.

"They are going to hear us coming," Kerney said. "We might not get there quickly enough."

Leo grinned. "Didn't I tell you? One of my deputies is an ex-jarhead sniper. He'll be on the lead ATV. If the plane starts to taxi, he'll stop at a thousand meters out and put rounds through the engine."

"That would be hard to do without a spotter," Kerney said.

Leo handed Kerney a bottle of chilled water through the open window. "If he misses, the helicopter will force the plane to stay on the ground. Take a load off. It's two hours until sundown."

"Is your deputy really a trained Marine sniper?"

"Fowler? You bet. One shot, one kill.

He's a Gulf War One vet. I call him my one-man SWAT team."

"What's his weapon?"

"A civilian version of an M40A1 with a ten-power scope and tripod."

"Let's have him leave his ATV behind and low-crawl into position at sunset. Tell him to get within five hundred meters of the landing strip. Closer, if he can manage it. He can hide in the tall grass."

Leo nodded in agreement and called Fowler.

After sunset Buster Martinez arrived at the Harley homestead on the Granite Pass Ranch to find Shaw waiting for him outside the barn next to his panel van. In the beam of the truck headlights he could see that Walt was wearing a holstered sidearm.

"Why the *pistola?*" he asked as he got into the van.

Shaw wheeled the van onto the ranch road. "With Kerney snooping around I'm taking no chances."

"You'd shoot a cop?" The thought of it made Buster's stomach churn.

"It's just a precaution," Shaw replied. "Chances are we're the only two people in the Bootheel not at the Playas ballpark for the free concert."

"That's where I'd like to be," Buster grumbled.

Shaw braked to a stop. "Go ahead and go."

"I just meant it would be something nice to see."

"Then just shut up about it." Shaw gunned the engine and accelerated. The van jarred over the ruts as it picked up speed.

Buster clamped his lips together. The van headlights froze a rabbit in the road and a front tire thumped over it. He glanced at Shaw. In the glow of the instrument panel Shaw looked pissed off. He'd been acting that way toward him all day. Probably still steamed about the saddle, Buster thought.

He unwrapped a piece of gum, popped it in his mouth, and started chewing. It kept him from asking Shaw what in the hell the big hurry was all about.

To keep himself alert and entertained Kerney used night-vision goggles to watch Fowler, Leo's deputy sheriff, ex-Marine sniper, one-man SWAT team, crawl toward the landing strip. In the gathering darkness, with the waning moon yet to rise, he wondered if Fowler's effort would be worth it. Other than the officers on the stakeout there had been no hint of human activity in the valley since their arrival. Additionally, the operation was premised on nothing more than an educated guess. There was no guarantee that a plane would be landing at the strip tonight.

Fowler was good; he stayed low, used his elbows, knees, and belly, and moved to the best concealment points. Soon he'd be in position, five hundred meters out, covered in sand and grit, pricked by cactus spines, bitten by fire ants.

Inside the four-by-four Leo had his headset on and was talking with the troops in a low voice. Throughout the wait he seemed perfectly content to remain sedentary and had exited the vehicle only once to relieve himself. Kerney didn't know how the man could sit so long without getting antsy.

So why was he on edge? Over the years he had calmly pulled more than his fair share of stakeout and surveillance assignments. He should be sitting back waiting for events to unfold, not prowling restlessly back and forth under the camouflage netting. Like a spasm the thought hit him that he had no business putting himself in potential danger, not with Sara in a war zone.

What if Patrick lost both parents in the line of duty?

What in the hell had he been thinking? he asked himself angrily.

The door to the four-by-four opened. Leo eased himself out and handed Kerney a headset. "Time to plug in. Fowler is in position."

"Let's hope we're not wasting our time."

Beyond the landing strip headlights flashed into view and dipped out of sight.

"I don't think we are," Leo said.

Walt Shaw made a hard turn at the fence line, sped to the gate at the foot of Chinaman Hills, and ground the van to a stop. Buster jumped out to open the gate and Shaw went with him, shining the beam of a flashlight on the rutted dirt road. The recent rain had washed away all the old tracks and there was no fresh sign that any vehicles, horses, or people had passed by.

Shaw gunned the van through the gate and Buster had to pull himself inside on the run.

"We're gonna be way too early," he said, trying to make small talk. He'd never seen Shaw so uptight.

"Not tonight." Shaw downshifted as the

van bounced through a sandy trough in the road.

Buster put his hand on the dashboard to brace himself as the van jitterbugged down the road. Through the windshield he could see the flashing warning lights of the plane as it came over the Big Hatchet Mountains.

Shaw stopped at the end of the eighteen-hundred-foot dirt strip and blinked the headlights. The plane banked, descended, and engine noise filled the night air. It touched down, taxied to a stop, and the pilot cut the engine. Buster walked to the cargo door and cranked the latch. The hold was empty.

"There's nothing here." Befuddled, Buster turned and looked at Shaw.

Shaw laughed in his face and shot him twice in the chest at close range.

Through his night vision goggles Kerney watched Buster go down. In his headset he heard Fowler swear as Shaw picked up Martinez and dumped him in the airplane.

"Everybody go, go, go," Leo yelled to the teams. "Lights and sirens." He ground gears, jumped the four-by-four out of the arroyo, and hit the gas.

Engines revved and roared in concert with the slow thud of chopper rotors and first whine of the airplane propeller cranking up. Sirens wailed, adding to the din. Emergency lights splintered the darkness. For an instant Shaw stood frozen in the glare of the van as the backwash from the propeller rippled over him.

"I've got a head shot on the shooter," Fowler said.

"No, disable the plane," Kerney said.

"Ten-four," Fowler replied.

Kerney counted seconds as he watched Shaw scramble into the open cargo hold. The plane swung around for takeoff, but before it could gather speed, Fowler put three rounds in the engine and two in the front landing-gear tire. The engine sputtered, died, and the plane tipped forward. Shaw and the pilot bailed out and ran for the van.

Behind Kerney the chopper went airborne, its floodlight washing over the four-by-four. The teams from Chinaman Hills and the windmill bore down on the landing strip. By the time Shaw and the pilot were in the van and moving, they were boxed in.

Leo skidded to a stop on the landing strip. Kerney rolled out the passenger door, crouched behind it, and leveled his weapon at the van windshield.

Under similar cover Leo grabbed the radio microphone and hit the PA switch. His voice boomed over the loudspeaker. "Throw out the weapon, turn off the engine, drop the keys on the ground, and exit the vehicle with your hands clasped behind your heads. Do it now."

Slowly the men complied, and Leo put them through a by-the-book felony takedown. Surrounded by officers, they were cuffed and pulled into a sitting position. While Leo checked the pilot's ID, Kerney went to the airplane and took a look at Buster Martinez. He was facedown, leaking blood, and very dead.

He walked over to Shaw, hunkered down, and looked him in the eyes. "Six officers will testify that they saw you murder Buster Martinez in cold blood," he said. "I seriously doubt any lawyer could mount a defense against such overwhelming evidence. Want to tell me what this was all about?"

Chapter Fifteen

Walt Shaw wasn't talking, so Kerney decided to take a crack at the pilot of the airplane, Craig Gilmore. He walked Gilmore to Leo's unit in handcuffs and sat with him in the backseat.

A man in his fifties, soft in the face with a dimpled chin, Gilmore looked like the arrest had hit him hard.

"Is that your airplane?" Kerney asked.

Gilmore looked out the window at the disabled aircraft. "Yeah, I bought it ten years ago when business was good."

"What kind of business is that?" Kerney asked.

"I own a regional wholesale cigarette and tobacco company in El Paso. But I almost lost everything when the tech stock bubble burst in 2000. I took a real beating."

"How do you know Shaw?"

"We were in the navy together and stayed in touch over the years. I brought him in on the deal."

"When did you partner up with Shaw?"

"Four years ago. It was either that or declare bankruptcy."

"Tell me how your scheme works," Kerney asked.

"It's real simple," Gilmore replied. "I forge documents showing that American-made cigarettes have been exported, and then sell them at cut-rate prices to several distributors in New Mexico and Arizona. Because custom and state taxes aren't levied, we make a substantial profit on each pack."

"How much profit?"

"It depends on the state, and we split it sixty-forty with the distributors. In New Mexico our cut is fifty-five cents a pack, and in Arizona it's seventy cents."

"How many packs have you sold?"

"Eight million, more or less."

Kerney did a quick mental calculation. Gilmore and Shaw had each cleared seven figures from the scheme. "Domestic cigarettes are sold with state excise stamps," Kerney said. "How do you get around that?"

Gilmore leaned forward to ease the pressure of the handcuffs that ground into his wrists against the seat back. "The local distributors mix the unstamped stock in with the taxed goods and charge full price to the retailer. Nobody pays any attention to the stamp when they buy smokes."

"Where do the goods wind up for sale to the public?" Kerney asked.

"Convenience stores, gas stations, smoke shops, small grocery chains, mom-and-pop stores."

Because Gilmore and Shaw weren't bringing counterfeit cigarettes into the country, legally it wasn't smuggling. It was a theft, fraud, and contraband operation. "Who are your distributors?" Kerney asked.

Gilmore named them.

"Why run the risk of flying the goods here yourself?"

Gilmore snorted. "Until now there wasn't any risk. Customs doesn't give a damn about general aviation planes that stay north of the border. It's a hell of a lot safer to use a plane than to try to truck the product through the highway checkpoints around El Paso."

"Do you warehouse your inventory in Virden?"

Gilmore nodded. "Yeah. We keep fresh stock of the most popular brands on hand there for the Arizona run. It's our biggest moneymaker."

Kerney opened the door. "Okay, you'll

need to make a complete statement to the sheriff."

"What will I be charged with?"

"Murder one."

Gilmore looked shocked. "I didn't kill anybody. Can you help me out here? I'll tell you everything."

"Then tell me this," Kerney said. "What were you going to do with Martinez's body?"

Gilmore flinched at the question.

"Well?" Kerney prodded.

"Fly to San Diego and dump it in the ocean."

"In my book that's murder one."

"I swear I'll cooperate."

"Take it up with the prosecutor."

"Can you loosen the handcuffs? They're hurting my wrists."

"Sorry, I can't do that." Kerney got out and looked at Gilmore through the open door. "Try to relax. It will be a while before you go to jail."

He locked Gilmore in the backseat cage and joined Leo at the airplane, where he was watching a deputy take photos of Buster Martinez's body.

"Who's doing the Q and A with Shaw?" he asked.

Leo nodded toward a sheriff's unit.

"Fowler, but Shaw's still not talking, except to say unkind things about you. The ME and an ambulance are on the way. I'm releasing the state police officers."

"I'll catch a ride with them back to Lordsburg," Kerney said. "Gilmore is going to tell you about their contraband cigarette scheme."

"It's not smuggling?" Leo asked.

"Nope. They've been stealing name-brand domestic cigarettes and selling them cut rate to distributors."

Leo's forehead wrinkled. "Who would have guessed?"

"They keep their inventory at the Virden barn."

"I'll get a warrant. Was Martinez a smoker?"

"I don't think so."

Leo glanced at Buster's body. "Well, cigarettes turned out to be hazardous to his health anyway." Leo laughed at his joke. "I'm really going to enjoy making phone calls to ATF and Customs."

"Rub their noses in it, Leo."

Leo grinned. "You don't get many chances to do that to the feds."

Kerney didn't see Leo for several days, until the filming of the finale to the chase

526

sequence at the smelter. He showed up in time to see a stunt driver roll out of a squad car just before it went airborne and landed on the flatbed railroad car.

When the car exploded into flames, Leo nodded in approval. "Now that's more like it," he said. "I told you they needed to blow something up."

Kerney laughed. "It's a realistic slice of police work, Hollywood style."

They watched the crane camera shoot a crash between two cop cars before Leo launched into an update on the investigation. Over a half-million dollars' worth of cigarettes had been recovered in the barn in Virden, along with almost a million dollars in cash. Shaw had been charged with murder one and denied bail. He'd lawyered up and still wasn't talking. Craig Gilmore was also being held without bond on the same charge.

"I don't think the DA is going to let Gilmore cop a plea," Leo said. "We've got enough eyewitness testimony to sink them both. If it goes to trial, you'll be called as a witness for the prosecution."

"That's not a problem," Kerney said. "What are the feds up to?"

"They're shutting down the network and arresting the distributors. Then they'll take their evidence to a federal grand jury. I'm guessing Shaw and Gilmore will get hit with multiple federal felony counts."

"Good deal."

"This case is going to get me reelected by a landslide next year."

"You deserve to be reelected. But do you really think, in spite of your good work, that the citizens of Virden are going to vote for you?" Kerney asked.

Leo guffawed. "Hell, no, but I'll win anyway."

The two men watched moviemaking magic for a while more before Leo shook Kerney's hand, thanked him, and left. Kerney hung around until the police-related shots were done and then headed back to Playas. Sara had e-mailed him last night. In two hours she would be calling from Iraq. He couldn't take the chance that the call would be dropped because of poor reception. He'd pick up Patrick, drive to Deming, and take her call there.

Although the conversation with Sara was long and upbeat, talking to her only served to drive home her absence. It gut-wrenched Kerney, and Patrick took it no better.

"I want to go home to the ranch, Daddy,"

he said tearfully after the call ended.

"You know Mommy won't be there, sport."

"I know. But I don't like it here anymore."

"Let's see what we can do about it."

That evening after dinner, with Patrick at his side, Kerney approached Susan Berman and asked if he could be released from the remainder of his contract.

"I thought coming down here would be a good distraction for Patrick and me," he added. "But I think it's time for us to go home and try to get back to a normal life."

Susan nodded sympathetically. "Of course. Can you stay on until we shoot the mob scene in front of the police station tomorrow? Malcolm wants the police reaction to be as realistic as possible."

"I'll be glad to," Kerney said.

"Good," Susan said. She paused as if to say more, thought better of it, smiled down at Patrick, and walked toward the production office.

"We go home tomorrow, champ," Kerney said to Patrick as he hoisted him into his arms.

Patrick lit up. "When do I get my pony?" he asked.

"Very soon."

The script called for the mob sequence at the police station to be shot in the evening, after the rancher and his cohorts had been arrested at the smelter. Kerney, who had no intention of staying in Playas another night, packed up and loaded the luggage in the truck before rehearsals began. He dropped Patrick at the nanny's with a promise get him as soon as he finished, so they could leave immediately for Santa Fe.

At the set a hundred extras who played angry citizens, reporters, and bystanders milled around. The script called for all the lead actors and the supporting cast who'd participated in the cattle drive to be perp-walked to the police station. The mob would rush the cops in an attempt to gain the prisoners' release. Once the prisoners were inside, the crowd would overturn a squad car and break the police-station windows before order could be restored.

Kerney spent an hour with Usher as he blocked the sequence, and answered his questions about how the police would react to protect the prisoners and quell the mob. When Usher was satisfied with the blocking, he went to the bank of TV monitors and called for a run-through of each shot. Kerney stood next to him and watched the screens.

Usher made camera adjustments and lighting changes, and by watching the monitors Kerney got a director's view of the complexities of moviemaking. It was all about point of view, capturing different perspectives, and heightening the tension.

When it was over, Kerney said good-bye to Susan Berman and went to his truck, where he found Agent Fidel waiting for him.

"Bratton tells me you're leaving," Fidel said.

Kerney nodded. "I'm heartbroken that I couldn't be of any help to you."

"You served your purpose."

"Thanks for the kind words," Kerney replied. "You're a real piece of work, Fidel."

"What's that supposed to mean?"

Kerney stepped around Fidel and opened the truck door. "Have you busted the smuggling ring?"

"We have a plan in the works."

Kerney shook his head and got in the truck. "Another plan? Outstanding. I hope it succeeds. Did you come all the way from El Paso to tell me this?"

"And to thank you for your cooperation."

"Check your dictionary, pal. I think

you'll find that *cooperation* means that people act together for a common purpose and with a common understanding."

"Whatever," Fidel said.

Kerney fired up the engine. "Gotta go."

"Steve Hazen said you have something to say to me."

Kerney laughed. "Forget it. You don't strike me as a person who takes constructive criticism well."

The morning after their late-night drive home to the ranch, Kerney and Patrick spent time with the horses and did a few barn chores before heading to town to stock up on blueberries and other essential groceries his son had requested. At Patrick's insistence they had macaroni and cheese with ham bits for dinner and then went for a ride on Hondo.

Over the next several days they visited preschools and found one that Patrick really liked. The children were well behaved, the schedule was well organized, the teachers were kind and caring, and the activities consisted of a good mixture of cooperative play and cognitive-skill building. Convinced that Sara would approve, Kerney enrolled Patrick in the program, to start the day he went back to work.

One night, while Patrick slept, Kerney got on the Internet and researched ponies. He wanted a surefooted, intelligent animal that had a calm disposition and was sound of body. He settled on the Welsh pony. At twelve to thirteen hands tall it was big enough to be ridden by an adult, yet small enough for a child.

He surfed for breeders and eventually found one in northern New Mexico who had several animals for sale. A photograph of a six-year-old gelding caught his eye. It wasn't a pinto like Pablito in Patrick's favorite storybook, but it had four white stockings and a star on its forehead. That night Kerney called and made an appointment to see the animal the next day.

Kerney said nothing about the pony when Patrick got up in the morning. When the chores were done, he hitched the horse trailer to the truck and they drove to the Mora Valley, where the breeder had her ranch. Patrick spotted the ponies in a pasture off the highway and started bouncing up and down in his car seat.

"Look, Daddy!" he yelled. "Ponies. Lots of them."

"Maybe there's one here for you," Kerney said as he turned onto the ranch road.

Patrick grinned and nodded his head.

The six-year-old gelding was all Kerney hoped for and more. It had sturdy, strong legs, a deep chest, a broad forehead, and well-defined withers. After a thorough inspection of the animal Kerney reviewed the breeder's studbook and veterinary records. Then he put Patrick on the pony's back and watched as the woman trotted it around the corral by the halter. The pony had excellent balance and a smooth gait.

Kerney bought it on the spot and got the woman to throw in a used child's saddle and tack for an extra hundred dollars. He had to pry Patrick off the pony's back in order to load it in the trailer.

"What are you going to name your pony?" Kerney asked as they left the ranch.

"Pablito," Patrick said, grinning from ear to ear.

Kerney rubbed his son's head and laughed. "That's a *great* name."

At home Kerney saddled Pablito and took digital pictures of Patrick astride his pony to send to Sara by e-mail. He knew the pictures would make her smile but also break her heart. A child's first horse was a milestone not to be missed, a rite of passage every ranch family cherished and held firmly in memory.

"Mommy should see me," Patrick said.

"You are wise beyond your years, sport," Kerney said. He tied Pablito's reins to the corral railing and saddled Hondo. Finally Kerney understood the ache Sara carried for all the events in Patrick's life that he'd missed.

"Mommy should be here," Patrick said.

"Yes, she should." Kerney swung into the saddle and took Pablito's reins. "And when she comes home, we'll all go riding together."

"She can't go away again," Patrick said sternly.

"Never again," Kerney said as he reached out and opened the corral gate.

About the Author

Michael McGarrity is the author of the Anthony Award–nominated *Tularosa*, as well as *Mexican Hat, Serpent Gate, Hermit's Peak, The Judas Judge, Under the Color of Law, The Big Gamble, Everyone Dies*, and *Slow Kill*. A former deputy sheriff for Santa Fe County, he established the Sex Crimes Unit. He has also served as an instructor at the New Mexico Law Enforcement Academy and as an investigator for the New Mexico Public Defender's Office. He lives in Santa Fe.